I0554047

QUINRU CALIFORNIA

The wars of the 21st century will be fought for clean water-
Ismail Seraguldin

Dedication: This book is dedicated to my wife Judi. Thank you honey for participating in mandatory fun and doing the hardest job of all: Navy wife.

Authors note: To my old shipmates: sorry I used your names, but in most cases I gave you promotions! I would like to thank Patrick Tracey, Diane Rinella and William Weinreb. Patrick, thanks for asking me if the US could actually ever be invaded again. Diane and Bill, thanks for the help with the writing.

Other works by Michael Dirubio

Unity- 2013
System 112- 2014
The Journal of Daniel Alfredson- 2014
Empire Man-2015
Thief in Law-2016

Thief in Need-2017*

*forthcoming

Quinru California

US Military Hardware Description and designations

SSBN- Subsurface, Ballistic, Nuclear- A nuclear powered submarine capable of carrying nuclear missiles. The US has only one type, the Trident II, or Ohio class boat.

SSN- Subsurface, Nuclear- A fast attack submarine, capable of carrying torpedoes and a limited number of tomahawk missiles.

SSGN- Subsurface Guided, Nuclear- A Trident II submarine that has been modified to carry a huge number of Tomahawk missiles.

DDG- Destroyer, guided Missile, Gas turbine powered in the surface Navy. The US uses two main types- the older Arleigh Burke class, of which USS Hamilton is an example, and the newer Zumwalt class. The Zumwalt is much larger and carries the laser and rail gun improvements.

CVN- Carrier, Strike, Nuclear- The US has two types: the older Nimitz class and the newer Ford class. Both can carry eighty or ninety planes, but the Ford has improved launch systems and is better integrated.

FA-18 A thru G- Fighter, strike and air superiority. US Navy version, carrier launched.

F-16- Fighter air superiority. Ground based, fighter aircraft.

F-35- Joint Strike Fighter- three versions: Army, Air Force and Marines. Army is a land based fighter. Navy version is a carrier based plane with tougher landing gear. The Marine version is a vertical takeoff and landing jet. All three carry the newest weapons and the open architecture data links.

Tomahawk Missile- Three main variants, anti-personnel, bunker buster, and a general use low level air burst area denial weapon. The Tomahawk can be launched by sub, plane or ship.

V-22, Osprey- the tilt rotor landing craft for the US Marines.

F-22, Raptor- US Air Force air superiority fighter and strike mission plane. Uses aspects of stealth in its design. So called sixth generation plane.

F-117, Night Hawk- Fourth generation plane in the use of stealth technology. Older less capable model as a strike fighter.

B-52 H- US Air Force's oldest bomber. Its nickname is the BUFF: Big Ugly Fat Fucker. Capable of carrying nearly fifty- five hundred pound bombs
US Military Hardware Descriptions and designations

M1A1 Abrams Tank- The main US battle tank. Armored and uses a 105 mm long gun.

Harpoon- US Navy Anti Ship missile. Plane, and ship launched.

Hellfire- US Anti tank missile. Carried on helicopters.

Blackhawk- US Army, attack helicopter

Chinook- US Marine transport helicopter

Chinese Military Hardware Descriptions and designations

Han class SSN- Chinese nuclear Fast attack submarine

Chaing Class- Chinese SSBN, nuclear powered

J-31- Dragon- Newest Chinese fighter aircraft.

J-16- Shenyang- Older fighter aircraft, design stolen from a US F-15 base.

Z-9 Harbin- Main transport helicopter

J-7 Chengdu- Naval fighter capable of taking off from a ski ramp aircraft carrier

HQ-9 Anti air missile system. Composed of the Fang Dun missile and the HT-233 radar, the complete system is China's best long range anti air defense.

Type 001- Zhou aircraft carrier. Displacing 67,000 tons and nuclear powered, the single aircraft carrier is based on a Soviet Kuznetsov class design. Carrier has a ski ramp lunch system. Capable of carrying forty J-7 aircraft as power projection.

Type 52 destroyer- Lanzhou class- Chinas newest most capable destroyer. On a par with the US Arleigh Burke class ships.

Type 055 cruiser- Wanchu class- Chinas newest naval ship. On a par with the US Ticonderoga class missile cruiser, the ship is the anti air and anti ship defensive platform for the Vertically launched Missile system for the Chinese.

DF-26 Dong-Fang Anti ship Ballistic Missile. Launched from the new cruisers. The most advanced missile in the Chinese arsenal. Capable of sinking US aircraft carriers.

Chinese Military Hardware descriptions and designations

FN-6- Man portable shoulder fired Surface to air missile. China's largest exported weapon. Used by the Syrian rebels to shoot down Russian helicopters and Syrian fighters.

HJ-8- Chinese anti tank missile. Man portable system capable of destroying US tanks from four miles away.

Glossary of Terms and Abbreviations

Squid- A term the Marines call sailors. The literal dictionary definition is "a lower form of Marine life."
Jarhead- A term sailors call Marines. For obvious reasons.
Bubble heads- What surface Navy sailors call submariners
Targets- What submariners call surface Navy sailors
Grunts- What everyone calls Army soldiers.
Uncle Sam's Canoe Club- what sailors call the Coast Guard
Pop tall with a cheery Aye Aye- just a way you tell someone they'd better say yes.

POTUS- President of the United States
Sec Def- The Secretary of Defense
CNO- Chief of Naval Operations
COMSUBGRU 9- Commander Submarine Group 9- based in Naval Subase Bangor, Wa.
PAC Fleet- Commander Pacific Fleet- Based in Pearl Harbor Hawaii
CO- Commanding Officer
XO- Executive Officer
Eng- Engineering Officer
Weps- Weapons Officer
Nav- Navigation Officer
COB- Chief of the Boat (submarines)

1st MEF- First Marine Expeditionary Force- Camp Pendleton, Ca.
2nd MEF- Second Marine Expeditionary Force- Camp Lejune, North Carolina
3rd MEF- Third Marine Expeditionary Force- Camp Courtney, Okinawa, Japan and Kaneohe Hawaii

1st Infantry Division- The Big Red One- Fort Riley, Kansas
3rd Infantry Division- The Marne Division- Fort Stewart, Georgia
4th Infantry Division-The Ivy Division- Fort Carson, Colorado
7th Infantry Division- The Hourglass Division- Joint Base Lewis McChord, Lewis Wa.
25th Infantry Division- Tropic Lightning- Schofield Barracks- Oahu, Hawaii

CHAPTER ONE

The old farmer looked at the sky with a grim expression. Farmers often spend much of their time watching the sky and the weather and the man had decades of practice. His expression was always grim of late- also from long practice. Normally, rain after three years of extreme drought would be a welcome respite. *But this much rain? And for this long?*

The small farm was located in the heart of China's central farming province of Hubei, near the city of Yichang. The farmer did not understand the changes going on in his small corner of the world so he simply endured them. The rain, the drought, the dam, all of those things must be endured; kind of like the government in his mind. He'd always been a bean farmer just like his Bactu ancestors and hopefully his ornery grandsons would continue the tradition as soon as they returned from that fancy school. 72 years old and he had never travelled more than fifty kilometers from this little plot of land. Oh, he'd seen the dam. And the tourists who came to stare in amazement at the monstrous construction. The farmer appreciated the dam, but knew it's downsides as well. Living near the river had always contained ups and downs.

The Yangtze river was the blessing and the curse of central China. Life giving water and silt for fertile farmland, it also brought disastrous floods to the region. The 1954 flood when the farmer was a little five-year old boy, had killed three hundred thousand and made millions homeless. Cities as far away as Wuhan had been devastated.

But the dam had fixed that. The Three Gorges damn had stopped similar floods in 2008 and 2010. People still died- three thousand from mudslides alone in 2010, but not in the millions like before. The drought that starting in 2017 and lasted until five months ago, brought pain of a different sort. Three years of almost no rain had withered crops and left the country uneasy and starving. It was not the famine of the Great Leap Forward period, but it was devastating nonetheless. The old man had come close to losing everything. Only the American food had saved them.

Now the rains had returned. But like a rubber band snapping back into to place the gods had sent too much rain. The lower Yangtze basin was receiving centimeters a day, sometimes two to three or even more. And they had been for months on end with little break. The farmer had not been able to plant his beans. It was looking like another lost year.

First the drought and now the rain.

Endure. It was what he did.

The sound was the first thing to strike his consciousness. The low rumble was vaguely like thunder but not quite. *What is that?*

The question brought his head up to look around. His tiny 10-hectare plot sat north of Jinshi park and the new tourist area. His view was blocked by trees and the low blue roofed buildings the government people built to provide services to the Europeans and Americans who wanted to see China's new marvel. None of that concerned him or got his beans to grow, but the noise confused him.

The farmer took three steps towards the edge of the field when the rumbling sound changed. Louder and more menacing the rumble turned into a grinding roar. Sirens suddenly split the air. The farmer scrambled on top of the collective curing shed the locals used to make the bean paste that had made them famous, for a better look. From the roof the man had a clear view up the Xiling gorge.

The steep walled sides rose 500 meters above the river on either side and bulged out to his extreme left. Heavily forested with trees and very rocky, the gorge was a natural beauty. Carved from the endless flow of the river, that man had contained in his hubris.

The roar continued to grow for a number of minutes as he could now see people on the opposite bank. The river curved to his right where he stood on the building and then widened as

10

the gorge opened up to allow the city of Yichang and its two million inhabitants to spread on the northern bank. The people had been drawn to the river to see what the problem was.

The water was murky as the months of relentless rain had swollen the tributaries that dumped into the Yangtze at this juncture point. The Hangbai and the Bailin both had been churning a sickly brown as they added to the flow of the huge river.

The rain set a steady patter as the farmer stood transfixed watching the disaster unfold. The sound of snapping trees hit his ears as he realized the worst. *The dam had given way!*

Looking left, the farmer could not comprehend what he was seeing. A frothing, churning maelstrom of water and debris was moving down the gorge. At least a hundred fifty feet high, the water was scraping the sides of the gorge as it moved down with a terrible speed and momentum, causing the roar and a wind.

The figures on the opposite bank started to climb to escape the flood, but the farmer stood firm. He had no place to go and no reason to run. The river had always given life and he knew the bill would come due someday. So be it.

The sound took on a physical power as the wall of death swept up site seeing ships and barges alike and tossed them aside like play things, moving inexorably on.

Horror froze the man's face as he watched the flood reach a huge apartment complex across the river, directly opposite him. The complex was home to three thousand people in a series of connected red roofed buildings. Most of them were at home still on this early Thursday morning. Breakfast dishes, kids readying for school, parents preparing for work as the turbulent flood waters scoured the place from the map.

The bean farmer never saw or heard the tree trunk that killed him. One second he stood on the roof watching the flood and the next he was blasted off and into the void that the flood created. He was not the first to die nor would he be the last.

**

The situation room in the White House was packed.

I hate that fucking clock.

The disjointed thought was apropos of nothing and the distracted man who thought it was equally apropos of nothing.

The reality was that the clock wasn't even a clock in the traditional sense. And it wasn't a single clock.

The wall clock in the White House Situation Room main conference space was actually an electronic bar- a digital bank of six clocks. The red numerical readouts were large and programmable. The first three slots were always the same heading, number one was "Local time". Next slot held the time zone where the President was physically located, designated "The President" and then "Zulu". Zulu being Greenwich mean time. The next three slots were free to match whatever hotspot happened to be happening right now around the globe. The three were currently labeled, "Beijing", "Wuhan", and "Moscow".

China and Russia. Especially China. The Russians were only on the clock in respect to their response to the Chinese catastrophe. *Every time we get into this room we have to deal with China,* the man, Paul Marino, thought trying to connect the clock and China in his head. He sat in a small folding chair on the perimeter of the John Fitzgerald Kennedy Conference room located under the White House east wing. Commonly called the Situation Room, the space was constructed as a result of the Cuban Missile Crises. Kennedy and his staff struggled with obtaining real time information and passing out sensitive orders to his underlings while the whole world staggered towards Armageddon.

All this technology because Kennedy could not communicate with his men on the ground, Marino knew. The secured communications abilities of this room were second to none in the whole world. Eight huge monitors dominated the end wall opposite the clocks. The side walls held five big TV monitors each while another two computer screens flanked the news feeds currently on the TV's. Fox, CNN, MSNBC along with BBC America and Al Jazeera were shown to both sides of the room. The international flavor of the news was being pulsed. The huge center conference table held 18 plush chairs and another 30 or so chairs like Paul's ringed the interior walls.

Every one of those chairs held a very important butt. The eight video monitors held important faces, as butts would have been inappropriate. Army and Air Force Generals along with Navy Admirals and senior Senators stared out of those screens with hard, blank faces. The paper strewn center table contained the President, the V.P. and his cabinet. The Chairman of the Joint Chiefs and the Head of the NSA also graced the room sitting in the comfy chairs and matching the video people in the blank stare department.

The reason for those blank stares sat at the middle of the table. "I said, fuck the Chinese- we're winning," Ronald Drum, the 47th President of the United States said with his characteristic sneer.

Marino sighed internally for the millionth time since this man was elected, but he kept his face impassive. *How can this ignorant, narcissistic, asshole, be the leader of the free world?*

"Mr. President, he said patiently, it has nothing to do with winning." "The Three Gorges flood is a disaster on an epic scale." A deep breath allowed Marino to gather his thoughts. "Imagine if the Mississippi flooded and the city of St. Louis was wiped out. That is what happened to Yichang a city of two million people. It is a total loss, sir." "The Chinese are in a precarious position, given the number of dead and the possibility of millions more starving in the next months..." he trailed off at the look on Drum's face.

"That's my point! the President thundered. "Why should we give the food? The Russians can't help and the Europeans are pussies. We got them over the barrel." The man took a deep breath and said with a grin, "Paulie, the people of St. Louis didn't vote for me, any more than the Chinese did. Fuck em both!"

Several sharp inhales ran around the room. Political cold bloodedness was an expected trait but this was mercenary.

"Mr. President, we don't want to test the Chinese on this. We have already sold them hundreds of billions in beef, wheat, and rice. We have even run a trade surplus given their last three years of problems, but this…" Aly Mustafina, the new Secretary of Agriculture chimed in. She was a little unsure of her place in this room with regard to her ancestry and back ground.

Butts shifted uncomfortably in seats. The capricious nature of the President made any intrusion into his bubble of self-made reality an act of self-immolation. No previous President had turned over his cabinet at Drum's rate. Of course no previous President had been insane, like Drum.

Wellington Thomas, the bookish head of the NSA, tried a different tact. "Mr. President, the briefing my staff prepared for you on the flood response and the whole Chinese problem…"

Drum waived a small chubby hand at his spy master. 'How in the hell does that help me in the election?"

My god- it is always about him, Marino realized with a start as people stared in amazement. *How in the fuck…Why in the hell…*

Marino clamped down on this fruitless line of thoughts. He'd taken the Chief of Staff job because the outgoing Chief, Ronald Drum, Jr. had been a classmate and a good friend. Too bad he was an amoral asshole who was susceptible to bribery.

"Mr. President…" the people in the room stiffened as the vapid voice of Tamsin Starlin cut through the silence.

Oh boy.

"We just have to trust the great American spirit of the fine folks who toil for the prospect of liberty."

An awkward moment of silence stretched while this word salad of inane platitudes was absorbed by the audience.

'What the fuck does that have to do with anything…" Chairman of the Joint Chiefs General Stedman Graham muttered too loudly.

That was all they needed, another shouting match between the Barbie doll V.P. and the General.

Marino stepped in to cut off the spluttering woman. 'Mr. President, I know you have a speech in Cleveland today. You and the Vice President should do what you do best- "Make American Greatness a reality." "Let your staff deal with the details."

Drum washed a hand over his orange face. The fake bake tan almost glowing in the harsh lights. He leaned back in his chair trying to evaluate what was in it for him. Seeing nothing to be gained by staying and leading the effort to save millions of people from starving, the man stood and motioned to Starlin. She also rose and the two were bundled out of the room in swirl of Secret Service agents while the rest of the participants dragged butts from seats.

Marino exchanged glances with Graham and Speaker of the House Anders Young. Paul could read their thoughts on the faces: time for an end run.

Four roller coaster years had taught them that the best way to deal with the man was to do what needed to be done and slip the papers to him for a signature. He never read anything anyway. They'd only pulled out the 25th amendment section four letter- twice to force him in line.

"Mr. Thomas, General Graham, why don't you lay out the situation for everyone still in attendance," Marino sat after his soft, sad comment to the rest.

Thomas cleared his throat as his slide points came up on the electronic board. "Ladies and gentlemen, China is on the precipice…" The failure of the Three Gorges Dam has killed at least fifteen million people over the last week. Flood waters will reach Shanghai by next Thursday. We cannot accurately predict the dead."

Several cabinet members sat straighter in chairs.

Wellington shrugged his shoulders to the unasked questions. "The Chinese have spent hundreds of years building flood control levees and water diversion gates for the Yangtze." "The problem is that they walled off several huge lakes in the drainage basin that used to serve as flood water receptacles." He paused to let that sink in. "The net effect was to force the river into a channel and that has moved the flood surge further downstream." "That has put the twenty-six million people who call Shanghai home, at risk."

"Evacuations are ongoing aren't they, General Graham?", Secretary of the Treasury Sharon Stallings, the fifty-seven-year old Wall Street wizard who was now trying to keep the US from inflation panic, asked shrewdly.

"Yes, Ma'am, they are", the General answered, southern roots showing. "But as I say we have no way of predicting how they are going to move with the flooded roads and the crush."

"Is the People's Liberation Army mobilized to help?" The Chief of Naval Operations, Admiral Kevin Mooney asked the NSA head.

"As much as they can be Kevin, but even the three million of them are stretched very, very thin right now," Thomas concluded.

Everyone knew China's run of luck as of late. As much as that bad run had helped the US, the staggering amount of dead, and disaster piled on disaster, the ruin of China was no one's goal. The world economy and the world resources were being stretched ever thinner trying to cope with the crises.

Christ! First Super Typhoon Ma-On strikes Hong Kong and Macau, three years ago, Marino reviewed in his head the list of woe for the ancient country. The destruction from that category six storm was cataloged as the first trillion-dollar natural disaster. Seven of the top ten natural disasters involved China in some way. Marino shook his head. After the storm, the Southern city of Guangzhou and its twelve million, well now eight million, left to deal with the cleanup from the worst industrial pollution leak in history. The three large toxic gas and industrial waste leaks had seemed to spring out from nowhere. The dead laying wherever the wind and the contours of the land led the poison. China was paying for its lack of regulation and corruption at least in part with the severity of these self-inflicted accidents. *Now the flood on top of those, Jesus!*

Thomas gave way to Graham who went over the US military's aid and readiness posture.

Marino listened with half an ear. His head reeling from the scope of the disaster facing China. Every side of beef and ear of corn or bushel of wheat was being sent east as fast as the Midwest could crank it out. Three years of capriciously good weather in the US meant bumper crops available for sale to the Chinese.

And sell to them they had! The yuan plummeted and the dollar strengthen as the ships went east filled with food. Not many plastic gadgets came back as the manufacturing centers and the distribution ports were damaged. The pleasure/pain cycle of the disruptions to the world's economy was swinging over to the hurt reading when the flood hit. *Now what*? Marino zoned back in.

"Has anyone talked to Xi Peng?" Stallings asked another smart question. Her large nose holding her black framed glasses high on her face. She was pretty even under the pressure she was experiencing and displaying the kind of calm that put people at ease.

Marino shook his head. "We can't seem to get a hold of him."

"Oh, Christ…" someone muttered. Everyone in the room started buzzing. The gravity of the fact that the leader of a billion plus people being "unavailable" was daunting.

"People!" Sec Treasury scolded. "Focus." She paused to make eye contact around the room. "Everyone here will reach out to their counterparts in China and find Ping." "Report results to Wellington, check?", she nodded to the head of the NSA who took the assigned action item with a grin. Stallings just kind of did that kind of thing: assign tasks to important people. "General Graham you have the military ready for any eventuality, right?".

Graham nodded, not wanting to be the one who stood out.

"Anders, Paul, you two will coordinate Congress with the help of our Senate friends." She went on without waiting for a response from the Speaker of the House or the Chief of Staff. "We will run our departments to facilitate getting China back to a stable position."

Heads bobbed about the table and on video screens around the country.

"What about the President?" The Secretary of Homeland Security mentioned the elephant in the room.

"Fuck him," Stallings said getting on with the necessary work.

***

Fuck him, thought Andre Treadwell. *He might be my father but he was never around and now he wants money? Oh, hell no!*

Andre shook his head and said, "Nah, man." "You good." He shouldered past the hunched older black man in front of him outside The Brick and went into the bar.

T J Brickhouse, also known as The Brick was a tough bar on Adeline street in west Oakland near the Nimitz freeway. The red brick sides of the building were graffiti covered and the interior was dark and filled with the kind of desperation Dre saw all too often of late. A score of black men, all worn and older sat in ones and two around the small bar or at little tables. He was willing to bet that at 28, he was at least fifteen years younger than anyone in this place. Unconsciously, Dre sussed out who was who in the room. Just an innate glance around to see who was a poser and who were the real OG's. He placed men into categories and figured his ranking. It was something learned on the streets by every black man.

His large muscular frame fit easily on the chair at the table because his "narrow ass" really was just that. Six feet one, and a 175 pounds he was still in army condition even though he worked at the port now. Had worked there for five years. He rubbed the

18

1st ID tattoo on his shoulder, a large red "1" on a patch. The tattoo only hurt for a moment when he got it in Bahrain. The shrapnel from Mosul in his leg still did when the fog rolled in off the bay. *Six long years since Iraq*, he thought. Did he miss the Army? Hell, no! Well, maybe.

Born poor, and black in Oakland in 1989, Andre had no father to speak of, an overworked mother, some spotty classroom education and a hell of a rough upbringing. Gangs, drugs and crime were a way of life at the Oakland Housing Authority and it affected the young boy. It wasn't that the boy was dumb, he simply had no options, structure or role models. He was athletic, but not that one in a million that would let him out of the spiral of pain. Substandard education, from underpaid and overworked teachers who were all too willing to shove the kid through the system, didn't help. Without the guidance from his father and the struggle of his mother, Andre drifted into the under culture on the streets. Trouble followed inevitably. A stern judge had given an old option after some petty thefts: Join the Army or go to jail. He'd taken the Army and found a skill: large truck mechanic. A tour in Iraq at 19 and he saw and did things that no young man should see or do. He also got to see a wider world and a wider perspective. It changed him and made him see possibilities where none existed before.

And he did make friends. Some of them even white boys. The steady paycheck had gone mostly home, but he had saved for the G.I. Bill. The injury had ended his enlistment but had set him home with a new purpose.

The shock of being home in Oakland and still being under fire was devastating for him. His mother, Nancy Paterson, had moved from the Authority to a small place over near Lower Bottoms after his half-brother was killed by the gangs. The jumble of houses and apartments bounded by the curve of the 880 freeway as it joined the 80/980 maze, was just being squeezed by the incoming tech boom in the bay area. Andre's arrival, allowed her to stay in the duplex due to the extra income. It meant however that he had to work in addition to the small disability check he was getting. He put his army skills to work as a mechanic at the port and he was lucky to be working. Consequently, between the SDI, the G.I. Bill and his job, money for school and home was available, *just fucking barely. Thank god he graduated next semester.* He was going to get his Business Admin degree from Lincoln University. The small school cost 9,345 dollars a year and it took him five long, hard years but he was going to do it. Andre was ready to be on his own. He had a plan! Start his own truck garage and make some real money. He almost had his business plan ready.

And sure as shit his plan did not include giving money to his absentee father.

After a minute of sitting at his table a harried young woman sat a beer down in front of him with a wan smile. "Here you go, bay bay."

"Thanks Tabs, How're you?" He tried a smile. Tabatha was too young too hard and too busy being a mom to need a guy like him in her life.

"I'm good Dre. Walkin my feet off!"

"Sit a spell."

"Can't, I got to serve the drinks." "You gon' stay? I get off at three", she asked with a shred of hope.

"Can't, I got to get to class."

Dre was always runnin between the port and that school, she thought. That was what *she* needed, a brother with a job and a plan. He just needed a good woman to share that plan with. Tabatha watched him out of the corner of her eye. He was distracted, she could see.

Tabatha hauled up with a quiet "see you." She knew he would drink only one beer after an early shift at work and before his school.

Dre rubbed his shoulder and then his short close afro. The "see you" got stuck in his throat. He needed to be smoother before Tabs would notice him.

Dre turned to see the TV out of the corner of his eye. Perched at the top of the bar, the small set was showing the President from Cleveland during his speech. The scrawl across the bottom paraphrasing the politicians list of successes: unemployment down to 4.6 percent as manufacturing jobs came back to the US, wages up three percent in the last year, exports at record levels.

Yeah but the jobs are all computer related. It aint like the old days.

Dre certainly hadn't voted for Ronald Drum. He voted democratic when he remembered to vote, like all millennials. *Millennials. That's a term for white folks. Got nothin to do with our situation.* And to top it all off, the election was coming up soon. Today was the 21st of September, 2020. Seemed it could not be twenty years since the century turned. He finished the beer and flipped a five on the table. Tabs needed the scratch.

Thankfully his father was gone from in front of the Brick when he left. It hurt him to be part of such a negative stereotype: single parent African-American child. The *weight* of growing up without a father seemed to drag at his heels. Little shock reminders like today, when his ghost of a dad appeared asking for money was insult to injury. It added another rock to the sack he was carrying on his back.

But Andre Treadwell was going to drop that sack! Once he had his paper he was going to break out! He'd seen hell on two continents and he also saw a light. The battered Olds Cutlass turned under the freeway to crawl back to the bottoms. He had two hours to wash up, eat something and do some homework before night classes. Macro Economics tonight. His class of fifteen was intently debating and reviewing the US and Chinese economies.

He was struck by the interconnectedness of the whole machine that was economics. That analogy fit his mechanic's mind. Engines worked because parts fit and worked together. Economies were the same. Imbalances, or a lack of something made economies not work, that was basic.

The Chinese and US economies had been intertwined for the better part of a century.

***

Imbalances.

The discussion the class had been having last week was on the trade balances between the two huge countries.

"The dramatic shift in account balances happened starting in 2015 with the Chinese recession," his econ professor, Dr. Tompkins had lectured to them.

"I thought the Chinese economy just slowed from a really high rate of expansion, not a full blown recession?" Jen Lemurs put in a question and a comment. She was always commenting in class.

"The Chinese government may not have called it a recession but the value of goods and services went down, in real GDP terms," Tompkins told her and the rest. "We can't trust the numbers coming from the government. We have to look at other indicators." He paused to look around the class.

"Mr. Treadwell, you work at the port right?"

"Yes, Sir!" The army answer popped out of his mouth before he could think.

Tompkins smiled. "Andre, tell us how many shipping containers were at the port of Oakland in say, 2016?"

Dre thought back. "It seemed like millions. They was stacked up all along Harbor drive and the auxiliary lot."

"And now"? the professor prodded.

A frown spread on the young man's face as he answered. "Empty! The whole place is cleaned out. Just what's coming on from small ships and those goin' right back out."

'Those containers are heading back to China filled with food from the US, that's why the port is empty," the professor informed the class.

'So we can see from that indicator that the Chinese are importing more than they are exporting. Net exports are a component of GDP." The students furiously scribbled notes.

"We have other clues as to the extent of the recession, outflows of money from the stock market in China and the lack of investing in overseas projects among them." "All these mean a real slowdown in the Chinese economy." 'And what does that mean for us, Mr. Treadwell?" "Anyone?" Tompkins went on.

Scooping his dinner remains into the compost bin and replacing the pot on the stove for his mom, Andre remembered the answer: The drought and the disasters caused the containers to be shipped back filled with food and supplies. It was a boom for the US trade balance and farmers and hell on the Chinese. And at first the wealth had spread around to others.

"So the initial result of the slowdown was positive from Mr. Treadwell's perspective. The port was busy and he got a job earning decent wages and steady work." Tompkins watched the young and not so young faces of his class to see if they were getting the problem.

"But…" Andre asked, sensing the other shoe was about to drop like it was a sniper in Iraq.

"But the overall imbalances start to drag eventually, even on us. The price of food has gone insane! The professor complained. "That is just supply and demand at work." He paused again to let the note taking catch up.

"Eventually that inflation in basic things: food, gas and wages will trickle into everything else."

'Like what?" Mario asked.

"Houses, airplanes, computers, movie ticket prices, all of it." The man told them. "If wages and unemployment lag behind the core inflation rate we can get a phenomenon we haven't seen since the late 70's. 1970 you children!" Tompkins smiled. 'Stagflation!" "Ask an old person how bad that was."

"What's the government going to do about the inflation", Jen asked suddenly concerned.

The professor grimaced. "That's not the government's job, to worry about inflation. That is the Fed's problem. Remember our unit on the Federal Reserve and monetary policy."

***

Dre did remember the Fed and its response to inflation. He also knew that the rise in interest rates could fuck him and his business plans. He finished off his econ paper and uploaded it to his student account from the computer. The internet was being pirated off a Vietnamese family across the street. The computer was old and from a pawn shop.

He needed to get to class early to run his business plan capital loan projections by Tompkins. The era of cheap money was coming to a close and Dre knew the Small Business Administration was going to have a smaller supply of money.

Three months. I need the world to hold together for three more months till I get my shit goin,' Dre prayed silently on the way to class.

The cell was dark, dirty and soul crushing. It was meant to be all those things and more. Surely the sole male occupant of the cell deserved it for is crimes.

Xi Peng, sat on the edge of his small, thin, cot, back ram rod straight, staring at the cell wall.

Qincheng prison in Beijing was known as China's luxury prison, usually housing famous high profile prisoners such as the Dalai Lama or Mao's wife, Qin Jaing.

Those inmates stayed in the upper cells in relative comfort. But Xi? The old man was kept in the holes under the D block regular cells. The leader of Communist China had only been there a week. Hardly any time at all. The usurpers had not even had time to beat him properly. Yet.

The sound of the key scraping back the lock was suddenly loud to Peng's ears and it broke the still silence.

The door opened to admit three men, all in uniform.
Yuan Chinghung led the small procession. The thin General of the People's Liberation Army or PLA, was a spare man who had wisps of white hair sticking out from his ears even though he was just two years older than Peng. Yuan was also known by many

aliases, and was reputed to be a devious politician who always took the long view on any conflict.

The short fat form of Qi Jinyung followed Yuan into the cell. The oily hero of the PLA Airforce had 12 confirmed kills in some very dicey encounters off of Taiwan, Russia and Vietnam. The man was living well despite the deprivations going on in his homeland.

The third and last man into the cramped cell was the dangerous one. Yue Fei. Whip smart and still very handsome the youngest member of the Military Political Advisory Panel to the Politburo was the leader of China's Cyber forces. The youngest at 64, he was a ruthless, fierce adversary who had limitless ambition and drive.

Xi focused on Yue, ignoring the others and his own stench.

'Yue Fei, what fiction will you have me sign today?" He was proud of how calm his voice was.

Fei smiled grimly. "No signature necessary Peng. You are guilty of the greatest sin of them all- unluckiness."

Xi kept his gaze on the snake in front of him. "This isn't the old days. The people will see that you haven't helped them and they will rise up."

'The people will be perfectly correct," the snake spat back at Xi. 'We have no intention of helping them."

Off to the side of the two men, Qi slowly drew his pistol and pointed it at Xi.

"For crimes against the state…"

The single shot was loud and a spray of blood misted the air as the body of the deposed Communist Party Leader slumped to the side of the cot. The three men were used to death and they stepped lightly from the spreading pool of blood. Qi wiped the gore off his glasses and face.

The three new rulers of China, a full military Junta, gazed at the results of their work for a second.

"The others must be taken care of without delay", Yuan broke the spell.

Qi Jinyung holstered his gun and nodded. "I will coordinate reports and direct our troops to control the airport and the other physical structures we need."

Fei, the real leader of the Junta, allowed his two supposed equals to make their plans. He knew only two things mattered now: controlling the information and Lin Wei Bo. *It all rested on him now.*

"We have to announce our take over as quickly as possible," he told the other two as they left the cell. None of the three had any concern for the chaos engulfing their homeland.

"I got it!"

The words came out with a little more heat than she'd meant. *You don't talk to Admirals that way.*

"Sorry, Sir." Lynn Su Spiegal told COMSUBGRU 9.

"No problem, Lynn, just get it to me when you can and leave whenever you need to," Brent Kollmansburger, Commander Submarine Group Nine, told his admin assistant.

It was late in the evening and the conference room attached to his office still held dinner, his Deputy Commander and his staff. The conference call with General Graham and the Senior combatant group commands had been long, acrimonious and extraordinary.

Lynn knew setting DEFCON 4 plus was an enormous undertaking for the military. Any increase in the United States defense condition was critical and sure to be met with a response from friend and foe but these were dangerous times.

And the uncertainty was weighing on everyone. China, the US election, her divorce and her wayward son had all condensed into a snappy remark for her boss.

"We have to cancel the rest of FY 21 INSURV, ORSE and TRE's for the fleet, the Deputy summarized.

"Those CO's are going to be happy over that," Kollmansburger, a two-star Admiral grinned at his subordinates.

Lynn hid her smile. *Tommy was always complaining about the Tactical Readiness Evaluations,* she thought. She knew that an ORSE was an Operational Reactor Safeguards Examination which involved stressing the nuclear reactor on a submarine. Canceling those two inspections removed a major source of stress in a submariner's life. But it came with an increase in Optempo. Operational Tempo or more clearly, time at sea.

Seventeen years as a Navy wife, meant she'd picked up a lot of the lingo. One of her favorites was "mandatory fun." Several times a year the crew of a submarine would have a ship wide party or picnic. Because esprit de corps was so important, the Captains usually wanted all hands to go to these parties. So they made them mandatory.

As in --*You will have fun if I have to beat it into you!*
Hence the term mandatory fun. The good feeling didn't last as she was reminded of her split from Thomas Spiegal, a Fire Control Senior Chief on the USS Ohio.

"They ain't going to be so happy about the longer patrols and shortened refits," LT Manor told his boss.

The Admiral nodded. "I want the boats on full load outs. SSGN's full up with tomahawks, no Spec ops loads. Torpedoes are one in each tube and full rack stows. The boomers…" The Admiral broke off as he spied Lynn. She had no need to know what the load out of nuclear weapons would be onboard the west coast fleet of Trident missile carrying subs.

Lynn was grateful for the excuse to leave.

She drove home slowly off the huge base at Silverdale, Washington. Naval Base Kitsap-Bangor was an enormous facility that held eight of the traditional doomsday carrying missile subs and two of the converted "tactical Tridents" or guided missile carrying submarines. The base was also home to three orphan fast attack submarines of the Jimmy Carter class. The smaller fast attacks were not as good as the newer Virginia class boats, but they were miles better than the old Los Angeles class subs. But the Navy had stopped building them when the budget got squeezed after three hulls. So they sat at Bangor and did odd jobs for the Navy- like spy missions and provide Anti-submarine warfare training for the surface boys. Those crews spent a lot of time sneaking up on surface ships and they had embarrassed more than one Aircraft carrier CO.

Admiral Kollmansburger was responding to the CNO and the Chairman of the Joint Chief's order to take the US defense condition to a modified state four. More security measures and more surveillance of foreign forces with the added kicker of an increase in readiness posture for some forces. Namely, the subs and the forward bases. Like Japan and Korea for instance. Extraneous things like inspections had been canceled for them, but they could count on way more operational time at sea or in the field.

That sucks! Lynn thought as she turned up Ridgetop from the 303 in Silverdale, reviewing the situation in her head. She used to live right on the base when she was married to Tommy but now she had this twenty-minute commute as she and Noah were forced to live in the Ridgetop apartments. It wasn't that the new place was so bad, it's just that it wasn't a home yet.

Lynn regretted the divorce but she knew the reasons were real. For both of them. Thomas just spent too much time at sea. He had eighteen years in and was looking at six more. He wanted to be a COB. Lynn hated the responsibility that position held. Being the COB, or Chief of the Boat, meant being the senior enlisted man onboard the sub. It meant a 24/7 commitment to the young sailors of whatever unit was lucky enough to get him.

It also meant more time away from Noah. His son needed him as well. Tommy could see that but had told her he could devote the time their sixteen-year-old needed.

She doubted that. And that led to the fights and the divorce.

Opening the door to the small apartment she was struck by the reduction in their lives. Her high school aged son was folded onto a chair at the small dining room table doing his homework. His tall thin frame barely fit onto the wooden chair. *Our old table was much bigger* she thought.

"Hey."

"Hi, mom. Saved you some crock pot roast," Noah told her while typing furiously on his laptop.

"Thanks."

Lynn went into the kitchen after depositing her rain coat and umbrella on the stand by the door. The Puget Sound weather was always dicey, so she carried what she had to. She fixed a plate and joined her son at the table.

He continued to write on the computer while barely glancing at her.

'English homework, he explained. "Ten typed pages on Steinbeck's, *Of Mice and Men*. Discuss the themes with respect to our modern day lives," he quoted from the assignment.

It always amazed her how smart he was. She didn't ask but she knew he'd probably read the book within the last two hours and was now cranking out the paper which she was also sure was due tomorrow at 8 am. That drove her crazy but she bit her tongue. The young man had never let her down.

"Did you know there is a judge in Texas who used Lennie as a case study to determine a standard to which the death penalty could be applied?"

"No, I didn't", she replied and took a mouthful of food.

"Yeah, she argued that Lennie acted in haste and impulsively when he killed Candy and he could not formulate an advanced plan in the killing so therefore he should be spared." Fingers flew as he spun out the tale.

Lynn grunted. "What happened in the case?"

The young man stopped typing and looked at his mother with his Asian face and brown eyes. "What?"

"What happened in the death penalty case? Did the guy get life?"

Noah frowned. "No, they went ahead with the execution."

Lynn hated to do it but it had to be done. "It's Texas honey. They execute people down there." Doesn't matter if it's wrong or right, it's just what they do."

The boy watched his mother while trying to line up the facts in his head.

"Sometimes people do irrational things. Acts which they know to be wrong for whatever reason. They can get it justified in their heads." She related the real world to her boy.

Noah spent some time trying to figure out what was wrong with his mother. He let her eat while half his brain finished up his paper.

"What happened at work?", he asked her softly.

A sigh escaped the woman. *Too smart by half,* she thought. "The Admiral has to raise the DEFCON. CNO has ordered an increase in readiness posture."

Being a military brat brought a strange awareness and knowledge of things normally outside of a teenaged consciousness. Things like CNO and readiness posture.

"Dad is going to be okay", he told his mother. The two still loved each other- he knew that. Noah did not spend a ton of time with his father but they did talk. His dad was doing important work in the Navy. He personally didn't feel cheated but he knew his mom resented the time his dad spent away from home. And that had led to the divorce. Noah was aware of the divorce rate in the military. Ninety percent was a figure he knew to be true based on his friends and now himself.

With all the stress in the world given the election and Drum and the Chinese dumpster fire and dad and the Navy...

Noah was subjected to enough crap of his own due to his racial makeup and the adoption deal. The Sea Tac corridor was not as bad as the South but he saw the news and read things on the interwebs.

"I'm just worried in general", his mom broke into his thoughts.

The two discussed the world while Lynn finished dinner and Noah his homework.

'Well, Drum is going to be re-elected, especially since the Chinese coup last week," Noah said sagely.

"Pretty confident for a kid who can't vote yet."

"You don't change horses mid-stream, isn't that what they say in politics," Noah told her as they did the dishes. "Mr. Boeckman my history professor, says that it was the same reason George W. Bush got re-elected in 2004. Once the Iraq war started we didn't want to change the President in the middle."

Lynn agreed with that. "Yeah. The hell of it is, this marks the second time Drum has benefitted from an October surprise to help him in the race."

Nodding enthusiastically the boy dried the last part of the crock pot. 'That's what Mr. Boeckman called it, an October surprise. Last time, Drum had the whole Wikileaks scandal to help him win. This time he has the Coup."

"And we have to deal with the results of that action," Lynn said with a tired drain to her voice. She had to go in early to begin typing up policy statements and directives. The Admirals staff would spend the next day's ordering the new parts and weapons the submarines would need, but she had to help the whole base prepare for the reality of a new world order. One where the US was keeping a wary eye on China. But first she had to get her son through his homework.

CHAPTER TWO

The Chinese capital city of Beijing was home to twenty million people, the major Chines government institutions and the second worst air quality in the world. Only New Delhi in India fared worse in the number of airborne particulates race to the bottom.

Beijing saw 25 days a year where the number of cancer causing soot particles hanging like clouds, rose above the 900 PPB the World Health Organization called, extremely hazardous. Delhi rang up 30 days like that. The WHO had to come up with a new scale for the two cities: Black Zone. Beyond the red zone limit of 900 to 1000 parts per billion, the Black Zone was off the charts as far as the number of particles being breathed in by the unlucky inhabitants.

The city experienced at least 500 deaths due to bad air on those black flag days. That fact was not published anywhere- it just was.

The same pattern of not trusting official Chinese government numbers had to be seen in different indicators for the risky problem. USAID organizers and workers had been pulled out due to the danger. Same for Red Cross and other relief workers. Even the US ambassador had been recalled for "consultations" and the embassy staff reduced to the bare minimum of spies due to the unhealthy air.

Beijing had been abandoned by US and Europeans alike and left to the locals to slog around wearing the surgical masks that marked anyone who had to use lungs in the city.

That surgical mask itched Lin Wei Bo as he exited the private car and walked briskly into the Great Hall of the People. The five-minute walk was enough to turn the mask a shade darker as the fumes and soot rendered the air a brown, thick choking hazard. The General hoped the filters on the buildings air handlers were up to the task. He did not remove the mask until he stepped up to the check point. Security was off the charts as he had his body scanned and his brief case searched by hard eyed troops. *And he was the leader of these men!* The take-over by the military had brought out the natural

32

paranoia of the people. The city was in almost total lock down with troops on every major junction. Dissent was not being tolerated as the number of bodies were starting to pile up at the morgues. Wei Bo was young enough to have served as a second Lieutenant during the June the Fourth Incident. What the westerners called the Tiananmen Square protests. He'd done his share of head busting on kids who were his own age. *Peasants should know their own place.* Not very communist thinking but he'd always known the natural superiority of his own heritage and the rightness of his own actions. And now the cloak of the people was pulled back to reveal the wolf at the door: Hard line military leaders in charge of China.

Wei Bo passed thru the layers of security and picked up his aide, Lt Col. Zi outside the briefing chamber. Where the General was small, compact and trim, Zi was enormous. The man looked like a scarred Olympic weightlifter.

"Sir, the Officers are due in a half an hour. I have setup the presentation with the changes we made last night. The slides are correct as of three hours ago." Zi took his briefcase and handed him a water bottle and a wipe.

The General spent some time cleaning his face and ensuring his nose and mouth were clear of soot. He knew things were worse in other parts of the country. Surgical masks did nothing to keep out the poisonous gas of Guangzhou. Nor the flood waters of Shanghai.

'I will go in alone," Bo told his longtime aide. This was something he had to do by himself.

"I will meet you here right after," Zi told his boss.

"Very good, Colonel."

Bo continued into the secured small meeting chamber which was located deep into the building. Guards watched his every move.

The smaller, well-appointed meeting room felt and looked like an American court room. A raised bench sat at one end where the Military Ruling panel would sit. Wei Bo himself was at the small lectern opposite the bench set about twenty feet from the judges/Generals. In the gulf between man and Gods, sat a horizontally mounted display screen. His presentation would be looked down upon from the heights.

The General fiddled with the pointer on the podium as he went through the first few slides. Zi was his usual competent self and there were no problems.

A few deep breaths and he was ready. The next hour of his life would be the most important one so far.

***

But his whole life up to this point had been pointing towards this moment. Ever since, June the Fourth, 1989. A young second Lieutenant led his platoon of men to surround the senior leadership cadre of the student protestors and caught the eye of his superiors.

No one had ordered him to do this. The situation at 0230 that night was complete chaos. No one seemed to be in charge of either side. Despite having no communications with his superiors, Wei Bo knew that cutting the head off the snake of the student groups would quell the mob. The protestors would collapse without coordinated instructions telling them what to do. His men had followed his unhesitant charge into the swirling mass of bodies and flags towards the center camp area. Shooting some, shoving some and herding most, Bo and his men neutralized the main forty leaders.

Only 30 of them had died. Wei left a nice cache of prisoners for show trials. No one in Beijing seemed to care about the thousands that were slaughtered in the wake of Bo's actions.

The young army officer was lauded by the Party and the military, both. He was promoted and sent to the Central Party Tactical Officers School. Once there, his native intelligence and his natural leadership abilities moved him to the head of his class. Bo was sent to the western frontier on graduation to deal with the Uyghur problem. Yet again the Uyghur problem.

Major Lin Wei Bo had taken a hand-picked brigade of the toughest desert fighters that China possessed with him into the western empire. Equipped with small trucks and drones and small arms only, Bo had reported to the Western Command and quickly figured out the problem. China had no business running the Xinjiang region. Or even being there in the first place. The opium addicted Three-star General and the Party Leader who were corrupt as the day was long- were both killed. Bo set up the killings as

34

a revenge act for the killing of two Uyghurs the month before. Riots did break out but it was a nice excuse to kill a bunch of the native peoples.

Bo moved the military's defensive line back to the Gansu district. He allowed the Xinjiang autonomous region to be set up and he cut all information flowing out of the region. His last two acts were to move the ethnic Han back to the true Empire and poison Bosten lake. Travelling back across the Taklamakan desert, he thought his actions would either earn him another promotion or a bullet.

Back in Beijing, newly promoted Colonel Lin Wei Bo was awarded China's highest military honor for his actions. As a reward he was sent to the United States.

He studied with US Army Officers in an international school located deep within the Pentagon. Wei Bo enjoyed his time in the enemy capital. He was noted by his instructors for a "keen understanding of asymmetrical warfare and tactics." He also got several speeding tickets because the crazy Americans had very little traffic that he could not zip around. His courtroom experience was brief but eye opening.

That was fifteen years ago.

***

A small door opened and the three rulers of China entered without a word. They'd arrived early as a test for the Major General. The three sat at the benches with a minimum of fuss. Only the shuffling of the body guards that had entered with the men betrayed any noise.

Bo gazed steadily at the men. He'd been called here for a purpose. Six months ago, Yue Fei approached him as the country struggled and asked him to come with a plan. A very bold, and ambitious plan.

A deep breath and he started the briefing. "Comrade Generals, we can invade the United States west coast and take it for ourselves."

Small gasps came from Yuan Chinghung and Qi Jinyung while Yue Fei just smiled.

Bo advanced to his first slide and started to lay out his vision. "Our country is dying," he flipped thru intel reports of the recent tragedies and the economic storms sweeping thru China. "We have over 150 million dead in the last three years with another 500 million threatened," he said in a sobering reminder of just how bad things were. We have to jettison the aid efforts that the Peoples Armies are undertaking, right now. In fact, we should have done so a year ago." The subtle rebuke did not go unnoticed.

"We did not control China a year ago, General Bo," Fei said mildly but with a hard stare.

Bo knew he had to tread lightly. "Sir, I understand that, but we must disengage from the relief efforts and begin the training and logistics required in the gathering of our forces for the Strategic Counter Attack of the Western United States."

Bo smiled inwardly. *Strategic Counter Attack.* That was an interesting term. It was first used to describe the invasion of Vietnam in 1979. The small neighboring country was just coming out of its long wars with the west and the Central party saw an opportunity to carve off a chunk of territory from them.

That didn't go so well he knew. The Chinese had advanced 50 miles into a broad corridor from the coast up towards Lang San. The Vietnamese responded as they'd been trained to do: allow the invaders to get bogged down along the coast road to Hai Phong and let the mountain jungles tear up the tanks as they tried to threaten Hanoi. Well, Ho Chi Min City now he supposed.

Since the Vietnamese had not attacked in the first place, a "Strategic Counter Attack" might not have been the best name for the operation. The Chinese had to put all of their forces into a full blown retreat to prevent a catastrophe as the hardened guerilla army of the Vietnamese started killing Chinese troops and ending the invasion.

Yuan spoke up, his dry voice thin and reedy. "You are blunt spoken General. Let us be equally blunt. Let us call this what it is. Quinru. Quinru, California."

Invasion. The invasion of California.

Bo nodded to his superior. Yuan was the senior General of the People's Liberation Army. Wei Bo would only be the battle leader of the forces in the fight.

A cough from Fei and Bo continued the briefing.

"Comrades we are arranged in three phases: Phase one will be the disruption of the US as led by General Fei's forces. The goal is not the defeat of the US military, just to isolate the western half of the country to the troops already in place." He flashed thru slides showing the US order of battle and where the engagements would take place. The leaders asked several technical questions involving the timing and scope of attacks. Bo spent a full ten minutes reviewing his plans and the interlacing of his efforts with Fei's.

'Phase two is actually kicked off with General Qi's Peoples Liberation Army Air Force and their gambit."

The slides clicked thru with bullet points soullessly laying out the destruction.

Qi grinned. "We will do our part."

Bo nodded. "Thank you Comrade General. "My forces will be the second act of phase two." Again the maps and pictures and bullet points flashed out. Even Fei was daunted. This would be war on a scale not seen since the 1940's.

"Would the Americans respond with nuclear attacks?" Yuan asked quietly. Fei let a moment of disgust come over his face. They'd had this conversation before. *Of course there was a risk!*

Bo kept cool. "Sir, the risk is always there. But…

"But the Americans won't use nuclear weapons on their own soil and any attack on us would just ensure a full response from us. We have to make Drum see that," Bo drove on remorselessly.

Fei stopped him right there. "General, you concentrate on defeating the American conventional forces, let us worry about the US President and the nuclear question."

A bow from his head showed the deference that the Military Ruling Panel wanted from an underling.

Lin Wei Bo took full advantage of the time he'd been allotted to review his plan. It was his best work; he was certain of that. No one could have come up with a better plan.

'Finally Comrade Generals we have Phase three. The transport of 10 million technicians and farmers and workers to California will be a huge undertaking but when the only other option is a slow death by starvation, we will succeed."

The last of the slides clicked thru rather quickly.

The slim man at the podium paused for a second to gather his thoughts.

"Comrades, we did not ask to be put in this position. We can debate on whether it is our own fault or destiny to be where we are- but the fact is we are dying and have only two options: War or death." He let that sink in. "I have no illusions about what will happen if we lose. A quick death would be a blessing. The Americans have an interesting saying: If you want to see how hard a man can fight, back him into a corner." "We are in such a corner."

All four men knew the truth of that statement.

"My force needs and the supply requirements are summarized for the three phases. Time tables are also provided." Bo put down the computer remote and let the screen go dark. He gazed unflinching at the bench and its occupants.

Smiles and nods told Bo the answer: he was to proceed with his plans. None of the men paused to consider that they may have just signed the human races death warrant.

The Chief of Staff surreptitiously nudged the President to fully awake status. "Sir, PACFLT is waiting your go ahead."

'What?" President Drum snorted. He looked around. Admiral Mooney, General Graham, Stansfield Mussman, the Secretary of Defense along with Admiral Nickers, with his Pacific Fleet Command staff, all had eyes for him.

Assholes. I was up all night partying and enjoying some of the Hawaiian hospitality and now...

"Admiral you were saying?" Marino gave the man an out.

"Yes, Sir. We have completed the DEFCON 4 plus measures that CNO and the Joint Chief's instituted last week." The Admiral stopped to glance at Mooney and Graham. Those two just kept quiet. "I am increasingly concerned with the fact that I cannot contact the head of the Chinese Navy or a theater commander as has been established by the RIMPAC treaty."

The befuddled look on Drum's face told it all to the Admiral. *Jesus, this guy had no idea how these things worked, did he?*

"Mr. President, the RIMPAC treaty establishes a hot line for the highest levels of the militaries of the Pacific Rim nations to be able to call one another to express," he searched for the right word, "interest" in the others intentions."

'So?" Drum prompted.

"Sir, the fact that the head of the PLAN, is missing is at the least a cause for concern. At the most we should be readying for a potential attack."

Drum rocked back. "Hold on a second Admiral. We're winning! The Chinese just announced that they want a massive shipment of food. They're sending over at least twelve and more like twenty huge container ships for loads of food! This is the best thing to happen to the American farmer since the end of the dust bowl."

Paul Marino shuddered. *How tone deaf did you have to be to equate the end of the worst disaster to hit farmers as a good thing for today*? Profiting off the misery of others? He knew the reality of the Chinese need for food but the glee with which Drum was gloating over the starvation of millions was…appalling.

"I understand that Mr. President, but I have to look at the entire Pacific area. The Chinese disasters are destabilizing the whole region. The coup seems to have wiped out the moderate head of the PLAN." Peoples Liberation Army Navy," he added to the look from Drum. Nickers remembered the first briefing he ever gave the Presidential candidate over four years ago. It took them three hours to convince him that everything in the Chinese military was "Peoples Liberation Army" followed by whatever.

"So they have an Army Navy?", Drum had asked stupidly.

"Think of it like in World War II. Our Air Force was called the Army Air Corps, right?"

Christ, that took another twenty minutes to relate that the Air Force wasn't always called the Air Force. Drum also hated acronyms so sometimes it was very hard to talk to the man.

"Mr. President, I cannot speak to the man with whom I've had a relationship for the last three years as we have both been in charge of our forces in the Pacific Theater. Our satellite images show's some very strange movements of men and equipment in the southern areas of the country."

'The south? Aren't they moving troops in to help the flooded areas?" Drum asked.

"Yes and no sir. They were helping at first but two weeks ago they seemed to have just restricted their men to bases around Baoshan. And there seems to be some unusual activity around the Wusongku docks. The deep water port south of the city is also much more active than it should be."

"The satellites can only show so much, sir. The rest is Sigint and other data collected onsite." Nickers left it vague.

Drum showed no interest in it but the Secretary of Defense wanted the particulars when he made recommendations.

"Who's in there, Grant?" Mussman asked.

"Mr. Secretary we currently have the Bremerton in Hangzhou bay", the man told his civilian boss.

Kevin Mooney winced. "Bremerfish?" he said a little too loudly.

Admiral Nickers grinned at the CNO. "You should know all about her and I thought you were more respectful of the fast attack tough crowd."

Marino was confused.

"I was the Executive Officer on the USS Bremerton for three years back in 06. She was old then for Christ's sake!" Mooney related.

The Bremerton was indeed an old 688 class fast attack submarine. In fact, she was the oldest remaining submarine on active duty. CNO looked at PACFLT. 'We need to get one of the flight two boats in there. Or better yet, a Virginia."

The man wanted to get an updated and more capable Los Angeles class attack sub to take over for the Bremerton or even the newest submarine in the US arsenal, a 1.2 billion dollar killing machine like the USS Virginia.

"Bremerton just got in there and she is on station and functioning. We are getting the data, sir." Nickers volleyed back. "I don't want to pull her off and wait until we get another unit in there. We could miss something."

Drum had had enough of the talk he did not want to know about and being ignored. 'What the fuck do you need from me Admiral?"

Nickers stiffened. "Mr. President I need your go ahead to put South Korean and Japan US forces on a higher alert status."

That was the purpose of this meeting, Marino knew. Nickers, Mooney and Graham all feared an attack somewhere. They didn't want to be like Kimmel.

Husband E. Kimmel was CinC Pac in 1941. A bullet had famously struck his window pane and embedded into his office wall during the Japanese sneak attack. His comment that "it would have been kinder had the bullet killed me" was not far off the mark.

Nickers office was across the road and technically off of the base proper from where Kimmel had watched his career disintegrate, but the responsibility was his just the same.

Marino again did what he did best, head off the coming storm. 'Mr. President this campaign stop is pressing. We need to get to Kaneohe Bay to address the Marines and I know you have that fundraising function afterwards. I will coordinate with the Secretary and the Admirals to do what we need to do."

"Don't upset the Chinese too much Paul. I have had some great talks with that Fei guy. He seems to respect what I want to accomplish."

"No, Mr. President, I won't upset him."

The men and women in the room all stood while the Commander in Chief left to continue his vigorous campaign to lead the free world. Or to drink and play golf in Hawaii, whatever was called on for him to do.

"Mr. Marino, the law states that the President must be the one to increase the readiness posture of forces outside the US mainland." The Secretary of Defense stated the obvious.

'Write up what you want me to have him sign and it will get done. Give me an aide to run the paper." Marino said tightly.

"Admiral what are the Chinese doing?" he asked bluntly. Mooney took the cue.

"Paul, the plain fact is we don't know. We have some pretty extensive links into their nuclear forces. There has been no change or even a twitch in any of the procedures for the nucs." Everyone in the room seemed to relax a bit. "However the coup is roiling everything else. We get nervous when another country moves a bunch of planes and ships and troops around. I can't tell you what or where but something is happening."

Mooney shrugged. "I know that's kind of like the PDB that Bush got: Bin Laden determined to attack the US. That's not a hell of a lot of info to go on to connect the dots." The staff members were acutely aware of the famous Presidential Daily Briefing that Bush 41 got before 9/11. The failure to make those connections had killed thousands of people.

Marino absorbed that statement. The last time the information surrounding such a situation was this muddled, 3,000 Americans died. *What the hell could they do now?*

The Chief of Staff looked at the small, compact Chief of Naval Operations. Admiral Mooney was no more than five foot four and one hundred thirty pounds. Marino also knew from his file and personal interaction that the man was *competent.* He just exuded a calm air that said, "I know what to do*". Kind of like Stallings,* he thought. What's more, Mooney was a tough son of a bitch. His job before the Bremerton was in Iraq during the war. He was a strike force liaison officer. The job entailed daily decisions on killing people via drone and air strikes. And Marino knew that Mooney had been awarded the Navy Cross for doing that job. He also knew that Mooney had been on a sub that had crashed into the top of an undersea mountain. That was tough! To have survived that both physically and the career implications? Double tough.

"Mr. Secretary, Admiral Mooney, Admiral Nickers, you do what you think is in the nations' best interest and I will handle the President." "The election seems to be a shoe in in another three weeks so we might have to be dealing like this a bunch more."

"I know." He held up a hand to forestall the objections. These men did not like to do things the Constitution didn't tell them to do. They took the oath to the document not to the person after all.

'Who's my runner?", he asked Nickers. A young female Lieutenant came up when Nickers pointed her out.

"Get to Air Force One. She's parked at the Hickam secured strip. I'll have the signed order for you."

Marino took the typed paper from Grant Nickers.

The view from the door way to the headquarters of Pacific Fleet Headquarters out towards the water was breathtaking. The white colored office building was across the Kamehameha highway from the actual base and nestled on the flanks of the Makalapa crater. The deeply green sides of the volcano raised the building up about 600 feet and afforded a view west towards Ford Island and the lochs of Pearl harbor. The blue of the Pacific shimmered in the sun. Marino squinted. He could see south down the lava field plain towards Hickam air base and the edge of Honolulu International airport. The blue and white 747 was tiny at this distance but visible. He sighed and went to the black SUV that would take him over the H2 to Kaneohe Bay. The weight felt like more today. He supposed he owed a call to the other cabinet secretaries and the rest of his… cabal? Was that the right word? Shadow government? Maybe that described it better. Either way if the shit hit the fan, history would not be kind to any of them. Maybe he could climb on the plane and sleep for a while? That wouldn't be so bad would it?

The small boat chugged slowly along the south coast of Oahu. The blue and white sides of Air Force One stood out seemingly to be setting on the water from his vantage point. This low on the water his line of sight was limited to five miles or so.

Walt Tsuomo steered the 35-foot fishing boat, The Collen, past the small coast guard unit that was shielding the air strip from any naval terrorists. Not that the retired navy man was a problem. At least to the President. To tuna, marlin and mahi mahi he might be classified a terrorist, but you would have to ask the fish that question.

He was taking a load of soon to be sashimi to the fish market at the Port of Honolulu. The bulk of Sand island and its huge shipping docks lay ahead and to his left. The fish he was carrying would feed some of the hundred thousand tourists who were even now sitting on Queens Beach and Waikiki. *They should see it from this vantage point,* he thought. The native Hawaiian had lived on the island for all his five plus decades. Even twenty-six years in this man's navy had been spent on Oahu. A lifetime at sea made his skin deep brown and gave him a permanent squint. He even rolled his gait when he was shore bound, the natural rhythms of the waves so much a part of him even his walk was affected. His retirement was being spent as a fishing charter guide, showing the visitors the nooks and bays where the Ono hid. The whales were always a nice presence and a bonus. Two early season humpbacks played off his starboard bow even now.

A second Coast Guard unit moved past him heading south west. *Uncle Sam's canoe club workin hard.*

Having the President visit the islands was nothing new, since Obama. Drum only came to soak up the sun and the booze, *like the rest of the tourists.* But he couldn't really fault the man for that. He could find fault for what he was doing to the country however.

A staunch republican, Walt was going to vote democratic in three weeks. *Got to get someone in there who was competent with the Chinese thing happening,* he'd told his wife. He had two kids and two grandkids to protect and help. And by god he was going to do it!

The docks seem to be buzzing as he unloaded the small tuna into the tub for weight and grading. A young man grinned at him as he went into the market.

'Eh brah- howzit?" Walt asked.

"Matsun gon lay off some ohana, Uncle. Bummahs," the young man said without preamble.

He agreed with the bad feelings the loss of jobs would bring about. He felt for the mostly young workers at the shipping company. Walt hefted the tub and helped the younger man move the fish to the processing stations. Teams of women were filleting and cleaning the tuna and mahi. His mother had done this kind of work fifty years ago.

Walt wondered why the shipping company that was the main employer on the island- discounting the military- would be laying off people. He sought out Sammie Chow.

"Mr. Sam- howzit?" he asked the pidgin catch all Hawaiian greeting after catching up to the busy man.

"Walt, how are you man!" Sam was used to dealing with the haolies and the Japanese and Chinese agents on the docks. The man spoke five languages and could muster up words in another six or seven.

"You guys layin off?" he asked seriously.

"Got to Walt. The docks are going to be tied up for the next nine months."

"What?" he was flabbergasted. The small island counted on the bulk shipments from the Matsun companies to get all of the little things that they didn't produce for themselves. Things like oil and gas and wheat. Without the ships coming in the island would run out quickly.

Chow shrugged a bit. "We got a normal upgrade period on the berths and the Chinese have reserved some for aid ships coming and going. We gon deal with the Navy for pier space at Pearl to unload our ships."

Walt took that in. Weird. The cost of reserving three pier berths for three months was very expensive. But it ensured your ships got unloaded as soon as they came into port. And he knew the Navy would let the company berth ships at Pearl harbor for a while. As long as the carriers and the small boys could come and go as they needed to.

Well that was above his paygrade. He thanked the older man for his info and went back to his boat. His pay check was 975 dollars for the fish. *Covers my gas* he thought. It was getting late. He had another two hours to get back to Waianae. The working class west side of the island was nowhere near where Drum was living it up over on the east side. The Marines would just have to deal with the man. Not his affair.

"Fire- Marines!"

The 19 year-old marine private could not clear his weapon. The M16A4 tended to jam when sand got into the breach mechanism and Duarte's gun was fubared.

"Duarte!"

The surprisingly deep voice of the Sargent cut thru the late afternoon heat. Leather lungs was at it again. The squad braced for more yelling. Check that. Not yelling. *Instructions delivered at a high volume level.*

'Do you not understand the concept, Duarte?"

That kind of question had always confused the young Marine. Did it mean that he understood the question or that he didn't understand? Was it one of those questions that the person yelling at you didn't expect an answer- a whatchacallit, rhetercal question? Robert Duarte answered with his best "Uhhh…"

"Uhhh!" "Marines do not answer with Uhhh!" Snickers crept over squad faces glad to not be on the receiving end of the Sargent's instructions.

"I ask again Duarte, do you know what a fire team is, Marine?"

Finally! A question he knew the answer to. "Yes, Sargent." "A fire team is the smallest unit in the Marines. Made up of four or five grunts armed with M16's and the 203 grenade launcher!" Sargent!" he added as an afterthought.

"Then explain to me why twenty percent of one of my fire teams is not operational!"

Duarte admitted that his gun was jammed. The math part where one of five team members equated to twenty percent went right over his head. "Hold fire, Marines!"

The Sargent had the other four team member's safe weapons while Corporal Morrelli slid over one spot in the fire trench to help the newest member of their unit clear his weapon. After some futzing the bolt slid home and the pair were ready.

Morrelli slid back over in the trench taking his spot next to Privates Olsen and Hicks. Samson crouched on the other side of Duarte. Fire team Able was ready to resume training.

'Able team, resume fire at will, one magazine- Fire!"

Staff Sargent Connie Sanchez raised the binoculars to her eyes and watched rounds arc out down range. Each position had targets set up at 60 meters. About 40 percent hit rates she noted as the targets got torn up. The school system in Oklahoma might not put out the best mathematicians but they knew a fair piece about shooting and Duarte could hold his own.

"Cease fire! Safe and Clear! 'Baker Up!"

Five troopers scrambled out of the trench, after seeing to their guns and five more jumped in. This was Hill's team. The female corporal was the smallest, smartest, white girl, Sanchez knew. 106 pounds of freckles and fury. The sound of gunfire was muffled by her ear protection so Sanchez could concentrate on the fields of fire and the overlapping pattern. Nice. Hill had obviously been talking to her people before their turn. The girl would make a good Sargent if she chose to stay in. Sanchez made a mental note to talk to her. Sound her out about her plans and such.

A check of her watch as Charlie team started in on the live fire exercise. 1610. The afternoon sun was heating up the Camp Pendleton live fire range. Marine Camp Pendleton was a huge chunk of prime real estate right on the coast of California, just north of San Diego. Its 22,000 acres were home to the 1st Marine Expeditionary Force and a lot of scrub brush.

***

A Marine Expeditionary Force was a self-contained, self-sustaining fighting force of the United States Marines. Essentially it is an "Army in a Box". Nestled inside of the MEF was the 1st Marine Division and its 19,000 troops. Connie and the 1st Marines lived and trained at the main west coast camp for Americas elite ground fighters. Although some regular Army units might give you a hard time if they heard that kind of statement. The 3rd Marine Aircraft Group comprised the air part of the fighting force. The 11,000 flyboys and girls got to live at Miramar which was just north and inland from Pendleton. The last leg of the triad was the 1st Marine Logistical Group. It's 10,000 swinging dicks and vaginas got to bunk in the barracks at Pendleton. The very old and hot barracks at Pendleton.

The Army in a box concept was very apt for the 1st MEF. The force had everything it needed to wage a sustained, vicious war for 60 days. They had their own bullets, supplies, planes, tanks, bombs, and intel without relying on anyone or anything else. Hell, the 1st MEF even had its own lawyers. You know, just in case.

The Marines will tell you that a MEF is an awesome fighting force and they would not be wrong. The countries of Norway or Cuba could field a force equivalent to a MEF. *If they fielded their entire military strength.*

The United States has three MEF's. One at Pendleton. One at Lejeune, North Carolina and one in Japan. True- a battalion of those Okinawa based Marines were at Kaneohe Bay on Hawaii… Anyway you sliced it, that was a lot of young Americans with really bad haircuts ready to shoot your ass if the shit went down.

***

'Marines! We were so terrible at the live fire event that your reward is to hump it back to the Armory. We have to turn in weapons and get chow before 1730. Un ass now!" Sanchez delivered at a high level again.

The sixteen Marines of Orange squad led by Staff Sargent Sanchez began their three-mile journey back to the armory carrying a full tactical load. 35 lbs. of gear hung in various places on the soldiers. Even Hill, who grunted under the lighter weight of her twenty pounds of back pack, made the forced march with relative ease. The squad would join up with Red and Blue squads for their platoons turn at the chow hall. Pendleton's main chow hall, 33 area was drowning under the weight of the reinforced brigade of 4200 mouths to feed three times a day. Connie let her mind wander free while she went over the ramifications of why her unit was so large. *Lejeune must be a ghost town right now.*

The Marines had increased the op tempo and readiness forces of two if its MEF's: The 1st in Pendleton and the 3rd at Camp Courtney in Okinawa, Japan. Lejeune was reduced by about half while the other two MEF and the Hawaii brigade had received some plus ups in people. She knew she should be a little scared of that but she was not. Not really.

Growing up in east L.A. had been scary. Walking the streets of her neighborhood was scary. Iraq? Piece of cake. And now her job was to clamp down on the rumor mill and calm her subordinates and her direct superior if she was being honest. Second Lieutenant Pete Wilkins may have been a scared shave tail right out of Quantico but he was willing to listen, and that put him miles ahead in her book. *What was she always telling Duarte?* Trust your chain of command. She did. From Lt. Wilkins up to Major General Nethercot, she knew that the Corps had sharp minds running the show. It was an old Roman legion trick, even the lowliest cook in the legion could recite his chain of command from the general on down. That way everyone knew who was in charge. The person with the responsibility had the big red "X" on his or her forehead. That way if the shit got deep they weren't a rabble running around, they were a fighting force. Morale and willingness to fight went a long way towards determining who won battles, not just who had the most troops.

The Marines could hold their own with any fighting force in the world or even in history. That was especially exceptional since the people calling the forces into play may not have been the brightest. She hated Drum but kept that opinion to herself.

Watching her people turn in the stripped down weapons while sweating from the hike, she knew that the brass feared they might be called into some kind of action. *Korea. I'm betting the North takes action while the Chinese are down.*

Sanchez never let her thoughts intrude to her face while she policed her children. And she did sometimes think of them as children. Duarte, Hill, Morrelli, Hicks, Olsen, Washington, and Samson and all the rest were depending on her for guidance and leadership. It was something the 29 year-old took very seriously. Had taken it that way since she was a little girl. Her Abuela would kick her hind end if she didn't help. That's just what happened in her family. Her mother worked endless hours while her grandmother (Abuela Marta) ruled at home. Her siblings, Tino, Ariel and Abel the III, all did chores as she assigned and would inspect the efforts. It turned out to be perfect training for herding Marines. The stocky and tough woman always wore her brown hair in a braid and the gold cross around her neck looked good against her brown skin. The one thing her grandmother might not be too happy about would be the tattoo. "Death Before Dishonor" brandished her shoulder. A small souvenir from the desert of Iraq in 2011.

The Humvees deposited the squad in front of 33 area chow hall at 1718. *Cutting it close but they have to feed us if we get in before time.*

"Plenty of water with your meal, everyone. Hill you especially. I want to see some calories on that plate."

"Yes Sargent," Hill grinned back. Kid could eat anything she wanted and the weight shed off. Not that Concepcion Sanchez was jealous. She was a rock hard 127 pounds of lean mean fighting machine but she still had to watch it just a bit.

The woman grabbed a tray and three large glasses of water and juice and went to eat with the other squad leaders. The Marines fostered a rank structure so the officers would not be at the table but Sanchez would report back to the Lt. to tell him how the live fire training had gone. He would be eating at the Officers mess and then doing paper work in the offices. The shift in DEFCON had reduced her paperwork to a very little. A weird perk of the fact that they might be going in harm's way soon.

The other NCO's of Lima Company had no stunning insights as to the US military and its response to the Chinese problem and the world in general. She hadn't expected much in that way. Collins and Armster were a black and white Mutt and Jeff pair but they were not very curious. Armster was the company OOD today. As such he had all the keys and the radio. He also had to respond if any problem came up in the enlisted barracks tonight. *That sucks!*

Armster bitched about having to keep 120 very young, fit and horny Marines separated from each other and the general population. The base had put the regiments on rolling 96 hour lockdowns. So at any one time only one of the five regiments on base could be at liberty and hitting the bars in Oceanside or San Dog.

The NCO's would be on a different schedule but would be subject to the same lockdown. Connie was only going to get back home once in the next two weeks. She had Officer of the Day duty like Armster on her next free day. That part really sucked! So the rest of her squad would be out on the prowl while she was stuck at a desk. Not good.

Well you took the promotion.

"Hey, Sanchez, you got the absentee ballot forms right", Collins asked.

"Affirm. My squad all voted en mass two days ago."

'Who'd you have them vote for? Armster grinned.

Sanchez shrugged. "I let them chose for themselves. I told them that they could vote for anyone they wanted to as long as it wasn't Drum."

The two men snickered. Quickest way to get under Sanchez' skin was to mention Drum. The two idiots kept at it until Sanchez threatened to kill them.

That was how Armster knew it was time to stop. *Tease until someone cries or hits you. Then only one more twist, that's how that worked.*

The radio burst in with static. Armster had to go let some knucklehead into a barracks room because the idiot had locked himself out. Kids!

She finished her meal and went to find the boss. Connie wanted to turn in early. It was hard work molding young minds and bodies. Plus, she knew the whole 1st MEF had a live fire division wide training op coming up soon. That was going to be interesting. It was a rare chance to work with air, intel and artillery all at once. The only thing more fun in her estimation was when they loaded the entire division on the Amphib ships and let them practice invading some beach somewhere.

CHAPTER THREE

That is the hardest I've worked since Iraq, Andre thought, slowly wiped his hands on a rag. The grease stains were coming out from under his nails and off his skin but it was rubbing the dirty areas raw. The harsh cleaner killed his skin and cracked and dried it out something fierce. He was going to have to moisturize as soon as he got home. It was Tuesday November 3rd in the year of our lord 2020 and the past week had been the most difficult and rewarding week of his life.

Andre was at the Roadability pedestal at the port in the back area workers break room. His shift was ending at 3:00 pm and he still had another three hours to put in at home before school. Then he had more paperwork to do after he got back to the house at the Bottoms and then… *Yeah, I'm busy alright*, he thought. Oh and he had to vote today, so that was one more thing on his to do list. Jesus! The small building he was currently looking at to house his new business was isolated, old and expensive as far as he was concerned but… it was going to be his.

Tompkins really came thru, the man reflected again. Without his professors help the SBA loan would not have been approved. Six hundred twenty-seven thousand dollars. That is a lot of scratch to be trusted with. The hell of it was he would need every penny and maybe more to start with.

"Dre, can you help me, man?"

Manny, one of the Pacheco brothers, stuck his head in the break room door.

"Shit, I just got cleaned!"

"I need help to lift the tire, dude, please!"

"Where's your brother, I thought you was joined at the hip?"

"Tito is working on the wrecker- towing in a rig," Manny explained.

Dre knew that hooking up and towing a broken down tractor trailer cab was a very difficult and back breaking job. On the other hand, hoisting a tire onto the automatic tire changing machine out on the shop floor was not much fun either.

"Yeah, man, I'll help."

"Thanks!"

The two men went out onto the main shop floor. Roadability was a funny name for a station at the port but that's what they called the thing. Andre had been amazed at the operation when he'd used an Army connection to snag an interview down here.

***

The Port of Oakland was a giant sprawling complex. Situated on the northwest corner of the city, the port grounds bordered the Nimitz freeway and the rail yards to the east. Huge cranes dominated the concrete pier ways while the flat asphalt pads that held the off loaded containers spread out behind the massive white cranes. The rectangle shaped wheeled gantry cranes looked cool and kind of like prehistoric dinosaurs. Dre knew the story of a young George Lucas who saw the cranes as a boy back in the 60's. He'd taken the general shape of the cranes and adapted them to be the huge walking battle tanks in the Empire Strikes Back movie.

Several red colored newer cranes that were even larger than the white ones, rode at the far north end of the piers. To the uninitiated the Port was a confusing jungle of rail lines, weird looking wheeled cranes and trucks, all running around without apparent direction. In reality, the port was laid out in a racetrack configuration that was quite detailed in where and how tons of freight moved on and off the grounds.

Trucks entered the main port terminus at the south east end and presented paperwork on what they had or wanted. If a truck was dropping off and picking up the TEU or Twenty foot Equivalent Unit container, it went to the terminus to get paperwork authorized and a drop off pad assigned for the incoming load. Once the wheeled crane lifted off the empty, the truck cab would continue to the next terminus to get an Id track tag and for verification that the shipping company had both load ready and the okay to move it. The port authorities would then direct the cab to the pick-up pad where the load would be craned onto the truck frame. Since most containers were the 40 feet- 2 TEU type, the whole unit now had to undergo several inspections: Both to ascertain the safety of the load and the truck itself. That's where roadability came in. If the truck was not fit for the US highway system or if the container failed a check-such as it carried some kind of contraband or dangerous cargo, then the fixes were applied at roadability.

Once cleared by the inspectors and the shipping agents, the truck sped on its way out the port and down Adeline street right onto the interstate highway system for delivery all over the country. The miracle was that barring some mechanical problem or a hitch in the paper work a truck could pick up and drop off in less than two hours. And that happened *thousands* of times every day at the port. At all US ports. Long Beach, Sea Tac and Hawaii all operated on the same system. The same went for the major east coast ports at Jersey and Miami.

***

Dre grabbed a pair of latex gloves as he went through the shop to the tire changing machine. Manny led the way to the hydraulically operated machine. The 48-inch diameter tire was ready to be fitted to the rim already loaded in the machine. Both men were required to hoist the tire onto the mating rig. Dre and Manny hefted and grunted under the load as they lifted it up to chest height to position the tire up to the rim. The rubber tire didn't weigh all that much, just 30 or so pounds, but the thing was unwieldy and awkward to move so two men lifts were preferred.

Dre held the tire up and steady while Manny went to the bucket and applied some silicon grease to the inner and outer edges of the wheel. The tire changer was computer controlled so it took just a few moments for Manny to type in the size and model and the machine was soon doing its thing. In three quick minutes the wheel would be ready for balancing.

Dre watched while he checked his gloves. Not much grease on his hands now. Manny worked the tire machine with ease. That was at least fifty percent of what they did at roadability: tires.

The number of trucks running on defective tires and rims was astonishing to the man. And he saw an opportunity in the situation. Sitting next to the tire changing machine was a giant stack of tires, easily 200 tires of various sizes spread around waiting to be mated to a rim. An equal number of rims sat in haphazard pile next to the tires.

It was a problem he'd dealt with in Iraq. Rims got damaged fairly easily: bent and cracked and most commonly, the lead balancing weights came off. Dre had spent countless hours welding the rims, pounding them back straight and balancing them in the desert.

He watched with approval as Manny spun up the tire and squeezed on the lead slugs to different sections of the rims. The tires had to have this or when they got up to road speeds they shimmied. That caused the tires to wear and blow too often. Dre had seen too many "road gators"- strips of tire tread from a blown tire- to not know there was a need to have the wheels and tires mated and waiting on the trucks when they broke down. But the roadability crews were too busy to keep up. So Dre saw where he might make some money and get his foot in the door.

Moving over to the now mated and balanced tire and wheel, Dre helped Manny lower the unit and haul the much heavier tire off the machine and on its tread. The two rolled the tire over to the rig waiting to get the wheel mounted on its back axel.

"Manny, you and Tito happy working here?" Dre asked casually.

"Sure Dre. Any job is good right now man," Manny said coolly. His English was much better than his brothers.

"You know I been goin to school?" Dre asked as they positioned the wheel on the lug bolts.

"Yeah, you graduatin soon eh?"

"I am, man. Listen. I been talkin to one of my professors and I got a small business loan." Manny grunted in surprise. "They gave you a loan?"

Dre laughed. "Yeah, man. Sometimes affirmative action works in your favor. Anyway, got the loan and I been talkin to Mr. Jenkins at the port."

Manny Pacheco was very impressed by that. Jenkins was *the man. Dre was always using his head.* But he played it cool and said nothing.

Dre looked at the Hispanic man. "I got a preliminary deal to take over the old Hazmat inspection building and set up a repair shop. We'd start with tires first and then work up."

Pacheco thought long and hard. "You want us to work for you?"

Dre grinned and nodded. "You and Tito are the hardest working dudes I know. And you know the tire machine and the wrecker."

"You buying a machine and a wrecker?"

The two men spent a few minutes using the impact wrench to affix the tire to the axel. Manny asked some technical questions about the machinery.

"Manny, man the new tire changer is 15,000 on the hoof, man. Shit, a new Peterbuilt towing unit costs 500,000," Dre complained. That would be 90 percent of his loan without even starting to pay for the building and his labor costs. Not to fucking mention tools and tires and payroll taxes…shit.

'Dude, you don need to buy a new tower. Tito and I know a decent rig that's a 2015, you could get for 200,000, maybe. But I definitely think a new tire change machine is better. The new ones can hold the rims while we repair the units."

So Manny had figured the tires like he had huh? Good, Dre thought. He asked after the man's thoughts on tools and other aspects of the new business. Manny had some *fuckin good* ideas.

"What about Tito?"

"What are you paying?"

That was a tricky question. Time for some misdirection. "You guys are legal right?" Now it was Manny's turn to frown and think. "Legal enough. We'd get thru E-Verify." That was all Dre needed to hear. The US system for verifying the status of foreign workers was notoriously bad, but if the brothers could get thru then he would be clear.

"How bout this: I pay you guys a straight 20 percent of the profit."

'Fuck that!" "Won't be no profits the first year."

No flies on Manny! "Okay man, how's this sound: A set 20 dollars per hour as a floor, then we set a 10 percent of the gross ceiling. We figure it out monthly, right?"

"What about benefits?"

Dude!

The men hammered out an agreement over the next thirty minutes. Damn that felt *grown up* to Dre. Shaking hands with his first employee, they made plans to meet up at the Brick at 8:30 tomorrow to go over things. Dre was elated. Suddenly the concept of owning his own business went from abstract to real with a lurch. He'd better get going, he had shit to do.

The helicopter ride should have been appalling. The city of Shanghai was separated into little isolated islands of dry land floating in a dirty brown sea of flood waters. Even a month after the flood, the waters were still clinging to the low lying areas. More rain had hit the area and the water had no place to go. So it sat, and infested with debris and bodies and filth. The four men in the passenger compartment of the Harbin Z-9 helicopter were oblivious to the wreckage as the craft glided over the doomed city. The dawning sun was even now raising over the sea to the east. Fei and Wei Bo sat in the rear two seats and both stared out the windows without much chatter. Yuan and Qi sat in the front two benches and kept up a running count of the numbers of fires they could see. The count stood at over 570 as of now.

Wei didn't listen. The number of fires did not concern him. Nor did the number of dead, or of the problems in Beijing. His job was down here and *he was on schedule.*

"Drum was reelected least night, General Bo, are you aware of that?" Qi asked, his huge form filling the seat. Bo wondered if the man could still fly, fat as he was now.

"I saw the US news this morning, Comrade General." Bo told him quietly.

"How are the ships coming?" Yuan demanded.

"I am on schedule with refitting the units. I have all the required ships here and at the deepwater port." Wei related.

The aircraft banked over the Boshan section of Shanghai heading south. The University of Shanghai had numerous student housing buildings that sat on relatively dry ground near the Naval base that was their destination. A huge soccer and athletics field complex adjoined the housing areas. The lightening day showed numerous tents set up and a steady stream of helos and trucks coming and going from the tent areas. To the satellites ever peering eye, it looked as if the aid for the city was being coordinated from this spot.

That was wrong.

The port area of Wagakzu was south of the naval base and of the university. The land was protected by a man made berm that had sealed off the flood water but had created one of the island the view had shown the men. The docks themselves rode on floating piers so the tides could be dealt with. That had the added advantage of letting the ways ride above the flood waters as well. Twenty huge ships sat at the docks. The gantry cranes, gangly red cousins of the Port of Oakland type, swung the shipping containers off the ships and onto the clear pad area. Hundreds of workers swarmed the flat pier area and were working on the containers.

That was Wei Bo's doing. Col. Zi was down there even now, coordinating the efforts here with the similar efforts other people were making at the Deep Water port on Dazhitou Island.

The deepwater port was connected to the mainland by a long flat bridge that spanned 12 miles of Hangzhou Bay. The Z-9 Harbin helicopter followed the bridge out to the port to fly over the huge operation out there.

Ships. A further Twenty two of the giant container ships, sat at the piers or rode at anchor off the docks. The blue hulled Hanjin ships were not the largest container ships in the world. These were Post New Panama Canal ships, true, but they were not the "triple E" variety. As such they could *only hold 15,000 of the forty foot containers,* not the 19,000 plus of the new models. But what was critical for the Chinese was the fact that they were available. Since the Korean shipping giant Hanjin line went into bankruptcy in 2016, the ships had sat idle at various ports. The Chinese government had contracted for them on an emergency basis to provide aid for the disasters ravaging China.

The ships seemed enormous to Wei's eyes as the helo looked them over. 1200 feet long and 150 feet in the beam, the ships were 250,000 tons when fully loaded. That gave them a draft of over 50 feet. *Twice as bulky as an American aircraft carrier.* Wei's thought was very dark as he was worried about the American carriers.

But the American carriers did not seem to worry the other three. The Military Ruling Panel was very pleased with Wei's efforts. The short visit to consult with Wei was easily explained as a photo op to look over the disaster area and console the poor people.

The Naval Base at Boshan had almost all of China's blue water forces arrayed by its docks. The ski ramp carrier Zhou Lan rode at anchor while numerous missile cruisers, destroyers and frigates lay nestled three deep at the moorings. The large Amphibious transport ships were down in Dazhitou at anchor near the southern tip of the island. Wei's plan did call for those ships to be used in the invasion but it was a secondary role. The Chinese Navy would play a big part but it would be on China's terms.

The four men exited the helo as they landed at the athletics field back to the north near the base and the university. Wei's office/home/field camp was not luxurious and the Generals all disproved of the horrendous smell. Dead bodies have a way of stinking up the place.

"The only thing we need to know are the time frames, Wei," Yuan was the one stating the obvious.

"Comrade General, I am exactly on schedule as laid out at our earlier meeting. The slip to the schedule will come in loading the troops and supplies."

The remark was a sly insult to both Yuan and Qi who had to move the resources he needed to this area. Any slip to the schedule would by definition be their fault.

Fei smiled. General Bo was a very smart man. 'Comrades we are months from the opening moves." "None of the slip is of any consequence."

Wei let none of his inner turmoil show on his face. His plan was brilliant and bold but complex. There were a number of elements he could not predict. And that worried him. The carriers were only one of the problems he was dealing with. Just the idea of invading the United States and trying to take and hold land was intimidating. But Wei knew that a hundred years ago the very idea would have been ludicrous. Now?

Now the US lacked the manufacturing capacity to make the instruments of war needed to repel an invasion.

They were going to have to fight the war with what they had on hand now or what they could bring to the battle field. Not that that was a small amount of men and material but... Wei had used his plan to level the playing field wherever he could. But variables could still came into play. Especially when they were dealing with war.

"Now that the buffoon is in place, we have the beginnings. I will provide the smoke. Qi will handle the mirrors and Bo you are in charge of the hammer." Fei laid out the responsibilities and the men again refined tactics and plans. The plan was flexible in that it allowed the shifting of objectives once on the ground. That part was up to Bo. He would be on the ground in the US. It was his choice of where to confront the Americans. "The missiles are key," he said yet again.

The Council spent hours going over the details. The midday break was a small meal eaten off a camp table in the tent attached to the grass field.

'What about the weather for the transit and beyond," Yuan wanted to know.
Lin Wei Bo shrugged. "There is simply no way to know, Comrade General." "I have projections for the seasonal changes on the west coast but they are mere 'Dryer than normal," projections. The Army General scowled. He looked at the storm clouds gathering over the city to the west. It was weather that got them to this point and it looked as if the storm was ready to break.

Washington DC was slightly frigid on this November day after election day. The still Secretary of the Treasury, Sharon Stallings entered her office building the boring way: from the street off of 15thNW after her driver dropped her off. She much preferred the cool way: entering from the secret closet in her office that led to the stairs and down to the tunnels that connected her to the White House and the old Executive building across the White House grounds.

There had to be some perks to being in this shit show, she thought for the thousandth time. She was fresh from a meeting of the shadow US government. Marino, the cabinet Secretaries, select Congressional leaders and the Joint Chiefs all hashing out how to usurp power from Drum. None of them wanted to, but they all had made a pact to stick it out together to get the country through this trying time.

Her sense of *wrongness* was off the charts. As the head of International banking and investments for a major trading house, she'd come to rely on her gut to tell her when things were not as they seemed. Check that. Things were *never* as they seemed when dealing with the international money crowd, but she'd figured out when the bad feelings were the dangerous or illegal kind and not just the normal trying to get the better deal type of shenanigans.

She had an IMF meeting and a meeting with the heads of the Central banks in Europe and the US to deal with China later this week. Cracks were beginning to show in the markets as the strain of having a billion people and their money fluctuate wildly in economic terms put a strain to the system.

What she needed she told Marino and the others at the meeting, was for Drum to hold a press conference and reassure the internal and external audiences that the US was leading and dealing with the Chinese problems. Both in food aid and stabilization of the markets, for starters.

But that was asking too much of the megalomaniac. That seemed to be the general consensus of the members.

She'd remembered when the outgoing Sec Treasury had called her and begged, *Begged!* for her to take the job. "Only you can hold things together," the old colleague had said softly. The man wasn't flattering her, just stating the obvious.

Well she was truly dancing as fast as she could right now. *58 and going on 100* she thought. A quick check of the mirror and she saw the grey starting to show thru again. The dark circles under her eyes were beginning to show as well. Too many nights spent worrying. *Fuckin Drum aint sitting up nights worried,* she thought.

Anders Young, Marino and the Senate Majority leader together had tacitly figured out that the government would run on a series of continuing spending resolutions and stop gap funding measures.

Not the most efficient way to run things but it avoided the shutdown monster. The main problem was that CR's and stop gap funding could not respond to emergent situations.

Like what happened the other day.

***

The US Treasury had scheduled an auction of debt. Just your normal garden variety selling of debt to allow the country to do little things like pay its military and its senior citizens their social security checks. The problem was, the Chinese market bought only 100 million dollars of a 25 billion dollar offering. Europe was not much better, snapping up 2 billion at a yield of 3.9 percent. The internal US market got its normal 16 billion but that left 7 billion dollars on the table. Russia was sure as shit not buying anything, and the middle east was out of it still with oil prices at historic lows.

Sharon was left with very few options. Cut the spending of the US government by 7 billion or raise the yield to four or even 4.1 percent to entice more buyers. Either option was a problem. Spending cuts were difficult unless they could raise more on the revenue side, but raising taxes in this environment was nonstarter. So they could raise the yields by dropping the price of the bonds.

But that act was inflationary on its face!

The Fed was going to have a field day with that. They would be forced to raise the prime rate on loans. The economy would slow as a result and the spiral downward would start.

Stallings knew the pain that would cause people and tried to explain it to the others in the administration. The bitch of it was there were no indications that next week's auction would be any different. Or the week after that. *What happens when we start offering the magic five percent to people on long term bonds?* She knew all about the psychological impact of people locking in to five percent returns on their money. The sad facts were obvious: people believed the four percent withdrawal rate was the bell weather and if they offered above that?

The blank look on an aide's young face said he needed a refresher on economics 101.

61

The theory held if you had a chunk of money to invest you put it in a place where you could return four percent. You lived off that four point edge and kept the principle as safe as possible. For two decades now the only place to get that rate of return was in the stock market. And that fact drove US businesses. Drove them in their hiring and inventory levels and the amount of capital investments they made. Everything. When an investor could get five percent in the safest long term investment in the world why would they risk their nest egg on the Street?

Bottom line was they wouldn't. And once they yanked their money out of the market, the country was well and truly fucked.

Stallings had tried several times to get Drum to understand the seriousness of this problem. The orange faced asshole had stared at her the whole time. If she didn't know better she could swear he was preparing to short the US market. But that would be crazy. Right?

Sharon had briefed the other members of the shadow group as best she could. Most were up to speed but the military guys didn't understand. Money just came to them didn't it?

Marino promised to get the President to sign an executive order giving her flexibility to arrange payments as the constitution allowed.

That was an extraordinary measure. It gave her the power of the purse over everyone. She was sure Congress would have something to say about it when their pet projects started being delayed.

***

Can't be helped, she thought and set about ordering the priorities of where the money the government spent would go. She didn't have time to reflect that the last person to have this kind of power was Thomas Jefferson. She set about trying to stabilize the world economic systems.

***

Noah held on to his father for a brief second and then let him go. Man and boy were on the delta pier at Joint Base Bangor as Thomas Spiegel was getting ready for deployment. The misty rain was a constant companion this week as the sub had made its preparations for a run to the Pacific Ocean.

"Take care of your mom and I'll be home before you go down to San Francisco for the thing." Senior Chief Spiegel liked to tweak his son's interests by referring to the Internet intern program as "the Thing". His primary job in the Navy was as a Fire Control Technician targeting and running the tomahawk missile canisters but a collateral duty was running the intranet and the computer systems onboard the boat. The man knew a lot about the internet and computers. Maybe even more than his son!

Noah grinned and accepted the needle. He was glad to be able to see his dad in the tight window before he left for the May 1st[th] job and after he came back from this run. His school was going to end two weeks early for him so he could get the privilege of working in a windowless office all summer toiling on the internet infrastructure of the nation. "We'll be fine. Mom has been so busy with the Admiral I never get to see her."

"Your mom is running that office so you have to help out as much as you can, Noah." Tommy spoke to his son just like he would one of his sailors. The past month had been an endless series of appointments to get things taken care of: Change the oil in the cars, make sure the smog check was done, renew the license plates and registration. Base stickers, doctor visits, dentists, banks, all of the small crappy adult things that made modern life hell. But the sailors and he had to do this before they left. Tommy had also spent some time getting everyone on the sub to fill out a tax extension form. Even with an increase in DEFCON and a long period at sea upcoming, Uncle Sam was getting his taxes. It was just that they weren't even going to get W-2's until they returned to port in late April.

The gold anchor and star of his collar device stood out on his blue coverall poopie suit. Noah always liked the cool patches his dad had on the working uniform. The USS Ohio had a circular cloth path that sported a nose on profile of the submarine with USS Ohio (SSGN 726) emblazoned in white on a red border. The ships motto, "Always First" was on a blue banner while a gold Tomahawk and a special ops scuba diver in gold floating above.

Special Operations teams and Tomahawks. The Ohio carried both. Normally they carried them that was. Not this run. Today, she was full up on the missiles. 154 of the fifteen foot conventional missiles sat in canisters in the vertical launch tubes. The Tomahawks came six to a canister that slipped into the tube originally constructed to hold a nuclear ballistic missile.

63

The Navy had four of the "tactical Tridents" as they were known in their inventory. The arsenal ships had seen service in the Iraq war, launching missiles inland from the Gulf of Arabia. Since 75 percent of the population lived within 500 miles of a coast line, the places where a missile could not reach out and touch someone or something were very small. The four were now sitting at Bangor awaiting whatever orders the brass thought appropriate. Ohio was up first.

"I will dad, don't worry," the boy told his father.

Tommy swallowed the pain that wanted to show on his face. The divorce had been hard on his boy and on the parents but he was managing. He hoped the young man understood what had happened between the two adults.

"I'm proud of you, son." The words came out softly as the man embraced the thin frame of his son again.

The "thanks" was muffled as he squeezed. Noah smelled the industrial smell of oil and grease and sweat on his dad's clothes. He kind of hated that smell.

All over the pier, sailors hefted bags and walked thru the security gate. Noah watched for a long time as his dad was swallowed up by the low slung black tube.

Inside the huge submarine the crew was busy stowing gear and personal items. They had a long day ahead of them. The Captain was holding an 0900 meeting with the Admiral and his staff as the two SSGN's- the Michigan was the other, would put to sea and rendezvous with the John C. Stennis battle group.

The two subs were going to try some new stuff on this run. Tommy always liked it when they did new things. It was boring punching holes in the ocean just running around. The GN's were built to be used. They could deliver special ops troops or serve as an arsenal ship and then they could spy like a fast attack. They had a full complement of torpedoes didn't they?

'Senior Chief, report Weps Department status for ready for sea." The Chief of the Boat, Randal Mannis asked his friend.

Tommy looked up from the Fire Control console in the control room of the sub. "COB, Weapons Department is ready for Sea, all personnel on board and at stations. Equipment deficiencies are logged and all gear is operational." The formal litany was comforting as they knew a stressful test was heading their way.

"I have you off the watchbill, Tom, Mannis told him. "This op with the jarheads is going to be difficult."

"I have three extra techs on board, along with a liaison from the Marines, so we should be able to talk to them."

The two men discussed what was going to happen with the extra personnel.

"They are in the temporary racks on the second level, missile house."

"Go check on them please."

The control room with its computer stations and ballast control panel and diving stations was the nerve center of the ship. The Officer of the Deck stood watch in Control on the Conning station. The raised platform held the two periscopes and the announcing circuits for the sub. The Navigation chart table was off to the right. The radar and a host of other stations ringed the crowded room. Usually nine men and women stood a watch in this room. Right now fifteen people were jammed in ready to take the ship to sea, at Piloting stations.

The access hatch and ladder up to the conning tower and bridge was in the center of the room. The OOD and his look outs were even now stationed up there ready to go. The CO would be joining them very very soon.

Radio and Sonar were forward of Control on this top most level of the sub. Directly aft of the Conn was a room devoted to special ops planning and targeting for the tomahawks. Tommy ducked quickly into the room. He had special security clearance to get into the place.

The cool of forced ventilation designed to keep powerful computers at sixty degrees made him very thankful he'd put on his green submarine sweater. The wool was his best defense.

Several Fire Control Technicians were huddled around three central consoles as they monitored the missiles in their canister's. Any loss of connectivity or electrical power or a host of other conditions would cause an alarm. They'd been dealing with a balky canister connection to the umbilical in tube 16. Fixed for now, thank god.

A Marine Lieutenant was running them thru the newly installed radio and comms links.

'Sir, are you stowed for sea? Any issues with your rack?" Tommy asked the man.

Second Lieutenant Koster grinned at the Senior Chief. "No Senior, everything is fine."

"Sir, remember we are going to be putting the ship thru angles and dangles as soon as we submerge, so…"

The concept that this five hundred sixty foot machine would submerge under water and then raise and lower its nose twenty-five degrees was incredible to this man. Eighteen thousand tons of ship. *No they called them boats.*

"I'm sorry we couldn't get you in the goat locker or in officer's country, sir..." Tommy started.

"Senior, are you kidding me? I have a bed! And it's not on the ground in the mud. And no one is shooting at me!"

The techs all grinned at the young officer. Let's see if the guy bitched after being cooped up for a while.

"Aye sir." "You and I have to brief the Captain with the Weapons Officer in three days, are we ready?"

"Affirm Senior!"

Easy dude. Just be ready when the Commanding Officer starts asking questions.

Spiegel exited the ops room and went down the port side aft ladder to the second level passage way. Officer berthing and some equipment spaces were up here. Continuing aft he swung thru the water tight hatch into the mouse house. That being what the sailors called the missile compartment. The port side on this level on the out board side held a small walkway and rack after rack of cabinets for spare parts. In between the racks were dead spaces that the over stuffed sub had turned into spare bunks. The thin mattresses were thrown anywhere they could be jammed.

Of course it sucked for the person living in the small space. People constantly walked by making noise, lights were on 24/7 and whenever a supply guy had to retrieve parts they kicked you out of bed.

Better than hot rackin. I suppose, Spiegel remembered sharing a rack with another sailor when he was a young nub. NUB. Non Useful Body. A term given anyone who was not qualified on the ships systems so had not yet gotten his dolphins. The stylized dolphins were a source of pride for the sub sailors. Spiegel had worked his tail off as a 19 year old fresh from school. He'd gotten his quals done in one run. A very difficult task. Once you had your fish and got a watch qualification completed, you were no longer a NUB and life got better. Not easy of course, just less hard.

Spiegel stopped at the bunks of his new people about halfway down the 255 foot long passageway. His crew had received some last minute additions to augment his regular watchstanders. Two of them were qualified sailors rotating early from shore duty. The third was a NUB but who looked to be a hard charging sailor.

"Perkins, Ashley, you guys okay?"

The two second class petty officers looked at the Departmental Senior Chief and smiled.

"Yes, Senior. Only problem is we can't get stowed for sea with people checking on us all the time," Perkins related.

Tommy knew what had probably happened, Aikens, his leading first and Chief Gunderson had probably been by this morning already.

"Hey, guess what, CO, XO, COB and Weps, all gonna be "just in the neighborhood" and see what's going on", Spiegel told them.

Ashley, the taller skinnier one snorted. "As long as the Bull Nuc don't harass us we are golden."

Tommy laughed and told them they were unlikely to see the oldest nuclear trained Ensign onboard, commonly called the Bull, directing Weapons Department personnel. "Nucs should stay back aft- pushing- where they belonged."

The two sailors laughed easily.

Tommy found out that Zemora, the NUB third was stowed and over on the mess decks. He spent a few minutes going over the watchbill and the plan of the week with his newest charges. Ohio stood four section watches this run. Which meant that they were atypical for a submarine.

Normally, the Navy Submarine service stood six hour long watches, with three sections rotating thru. That way, you spent six hours on watch, six hours off watch working and then got maybe six hours of sleep. Repeat until the days blurred together and the only way you could tell time was by what meal the mess cooks were preparing. A four section watchbill meant that the sailors got more time for sleep, but they ate the same thing all the time.

If the meal had eggs or egg substitutes, it was breakfast. Dinner always had some kind of soup. Midnight rations, or mid rats always had one of two things: Beanie weenies or scagioli which was the Navy version of Chef Boyardee ravioli. It was VITAL that a US sailor know his or her food shapes. Round and breaded was a chicken puck. Round with grey color and rough texture could be veal or a hamburger. Square and breaded was fish. Fat, torpedo shaped and breaded was chicken cordon blu. Trapezoidal and white was index card fish. Wash all that fine cookin down with Ultra High temperature milk- sometimes called death cow- and you could lose fifteen or twenty pounds on a long run.

He did find Zemora on the mess decks, which was one level down from the temp racks and back in the forward compartment. The young woman was ready to go.

"I'll want you up in the planning room the whole run, Petty Officer," Spiegel told her.

"Aye, Senior."

The girl was no more than nineteen. *She could be Noah's girlfriend*, he thought. 'Run your questions through Aikens and Gunderson first, but if you need something find me and I will make it happen."

Zemora was reasonably happy for someone who would not see much of the sky for the next months.

"Station the Maneuvering watch!"

The announcement came over the ships 1MC circuit. The general announcing circuit ran the whole length and breadth of the ship and could be heard everywhere. The buzz of the ship increased as every person onboard had an assignment. Line handlers went topside. The navigation team all went to control. The damage control teams went to the mess decks with specialized equipment. Various stations donned sound powered phones and checked in with Control. Ships goal was five minutes for each space to be fully manned and on line.
Ohio took six as last minute details got ironed out.

Tommy went topside. Normally he would be running the line handlers, the crew of sailors who loosed the large mooring ropes that tied the boat to the pier, but this time he was "unassigned personnel".

The long flat black superstructure deck of the Ohio was broken at regular intervals as a six foot diameter circle cracked the smooth surface. The hatches for the Missile tubes stood out against the rest of the steel structure covering the smooth spherical hull. The Captain, Commander Greene came hurrying on board from his meeting.

No need to hurry sir, we aint goin anywhere without you, Tommy thought. Just back from his last meeting with the Admiral. Tommy had served with Admiral Kollmansberger when he was the CO of West Virginia, SSBN 736. K14 was the man's nickname, and Tommy knew him to be very sharp and serious. If the Admiral was worried, then he was too. He had special insight since Lynn worked for him. *Had special insight,* he supposed. The man put those thoughts out of his mind. Not much he could do about his marriage now. He was concerned and excited for his son too. Noah was starting to branch out and this internet boot camp thing in SF was going to be good for him. *Get him out of Kitsap county and let him see more of the world than just Navy towns.*

The Ohio took on tugs and started the long journey out of the Puget Sound and towards the straights of Juan de Fuqua. The first obstacle was the Hood Canal Bridge. The bridge was only three miles from the base so it was always the gathering spot for wives as they waved a last time at their husbands before going to sea.

Tommy looked to see the small figures up on the bridge waving and smiling. Suddenly he spotted two familiar shapes. Lynn and Noah straining and looking. For him.

He caught his ex-wife and son's eyes as the ship slowly slid under the bridge. A lump formed in his throat as they waved and cheered. He waved back.

That act of kindness and love from his ex-wife sent his mood soaring. She didn't have to bring Noah to the bridge. He'd been on many, many deployments, so it wasn't like he needed the boost but still, it was so damn decent of her, that he felt good and knew he would for days afterwards.

The Ohio had been busy on the six days it took her to get into position for the op. Lieutenant Koster, was spending every waking moment on the ops room with Spiegel, the CO XO and the Weps. The men knew a hell of a lot about the new gear but not everything.

As an arsenal ship the Ohio had weapons aplenty. In addition to her torpedoes, she had four basic variants of the Tomahawk cruise missile. A land attack version with a single large warhead. An anti personnel version that had bomblets dropping off over a large area. A bunker buster variant that could penetrate hardened concrete targets and a special air burst variety that could do a lot of damage Spiegel supposed.

***

Lieutenant Koster had briefed the CO four days ago on the upcoming mission.

"Sir we are going to test the interoperability of the SSGN launched tomahawk variants with various operational units." The Marine accompanied the bullet points with slides in the Officers mess. The small table could hold fourteen and the room was packed to beyond capacity. 18 men and women jammed into the room to see how the new gadgets the Marines brought on board would work.

"The problem the GN's had during the Iraq and Afghanistan conflicts was the lack of real time target detection, selection, and prosecution."

The CO grimaced. "Can the buzzwords, Lieutenant. Tell me what we are going to do."

Koster gulped. "Sir we are going to launch tomahawks on targets designated by various Marine, Navy, Army and Air Force units."

"What's more sir we are going to practice passing control of the missile back and forth across multiple platforms and users until a target is identified and destroyed."

Silence gripped the room. *That's gonna be a neat trick,* Tommy thought.

"Go on, Lieutenant," the Commanding Officer said.

Koster reviewed the subs current targeting and guidance link package. "The Link 11 data and designations flow from the radio mast thru the radio room and down to planning and missile control system and then finally to the missiles." Pictures of the second level forward missile control room which was located underneath the planning and ops room flashed in the officer's mess. "Up to this point it has always been a static link: Only the National Command Authority could input the data, transmit it and the missile flew to completion."

"TOMCOMM has changed that." And innocuous box was flashed on the screen. Small, metallic and with a thick stub antenna poking out the unit also had several input output attachment jacks. TOMCOMM is a universal send receive interface with the missile for real time targeting and coordinate updates."

"Whoa." The XO was impressed.

"Yes, Sir, the test plan calls for a total of 24 missile firings by the Ohio. All variants will be tested. Range safety calls for inert warheads on all munitions and sub munitions," Koster related.

Spiegel twisted as the test plan called for a series of firings in an 8 hour period. Eight in the first two hours, four in the next hour. A one hour silent period and then another four in one hour followed by eight in a free fire forty-five minute period. The remainder was also silent.

"Why forty-five minutes?" The Weps, Lieutenant Archibald asked.

"That's fuel limited. "We figure the birds have about a forty five minute free flight fuel window after launch. Zebra test is going to ripple fire eight weapons and have them loiter in a race track formation over the battle field. Command wants to see if we can detect target and destroy in a real time test with different controlling units."

Grins spread around. Yeah that was going to be fun.

"Yoke test has us passing control back and forth as many times as fuel can with stand," Koster related. Yoke test was one of the four missile batches in the hour. Xray test was similar to Yoke but the targets would be changing in addition to the control of the flying bombs.

"Will control ever come back to us?" The CO wanted to know. Koster grimaced. This Captain knew the guidance for the test didn't have that as an implicit goal but both Greene and Koster knew the Command Authority liked to challenge its people.

"Unknown sir," he admitted.

"That's a yes", Greene told the XO to general laughter.

Is it funny because its funny or is it funny because he's the Captain? Tommy wondered.

Greene turned his gauze on the two men on his left. "Weps, Senior, you have the football. I want to be able to pass control back and forth just like any other unit. Figure out how we are going to get the real time Link 11 data and the drone feeds off the TOMCOMM and integrated back into our fire control system."

With that tough task laid out the CO moved on to the COB and started discussing the ships personnel and the positioning of the battle stations crews.

"Port and starboard sections for the crew, sir. We switch them out during the one hour dead period, the COB told his boss.

"Nav, do we own the water?" He asked the Navigator about the positioning of the ship during the test.

"We do sir. We can go in any time after 2400 hours tomorrow. No depth restrictions and we have no other opposition units or submerged interference." "The coasties are keeping the surface units out of area."

That was easier on them than normal and Tommy was surprised. Usually when they did these kinds of tests the Navy liked to put another submarine in the area to harass them, or some cruise ship moved right thru the middle of what they were trying to do. *They must want us to concentrate on the birds*, he thought.

"Who's the Command Authority for this, son?" the CO asked the Marine.

"General Nethercot," Koster told him.

The man held silent for a minute. "Okay. We have the test plan and Lt. Koster. It's pretty simple for us: get in position and bomb the Marines in California." Snickers around the table. "Seriously, we do not want to be the person who is not holding up their end of the octopus."

"COB! We probably need a field day to clean the boat before we commence with the tests, huh?"

"I was just thinking that, sir!"

"Sir we don't want to be the low man on this" Sargent Sanchez told Lt. Wilkins. Lima Company 3/5 of the 1st Marines was dug into positions on a low ridge looking down on the scrubby flats of the missile range built on the huge Marine Air ground battle range on 29 Palms. The huge desert training facility was hell and gone from San Diego and anything else, located east of the population centers by 100 miles. Army and marine units trained at 29 Palms for desert warfare. A series of concrete "enemy buildings" stood in a line three kilometers away from the Marines. Several faux tanks and armored personnel carriers were strung out in a skirmish line opposite the forces of the 1st MEF.

This was a serious op, Sanchez realized. It had started this morning when Lima company was picked up at a rally point, several miles from Pendelton on the Miramar staging area. Fully forty Marines carrying a full weapons and ammo loadout packed into the Marines newest battlefield toy, the tilt rotor V-22 Osprey. They still went into the twin rotor chinook helo's of the Vietnam era, but now the Osprey could whisk them on and off hotspots much faster. The Osprey competed with other aircraft for airspace on the range as the FA-18's and the stealthy F-35 Lighting streaked by on close support missions. The Lightning was untried in battle and had a very sketchy reputation with the pilots. The saying went that it had done its worst damage to the Pentagon's wallet.

Sanchez could also spot the units' intel drones buzzing a few thousand feet in the air on the edge of the battlefield.

The exercise had started per normal, a series of coordinated artillery barrages, a few air strikes and then the ground troops practiced moving in on entrenched positions with the Bradley's and the tanks. No big deal.

Olsen, Hicks, Duarte and Morrelli were sweating and taking a drink/ration bar break while she went over the next portion with Lt. Wilkins.

"I've never done this before, Sir. We can laze the targets but "Pass operational control from designated units?" "I'm not sure what that means."

"Sargent we have the laptop and the TOMCOMM unit," Wilkins told her. The young Officer was white and about ten inches taller than Sanchez. She hated looking up at him all the time. "We just have to drop and take control as directed."

Armster, Hill and her fire team moved up next to the pair as they looked over the material for the tests. Whiskey test was in fifteen Mikes. A series of eight firings in two hours. Sanchez and Lima company got the honor of marking a preset target with the laser designation unit. That part was easy. What she was worried about was the Zebra test much later in the day. The brass expected that her unit take operational control of a flying missile and put it on a target that "Presented the most operational advantage."

"How in the hell are we supposed to know that, Sir!"

Pete Wilkins crouched down near his staff Sargent. "Sanchez, we use our best judgments. It has to depend on the weapon and the warhead and the situation. During these Whiskey shots we can use the TOMCOMM to monitor what and where and who has control of the missile. Roger that?"

"Oh rah! Sir!"

It was all a little video gamey for her tastes. Connie liked to shot at people right in front of her. That's how they did it Iraq. That's how it would go down once they got to Korea, whenever that little MF'er over there got the balls to attack south. Until then, she would do her best like always. Wilkins and Sanchez dug into the manual and the laptop files to figure out how to Buck Rodgers this thing.

"Dammit Weps, what menu option was that again?"

Tommy could not figure the TOMCOMM laptop menu system fast enough. It was several layers in where the control code was inputted to allow an outside unit to take over control of the missile. Since the sub never took control back, its normal fire control software just inputted the coordinates or the laser designation option right on the main screen.

USS Ohio had been at battle stations missile for the last two hours. The sub hovered at launch depth about fifty miles off the coast of Southern California. The ship was barely crawling along and just turning the screw enough to overcome the Humboldt current that tried to sweep her back north. Several masts were poking their little heads above the surface of the calm waters of the Pacific at this midmorning hour. The periscope, and two radio/comms masts were raised and their trail feathers could be spotted. If anyone was bothering to look for them.

"It's under the "input desig/code- option five" on the Input Output menu," Lt. Archibald told him while Lt. Koster nodded.

"Okay. Got it." Tommy pressed buttons on the laptop and the fire control system while the two offices looked over his shoulder. The two console techs reported green status on the units after the missiles accepted the new commands. "Control, Ops, all birds, status green. Control is ours. Whiskey flight will commence time 1034 local. 1934 zulu."

"Very well ops." The CO 's voice was clear and calm over the open mic system. Instead of using the dedicated ships announcing circuit or the sound powered phones, the crew had installed a simple Radio Shack wired mic and speaker system to SONAR, Radio, Missile Ops Planning and Control. It allowed the CO to split his communications into three areas: the MC circuit for ships orders and engine orders, the 1MC for emergencies and the open mic system for the weapons test.

Koster queried radio to confirm the open comms line with command authority and his fellow Marines on the ground on the other end of the missiles track. Radio supervisor reported in direct comms with General Nethercot.

"Command Authority, this is Sierra unit. All green. Request permission to commence Whiskey at time 1934, zulu. Launch spread at twenty, repeat two zero, minute intervals until completion." Captain Greene spoke directly into the mic unit to transmit to the Marines ashore his intentions.

"Sierra unit, this is Command. Understand Whiskey at 1934 zulu, two zero minute interval until completion."

The Marines waited a full minute while this request went thru the chain of command and out to the subordinate units in the field. "Sierra this is Command, you have permission to commence at 1934 zulu."

"Command, this is Sierra, Aye, aye."

Koster grimaced as Greene used the Navy "I understand and I will comply" reply. Marines tended to hate that. Spiegel grinned. Just because the guy was a three star General, didn't mean he wasn't an asshole.

Time sped up as the ship anxiously awaited the launch window. The ship set Battle stations missile-ready, at 1020. The huge hatches on three of the tubes swung up, exposing the tops of the missile canister packs. At 1030 local, the Captain ordered "weapons free." Tommy acknowledged and the final ships position and targeting data was inputted via radio link thru the umbilical and to the missile. As the canister reported the uplink complete, the umbilical retraced to allow the weapon to be "free" in its canister. Everything was internal now. At time 1034 exactly, a signal went from the canister down to the rocket motor in the body of the missile. The motor cooked off in micro seconds. The thin metal film protecting the top of the canister ripped open as the missile roared off. A second bird in another tube unit ripped out of its protective cover at nearly the same time. Both units punched out of the ocean with a fiery roar and hurtled skyward. Protective covers flipped free as the missile cleared the surface and flew off. The debris would fall back into the ocean near the sub and could be a hazard to other birds in a ripple launch scenario. In this case there was plenty of time to clear the materiel and launch without problems.

"Whiskey flight volley one away!"

Spiegel's report was passed to Command. Ohio had done her part at the start of the op.

"Here they come!" Wilkins voice rose as he got excited. The one hundred fifty mile flight plan would only take five minutes, so things were going to happened quick.

The TOMCOMM unit blinked away serenely but the laptop pretty well freaked out. Data flashed on the screen as the unit got into synch and contact with the two incoming birds.

"Green Comms!" Sanchez reported as the missile designated for Lima company blinked into being on her screen. "Morrelli, Duarte, steady Laze the target, tank cluster, designated Whiskey Volley one, Able unit." She told the young Marines what she wanted as the target, (the cluster of tanks) what she was calling the incoming missile (whiskey flight volley one the first of two units) and how they should paint the target (steady laser versus a flashing pulse).

"Steady laze, cluster of tanks, whiskey volley one able, Roger that!" Morrelli answered with just a hint of his accent. New York is hard to get out of one's voice patterns.

The two Marines positioned the small laser designator box at the top of their sand bag berm and flipped the power switch. The green lights came on in seconds and the red "LASER ON" light illuminated almost immediately after.

Wilkins reported up his chain of command what was going on and the squad had about forty-five seconds to hold their breaths as the time counted down.

The contrail was the first visible thing. Two white lines stitched themselves from the sea towards their position inland. There was no sound as the white line dropped down and came on towards them.

Sanchez shifted her gaze to the target. She'd picked a group of three of the fake tanks parked down below them. The theory being that a hit with the six hundred pound warhead anywhere in the general vicinity of the three vehicles would be fatal to all.

The 20 foot long subsonic missile was painted bright orange but was still barely visible as it buzzed into the field. The huge dirt and dust cloud it threw high into the air was much more impressive. The hard sided steel of the targets pinged loudly as dirt clods bounced off.

"Hit!" Wilkins crowed and reported.

Sanchez had the fire team switch off the designator unit to save the batteries. "Nice work, Duarte, Morrelli."

The Lima company and Sanchez could relax for a few minutes while other units took their turns in the hot seat guiding the missiles into the targets. Duarte loved the part where the sub munitions popped off the flying missile to cover a huge swath of ground with tennis ball sized bomblets. Sanchez told him he did not want to be on the other end of that attack. "The grunts absorbing the bombs are going to have a very bad day."

Better to be the hammer than the nail, she thought. "Orange squad, strip weapons and pack gear. We move out on the humvees to the other side of the ridge in four hours for Zebra test." Her kids still had more work to do.

"I think we can do that Captain."

Spiegel and Mannis were in control after the last of the Yoke flights had been released. Not a bad day for the sub. 16 missiles launched with only two slight hitches: one bad data link- which caused the missile to go back to default and follow a preset hard target choice. And one bad control link which had the Marines scrambling to pass control to another operational unit.

The CO was irritated by only one thing: he was basically in the dark here. He had no visual look at the battle field. Not that Greene was some kind of tactical genius but he still wanted a look at the overall picture. The sub had received a low resolution, drone still picture over a limited band width link from Radio but he was not at all satisfied with that.

"I can't make out shit on that- can you XO?" Both men looked at the picture and tried to puzzle it out. "Senior is there a way to port the vid link from the TOMCOMM unit?"

Tommy exchanged glances with the Weps who shrugged. "I think we can do that, Captain." Spiegel knew that Air Force pilots on low tech older planes often used the cameras from their missiles to use as battlefield surveillance units.

His techs busied themselves attaching a tap line on the TOMCOMM unit. The unit they were strictly NOT supposed to touch. Within minutes the video static was being displayed on the laptop. "The screen is static right now, Sir. The bird is inactive, but as soon as it goes hot right after launch we should have pictures". "We will only have the picture from the unit we control, Captain."

"Right Senior. Weps can we pirate that laptop line out to the Conn?"

The Weapons Officer smiled. "Yes, Sir, that part is easy."

Soon enough the CO's video monitor was showing the same static. The large video monitor in control was what the Officer of the Deck used to scan the surface of the sea when the ship was coming to periscope depth. A sub was very vulnerable when heading from the depths to the shallows. Even with all her sophisticated Sonar and tracking gear collisions while coming shallow happened.

"All hands this is the Captain. We are going to ripple launch eight missiles in approximately 22 minutes. We haven't done this big a launch since the test trials 12 years ago. Be vigilant on stations and if something is abnormal, sing out and we will figure it out. Carry on."

Green hung up the 1MC mic.

"Officer of the Deck, increase speed to ahead one third, turns for three knots."

"Ahead one third, turns for three Aye Sir," "Helm ahead one third, turns for three knots." The OOD repeated.

As maneuvering answered the engine order telegraph at the helms control station, the ship vibrated just slightly as Maneuvering made enough revolutions on the ships screw to make the ship go three knots of speed through the water. The Captain was increasing speed to help clear the debris field as the Tomahawks were hurled off the ship.

"Officer of the Deck, ship has 42 minutes on this course," the Navigator reminded him. The ship was going to be outside of its assigned waters if it remained on this course for the full length of the Zebra flight test.

"Aye, Nav, I'm going to put on a slight right turn to move us seaward," the OOD confirmed. Both the Nav and the CO nodded to this statement. The miniscule three degree turn would put the ship in a huge circle and they could concentrate on launching the Tomahawks.

Again the time seemed to fly by as the Yoke and X ray tests went sort of smoothly. Units that were used to controlling weapons systems, like drone pilots and aircraft were familiar with the Navy/Marine Corps Tactical Interoperability Net, so the AN/UPR-134 R TOMCOMM unit was nothing to them. To submarine sailors and Marine grunts? Not so much.

"Weapons Free!"

Ohio shuddered as a ripple of eight launches in under a minute leapt off the boat. The weird "clunk" of the missile protective fairings bouncing off the superstructure unnerved some of the crew.

"Ops we have picture," the CO announced over the open mic.

"Yes, Sir we have it on the laptop. Adjusting." Tommy reported back. The view from the flying bomb was pretty bad. A blurred blue swath was all they could see.

"Order the camera to zoom out," Koster told Archibald. The powerfully built Weapons Officer tapped on the laptop and the view suddenly cleared a bit to show the ocean streaking by.

"Flight plan calls for the birds to go to a cruise altitude of 10,000 feet and orbit over the Strike Range on a ten mile race track." Koster acknowledged the reminder report from Tommy.

"Weps that's better. We can see the coast coming up." The CO and the whole control room party were pleased. Watching TV was always fun.

"Missiles incoming!" Lieutenant Wilkins told Sanchez. Forty Marines were arrayed around the pair watching them struggle with the laptop. The radio Hicks had was pressed to his ear to get orders from Nethercot and his staff.

"All designated units standby to take command per the test plan!" Hicks relayed the orders.

"Sargent?" Wilkins was concerned.

"Got it sir, Code ready for Zebra flight unit five. Target to be determined." She mashed buttons on the laptop like they owed her money.

The contrails were converging and the different spacing levels of the missiles showed. The eight birds went into a two and two formation, with a five hundred foot separation pattern. The leader missile about 2,000 yards in front of the trailer. Nethercot and his underlings let the missiles fly two complete race track patterns before ordering the individual units to take control.

"India company, 1/1, Control unit Zebra one, 2,000 feet ascent and continue race track."

Lima Company watched rapt in attention as a contrail split off from the others and rose dramatically higher than the other seven birds. Ohh Rah!

More orders came for other companies, and then-"Lima, 3/5, Control unit Zebra five, 2,000 feet descent and race track orbit to the north."

Sanchez input the commands and the codes into the TOMCOMM. Wilkins checked them over and said "Affirm!"

After she hit enter, the bird glided down effortlessly and established itself in a unique orbit north of the other missiles.

A full fifteen minutes passed while Command Authority ordered a series of maneuvers and target designations with the flying bombs. Sanchez let the other NCO's type in the commands while Wilkins kept an eagle eye on the thick fingered grunts.

Hicks squeaked as he repeated this order. "Lima 3/5, Zebra five, trade operational control with Unit Sierra. Coordinate directly."

Sanchez goggled. "Unit Sierra, this is Lima 3/5, Zebra five, surrendering op control." *Was she really talking to a submarine at sea?*

Hicks' mouth went wide in a smile as he said, 'Sierra acknowledges and has control."

The Marines watched their Tomahawk rise up and move back to the south under control of the launching submarine.

Nethercot decided to get really cute with his charges. "Command Authority is dead."

The silence over the radio unit built to an unbearable level until, "This is Colonel James. I have Operational Authority, code Oscar, Oscar, Oscar."

Wilkins furiously dug into his vest to retrieve the laminated Op Board. The small pamphlet held radio frequencies and passwords and codes for just such occasions.

"Affirm!"

Hicks relayed Lima Company's status to his new chain of command while the other Marines around him breathed a sigh of relief.

James decided to change target designations on individual units, just to fuck with people.

"Lima 3/5. Control unit Zebra five, change target to fifth on established objectives."

Wilkins had Hicks "wait one" to command while he verified the objective to ensure the order was carried out correctly. The objective order numbers had changed twice during the day.

And now he was unsure which target was fifth.

"Sir, recommend we take op control and then check target with Command." Sanchez kept her voice low.

Wilkins processed the request. To his credit he immediately recognized good advice. "Take control, Sargent."

"Hicks, to Command, verify objective five is target designation building six Yankee," the Lieutenant told the radio operator.

Sanchez retrieved the missile control from the Ohio while Hicks and Wilkins talked to Command to ensure they had the right target. They did.

She knew Wilkins was going to hear some chatter about not knowing the target changes off the top of his head. But she also knew the young Officer was right to check in with the Staff to confirm. *Better a quick radio call than a friendly fire incident.* People got killed if you didn't have enough sense to admit what you didn't know.

Another ten minutes of rotating control as the missiles flew out to a rally point and then made one by one target runs on the hard points on the 29 Palms range. Zebra five made a humdrum splash into the dirt and a confirmed kill.

"Hicks, tell those squids- thanks," Sanchez told her squad member.
Wilkins nodded along, "Sargent lets regroup and police the area before we hit the Humvees back to the landing point. The Osprey is landing in 45 mikes."

"Orange Platoon!" "You heard the man!" Leather lungs was at it again.

"Sir, General Nethercot sends his regards, all objectives met on the test plan and he is quite pleased," Koster reported to Greene as Ohio went deep and headed west southwest to form up with Michigan and the Stennis group for their transit to Hawaii. The sub still had a few months underway to get more work done. Tommy sighed. More work to do.

CHAPTER FOUR

Washington DC was clear and cold on Inauguration day, 2021. President Drum wore a stylish black overcoat on the dais as the Chief Justice of the Supreme Court, John Roberts administered the oath. Roberts did better than he'd done on Obama's first try in 2009. Today he read the oath from a discrete index card in his hand. Drum smiled broadly as the V.P and dignitaries all looked on. His speech was a typical mishmash of campaign stump speech and rambling un connected thoughts.

'Today marks the beginning of the United States ascendancy in the world order. Trust me, we are going to regain our rightful place as the economic and military power in the world. The Chinese are paying the price for their undemocratic policies and their attitudes. These next four years will be a lasting period of peace and prosperity in the country."

The crowd clapped politely at appropriate spots. Marino and Stallings exchanged looks in the last row of the reserved guest spots. *These next four years was going to test them like no other.*

At the same time as the President's speech, United flight 808 landed at Dulles in from Beijing via SFO. The triple seven aircraft held 365 passengers on the Eighteen-hour flight. Government types coming and going and a slew of business travelers joined the few winter tourists heading from one capitol to another. Seven single Chinese men all between the ages of 35 and 45 exited the plane separately and got thru customs and passport control with a minimum of hassle. None of them appeared to be traveling together as they were met by cars and whisked to different parts of the DC area. From there they would join other agents and support people as they embarked upon phase one of Wei Bo's plan. General Fei had briefed and helped design and plan the missions for these men personally.

Zhou Chan was a typical agent the Chinese managed to insert in the country. He was met at the airport and taken to a safe house in the city of Fairfax Virginia, near George Mason University. His contact was an adjunct professor at the college. Several high powered rifles with plenty of ammunitions were bought legally. The AR-15 was very much like Private Duarte's Marine M16. Both held 20 rounds in a large banana magazine and could spit out the 223 grain bullets at over 2000 feet per second. It was only perfect irony that the gun shop the terrorists bought the weapons at was near the NRA National Firearms museum off of I-66. Since no database existed of people on the terrorist watch list, Chan raised no flags.

His target was relatively simple: Three large substations along the 495 beltway. The plan was absurdly easy. Just shoot the hell out of the power transformer at the substation. The facility was unguarded and the power transformer was custom made for each station. Since no repair was available, the ISO grid operators had to route power around the outage. That worked for a single station but with multiple substations shot up?

The test run they'd undertaken years ago in California was very illuminating. The San Jose substation was attacked at 2:30 in the morning. The sixteen shots fired from a high powered rifle, tore up the transformer with ease. No video of the attackers was ever found. It took the utility company 27 days to fix the damage. The ISO grid operators responded with true government indifference. They did *nothing.* Installed no cameras, built no fences higher or hired security people. Nada.

After he took out the substations the man had secondary and tertiary targets a plenty. Chan was ready. He was certain he would be able to meet all of his objectives and join General Bo on the west coast. He just had to lay low until D day.

Dre tore his eyes from the TV and got back to work. *Don care who the President is, I got work to do.*

"Manny, Tito, can you come in here a minute?!" He called out to the work area from his office. *His office!*

The two brothers broke off from the tire machine and tramped the several steps into the boss's office. They had to step lightly around the mass of tires and rims they were sorting together. The new guy, Amir, an Indian from Fremont, was stacking the tires according to size. Three days here and he'd done nothing but run tools and haul rubber. *Got to start at the bottom,* Tito's grin said.

"Hey, yeah Dre? Manny asked sitting heavily in the ratty folding chair in front of the battered desk. The TV was the only decoration beside the four framed plaques: Three ASC Mechanics Certificates and one degree from Lincoln College in Business Administration, all hung on the wall. The dirty grimy walls. The phone and the computer were clean, however. Manny's brother just leaned on the door jam. There wasn't much more room in the office.

"Just got a call from Jenkins. Rig down on the approach on Adeline street, wants to know if we can take it? I told him yes." The brothers grinned. Tito can you take Amir and tower over to see what's up?" The large Mexican American grunted his yes. But Andre had more good news.

"Manny, Jenkins also said he had four rigs down for tires and wants to know if we have two 36 inch P295s, a 38 P275 and a 44 P300?" Dre was not sure what they had mated up, yet. His sophisticated inventory system which called for the workers to update a clip board was not up to speed quite yet.

Manny rubbed a tired hand over his jaw and mouth. "Got to check but I think yeah."

"The rigs gonna limp in in the next ten minutes. We got to turn them quick, Ya?"

This was the critical moment in his new business and Dre knew it. The past two months were very, very, slow. It seemed to Treadwell that it took three times as long to get things done on his own compared to working at Roadability. The shop took a full three weeks to set up. They'd had trouble with the hydraulic lift unit. The compressed air line was rotted initially and the new tire changer was a week back ordered. The three of them spent hour after hour scrounging for tools and parts and supplies, from any place that would let them have some. The old Hazmat building stank when they first opened the door but a few hours with cleaners had taken care of that. Dre learned a new business term when he complained to Tompkins how tough they had it. *Burn rate.* "It's how much money you are spending each day and how many days you can keep spending that money until you run out." The professor had told him.

Not fucking long was the sad answer. The paychecks to the brothers the first month was hell to write. Not that they hadn't earned the money, they had! It was just there was only 2,000 dollars of revenue that December. The first three weeks of January were better. The new year seemed to bring the port some business. And with the increase of business the new repair shop got some new exposure. They repaired a few sets of tires and gotten them done right. Trouble was, it was spotty pickings. Dre needed consistent work.

And now came the test jobs from Jenkins. Do these tasks and do them right and the man would know he could count on the boys from Oakport Truck Repair. Dre could feel this in his bones. They were busy enough to need a tool runner and Amir had just been hired. Dre watched Tito and Amir drive out in the tower rig. The refurbished unit cost 189,000 fuckin dollars! About time it started earning its keep!

"Dre! We got em," Manny reported. Help me line them up and we can process them quicker."

The men readied the tires as the first rig drove off the race track and headed towards the building. The second 18 wheeler was behind by just a few hundred yards. Dre and Manny bent to and started working. The third driver asked Dre if he worked brakes. "I got a chattering on the front axle," the white, heavy set man told him.

"Sounds like the calipers or the pads, Dre opined. "I can turn the rotors and install new pads," he told the driver.

"What's the rate?"

"65 an hour labor plus parts." Dre informed him and held his breath.

The driver knew Roadability charged 75. "You guarantee for 90 days?"

Dre nodded yes and remained silent.

"I can bring it in tomorrow. Can you have it done in a day?"

"I can," Andre stated with certainty. He got the details on the truck so he could ensure the shop had the parts.

Manny grinned at the tire machine over the exchange. He worked feverishly. The fourth driver asked for a Freon charge for his refer unit. Dre thanked his lucky stars Manny had insisted on getting a Freon rig. It was hell to dispose of the spent gas but they charged an arm and a leg for the service. A few more minor repairs to the third rig and the two men were just finishing up as Tito and Amir drove up in the towing rig. Without the broken down truck.

'Aux power unit in the cab," Tito told him. "We replaced it. He paid Visa." The man handed Dre the slip.

Dre took it and told him, "Nice work. Can you check supply on a rotors and drums for a Peterbilt 367 a 2016?" "Brake job tomorrow."

"Yeah, sure. Amir, come with me I can show you how to look up parts and order what we need." The wiry man followed the older mechanic into the shop floor.

Manny came up next to Dre as the phone rang. A truck was just pulling up and the driver yelling out the window, "I got a slow leak, you guys got a 42 inch? P 295?"

"You get the phone, boss, I get this guy taken care of."

Dre hustled to his office. His shop had just made 2500 dollars. A job tomorrow and another on the phone. Shit! He still had paper work to take care of tonight. Being too busy was a problem Dre could deal with!

As he dealt with Jenkins, he watched the spindly looking cranes outside his window swing containers off a huge ship. Shit that looked like easy work!

"Jesus, I've never seen water this color before... OOD what is that- baby shit brown?"

The CO of the USS Bremerton handed over the periscope to his Officer of the Deck. The young Engineering Officer was newly qualified and the CO liked to hang around on his watch- for Justin. Justin Case.

The Bremerton was someplace where she definitely shouldn't have been. *Good thing the water is this crappy color. Anyone spots us and its World War III,* Captain Kosinski thought.

The sub was barely going fast enough to maintain periscope depth. She was trimmed heavy to ensure that with any problems they could sink out and disappear.

"Dive, watch your bubble." Kosinski directed.

The bubble being the angle the ship currently maintained. Bremerton was at an up angle of about two or three degrees. It was tricky in shallow inner harbors like this, the CO knew, to maintain the trim.

The view from under the highway 40 toll bridge to Changing island was fairly restricted. The shipping docks were off the subs port side and they'd gotten some pretty good video of the massive port and the ships docked along side the ways.

But the sub wasn't interested in the huge merchant ships and the fucking cruise ships that moved back and forth from here to Dazhitou island. Kosinski wanted a better look at the Baoshan naval base. The forty or so ships moored there represented a huge percentage of the Chinese blue water Navy and he wanted intel on them.

Unfortunately, the Chinese were not being agreeable. Bremerton had taken three days to ease herself up the channel to a point opposite the navy base. They got some video and pictures but the ships were quiet. He wanted sonar signatures so they could track the ships in the open ocean. They had some of them cataloged but not much other data. He didn't know if it was worth the effort. Plus, the sub had to keep dodging the incredible ship traffic in these waters. Jesus, the number of helo's and scows ferrying shit around was daunting. Just one of them smacking into the hull and they were in deep trouble.

'All right OOD, ease us back out. Let's go south and see what's happening at the deep water port again."

Kosinski frowned and looked around the Control room of his command. His sailors were preforming their duties but the ship had seen better days. Half the hydraulic pipes running in the overhead weaped oil at the value junctions. The displays for the watch standers were not the spiffy flat panel vid screens of the Virginia class boats, but the tired old phosphorescent green waterfall displays from 25 years ago. Hell, half the time the main updates to their intel came on a cell phone versus a data link. Bremerton only had another five weeks on station. She had to gather as much data as possible and then head back out to the Yellow Sea to transmit the bulk of her intel back home. Pac Fleet had left them in place, and even a lowly fast attack captain knew that they wanted a more capable intel platform on site for this op. *"More technologically capable but not gamer!*

Bremerton might be old and held together with EB green, but she had a fine crew and Richard Okane's cribbage board. That fucking counted for something! Kosinski had a running bet with the XO. Just one time he was going to snorkel right here on station.

The channel here was so noisy that running the diesel engine to re charge the battery or swapping out air in the sub, commonly called snorkeling, was not the loudest thing in this channel. The real problem would have been the exhaust smoke. No way to explain that. The XO would not take him up on the bet. Kosinski was just crazy enough to do it. *Too bad this was his last run with the old girl,* he thought sadly. Kosinski was due to rotate back to a shore tour after this. A Pentagon staff job awaited. If he wanted that star, he was going to have to play the game. Meantime he had some spying to do.

Wei Bo walked the docks at the Deepwater port of Yangshan on Dazhitou island with Colonel Zi. Both men watched the welders swarm like ants over the shipping containers. Sparks flew and the pipes outfitted to the outside ends didn't stick out very far. The vent holes were crude and looked like claw marks in the steel. A series of four slashes about three feet long on each side of the red painted 2TEU units were difficult to spot if you weren't looking for them

"It is taking a long time to containerize the missiles", Colonel Zi observed.

"We have to have them. Whatever time it takes will have to do," Bo told his aide.

"The ruling Panel might not be too happy."

"They have much more to worry about than a five day slip to my schedule," Bo told his friend with a mirthless smile.

Riots in Beijing were forcing the Generals to crack down on the civilian population. That was taking men away from the plan. None of the front line troops had been affected yet but some of the reserve troops were out of position. Wei Bo was counting on those men!

He sighed heavily. Days and nights with little sleep had turned into weeks. God's! it looked like the trip over might be the first time any of them got any sleep! Neither man looked to the channel to see the tiny periscope taking pictures of the doings.

The ride back to Baoshan base was an uneventful hop over the inner bay. Some of the flood waters had drained off but the retreating deluge left a mud stained ring around the bathtub that was the city of Shanghai. His men still spent most of their time in tents as the time for loading was still aways in the future but Bo could see the momentum gathering. He was due in Beijing in four weeks to brief Fei and the rest of the Council before Fei left for America. The Summit was all part of the plan. Fei wanted to meet with Drum to gather sympathy and announce the aid ships coming to get US food for the starving Chinese people. Neither Fei nor Bo thought the summit would actually achieve anything. Both men planned to stroke the American President's ego to keep him blind to the coming blow.

In contrast to Hangzhou Bay, the water off of Iroquois point in Hawaii were crystal clear and a stunning blue color. Walt Tsuomo steered the Colleen towards the east loch and Ford island thru the man made channel in the coral reef. The three hundred yard wide channel was very deep and the entrance to Pearl Harbor Naval Base. At least eighty feet of water was under the keel at this point. The Colleen had three visitors who'd spent the day whale watching and fishing off of Kaena Point. The extreme western point on the island of Oahu was famous for its humpbacks and its waves. Today was only a mild chop out there as compared to some where the waves broke very large indeed. Still four hours out there had left the mainlanders windblown, sunburned and tossed.

A side trip to visit the USS Arizona memorial was a welcome suggestion to the couple and their teenaged son. Walt had the boy driving the boat. Standing up on the flying bridge was always fun and made any young man feel like a full bird captain.

"Just point the bow between the buoys okay, brah?"

"Okay, dude," the boy told the Hawaiian.

Walt busied himself with harbor control getting permission for his people to round Ford Island and head to the Pearl Harbor Yacht club. From their it was a quick walk over to the Arizona Boat pier to catch the tourist boat over to the sunken ship itself.

"Steer course north for a few minutes, Bradley, we have permission from the harbor master," Walt told the boy. Brad's parents Alice and Mary hauled up the small ladder to join the other two on the now cramped bridge. The view was much better up here!

'Why can't we go to the right and go by the base? Alice asked.

"The Navy won't let us, ma'am. The Stennis battle group is in port and they have three big merchants also taking up space," he told the ladies.

Brad was disappointed. "I would like to see the carrier."

Walt grinned at him. "Still plenty to see, bra!"

As the ship started its sweeping right hand turn to round the Ford Island community center, the mothballed ships of the middle loch became apparent. The tourists made the appropriate ohhing and awwing noises at the rusty old ships. "If you look over the low lying ground right there, Walt pointed, you can see the superstructure of two submarines. That is the Michigan and the Ohio getting load outs at the West Loch weapons compound."

Craning their necks in the opposite direction, showed the inner docks of the Navy base and the three huge and futuristic shapes of the new Zumwalt class destroyers parked there.

"What the hell is that!" Mary asked excitedly.

The Hawaiian captain grinned back at her. "That's the Floating golf ball! 2.2 billion dollars of your tax dollars at work!"

The Colleen continued up the west side of Ford Island towards its northern point. Moored alongside the island, tucked away on an innocuous pier, floated an enormous platform. The size of an open ocean oil drilling rig, the platform held on its top a white, 150 foot diameter ball. It looked cool and futuristic until you saw all the rust.

'The Navy tried to develop an X band Radar to track incoming missiles from rogue states like North Korea", Walt explained. "The platform takes a huge amount of fuel and it never worked properly so it just sits here and gets used as a movie prop set."

The tourists felt dwarfed by the 18 story tall platform. Viewed from sea level it looked even bigger.

"They filmed Die Hard 6 on there!"

Brad was very impressed with that. Taylor Kitch was one of his favorite actors.

Tsuomo tied off the Collen and bid farewell to his guests. The Yacht club was an unofficial meeting point for kama aina and he spotted someone he wanted to talk to.

"Sam Chow!"

The portly Chinese man turned around when he heard his name.

'Walt! Howzit? Brudda"

The two men exchanged pleasantries. He asked the agent about the work on the docks.

"Workin along fine, man, fine, the man told him. "The upgrade is only two weeks behind schedule, so that won't be a problem. The Chinese government is still loading three big merchants in the May time frame. Hey, got me a big sit down with the new man in China." Mr. Chow told Walt in a conspiratorial voice.

"What?" The ramifications of that sunk home for Walt. "Who is the man?"

"The General, da kine called Fei" Mr. Chow named the member of the Central Military Ruling Panel.

"He da head cheese, Mr. Sam." Walt told his friend. What he coming here for?"

"The China shipping company, they call me, say, Mr. Sam, The General comin on his way to Washington. Gon stay on the island 2 day to rest. He want to talk to you about da kine."

Chow meant that the General wanted to talk to him about "issues".

What the hell? This whole thing felt off to Walt. If the Chinese wanted to ensure their ships got good treatment, the agent for China shipping lines, Lau Tzu, would just stuff an envelope in Mr. Chow's pocket. The man would spread the wealth around to his workers and boom, "long time" would turn into "short time". Walt never held to the islands philosophy of "can't do it today, bra, waves are up" when it came to work. The tides and the sun told you when to work. It was Mr. Chows job to make sure that ships got in and out on some semblance of a schedule.

But why would the head of China want to talk to a local?

He wants some intel. Direct intel. The realization bloomed in Walt. And just as that realization bloomed, he feared for his friend. And he feared for what that meant for the island.

"Uncle we got tell da kine about this."

Now it was Mr. Chow's turn to frown and think. Walt knew people. Navy people.

"You serve with the head cheese, eh brudda?"

He had in fact served with Admiral Nickers. Knew him when he was a lowly Department head twenty five years ago on the USS Cushing. Well she was now razor blades and Nickers was PAC Fleet.

The Admiral needed to know about this meeting.

"Mr. Sam we gots to go to Makalapa."

The first week of March, 2021 saw the cherry blossoms open almost a full month early. The wet winter and early spring had given way to a full blown heat wave. *Eighty degrees was too hot for March,* Paul Marino thought.

The State Dinner was in full swing. 150 guests sat in the formal splendor of the State Dining room eating off the Eisenhower china. The Chinese contingent and their forty or so people were interspersed among the US government and civilians who were lucky enough to have scored an invitation. The head of Archer Daniels Midlands sat with the US Secretary of agriculture and the Chinese Interior Minister. The Chinese were in strict formal tuxes not uniforms as they wanted to downplay the military aspect of the take over.

Drum and Fei sat at the head table with their wives. The computer science major and the TV fashion show host did not have much to talk about. Neither did their husbands. The President looked bored. Fei had insisted on private one on one talks with Drum all day today.

The shadow government almost came out of their shoes saying no to the Chinese request.

"Jesus, he'll give away everything!" Stallings had complained to Marino. The Presidents right hand man told her no, "anything they agree to has to go thru us for implementation so if we don't want to do it, we just won't."

"But the information he can give them!" Stallings was scared that Drum, a man famous for his loose lips was going to tell the Chinese a bit of vital information. Marino and the Secretary of State, Hollings Hempsted, knew that Ronald Drum was not getting the full intel briefings that previous Presidents had been given. Obama was especially famous for digging at the daily briefers for every facet of information they possessed. The main problem he'd had was that there were just so many unknowns when the CIA and the NSA came to call. Drum liked known things.

Drum was not burdened by the same intellectual curiosity as Obama and was not getting the full picture. Marino was up to the West Wing after the meetings to sound out the President while he dressed for the dinner.

"Fuck, Paul, I don't know. He just kept yammering on about how the Chinese were grateful for the cooperation of the American people."

Marino scrunched up his brow. *What was the Chinese man after?* "Mr. President you know your opponents are worried that meeting with this man so soon after he deposed the democratically elected leader of China,…"

"Democratically elected my ass," Drum broke in.

The idiot has a point there. "True, Sir. But Fei did take over China. And he is part of the ruling military council. So it goes without saying that he has an ulterior motive in coming here."

"Yeah he wants to invest in my kid's company!"

Marino almost bit thru his lip.

"Sir, that would be very unlikely and illegal to boot."

The President frowned and adjusted his bow tie. "Why the hell is it illegal for me to throw some business at junior?"

The sigh slipped past his lips. "It is pro forma pay for play, Sir."

The insolent grin never touched the eyes of the man. "Paulie, that's what is so beautiful about this! I don't have to play ball at all for this." 'They just want to be able to buy food"

"Of course, Sir."

And the agreement would go out tomorrow at the joint press conference: Several huge container ships were coming to America to load up on US farmers' bountiful harvests. Every bit of winter wheat and the entire California rice surplus was going to the people of China.

And Marino knew they needed it. Food riots in Beijing. Strict rationing in the south. The western part of China was turning into a dust bowl. And Fei seemed powerless to stop it. Sec Def told the shadow group in secret that he thought Fei and the other two had less than two years to run China before the people revolted. General Graham seemed to agree.

Paul watched everyone eat over the clinking of glasses and wine cups. Per protocol Tamsin Starlin was not here tonight. The V.P. was in a secure bunker in case something happened. He shuddered thinking about the problems that would cause: Tamsin Starlin as President of the United States.

"Mr. Marino are you okay, sir?"

His Chinese counterpart, Yue Fei's Chief of Staff, a Mr. Lin Wei Bo, asked out of politeness as his seat mates face went white.

The smile was very small. "Yes, just a chill this evening."

"Of course." The lie came smoothly to his lips.

"Did you enjoy Hawaii Mr. Lin?"

A probing question. While it was not unheard of for foreign leaders to stop on the long trip to DC, most got to Washington and slept a day there and then went into the meetings.

Nickers, Mooney, Graham, Stallings and the rest had gone into over drive when Fei met with a local in Honolulu. They had it right from the man himself: The main thing that the leader had wanted to know about, was if the docks at Sand Island could take the huge Hanjin post Panama canal treaty ships they were sending? Oh, there were some follow up questions on how many men would be un loading the empty containers and such but it was pretty logistical. The local, a Mr. Sam Chow, was adamant. Nickers was sure of their source and his loyalties. He'd told them all about the meeting.

"I did, sir," Bo answered. The weather was so nice and the water lovely. It was refreshing to be able to swim and take some sun. The only problem was the crowds of military people on the roads. The increase in DEFCON made the island look like a fortress."

There it is. Typical Chinese opaqueness. Marino reevaluated the man. Short and slim the black eyes were held in a square face. Just a hint of grey in the black betrayed the age. A sense of calm and strength radiated from Bo. *So he wanted to know how long the DEFCON increase was going to last, huh.*

Well, Sir I'm not at liberty to discuss that. The Chairman of the Joint Chiefs and the Secretary of Defense might be better able to tell you…what you want to know.

Marino trailed off. *Fucked that up!*

He hadn't meant to say that. The answer should have been: The President will decide that. But Marino was used to not checking with the President on that kind of thing.

And now Lin Wei Bo knew that. *Shit!*

He managed to get thru dinner without any more slips. As soon as was feasible he couched Stallings in a corner and told her what had happened.

"Who is this Wei guy?"

Marino glanced around. "He's a General in their Army. Supposed to be the Chief of Staff. I thought he was here to spy." 'And now he and the Ruling panel suspects that the United States President is not ordering the increase or decrease in military readiness posture."

The sour look on Stallings face said it all.

Trying not to raise suspicions, Sharon left Marino and went over to Stedman Graham. A whispered conversation moved the two of them over to Wellington Thomas. Thomas broke off and went to speak with Sec Def and Hempsted. They in turn went to others. The consensus was that the Bremerton was due back to Hawaii in two weeks. They would have more information then. Until then they would keep the President out of the decision.

Each person in room of VIP's has an orbit. A space into which people move in and speak and move out of. A trained spy can catch the subtle underpinnings of alliances and factions just by watching who speaks with whom and who is rejected. Bo had always found it fascinating.

He carefully noted the movements of Marino and the Cabinet Secretaries. Fei had told him that Drum had readily agreed to restore the DEFCON level to five during their talks. "The man seemed to be surprised when I informed him it was not already there." Fei remarked before dinner.

Interesting.

Sometimes when you hunted birds you set a dog loose to see where the flock went to roost.

Noah Spiegel closed out the email connection. His dad was okay and that's what counted. They'd gotten a break in the training schedule for the battle group and were back in Hawaii while the big boy got some work done. The young man knew "the big boy" was the USS Stennis. The air craft carrier was always having work done on her steam catapults. The newer USS George H.W. Bush used an advanced electromagnetic system to throw jet planes off the deck. Meanwhile the old Nimitz class flat tops sailed along using the old technology. When it worked.

Most times the Battle group ships stayed out if the repairs looked to be quick but they were due for a port call, so the sub pulled in. Thomas Spiegel mentioned he was getting sick of West Loch in his email because that's where they kept the tactical Tridents. It made his young sailors miserable because they couldn't get to Waikiki so easily. And that's where the horny thirsty kids wanted to go.

Noah remembered his visit to the 50th state. Even at twelve he'd been offered some weed. He still chuckled remembering how his mom had choked at that. His dad had just brushed the guy off. *Ahh, good times in Waikiki.*

It was past seven in the evening. A fine March mist was enveloping everything in the Apple state. His homework was done and he stirred up the casserole in the oven for his mom. *Something must be up because the Admiral has been keeping her late this whole week.*

And he had things she needed to sign. And money had to be spent. If he was going to get what he wanted. The keys rattling in the door signaled she was home and he prepared the ground for the battle.

"Hey- you're late.'

"Sorry sweetie, the Admiral needed some things typed and sent out."

"Yeah. I saved you some dinner, it's in the oven."

"Thank you. Is your homework done?", she asked with a hint of suspicion.

"Yes, it is. Just some math. We have the big test on Monday." He tried the first probe. "I have three full nights to study for this test."

"Uh huh," Lynn said getting a plate and sitting at the table.

"I've been studying with Tracy Chin, so…"

She didn't say anything. Better to let him come out and say it.

"So I want to use Dad's old car." He blurted it right out.

Lynn counted to ten. And then did it again. Noah watched her do it. Thirty was as high as she'd ever gotten to.

"Let's talk about this."

Her seventeen year old genius rolled his eyes and put on the tone that only HORRIBLY DEPRIVED TEENAGERS COULD ACHIEVE. "Mom!"

"A car is a big responsibility."

"I know, but dad says it's alright."

The count to twenty was slower. *Thomas Spiegel was gonna be a dead man when he got home.* 'Did he say it was alright or did he say "talk to your mother it's alright with me, if she says yes?"

"Kinda that last one. I was just emailing him. Ohio's in Hawaii."

"I know that honey. I talked to him this morning."

Noah did a double take. It was no fair that they *talked to each other!* How could he play one off against the other if they talked?

"Mom the car is practical for me. I could have been over to Tracy's house and practically on my way back home right now if I could drive." "That way I don't have to bug you."

"I like being bugged by you."

That line didn't go over so well.

"What's more, mother, I would not have to wait on you to get home from work…and I could run errands and…"

"No! You are not taking the car to San Francisco this summer!"

"But mom!"

The two argued for a few minutes. He had some decent points. The boy had obligations and this intern job was going to be a real job with adult responsibilities.

"And Mr. Boeckman said that Big Sur is only three hours south of San Francisco and Muir Woods and the Golden gate bridge…" her young man glowed with the allure of the big city. Tears formed in her eyes. He was vibrating with the possibilities of a summer away from his parents. A summer where he was going to be working on cool things and hanging out with cool people and…not with her.

She turned rather than let him see her cry.

Noah stopped chattering. He reached a hand to her shoulder across the table. "Hey. I'm sorry mom. I don't WANT to go to San Francisco." I mean… I don't want to leave you."

She smiled and looked at him with watery blue eyes. "Yes, you do!"

He smiled sheepishly at her. Now was the time to strike. "So I have these forms from UC San Francisco. If I'm going to get a parking pass I have to have you sign and put up the 450 dollars for the spot.

That part didn't go over so well. It was already going to cost them a nominal sum for the dorm room.

"This job is going to end up costing me money!"

The kid grinned at her with those white straight teeth. *The ones that cost me a fortune in dental work!* He was going to live on campus and eat there as well. Three months in the city. She'd be lucky to survive it.

"I can't wait for May 1st!"

Where in the hell did that five thousand come from? It was twelve midnight and Dre was bleary eyed. Closing out the month of March on Quicken. The very busy and profitable month of March. Oakport Truck Repair was a company to be on the lookout for. Andre's six (Six!) employees had left earlier that evening. Tito and Manny were very pleased. That ten percent of the gross as a ceiling turned out to be a mother fucker! The shop had done a cool one hundred twenty thousand for the month in gross. Shit that was six thousand apiece for the brothers. Sixty five hundred covered his other labor costs. Thirty five thou got plowed right back into the business for parts, tools and supplies. The rent and the loan nut cost him twenty five large. Dre really balked at the ten grand he put down for health care costs, insurance, and some upgrades to the building (that new break room was needed). Another ten out to the mother fuckin government for taxes. Now he knew why people bitched about them.

So, adding it all up; he did give himself a decent salary this month- Sixty five hundred- he had bills to pay any way and that should mean…
Damn. He had five thousand left over.

Where in the hell did that five thousand come from? A re check of the math showed he was right. *Well that's the bosses' money. Right?*

Or was it? For the first time in his life temptation hit Andre Treadwell. Not *I wanna cookie* temptation. Not *that woman looks fine* temptation but, real *devil* temptation. The kind they told you about in church. The kind of choice where you've worked really hard at something and now you got it and hell yes! I deserve that money. But some little voice inside him said maybe he didn't deserve that money. Maybe the workers deserved that chunk. Tito and Manny and Amir and the others been bustin hump! He knew that. They'd sweated right alongside a brother. Maybe they deserved somethin.

Wild thoughts began to fill his head about what he could do with five G's. Clothes. A newer car. A no shit vacation! One like white folks took. Go and see some of the world. Not like the Army! But like a tourist. Hawaii maybe Vegas. Anyplace. He'd worked hard and…

That little voice was sounding again in his head. *Maybe he should…*

In the end, he decided to split it. Three thousand among his six employees worked out to five hundred each. That left him with two grand and a clear conscience. He'd talk to Tompkins. His professor would know what to do with that money.

Closing up shop, he drove the cutlass past the Brick. Tabatha was standing on the street corner looking down at her shoes. Dre coasted up to a stop next to the woman. He could see she was crying.

"Hey! You okay?"

The woman slowly raised her head as she became aware of Dre.

"Dre, that you? Aint seen you around here much lately."

"Yeah been workin. Hey finished up my degree! Got me a shop out to the port"
A wan smile lifted the corners of her mouth. Tabatha nodded. "I heard, I heard."

"What's wrong girl?"

A shrug answered that question. "What aint?"

Dre took that in. "It aint all that. How bout a cup of coffee?"

She hesitated. "Its late. Don you got to work in the morning?"

"I do. But it's just cup of coffee. Don't got be a big deal."

She got in the car. The two drove off to the nearest Denny's. For Tabatha it was better inside the cutlass than it was to be outside the cutlass.

For Dre it was just nice to be able to share his success with someone.

Secretary Hempsted felt like he was the last option left available to go to China. Stallings was over in Europe dealing with the IMF. Thomas was shut away with his computers trying to figure out what was going on in the world. Marino was riding herd on Drum trying to keep him from ending the oldest and closest "special relationship" in the world. *The Brits are going to have to get over Drum. They inflicted Boris Johnson on us after all.*

The C-5 galaxy transport plane was half full. Mostly farm equipment destined for the interior. The twenty odd passengers were split three ways: State department staff, farm folks and spies. You could tell the spooks because they never searched for an answer. "Hey where you headed?" Hempsted asked one of the farm people. The guy, a tractor expert, just moved his shoulders up and down. "Damned if I know. Some place inside China. Try to help out." The spooks could rattle off the name of the village, the province and the local contact. Idiots. Even the best expert knew only a sliver of what was really going on.

Hempsted was being sent by the shadow group to ascertain if the situation in China was as bad as they thought.

The stopover in Hawaii had allowed them to get off the noisy airplane and stretch some legs. Hempsted was driven directly over to PAC Fleet for a briefing.

Mooney was there. As was Grant Nickers. Their staffs crowded the table as well as two out of place civilians. *WTF?* The last character involved was the CO of the Bremerton. CDR Kosinski. It was his intel after all.

"We never saw much activity in the way of the Chinese Navy. They stayed at Baoshan. Plenty of helo activity and ships, but no masses of troops anywhere we could see." Kosinski looked at every eye watching him as he told them of their spying mission. "We did get views of troop tents." The vid and pictures flashed on the screen. Admiral Mooney backed that up with some satellite views of the tent field of Chinese troops.

"We also got some shots of the devastation in Shanghai." A sobering series of low angled shots of the waterfronts of the city were flashed on the screen.
Yeah things were as bad as they said. *Why send me then? Oh I get to convince the ruling Junta that the US is going to raise DEFCON back to five.*

"What about the merchant ships?" a civvie, some guy named Walt asked.

Kosinski nodded coolly. "Tons of them. Both at Youshang for the Deep water port and Waingzhou docks near the naval base." "The Chinese are working overtime to fit out the ships and get them filled with empty containers for the trip over. You could walk over to the US on the containers."

Nickers faced Mooney and Hempsted. "We do not have any images of them massing troops and tanks near any border. They aren't loading troops onto amphib ships. No groups of planes taking on weapons packs." "Just merchants."

That seemed to mollify the staffs but the brass was nervous. The second guy- the one who'd met with Fei here in Hawaii, relayed what he knew: Fei wanted to know that the cargo handlers could take the capacity to unload and reload as quickly as the Chinese people needed them to. Mr. Chow was limited on crews but had provided the Chinese his numbers of workers and a time frame for the operations. That was all.

"So we go back to five?" Hempsted asked when the civilians were shuffled out.

Mooney nodded reluctantly. "We do. The Chairman and the services heads have discussed it. We are burning thru our op budgets, so we go back to full peacetime level. But we got a few tricks to pull yet," he didn't elaborate those tricks to the Secretary of State. The man couldn't divulge what he didn't know. After Marino's gaffe the group was playing it close to the vest.

Hollings tiredly re boarded the plane and tried to sleep on the way over to China.

The Chinese delegation at the Beijing airport was formal and grim faced. Sec State greeted the Chinese ambassador, Liu Zhone with a firm handshake. The men were very similar in build and temperament. Short dark hair, brown eyes and angular faces. Only the eye cast was different. Even their dark blue suits with red ties looked the same.

Despite the diplomatic dance that had to be performed for the cameras, neither man wanted to stand on ceremony. Plus- Hempsted did not want to breath this air for a second longer than necessary.

Safely out of the fumes and into the Grand Hall of the People, the American diplomat's security detail, eyed the Chinese military guards like strange cats.

The frown on the Secretaries face was properly interpreted by Liu.

"Mr. Secretary the guards are entirely necessary in these times."

"Mr. Ambassador, my purpose here is to review the situation in Shanghai. My government wants assurances that American aid is reaching the people in an appropriate manner."

"We will fly to Baoshan and you can see for yourself the situation and our efforts."

"The Navy base?", he could not keep the surprise from his voice.

The Chinese man bowed his head a bit. "The civilian airport was damaged in the flooding and has not yet been returned to operational status."

Interesting.

The flight south was only marred by a freak accident. Hollings cut his palm on the side rail of the roll out ramp the Chinese provided for his plane. It didn't look bad but it hurt like a mother!

A quick first aid wrap and the five-man American contingent was led by the smaller Chinese team onto the twin rotor Harbin helicopter for the tour of the stricken city. The whole scene reminded him of a war zone. The grey overcast skies seemed to merge into the smoke haze. The recent cold snap had the population scrambling for warmth. It looked miserable down there.

The helo banked over the tent field he'd seen in the briefing. It looked the same to his eyes. Hempsted commented on the number of troops and the amounts of military check points that graced every major street crossing. "Will that impede the food distribution, Sir?"

Liu shook a quick no. 'The reality is the troops are protecting the convoys to ensure there is no hoarding or fighting over the foodstuffs."

The silence in the craft built for a few minutes until the ambassador showed his hand.

"Perhaps the number of troops in the city could be reduced if your own defense posture was lowered to a reasonable level."

"That's a pretty phrase, Liu- a reasonable level. Our forces are responding to a military takeover of the country with the largest standing army in the world. I would argue that DEFCON 4 is totally reasonable. There are some in my government who advocate for DEFCON 3 with a Nuclear deterrent level 2."

The hammer came down.

Liu reacted sharply. "Surely you do not expect us to attack you?" Our troops here are purely an internal matter and as a response to the disaster. President Drum said nothing of this to General Fei in Washington."

The American grunted a response. He did it because he had no good response to that statement. He could not admit that Drum wasn't setting the agenda for the US military. The strange convergence of an illegal act done for every right reason hit him again. *The Commander in Chief was not running the military. This sucks.*

"Are the ships ready? More importantly when can we expect them?" He asked the questions one on top of each other. Not exactly the finest diplomacy.

'We had hoped the first of May, but as you can see the containers need more prep work."

The fact that the ships were not ready was evident even to a layman like him. Cranes and gantry haulers were swinging the 2 TEU rusty units on and off of ships. The whole dock area was organized chaos. "I think that we have our assurances that the aid of the American people will reach their brethren in China. Mr. Ambassador I also believe that the US readiness level will return to full peace time status within a short period of time." He delivered the message just as Stallings and Graham and Mooney wanted him to. God help them all.

The ride ended back at the runway where the huge C-5 dwarfed the smaller Chinese fighters the PLA Air Force had provided as an escort, was in silence on both sides. Liu quickly took his leave of the group pleading work after a perfunctory farewell.

That was fine as Hollings had to get back to DC and brief the rest. His mission was a short one. Secretaries of State specialized on quick trips.

Unfortunately, this was Hollings Hempsted's last plane ride. Two days after returning he was feeling rotten and checked himself into Bethesda Naval Hospital. Two weeks later he was fighting the infection that would eventually kill him in June. He was the first casualty of the war as the drug resistant super bacteria the Chinese put on the raised sliver of metal on the ramp side rail, wrecked his immune system.

CHAPTER FIVE

April 28th was the type of day that made the Chamber of Commerce drool in Seattle. Mid seventies with cobalt blue skies and a slight breeze. Hordes of boaters crowded the sound as everything that could be on the water was on the water. Blinking Seattle hippies grouped into the morning sun as the Emerald City came out of a wet winter to a few days of soak it all up, sun.

Tommy stood in the driveway of his house on base at Bangor. He wore shades because the bright sunshine hurt his eyes after so much time in the gloom. Noah filled the old Toyota Camry with luggage and computer gear with barely contained excitement. Dad was stoic but mom leaned off to the side, fighting every instinct to hug her son on every trip from the house to the car.

The death stares she was giving Tommy didn't hurt, they just made him laugh.

He edged over to stand next to her.

"He'll be fine."

"You better hope so, because if one hair on that head is hurt, I'm comin to find you."

"Whoa, momma bear!"

The two shared a small smile at the little nick name. Lynn wasn't that bad, just a normal amount of over protective.

'He's smart, level headed and has a good sense of right and wrong," dad reminded her.

Crap! That was supposed to make her feel better not tear up!

He put a tentative arm around her shoulders. She stiffened at first then relaxed into the hug.

Noah was SO EXCITED.

Three months in San Francisco and he was driving down today with a stop in Portland and then he checked into UC San Francisco to get his room assignment and he had already talked to his roommate who sounded cool and he was going to meet the internet people on Monday and don't worry he was going to drive sparingly in the city and...

"Maybe you should take a breath, kid," Tommy told his son.

"Crap I forgot my ipad!" he zoomed back into the house which was serving as the staging area for his assault on the Bay area.

As the young man made his final preps, Tommy went over some rules. "I've arranged the hotel room off of the I-5 just south of Portland. You should be there in eight hours or so, but if there are any problems call them and tell them you are going to be late. Then you'd better call me and explain what happened, right?"

"Yes, sir."

"No hitch hikers, ever!" No texting or phone calls while you are behind the wheel and we don't even need to speak about drinking yes."

Noah nodded.

"Let me hear it, please."

"No texts, calls, drinking, wild animals, hitchers, or anything in the car."

"Good."

Lynn came up to stand beside Tommy. Noah thrilled to see his parents this close. "We are trusting you with this crazy idea because this is the kind of program that can get you into a good college and then get an inside track on a career." 'You work hard and do what they tell you to do…" "And call me when you get there."

"Mom!"

Tommy grinned and the two men hugged it out.

Lynn squeezed so hard Noah "uurrpped". He escaped behind the wheel with a last wave and drove off for a glorious summer away from his parents!

The two adults stayed in the driveway for a long time after the car disappeared. Both of them figured that this moment would come in four or five years after the boy was done with UW.

"Want a cup of coffee?", Tommy asked casually.

Lynn searched for the hidden motive and message and then said, "what the hell."

The house was almost the same as when she'd left a few months ago. Same half dead plants. Same faint amine diesel engine smell from his stupid Navy clothes, same pictures of the three of them with those stupid grins. She missed it all.

"I have three weeks of temp duty at SWFPAC", he told her while the Kurig did its thing.

"I typed up the orders on Admiral Kollmansburger's say so," she informed him.

She probably knew more about his assignment at the Strategic Weapons Facility Pacific than he did. All he knew was he was going to work on refitting both the tomahawks and the

Trident missiles. The brass had a huge team assembled to work on something big. And it was a typical, "do it now" kind of job.

"The old man know what is up with the DEFCON thing?" The question was more to get her talking than getting real information.

She was silent for a period. Not that she didn't trust him, just she was closed mouth about these things because she was a professional. Tommy was cleared for the data classification level but he had zero need to know.

'Sec Def and the Joint Chiefs are going to arrange for some "training ops" to ensure some units are in a continuous upgraded Operational readiness posture."

A heavy pause. "That might also mean the tactical Tridents are going right back out after they finish up the load out and the work you are doing at the weapons facility." The boomers too," she added.

Tommy whistled slowly. That was heavy, and Lynn was trusting him with the knowledge. He knew she was working her ass off for the Admiral. That was how she rolled.

"Why don't you stay here? No sense in going back to that apartment by yourself. If you lived here again you cut twenty minutes off your commute. That's more rack time." He said that with a grin. Sleep time was very important to US sailors, and busy administrative assistants.

Her face betrayed nothing as Lynn mulled over the offer. Giving in was actually easy for her.

"Okay."

Tommy glanced at her over his cup. He'd missed her. This part had to be done delicately.

"You take the big room. I'll shift over to the guest bedroom."

Lynn nodded not trusting her voice.

"Probably won't be seeing each other over the next month, anyway, with work and all, Spiegel confided to his ex-wife.

She knew that to be the truth. Too bad, sort of, she mused to herself.

The smell inside the tent was musty and had the foul underpinnings of death. The five men inside had all smelled the stench of bodies before so they ignored what had to be ignored. Fei, Yuan, and Qi as the ruling Council got to sit in the rickety chairs while Zi and Wei Bo were made to stand on the opposite side of the table. The maps and pictures of the US west coast covered the table so none of its scarred surface shown.

"We are at zero hour, comrades." Bo announced quietly. He was gaunt from work, lack of sleep and poor food. But he had succeeded.

"Our forces are here, virtually undetected by the Americans. We have the loadout of supplies and ammunition as well as the required supporting items. General Qi has assured me the planes are ready. General Fei, are we ready to implement phase one?" He bowed and waited out his superior.

Fei nodded gravely. He knew what this moment entailed. "General Bo we are. I will dictate the orders to our agents based on your timetable."

"Excellent sir. D day will be the 18th of May. That is based on weather reports for the US and on the Pacific Ocean northern basin. General Fei, D minus 10 for your disruption forces, Sir."

Fei nodded agreement.

"General Qi, D minus one for you?"

The fat man said loudly, "we will be ready."

"General Yuan my men are loading on starting tomorrow. The Navy goes out and then we proceed per plan, yes?"

The PLA leader also agreed. At this point he could not stop anything. Even if he had misgivings in his heart. He could not show weakness in front of these men.

The council consulted their ground General for his plans. "We are invading California to establish control, therefore my objectives will likely depend upon the American response," Bo reminded them.

Colonel Zi was very quiet during this meeting. The big man had total faith in General Bo, so the thought of failure did not enter his brain.

"Col. Zi and I will move aboard our ship in the next days. All our communications will be thru the encoded system." Bo reminded them.

The ruling council remained only a few more minutes with Bo. In reality the men had abandoned Beijing. The riots and the scarcity of food caused too much chaos. Baoshan was much safer for them. From the main Chinese Naval Station, they could coordinate the attack and maintain control on China's nuclear forces. The army missile silos in the far west had already been written off. Several had come under control of local military units. Fei was dispatching shock troops and special operations people to disable the missiles. They could not risk some rogue Colonel deciding he was a new warlord and launching a preemptive strike. A strike that might be on mainland China or the US or anywhere. Fei cared only for the submarine launched missiles. The five Chinese boats were hidden and controlled by his loyalists. Those bombs were his ace in the hole.

"Why in the hell is the stock market going down?" Drum asked yet again in the cabinet meeting.

Sharon repressed the sour look that wanted to go on her face. "Mr. President the world is reacting to the Chinese problem. Uncertainty drives the market and without assurances that the US is going to help stabilize the region, the markets will feel downward pressure."

Too high brow, Sharon, Marino thought. *He won't understand that.* Tamsin Starlin certainly didn't. Her face had the puzzled look of someone who'd just heard a new language.

The President would not admit that he hadn't understood the Secretary of the Treasury so an awkward silence built.

"I think the important thing is what can we do about it", Paul said to move things along.

"I think a speech to the UN would help calm nerves", the Deputy Secretary of State said. Mike Lisbon was new to this table as Hollings was laid up in the hospital. Sharon surely missed his wise voice right now.

The scowl crept onto Drum's face. He didn't like talking to the UN. He didn't like the UN being on US soil. He just hated.

"Mr. President let us deal with the optics of the situation. Television pictures of US grain being loaded onto ships bound for China will go a long ways towards bringing the market out of bear territory."

"You better hope so Paul."

Drum moved off with the Vice President without so much as a see you later. The Secretaries were used to this treatment by now. They also knew to stay in position as the group was joined by General Graham and Wellington Thomas. Anders Young the Speaker of the House would be a few minutes late, traffic on the Arlington Memorial Bridge.

"How soon on those merchant ships, Paul," Sharon asked, leading the shadow government.

Marino pursed his lips. "Two weeks. Drum talked to General Fei late yesterday and said his ships are moving now."

Graham snorted. "Baoshan emptied out over the last three days, did the bastard say anything about that?"

"Protection for the merchants", Paul told him and the rest at the table.

"Things are surely sliding off the deep end," Thomas told them, sweat on his brow.

"Well what can we do to arrest the slide and how are we going to coordinate our actions? Sharon refocused them.

The group debated the proper response. "General Graham are we as prepared as we can be?" Sharon knew they'd come back up with the DEFCON level but the military had some projects going on, training ops and such to get units ready to move out in a moment's notice.

"We are Madam Secretary. I have the third ID moving equipment to RO RO ships to prep for Korea, among other things."

Stallings frowned. If Drum was incapable of admitting when he was clueless Sharon had no such problem. "General, pretend I'm a civilian stock broker and give me that again, please. Graham couldn't help but laugh. "The Third Infantry Division is one of our heavy mechanized units." "Tanks, big heavy tanks, and lots of them," he told her to forestall the question. "We can't just pack the Abrams on a plane. The big guys need a big ship. So we have Roll on roll off ships from the military sealift command ready at ports waiting to take the equipment to wherever the men will be needed." "They mate up and off they go."

Sharon was impressed. "Good." "What else."

Money the subject always came down to money. They needed Young to work his magic checkbook and pay for some off budget items.

The vibrating cell phone went off in Paul's pocket. No chief of staff ever had his phone off completely. As he reached in to check it two other phones went off. Suddenly every cell in the room was insistent on being heard.

Uh oh.

Faces went white. Marino quickly read his text: Speaker involved in crash. Bad.

'Shit!" "Are you getting this?" he asked Stallings.

She read her phone. "Anders Young was in an automobile accident on the Arlington Bridge." A long pause while everyone watched her. "My staff says CNN is saying he may have gone into the water."

Chaos erupted as people scrambled to contact the DC police and staff and others.

"People!"

Her voice cut through the noise. Stallings started giving out orders. "Paul, inform the President. And the Vice President", she said after a beat. *They didn't know much at this point but better to be careful.*

"Thomas, General Graham, please coordinate with the DC police to establish secure lanes for critical personnel to get to the capitol." "Homeland you will help with that, check?"

"Aly, can you call your friend Senator Belkins to have him call me?"

People got moving on assignments. The cabinet Secretaries stayed in the oval office conference room while the President was moved to the situation room. Marino was kept hopping as he shuttled between the two groups trying to push and prod the President to do what Sharon wanted.

Information was sketchy forty minutes later when official word came down that Anders Young, third in line for the President was killed when his car was hit and careened off the Arlington bridge. He died from drowning as did the occupant of the second vehicle. That body took two weeks to identify as there was no id and the car stolen. Finger prints finally id the man as Zhou Chan a Chinese national who'd entered on a tourist visa and was here perfectly legally. By then it was too late.

"Sargent, what's that?" Duarte asked Connie if she knew what the line of people standing outside the US capital building were for. People and umbrellas stretched the length of the steps and down the sidewalk as the TV in the classroom/office was on the news.

"The body of the Speaker is lying in repose in the Rotunda before the funeral tomorrow, she answered. "Repose means lying in a casket in this case and the Rotunda is the round chamber inside the Capital dome," she explained patiently. "Those people are waiting to pay their respects."

"Ohh."

Orange squad was taking a rare down day. Wilkins had all of them updating records at the Lima Company headquarters building. It was strange to think of Marines with an "office" but they did need it to fill out paperwork and hold classroom training and similar things.

Sanchez was very pleased with Duarte. Her baby Marine was growing up. The last few weeks had seen the young man actually use his head. For something besides holding his cap.

Command was very happy with their live fire exercise performance. Lima had been singled out as an exemplary performer. Nethercott himself handed Wilkins a piece of paper that said so, so Duarte knew it must be true.

"All those people getting soaked for a guy they didn't know?" Morrelli chimed in. The North eastern seaboard was getting socked by a spring storm. Sheets of wind driven rain were testing those umbrellas.

"Yeah. Someone high on their chain of command just died, so the government workers stand in line," Hill fired back in her squeaky voice. Sanchez was glad the girl hadn't cussed. It disturbed her to hear Minnie Mouse fling F bombs.

"Don't you think we'd be standing if the Old Man died?" Olsen said in his Louisiana Cajun twang. The tall man was hunched over the table scribbling without looking at the rest.

Sanchez let the bull session go on. Her time in Iraq had taught her the importance of establishing some connections during less stressful times. That way when her Marines were under fire, there was a trust built up. If not a trust, an understanding of the person next to you in the fire trench. It was the same way friends built bonds: with time and shared experiences.

Armster and Collins had their squads in adjacent classrooms working the same paper drive. The early morning sun was out now that the marine layer of fog had burned off. The southern California coast could be gorgeous when the dew glistened on the brambles.

"Sargent, what am I going to do with this?" Duarte held out a piece of paper.

Sanchez closed her eyes rather than roll them at her charge. She took the letter and read.

"The state of Oklahoma wants you to pay taxes. No, check that, they want you to file a return."

The young man was confused. "I have to pay taxes every year?"

Snickers sounded around the room. *Here it comes.*

"Yes, Duarte, every year if you worked and earned over a certain amount." "Look, you have to file taxes if you earned more than say, 12,000"

"But I didn't. Those were just fast food jobs, when I was a kid."

Sanchez didn't comment on whether the man was still a kid or not. "Yes, but there was still withholding." She went on to explain how the state was taking money out in advance. "That is the same as the Fed's right? We set up your W-2 to make sure you have enough coming out so you get a refund at the end of the year, remember?"

Duarte did. The seven hundred dollars back from Uncle Sam was a very nice bonus for him last March. He still had five hundred in his savings account. That was the most money the man had ever managed to save.

The rest of the squad was listening without snickers now. The Sargent was going to explain something.

"So Duarte, you don't have to file taxes if you only earned 3,436 dollars in calendar year 2019. But…

Everyone leaned in.

Sanchez waived the letter. "The State is doing you a favor. They have 122 dollars of your money that probably belongs to you. If you file for it, you get it back."

One hundred twenty-two dollars could buy some beer. A lot of beer actually. If that much money was lying on the ground, he would stop and pick it up- right? And all he had to do was fill out a form?

As Sanchez went to explain to Wilkins what was in the letter and how she was going to handle it, Hicks slid in next to her as she walked the hall. 'Sargent, I may not have filed in Louisiana three years ago."

The sigh was long suffering from the Sargent. She missed the increase in DEFCON. More shooting, less paper work.

The huge 747 lined up on final approach to Andrews Air Force base fighting the wind at every turn. Air Force One is normally piloted by one of the services most senior pilots. L.t Col Andrew Jacks (call sign Black Jack) was not that guy. Drum had fired the two previous pilots for "insubordination." That was what he called it when they did not do what he wanted.

This was exactly the situation that got Colonel Lemers fired. He'd refused to take off at Orange County airport during a Santa Ana wind event. It was the end of a long day of fund raising and Drum was tired and just wanted out of California when that asshole Colonel decided he was too afraid of a little wind to fly. *Gusts to 60 MPH was too much for the pussy.*

The plane was heading back from Florida after a night of partying at the resort. Drum was half asleep in the stateroom but Starlin and the Senior Senator from Florida were also onboard and in the midsection seats. *Marino would have freaked if he were here*, The President knew. His Chief of Staff was always telling him what he couldn't do. He knew the Vice President was not supposed to fly with him, but Tamsin was from Florida. Those people were not going to donate without her and the little guy being at the party. Drum had to come back from Florida early for that assholes funeral.

Black Jack and the copilot pulled and pushed at the yokes. There was no wind shear being shown on the radar but the cross winds were fucking *bad*. Even computer aided flight was having trouble.

"Abort landing, go around."

Jacks thought furiously. The backup landing strip that offered the best path out of the storm was maybe Dulles. In truth the storm was big enough that the whole region was in the same wind field. Jacks did NOT want to go to Pittsburg. Nor did he want to swing the plane around.

'I have control" he said authoritatively. He and the copilot concentrated on getting the plane down. The copilot shot him a quick look. They'd discuss with their fists afterwards on Black Jack's decision and if it was a good one.

He almost made it. The rear wheels had just touched down when a gust hit the right wing tip and forced it up. At least fifty miles an hour, the wind kept the tip rising for a few agonizing seconds. Yanking the stick and gunning the engines just could not compensate as the plane lifted a few feet off the runway. Once the plane went over 50 degrees in the vertical, the die was cast. The left wing tip dug into the ground, gouging out a huge tear in the earth and cartwheeling the plane down the runway at an angle. Fire bloomed as the engines exploded on that side and threw pieces of metal and people all over the place.

The President died instantly enveloped in huge fireball, barely able to comprehend what was happening to him. He only had time for one brief scream. The Vice President and the President Pro tem of the Senate died a few seconds later from blunt force trauma. A further sixty-five staff people also perished along with the pool reporters and support personnel.

The worst constitutional crises in its history, hit the United States.

The Secret Service men burst thru her door and flanked either side of the desk. Sharon Stallings the 46th President of the United States, looked up as her phone started buzzing.

"Ma'am you need to come with us." "Cobra is on the move." The agent spoke into his cuff mic.

Cobra?

The disjointed thought kept her from saying, 'what the fuck?' so all she got out was a strangled "Uuurrk."

The two men grabbed her and shoved her thru the closet door into the stairwell for the secret tunnel.

"Libby! Follow us!" Sharon screamed at her chief of staff. The bewildered woman watched horrified as the three disappeared and then she ran to catch up.

Stallings wrenched away as the group rushed down the lit corridor. "What happened?"

"Condor is down, so is Cat."

'English please!"

"Ma'am the Presidents plane crashed on landing five minutes ago, the Vice President was with him. Both are assumed dead."

Her mind reeled with the news. Drum? And Starlin?

But what about…holy shit Anders Young died four days ago. And Hollings was laid up…That meant?

"Wait, it's not me! You made a mistake. Senator Gonsolvo is Pro Tem."

"No ma'am. Camel was on the plane as well."

She slowed to a normal walk as some of the enormity sunk in. "They aren't code names, they were people! Dammit."

The agents said nothing.

"I'm going to do what you tell me as far as security goes- but I'm different than Drum!"
"Libby!"

The agents allowed the woman to get closer while still keeping an eye on her. Neither had pulled a gun but Sharon didn't put that past them.

"Start making calls", Sharon told the woman. Everyone on zulu list."

She was extremely grateful to see Paul Marino waiting at the White House end of the tunnel with more security and staff.

'Madam President."

The surreal nature of that statement rocked her mind and her answering smile was very small. "Do we have confirmation on that?"

Marino shook his head. "No, but I have a report from on scene. There is very little chance anyone survived."

"Paul, terrorists?"

The sixty four trillion dollar question hung in the air as they entered the West Wing. Marino shrugged. "We don't know."

More people joined them as the power vacuum swelled.

'People," she said using her familiar phrase to quell the noise and confusion.

"Paul, I know we have an emergency transition plan developed, check?"

The man told her that they had an outline of what to do in this situation.

'Well dust it off." Her voice rising, The President was going to give some orders. "We have a plan on how this is supposed to go. I want you all to follow that but use your best judgement on when something needs to be adjusted. Ask me if you have questions…after you try to solve it yourself!" she said to quell the rising tide of hands starting to flutter up to get her attention.

"Now! Someone please tell the first lady I'd like to offer my condolences. I'd like her to stay here rather than go to the scene. Paul is still the Chief of Staff. Libby will coordinate my people to you. I will be in the situation room unless I need to move. Everyone will bring me what I need to do or sign or whatever in there." "Questions?"

"What should we do with Anders Young and the funeral?"

"What do you recommend, Mike?"

The Protocol Chief frowned. "We should postpone the funeral until Sunday. I'll coordinate with the family to remove the body and do what we need to do."

"Excellent."

That exchanged established how Sharon dealt with the crises. As she moved down to the situation room the deputy communications director inquired about when she should speak to the nation.

Again she asked about a recommendation.

'We should put out a preliminary statement right away. The whole line of succession is going to raise some serious issues," Gail told her immediately.

"The Constitution is clear, she told the woman. "I'm next up."

The new Communications Director, since her predecessor went down on the plane, shook her head. "There will be some questions." "I'll have two preliminary statements in twenty minutes and your address to the nation on your desk in two hours. We will go over teleprompter, hair, makeup and clothes then."

Stallings inwardly shuddered. Thank god she was dressed well today. She was usually fairly casual but she favored some of the Donna Karan line of female power suits and had one on. Her long time boyfriend called them her 'bitch in heels" clothes. *Oh shit she needed to call Coleman.*

The next hour was a blur. Little scenes kept impinging on her conscience. The almost bored look on Drum's third wife's face as she said polite words back to Stallings. The way the pool reporters shouted the same question at her even after they'd gone over the succession line five times. When the replacement nuclear code briefcase made its appearance at her side later on it hardly caused a ripple.

Marino sat next to her at the conference table. She hadn't named a V.P. yet. That part was a little fuzzy. "Madame President the emergency plan does call for you to be at a more secure facility."

"Paul, if I'm not safe in my house, then what American is safe in his?"

She was gutsy, Paul thought.

Stedman Graham and Wellington Thomas got off the phones and approached her seat. "I talked to Kevin. He is going to sorte some of the Navy, namely the aircraft carriers that can be sent out along with their battle groups." Graham said.

"We should get Sec Def on this."

"He's at Andrews leading the efforts there," General Thomas informed her.

"Okay. If we need to consult we can call him."

"What about recalling troops or canceling leaves or any of that?" She was not quite up to speed with how the military worked this kind of thing.

"I don't recommend doing anything like that. We want to be as normal as we can possibly be. "We don't have any chatter that this is a terrorist act. No one has credibly claimed responsibility for it. A small fringe group said one of their missiles brought down Air Force one but that is untrue, of course." The head of the NSA laid it out for her.

"How do we know this?"

Paul coughed, "Madam President, Air Force One is filmed every time it takes off or lands for just this kind of occurrence. We have the video and one of Wellington's analysts…"

The young man looked shaken to be in the situation room. Normally he got to do this in the puzzle palace but now he was out in the daylight so to speak.

The video was flashed on the wall screens.

"Ma'am you can see here the wind pattern as it hits the right side of the plane. The pilot was over maximum cross wind speed of 42 kts by at least ten and maybe twenty knots." The analyst tried to be clinical but his voice cracked a bit.

Sharon looked over the table to the people in general as the horrible crash was shown. "That does not get out until the NTSB makes its findings." "Go on."

117

"There are no tell tale sparks of bullet strikes or any indication of a missile hit at all," the analyst said. "This was just an accident, he said sadly. The guy made a poor decision."

"Thank you, she waited until the analyst was out of the room. "Gail we need to leak that this was an unfortunate accident by our preliminary assessments. Also work into the speech that normal functions of the government are still going on."

It was just three O'clock here in DC. They been at it a while and the whole shadow group had more to do. Shadow no more actually.

"Holy shit, Dre! You see that!"

The new guy Jeremey, was very talkative. The eight employees of Oakport Trucking were all crowded around the small break room TV. The news was showing the video crash of the plane on an endless loop.

"Yeah I seen it." The dude was surely dead. Dre had not liked the man, but going down in a plane was not a good way to go. All eight of them puzzled over why the lady was now the President. Seven sets of eyes turned to Andre. He was the college man after all!

"The Constitution say she the President," he told the others.

"Yeah but who is she?" Amir was fuzzy.

All of them were. It took a long discussion on cable TV as to why the swearing in had to wait three hours until the Cabinet could bang out a letter that Hollings Hempsted was incapacitated and unable to perform the duties of President. The Supreme Court with Roberts in the lead had signed and validated the letter as what the government had to do in order for the succession to be valid. Sharon Stallings was sworn in as President at Bethesda Naval Hospital in the corridor with Hempsted's family in tears along with Drum's widow and the Supreme Court, select leaders of Congress, and a slew of security people.

"She four or five in line?" Manny asked.

"Fourth in line starting with the Veep."

"She dead too!"

"Who's next?" Tito asked.

Dre frowned. "Don't know. White folks be droppin like flies. I guess she got to name a Vice President, then they got to get a new Speaker and a new Senate dude."

"What if somethin happen before that?"

Dre scowled. "I don't know. And I don't care. We got to be ready for those ships in the next week. The rigs are pulling in already."

In truth they were. The port was open and ready. The close-in, flat concrete pads in front of the gantry cranes had been cleared for the incoming containers. Trucks had been moving shit around for the last three weeks getting ready. It was very uncommon to have three of the big ships hit at the same time. They were due at 10:00 11:00 and noon. The pilot's union would not bring them into port without one of its members on board. Even the Chinese had to deal with the unions.

Dre's people went back to work. The shop was busy with the Chinese coming to town.

The view from the huge ship's bridge was stupendous. The small white caps and the little waves did absolutely nothing to the motion of the ship. The Pacific Ocean could toss around a ship this big but it had to be a monster fucking storm to do it.

Lin Wei Bo could feel the engine throb in his feet as he looked out towards his fleet. This was a large group of ships. Bo wondered where this fleet fit in history. He was fond of trying to put things in their historical contexts. The twenty ships were arranged in a loose column in this patch of the northern Pacific 3oo miles east of Midway atoll. A full sixteen of the ships were the large two hundred thousand gross ton container ships like the one Bo currently stood on. The other four ships were the white multi decked ubiquitous cruise ships that Americans favored for their vacations. Another twelve ships set in a trailing convoy some miles behind the vanguard. To top that all off, another twenty-six container ships stood to near the Deepwater port where they'd come out of off of Shanghai. Fifty six ships in total. Not to mention the Naval ships that were going to guard the second wave. The metric tonnage would measure up to any fleet in history, Bo thought.

The Great White Fleet of 1907 had sixteen large battleships and they circumnavigated the globe to announce the Americans as a major world power.

His fleet was bigger. The D Day invasion was probably bigger in terms of numbers of ships but he felt that he had them on numbers of troops.

Let's go back in time, he mused. The Spanish Armada? Three hundred thirty ships but they were tiny. Actium? Marc Antony had two hundred thirty large war galleys but as spectacular as the sight must have been, they were toys compared to his behemoths. The Persians? Ecnomus? The Greeks at Troy?

He had the power with him right now to defeat the greatest military power the world had ever seen. He could do it!

Colonel Zi moved to his side to show him a laptop.

"What?" *"What!?!"*

Bo could not believe his eyes. He searched Zi's face to see if this was a cruel joke. *Did Fei do this? Why?* He struggled to understand the news. The American President was dead. A plane crash apparently was the cause. 'Get me Fei." "I must confirm this."

The encrypted radio phone was a military version of a cell phone. Not the most secured method of communication but he had to consult with the General.

"It is Zheng He. I have heard the news." "Did your people do this?" Bo used his code name. Zheng He was Chinas most famous explorer and Naval Commander. The Treasure fleet he led to harass the Japanese was the largest in the ancient world. Bad luck came in the form of a typhoon which scattered and sunk most of the fleet. Bo was certain that would not happen to him.

"Why do you ask this question? No! We wanted the other man in charge. A twist of fate, that is all."

Fei was pissed off. The plan did not hinge on the incompetence of Drum as the Commander in Chief but they did prefer him to anyone else.

Bo was satisfied that the Presidents death was a coincidence. "All proceeding well, targets are within reach. Days now." "Zhenge He out."

Bo broke the connection. He might well be assassinated at the end of this but he did not care. Fei did not have his disrupters kill Drum, he was certain of that. As the man had said, a twist of fate only. He was left to deal with the consequences of that twist.

"Have the cruise ships split off to form up." They are to proceed per plan in a separate group."

"Are you worried about submarines, Sir", Zi asked, thinking Bo was having the smaller cruise ships break off to attract less attention.

"Not as such, Colonel. I am worried about them in general. If they want to sink us we have no defenses to employ. But they have no reason to suspect anything. Our agents report just minor adjustments to the defense posture of the country. The effects of the Presidents death remain to be seen and felt but Fei was confident."

No, Bo was not that worried about submarines. He was worried about B-52's. Not that the huge ancient planes could sink his ships at sea but if the Americans reacted quickly after they landed, but the incredible amounts of bombs the planes held could blow their landing points out of existence. If.

If the enemy chose to bomb their own cities.

That was a hinge point on his plan. The first critical moment. If the new President deduces what is going on quickly enough she can order the old bombers out of Diego Garcia and to destroy the ports where they were going to land, before they could mix with the civilian populations inland.

Once they were in with regular American citizens, he thought the government would not want to indiscriminately bomb US cities. That gave them an advantage. Bo knew there were other critical points where things could go wrong. Hell, The President could order a full scale nuclear response but he did not consider that possibility seriously.

Eighteen to twenty-four hours in. That's when it's dangerous.

He hoped the men were faring well inside those containers. Another week to go.

"How are you getting along?", Lynn asked her son, moving on from discussing the shocking news of the Presidents death.

"Mom, I told you, just fine." Noah was juggling the phone and his keyboard at the same time. "We are getting overloaded with calls and traffic on the news this morning."

Lynn noted the "we". Her phone calls to her baby had found him working fourteen hours a day. "What are you doing?"

"It's complicated, mom. I work as part of the team that monitors and controls the companies digital phone network and internet infrastructure." "And I get coffee."

She had to laugh over that. "That's how it works kiddo." "Show everyone you can get the drink run right and they move you up to delivering mail. Show up for work on time and dressed appropriately and they will let you stare at a screen for eight hours a day. Prove you can do that and they will let you write code until your fingers bleed. Do that well enough and you finally can make a decision."

Noah grunted out his agreement. "My team lead, Rammy Pak, says I'm doing well and she is going to let me help run the networks on the weekends sometime."

"That sounds good but you do want some free time."

Noah inwardly shrugged. He kept his voice neutral. "I'm just concentrating on the work for the time being. The site seeing and other things can wait."

The young man was finding out some things. In truth the trip down was scary and the city itself was very intimidating. The fleabag motel turned out to be worse than he'd imagined and way worse than his dad had thought. *If his father had actually seen the place, there is no way he'd have let him stay there.* But his father expected him to stay there so the boy had gritted his teeth and endured.

The rest of the whole Intern experience was disappointing and eye opening. The dorm rooms at UC SF were almost as bad as the motel, there were enough homeless people lying around campus and on the streets to make him cringe and to top it all off his roommate had lasted exactly two nights before bailing.

So he was alone and depressed in the city. The job became his whole reason for being. Even that part was tougher than he'd expected. Not the work aspect but the social. Rammy was cool but no one in their five person team had time for a high school senior. They all had lives and friends and bars to hang out in at night, so Noah sat in the basement office on Folsom and 10th alone most of the time. The huge glass and concrete building was SOMA, or South of Market in cool San Fran slang. He'd learned that the natives *hated* "frisco" and he should never say that. The walk to work from the campus was very easy and beyond one frustrating drive around the city in traffic, the car had been parked the whole time. Noah figured out the BART and the Muni systems very fast. He even went down to AT&T park to stand outside and listen to the crowd. He couldn't get tickets to get into the actual game.

"Free time has been pretty scarce so that won't be a problem. "How are you and dad?"

"Things are crazy here. Oh, I'm back at the house if you need to reach me. Don't!" She warned trying to head off the million questions the boy would have. "Your dad is probably going back to sea soon anyway. He's TAD on an assignment for a while and then gone." Noah felt the hope bloom in his chest and tried to play it cool. He knew that TAD was Temporary Assigned Duty and that if his mother was back at the house things were moving nicely. *Now if something doesn't come along and ruin it.* Something like their son whining about his intern job.

"Okay mom. Just say hi to dad and tell him everything is going fine. I gotta go, my boss is motioning."

Rammy Pak the Korean American company lead for the network ops team waived Noah into her office through the crappy door window. The whole basement was utilitarian tech and worn. A raised square paneled floor which allowed for cable runs underneath showed all the dirt everyone tracked in. The half walled cube farm looked like every other American office with six desks. The server farm was off to the left and was ice cold from the forced ventilation system and cooling water. The rest of the office shared that cold. Rammy had on jeans and a sweater. At 26 she was young and smart and driven. Straight short black hair and the flatter but still lovely face of her ancestors held brown eyes and a smile. She liked Noah. Kid was smart and eager and teachable. Good combo.

'What's up?"

"I need you to run a search on the network. Internet and email plus phone. Keyword: Zhenge He."

Noah nodded and wrote it down when she spelled it for him. "What's that?"

"Not what, who." "Zhenge He was a Chinese explorer and sailor and admiral." "I need all the traffic that mentions him."

The request came out lightly but Noah picked up on the vibe.

"Can you speak or read Chinese?" she asked the young man.
"I know some words and phrases. My friend Kimmy is ABC and she is fluent. She was teaching me this year." 'What time frame?" he kept it professional.

"Better go back at least a year."

As he turned to leave the office and go back to the work cubicles where they could access the network, Tammy stopped him with one more request. "Bring the results to me ASAP and no one else."

That bothered him. A lot. He tried to hide the frown as he left but Rammy did see it.

The main frame computer in this building processed almost all of the internet traffic coming and going from Asia. Phone communications was for the western half of the US and the Pacific rim. The amount of data and traffic was daunting. Terabytes of information flowed in and out on an hourly basis.

And he could tap every bit and byte.

Not of course that doing that was legal. Ask Snowden. Or the NSA.

Noah typed the search terms into the computer. He put in several alternate spellings of Zhenge He. He also narrowed the databases he initially put in the playing field. Tammy said ASAP. He also intended to look at the first few hits and see if he could deduce a pattern of who was using the key word. It was possible that Zhenge He was the name of some role playing character and it was going to show up all over the place, but...
If the name kept popping up in relation to a certain area. then he could widen the search to include that data.

Noah had come to learn that with data, nothing is deleted and nothing is private. Screen captures got all of those tweets that people never actually meant to send. Emails and even phone calls were backed up. Oh, it took some time to do, but the data was available and it was easy. So easy an intern could do it.

All you needed was patience and a keyboard.

"Hey Walt!"

Sam Chow called out as the short, round and brown Hawaiian walked across the busy parking lot. Temura's market in Waianae sold the best poke and pipikaula on the island and the lot was crowded. Of course many home cooks would question that statement about the poke, Walt's wife among them.

On hearing his name, Tsuomo turned and saw the Chinese American man weaving his way towards him thru the people and cars.

"Howzit."

"Not bad, Mr. Sam. Funny see you here. Thought you be down the base moving all the ships around so the Navy can scramble."

"Bruddah, just came back from dere. The place be mad busy!" Carrier group gonna be gone this morning after the news came on Drum." "I think they be back in a week or so after everything calm down."

Neither man was particularly sad about the President, just the normal amount of worried that it was another terrorist attack and the nation would be plunged onto another 9/11.

"Look like the plane just went down in the storm, was what Nickers told us this morning when we was down dere. Matsun gone move two ships in tomorrow."

Walt was pleased his old shipmate the Admiral was keeping everything calm. He knew if PACFLT was on the case then the situation was handled.

The gunshots were very loud.

People in the lot instinctively ducked, including Walt and Sam. The five shots were followed very quickly by a flash from the substation behind the market. The small chain linked fenced electrical works was mauka side of the Farrington. Mauka as opposed to Makai. Mauka meant that something was located towards the mountains rather than the beach (Makai). The transformers and converters were relatively small but very important for this side of the island. The arc flash of the transformer blowing up dropped the market into blackness. Indeed, Walt could see that the whole corridor along the busy road that ran the length of the west side of Oahu was now without power. *If the power's out, the lights are out and its gon get hot and traffic gon be bad.*

Neither man had seen where the shots were fired from but Walt knew an act of terrorism when he saw it. Two calls he had to make. His wife and Nickers. Both needed to know what was happening.

Mr. Sam rushed back to his car. He had to get to the docks. The drive would take him almost two hours but he had to get back to see what the effect was on that side of the island. Waikiki and downtown would be isolated but if any other electrical works had been hit, it would be bad for the incoming container ships. He suspected he would be busy over the next few days.

CHAPTER SIX

The nights were the worst. Dragging herself into bed after dealing with the tremendous pressure for eighteen or twenty hours was bad enough, but to wrestle for a few minutes with the tremendous self doubt was new. Sharon was used to pressure and multi billion dollar decisions but this was different. This was life or death. And it was surprisingly up close and personal.

The last four days since Drum perished were the hardest she could imagine. Stallings liked to start each day with her daily intel brief sometime around six am. The briefer from Wellingtons agency was not the same young man who'd shown her the video footage on the Air Force One crash. It was her suggestion that he be the one to do the briefs, but a much more senior briefer who knew the kinds of questions Presidents wanted to ask was brought in. The balding fifty five year old looked like a dentist, not a spy.

"We have had intermittent internet attacks and denial of service hits on websites. Face book and Twitter have been experiencing outages. So far no major banks or financial firms have been hit but some government agencies and defense contractors are under pressure."

Stallings read thru the list. Lockheed and BAE. IBM, Boeing and others were on as well. She looked at Thomas. "It has the persistence of state sponsored attacks." He looked up from his notes. Senior staff and the major players were in the oval office. She still had trouble walking into the room, but she could not let anyone see that. Weakness was for at night in bed with Coleman. He just held her and let her deal with it. By day she slipped on her big girl panties and got the damn job done.

"Who do I need to threaten today?"

Thomas smiled. "China and Russia."

Putin and Fei. Those two dicks were peas in a pod.

"Paul, call Fei. Tell him that the Coast Guard is going to do open ocean seaworthy inspections on those merchants heading our way if they don't knock off the shit."

"Yes, ma'am."

Stallings was much different than Drum. Everyone was finding that out. She'd used the funeral of Anders Young to start the ball rolling on her choice for Vice President.

The notion of her appointing a Vice President was still pretty new. There were several instances of the President operating without a Second when the office was vacant. Truman went three years with no V.P. after Roosevelt died. LBJ did not have one until 1964 when he won election outright. Ford had no second in command until the 25th amendment was ratified and he appointed Nelson Rockefeller.

Now Sharon had a chance to bring some of her work with the Congress into the fore ground and appoint someone she was used to dealing with: Senator Richard Belkins. The man had been helping ram thru the spending bills and stop gap funding measures to keep the government functioning while Drum screwed around. And now she wanted to reward the man. But he was from the other party.

She made personal rounds of several house members and the leaders from both parties. "The casket summit" it was coming to be called by the press. And it looked like Belkins was a shoe in.

"Bobby give us the room please," Thomas nodded to the briefer. The man gratefully left without a word.

"Madam President we have a serious situation unfolding. You saw the collapse of the highway 17 bridge in Savannah last night?"

Silence gripped the room. "Yes. I thought that was an accident."

General Thomas the head of the NSA got paid to be paranoid and he was feeling very twitchy now. "The boat that hit the north piling was carrying fuel that exploded, yes. Our initial assessment was that they had the proper permits. And they did have permits to carry the gas, but there was no known reason for them to be on the river."

"Jesus!"

"We are still investigating but the bottom line is this: The 3rd ID is trapped in Ft. Stewart. Their gear is okay and the ships are fine, we just could not move them for another six to eight weeks. If something happens in Korea like we think…"

Sharon went over the ramifications.

"Plus we have had sixteen attacks on power substations or radio towers around the country. Disparate and random attacks. Hawaii, Frazier mountain in So Cal, and downtown

Seattle have all been hit. The eastern half of the power grid and the whole communication system is under attack."

'Who?"

Thomas hung his head. "I don't know for sure."

"Wellington, what aren't you telling me?" Sharon said softly.

The man struggled. He finally straightened and said, "Ma'am we have an asset at a facility in San Francisco. The young woman is monitoring cell calls and traffic on a Chinese operation. The pertinent code name is Zhenge He. Chinese explorer and naval admiral."

Who was going to ask the get out of jail free question?

The President herself said, "I'm assuming you don't have a FISA request on this?"

Thomas looked her square in the eye. "No ma'am." "I was doing what I thought to be in the best interests of the United States in the absence of leadership and directions from an incompetent President."

Marino could see the weight settle on the woman's shoulders. Sharon stiffened her spine and said, "All right, I order you to gather all intelligence on operation Zhenge He and whatever Chinese programs we can find out about. It seems to me that an attack on South Korea is imminent and these pinpricks by the Chinese are a deflector. I want us at full DEFCON 3."

"With all due respect Ma'am. Three is a half measure." General Graham spoke up for the first time. "Two means we cancel leaves and confine everyone to base because we think an attack is going to happen in the next 72 hours or so. Can we say that?" Heads shook no between the rest of the staff and participants in the conference.

"So we can't stay at 2 for a long length of time but three isn't any real difference in what Kevin and the other service chiefs are doing now." "Better to stay right where we are." That way we don't give away that we are ready for the Korean attack."

"Where are China's forces right now, General."

Graham laid out the Naval position. "The bulk of the Chinese Navy is off Midway playing nurse maid. They aren't the threat. The land forces aren't massing near the Yalu or the border area so this looks to be an air battle."

The classified computer flipped thru several pictures of Chinese air bases with increased activity levels all along the north and the south theaters of command.

"Who's the theater commander for Pacific?"

"Grant Nickers is PACOM and PACFLT right now." All eyes swiveled to the Chairman of the joint chiefs. "Drum didn't get around to nominating a replacement for Walters when she left."

Damn him! Sharon was outraged. They were going to keep finding these little speed bumps as they worked to undo years of Drums actions. Or inactions.

"Kevin Mooney is in Hawaii, helping out and General Zapata has his best air campaigner out there to coordinate the air forces in the region. Schofield Barracks and the Marines are just support so they won't matter", Graham assured her.

"Can we move the carriers?" Paul asked.

Stedman raised his shoulders up and down. "We can move the two Gulf groups thru the Straits of Hormuz and into the Indian Ocean. From the Indian Ocean it will take two to three days steaming to get them into position to help out in the far east."

"Kevin gonna be mad you move his toys without telling him," Paul warned.

Sharon laughed along with the rest. It *felt good to laugh again even for the moment.*

"Okay people."

Pads came out as work orders were coming down. "Paul, I'll call Fei myself and discuss this with him. Have the Dep Sec State sit in with me," she said as an aside to Libby.

"Graham, call Admiral Mooney and break it to him that I think it's a good idea to move those carriers. If he has a compelling reason, I can be talked out of it, but it better start with, MY GOD THAT WILL KILL US ALL!"

More chuckles from around the table. "Wellington, I want to know who your source is on the comms thing. If we have to go to FISA we will, but we need to pin the Chinese on these attacks." "Have your spy do some more digging." Libby we need to get the Congress going on Belkins thing. They are going to have to move fast on some of my nominations and bills if we are going to be ready for the opening of the stock market tomorrow." "Check?"

Admiral Kollmansburger had his boat CO's and their department heads arrayed before him in Explosives Handling Wharf number 2. The giant EHW was where the base loaded torpedoes and missiles on the submarines. Number two was twenty years younger than number one EHW which was just a few hundred yards up the sound. Bangor had seen a number of the

129

Trident submarines ship over from the east coast when the main threat axis was seen to be the Pacific theater as China developed around the beginning of the century. The extra handling capabilities had come in handy as the eight SSBN's were joined by all four of the tactical Tridents. Georgia and Florida mated up with Ohio and Michigan as Kollmansburger had operational control of a great many weapons.

He also had control of well over half of the nation's sea based nuclear deterrent triad leg. If the admiral was a country he would be the fourth largest possessor of nuclear weapons behind only Russia, China and the US.

The CO's along with their Exec's and department heads all attended the briefing. The senior enlisted from each boat also came in for the discussion. The men and women seemed to segregate themselves by ranks, the twelve CO's, all Commanders ringed very close to the Admiral. The XO's and their gold oak leaf's that marked them as Lt. Commanders came next. Mere Lieutenants made up the vast bulk of the department heads which were the most numerous of the crowd. The last ring was the enlisted COB's and department chiefs. Most of them master chiefs with the two stars over the anchors on their collars. Tommy stayed in this rank and was very quiet.

And now K-14 had to get the fleet out to sea. Orders had come down from DC.

"This is simple and hard. Ohio is the most ready ship. She leaves first. 0700 tomorrow. Boats sorte at one hour intervals. West Virginia, you leave with whatever we can get on you in the next 24 hours and are last in line. I want you all buttoned up and submerged as soon as you hit the 100 fathom curve." The Admiral looked his men and women in the eyes.

Stares came hard from the assembled CO's. The fiord that was the straits of Juan de Fuqua meant that the narrow water way was also very deep. The ships would be able to submerge very soon after entering Puget sound. But that was not normal. Very abnormal in fact. The sound and the straight were crowded with ships and it was easy to get ran over.

"The Coast Guard is going to have force protection out, same as they did for the Stennis group that left this morning."

"What are we going to do out there, Admiral." The CO of USS Nebraska spoke what was on everyone's mind.

"Same as you do every run. Make silent holes in the ocean. Clear the broadcast every six hours. When you get the order, if you get the order, you rise up and kill whatever we say."

An aide spread an oversized chart of the northern Pacific basin on the vap board standing next to the admiral. The giant red lettered sign that said "top secret" was jarring.

"The simple part: This box is boomer heaven. You all have assigned waters in here." The admiral sketched a huge square far to the east, past the international date line much closer to the Chinese mainland than Tommy ever wanted to go. *Thank god he was not going there.*

"As for the GN's, the man swept a hand much closer to the US mainland. "The Stennis is going to be meeting up out here with Bush and Regan battle groups when they head out of San Dog, sometime in the next two days. You are to trail. These are rough obviously, but you will have safe zone stove pipes here, here and here." A thick finger stabbed the chart. You all have the real chart and the coordinates. Do not fire into a stove pipe!"

"Did someone tell the surface targets that?"

The sailors all chuckled. They knew a stove pipe was an area in the ocean where a submarine could operate safely from the surface to the deepest they could go. No friendly unit- surface, plane, or sub was supposed to fire into a stove pipe. *Theoretically.*

The laughter ran down quickly.

"Admiral who is the enemy?" The Chief of the Boat for USS Maine asked pointedly. The woman spoke her mind at every turn. She got a little leeway as the Maine was the battle "E" boat for the squadron. Battle efficiency ribbons were permission to ask hard questions.

"That is the hard part. Master Chief, I don't know."

The frank admission stunned everyone.

"I won't speculate. Every contact is to be regarded as hostile until proven friendly. We have de conflicted any NATO or Rim Pac force units."

Frowns greeted this as the troops worked thru this. De conflicted meant that the other countries ship's and subs had been moved out of the area. *The whole Pacific?*

NATO and Rim Pac? That meant that the only two countries that were not in either force structure was North Korea and China.

Shit.

"Ladies and gentlemen, I have spoken this morning to both Admiral Mooney and the President. Both have asked me to convey their confidence in you. These are the Presidents words: "Your country is asking a very difficult thing of you. I send you out without a clear objective and a clear mission because I have faith that you will respond as American sailors have always responded: With honor courage and commitment."

The group broke up as everyone moved to get on with their responsibilities. Tommy got about thirty seconds with Lynn who was down assisting her boss.

"The CO is going to give us about eight hours at home tonight. Are you going to be there?"

Lynn searched her ex-husbands face. He was not scared, just acutely aware of what was possibly happening and the seriousness of it all. *This was crazy! The press had nothing on this. It was all Drum and the bridge and Young and Stallings...*

"I can be home by eight or so, I want to talk to Noah," she said reaching up to hug him.

"I need to talk to him too." His voice was muffled in her hair. The two held each other.

"We need to talk, Noah." Rammy yelled, motioning him into the office. The kid was working on something and not being very secret about it. *Maybe recruiting a high school kid as a spy was not the best move, she'd ever made.*

Problem was she was overwhelmed with requests to run searches and she could not trust anyone else in her group so that left her with...

"Coming!" The boy- no young man, scurried in carrying his laptop and a sheaf of papers which he dumped on her desk.

'Look at this," he dropped the computer and showed her a particular paper which turned out to hold translations of conversations. Chinese conversations of cell phones and radio phones. "Oh- who do you work for CIA or NSA?" he asked while she read. The voice was very nonchalant. Not even very accusatory.

Noah plopped in the chair while she did the carp face back at him. *Fuckin kid.*

Without waiting for her to answer or even allowing her to draw breath, he went on. 'These Zhenge He things are serious- look"- he pointed and quoted: Proceed with phase one- Zhenge He out.

"I had a long talk with my dad just now. He says to have you get these to your boss and funnel the intel to the military."

Ms. Pak buried her head in her hands. "Noah! Came out muffled. She raised her head and shook it. "One, how did you translate these much less decrypt these. Two, why did you talk to your dad? And three what am I going to do with you?"

The answering smile on the kids face was cocky. "In order: it's called google translate, duh… my dad is Navy, he has a TS and NATO ComSec clearance level. He confirmed what I thought- that you were a spook. And finally, the last answer is nothing. You can't kill me, I'm all you got."

He gestured around the empty office.

Thursday night at 8:37 pm on the 14th of May and no one else was in the building except some janitors and them. San Francisco was seeing beautiful weather after some heavy rains and everyone had bailed on them.

"I don't care what clearance level your dad has, he has no need to know," she began when he cut her off.

"Uh uh. Everyone needs to know about this." Spiegel was adamant.

Ms. Pak began organizing his papers into cognizant piles.

"Let's say for shits and grins, I agree with you and I can get my bosses to listen, who and where is Zhenge He. More critically what is the next target or move?"

The young man had no real answers on that score. The two of them batted around ideas and suppositions. *More substations? Internet? Communications towers?*

"DC is really worried about a 9/11 style attack with mass casualties," Pak said sitting back after two hours of work.

"That's not what is happening. The Chinese are not inflicting much in the way of casualties, just targeted infrastructure hits," Noah noted.

He watched her encode a report back to the home office, fascinated. Their best guess was that Zhenge He was directing things and was either in the US or very close, possibly Mexico. The trace program showed him using southern California radio towers until Frazier Mountain was destroyed. Now the signals were being bounced around Mexico and Arizona before going back to the west and overseas.

He was invested enough not to be scared. Or excited that his mom and dad might be back together again. Or scared that his dad was going to sea again to face who knew what? Or excited that he was hip deep involved in something that was uber cool. Or scared that Rammy and he would get arrested for spying without a license.

He got back to work. It was going to be a long night.

Bo paused a moment on the ladder up to the bridge. A crazy thought went thru his head. *You don't have to do this. Turn around and jump and no one else has to die.*

The thought was crushed out as all doubt had been throughout his life. He was committed. His country was committed. Let us see if the Americans were as well.

"Zhenge He here. All forces in position. Code eight, eight, eight." "I say again, Zhenge He- Eight, Eight, Eight."

Colonel Zi took the radio phone from his hand. Both men stood on the lookout sponson of the Hanjin Ship, Dragon. Her sister ships Leopard and Tiger were ahead and off to starboard by three miles. The cruise ship was port side of Dragon running parallel. The reserve merchant, Elephant was back another fifty miles along with the second cruise ship. All were heading for the Golden Gate twenty miles in the distance. Hidden by the fog and the dark, their objectives lay inside the bay. Committed by the call Lin Wei Bo had made and the madness of men.

Less than forty-five minutes later, General Qi's first wave of planes took off from bases in the south, near Shanghai and Guangzhou. They had further to travel than the forces scattered around Beijing. Five KJ- 2000- Early Warning and Control planes with their distinctive spinning dishes mounted topside, took to the skies to begin running race tracks between Dalian and Yantai. Those two peninsulas provided the choke point that separated the Bohai sea from the Yellow. It also established the AWAC's craft equidistant east and west from Beijing and Pyongyang. A flight of twenty airborne refueling tankers soon established themselves on a perpendicular path ten to a side of the line. Overtop of all that was an orbiting squadron of sixteen of China's best fighter aircraft, the J-31.

The Chinese plan had called for, and they executed a classic air superiority zone over the Yellow sea near North Korea. They now had the protection, the command and control and the fuel to conduct sustained operations in the theater.

The situation presented a force structure that would never be missed by US and Japanese air controllers and intel analysts. Before the J-31's, Fierce Fighting Dragons, the communist countries answer to the US F-35 Lightning, even completed one orbit, the phone lines were burning up to DC, Tokyo, Hawaii, Taiwan, London, Moscow and Beijing.

It wasn't a phone call at 3:00 am like the political ad said. It was the Secret Service agent that burst through her bedroom door that woke up Sharon Stallings.

"Madam President, they need you in the Situation Room."

The President swam up from sleep her heart in her throat, papers scattering as she'd fallen asleep on top of the cover doing some light reading. Looking over she eyed the empty spot in the bed. *Coleman? In New York, dammit.*

Her stretchy pants, tank top and moccasins competed with her scrunchy to scream the loudest, "I'm in relaxation mode!"

But her face didn't say relaxation mode. The face said, "Bring it on."

"What?"

A brief discussion and Sharon led the growing phalanx of people down the hall to the elevators after grabbing some better clothes.

Libby, Paul, and Colonel Stoerman, joined her security detail, Todd and Robert. All of them nodded without speaking. The group emerged from the elevator into the eye of the storm.

Grant Nickers was visibly upset on the wall video screen. "I have to have permission!"

"Permission for what, Admiral?" Sharon asked sharply stepping into view.

"Madam President, the Chinese are beginning a major military operation." He sketched out the air superiority zone the Chinese had established. No one needed to be reminded of the scant 120 miles between Seoul and Pyongyang. *That's about ten minutes flying time for one of those jets*, Sharon thought. That was a very short time to detect, analyze, and shoot a hostile.

"I need permission to contact Tokyo and Seoul to have them coordinate forces."

The President nodded. "You have permission of course, Admiral. Hang on let me get some things working here." She was locked in and decisive on what she wanted now. "Paul, Libby let's start waking up Congress people. Where are Stedman and Wellington?"

"Ten and fourteen minutes out respectively, ma'am," the duty comms person told her. She threw a quick thanks at the young airman.

Getting back to Nickers, she asked, "Admiral, is Kevin Mooney with you?"

"He's on his way ma'am. He's over at the Officers barracks at Hickam." A piece of paper was handed to Nickers. "Ma'am, I'm alerting the Nimitz and the rest of Yokosuka. I've put the 5th Air force at Kadena air base in Japan on five-minute alert. The Marines at Smedly are next."

"Excellent, Grant. Why don't you let Sec Def and the Chairman handle the statecraft with the Japanese government and the Koreans?" "You concentrate on US forces."

She could see him struggle. He was supposed to do the coordinating but she knew he was having a hard time dealing with the complexity. She did not want a superman trying to do everything by him or herself. 'Check?"

Nickers nodded gratefully.

"Now can anyone show me what we are dealing with here?"

All eyes turned to the wall screens. The Air Force liaison led them thru the radar data with an overlay of the satellite picture merged with a schematic map of the area. Colored triangles were put over aircraft that designated types and descriptions. The screen was rapidly filling.

"Holy shit, he's bombing the North!"
The Chairman of the Joint Chief's, Stedman Graham burst in with Thomas hard on his heels. No one could find Stansfield Mussman, Sec Def right now it seemed. The General knew his battlefield tactical picture pretty well. Scores of planes represented by blue squares were taking off from the eastern half of China and forming up for the almost due east trip to the North Korean capital.

"Those are J-16 Red Eagles, he told the President sitting opposite her. "Pieces of shit airplanes, actually. They stole the design from us. It is an F-16 knock-off but the engines are underpowered for the weight. Thing is a pig in the air." Graham was chattering to deal with the nerves.

136

"Why's Fei doing this?" Stallings asked for opinions as the room grew crowded. All of Washington's night was ruined. Not to mention the Koreans. The answers she got were not very illuminating.

The phone call to Fei was a mockery. "Madam President this is a purely internal matter. We will not stand by and be threatened with nuclear weapons by a dictator." "Do not interfere." The blunt warning was not received well. If Fei thought she was like Drum, then he was severely mistaken.

"General, this situation can easily spiral out of control. Seoul is only 38 kilometers from the DMZ. We are forced to put fighters in the area to counter your forces. If a stray missile were to hit an American or South Korean plane, the consequences would be devastating."

"If you were to allow us to conduct our affairs without interfering …"

"An attack is not "conducting affairs," I'm afraid."

"We assumed you would be happy with our taking out a dangerous unstable regime." "Not this way, General. There are better ways than killing innocent people."

Fei was not convinced. "We will not be threatened by anyone, Not the Koreans nor you." He broke off the phone call.

The President corralled a group of congressional leaders in the corner of the room. Normally the leaders would not be here but this was a trick she'd learned on Wall Street. Bringing the Board of Directors onto the trading floor during a huge downturn day was eye opening for the Directors. They were unused to the up close carnage of losing money. They'd been immune too long. It was the same with the Party Leaders. Delaying a confirmation hearing was normal business. Watching a possible war break out was another. "You see why now I need my V.P.? Senator Belkins would be on the phone right now briefing you all as to the situation, announcing our intentions to our allies, soliciting ideas." She told them all this with no guile or pretense. The House members were shaken.

The first hour of the attack was a straight bombing run. The Chinese concentrated on the North Korean nuclear sites with the added bonus of taking out the launch pads and the missiles. The North put up token resistance but it was ineffectual. Other than two Chinese planes that went down due to mechanical failures, the small numbers of Mig 31's the tiny hermit kingdom put in the air were quickly shot down and took no enemy planes with them.

The US and South Koreans put up planes along the line of the border with the North. The South put up every one of its combat ready fighters. 170 F-15's and F-16's hit the skies with a smaller thirty-two plane flight of more advanced F-35's. The Fifth Air Force based at Kadena in Japan could field another forty F-35's. The air craft carrier Nimitz had 80 planes split between the venerable F/A 18 super Hornet and the newer carrier variant F-35 Joint Strike Fighter. Admiral Nickers and Mooney established an Early Warning and Command and Control element of their own in the form of the newer E-8 JSTARS Air Battle Management planes. Four of the giant Northrop Grumman planes were out over the Sea of Japan trying to keep an eye on the five hundred Chinese planes currently in the air as well as the multinational friendly forces. One huge advantage the US/Japanese planes had was the JDAGE system.

"Explain again what the JDAGE System is, Stedman?" Stallings was not afraid to admit her ignorance on the new weapon.

"It's not really a weapon, Madam President. It is an integrated sensor suite used to detect, track and shoot down ballistic missiles from North Korea."

The President was suddenly deflated. She'd thought that they had an edge here. Stedman grinned at her. "Luckily for us it will work against regular airborne threats, like planes."

"What? How?"

"The system will talk to ships at sea and planes and land based missile systems. Once a threat is designated the targeting data is sent out and the selected weapon will lock on and destroy the threat."

Sharon was impressed. "Who do we need to talk to in Tokyo?"

Graham cast a jaundiced eye to the corner. "No one. We have no Status of Forces Agreement with the Japanese. It's being blocked in Congress. Nickers has been pushing interoperability and cooperation on a daily basis by himself." 'That's why he wanted permission to talk to the Japanese."

The ranking House member spluttered and then went silent under the looks of the room.

Sharon took no pleasure in the dressing down. "We need a clean bill pushed thru ASAP."

"Can this JDAGE thing talk to our E-8's?" She asked her General.

"Yes, Ma'am."

"Okay, get the JDAGE up."

"The Chinese are hitting the city!" All eyes turned to the display.

The wall screen showed the air to ground missiles and bombs taking out the Palace of Kim Jong Un. Waves of planes swept over the capital as ground based systems fired off missiles randomly at the attacking planes. Sheer luck caused three hits to the aircraft and the flaming wreckage fell over the city igniting fires.

As the sun started to rise over DC it looked like the battle was winding down. Planes were greedily sucking down fuel on both sides. The average fighter can last about two hours under full afterburners. The KC 135 tankers of the 909 refueling wing was seeing land office business east of Japan. Things seemed destined to remain localized until someone got twitchy.

The swarm of missiles that was fired from the J-31's who were protecting the strike fighters, had no provocation that anyone could see. Without warning sixteen missiles were streaking south towards the Korean F- 15's and F-35's patrolling their air space.

Multiple warning blared in the cockpits as the sky went ape shit. Counter measures popped off and hard turns saved eight of the Koreans but seven hits from the Chinese Beyond Visual Range Air to Air Missile's (BVRAAM) shredded airframes.

"Son of a bitch!"

No one would ever take credit or blame for that epithet that went out over the US flight network comms link. The pilots of the 44th fighter squadron-the Vampire Bats, all heard that call and came to action. A four plane element turned north and charged at the Chinese. In a target rich environment like that the ABM's, or Air Battle Management technicians had their hands full. The E-8 crew members assigned targets to the fighters based on complex geometry and chances of success. Computers picked up orders and slaved weapons.

"Vampire Vampire Vampire!"

Normally the incoming missile call was a sign of being attacked but in this case the 44th was getting some payback!

Each F-35 launched four advanced Aim 120 Air to air missiles at separate Chinese targets. The wait was not very long.

Splash sixteen.

A moment of silence gripped the White House and the comms link.

All fucking hell broke loose over the Korean peninsula.

Modern air combat bears little in common with the plane to plane visual dogfights of World War II or even Vietnam.

Advanced jets require long range radars and computers to help them analyze the targets and figure out how to approach without getting killed. US strategy has long been: see first, shoot first, kill first. The air superiority fighters of the US military have the most integrated avionics suites and sensors in existence. Combined with stealth technology, and advanced weapons today's fighters are lethal. Guided by their handlers in the AWACS planes, the average US pilot has a huge advantage in tactical and situational awareness over the enemy. No one is better trained and equipped to shoot down the opposition in that environment.

The problem for the US in this battle was one of that advantage. This time they didn't have it.

The Chinese had managed to get control established with their own AWACS and ABM people. *And they had numbers.*

The three hundred sixty two strike fighters left in the Chinese force converged on the allied planes. A full hundred broke straight for the E-8's running to the east of them. The AWACs were guarded but at sixteen vs a hundred it was no contest. Even with the enormous advantage of some ground based fire from JDAGE, all sixteen F-16's from the fighting fifth air force went down. They killed the enemy at a four to one ratio but the last eleven enemy planes managed to shoot down all four E-8's.

"Jesus how many planes do they have?"

The F-35 jock from the 67th fighter squadron asked his wingman. "I count forty three in radar range." "I have locks on twenty two," was the professional reply.

Captain Hard Jack McNauhay repeated this info on his net link. The pilots of the 67th air squadron, The Fighting Cocks, had just refueled after a boring turn south of the DMZ when the shit hit the fan.

"Cocks, Listen up!" The squadron leader Major Tammy Balin (call sign Ball Buster) alerted her charges on the net. "Switch to data share mode. We have trained for combat without the AWAC minders. Four plane formations. Senior pilot will mark targets and direct. Get hard Cocks!" Jack and his friends went to work.

The F-35 Lightning is a one hundred million dollar plane and most expensive fighter ever mass produced. Some call it a boon doggle, but you get something for your hundred million. In this case the Lightning's could act as a mini battle management system by themselves. They can share targeting and sensor data over an open architecture link. And that link runs throughout the services. So when the Marines showed up to the battle, their F-35's could link with and support the Air Forces planes. Same with the forty fighters from the Nimitz that flew in eighty seven minutes later.

So the battle was not quite a furball like the Chinese wanted. It got more confused when the Vampires managed to down four of the five KJ-2000's and chased off the last one. The superiority of the US planes stayed in the game at around a five to one kill ratio, but the US and Japanese planes went down as well. The skies over the Sea of Japan and the Yellow Sea was criss crossed with missile contrails. The slowly unfolding battle took place over six hours. Planes from both forces refueled and rearmed to get back in and deal out death.

A final wave of four hundred J- 31's took to the skies to finish off the last of the Vampires and Cocks of Major Balin and her friends. She died an ace, but that was of little consolation to her family.

The last forty fighters from the Nimitz were saved in the end by The President. And the USS Zumwalt.

It was her call to the leader of Taiwan that invoked the mutual defense treaty and put their two hundred and fifty planes in the air. The Taiwanese were not nearly as aggressive or competent as their US or Japanese counterparts but they supported the Navy and what remained of the Air Force far east fighter components.

The Zumwalt was part of the Nimitz battle group but their CO charged the new destroyer into the Yellow sea from the tip of Hokkaido as the battle progressed. The ship was out to sea while the carrier was in port when the call came to sorte from PAC Fleet. The captain quickly figured where he needed to be based on the tactical picture if he was going to provide some anti air support for the zoomie's.

And the destroyer brought a new toy to play with during the party.

Like something from a science fiction story the Zumwalt was equipped with a laser anti air weapon.

The laser had never been used in any combat situation or even an extensive test scenario but the man knew if he didn't do something quick, the Navy was going to be picking up dead pilots for a long time.

The first few shots (blasts?) (Zaps?) (no one knew what to call them) from the laser were anti climatic. No visible light or heat or sound beyond a waring siren.

The effect was also not as fruitful as they'd hoped. Of the first three Chinese planes targeted, only one broke off from formation. It didn't crash, it just flew back to base.

Not spectacular but the crew would take it. They finally figured out that the distance and atmospherics were diluting the effectiveness of the laser. A quick reposition and the clearing of some clouds and suddenly five directs hits with pure structural break ups greeted the firings.

"What the fuck happened to them?"

The Nimitz based F-18 pilot had little time to puzzle thru the problem. One second a plane had tone on him and then it was gone. Good for him- bad for them. The man had more pressing concerns.

The Zumwalt kept firing until the laser overheated. Splash forty one by the CO's estimates. That was the most planes brought down by any ship in the history of the US Navy. *By a factor of ten!*

Hours later as the last of the attackers disappeared back west, the sides took stock. Four hundred eighty three US, Korean, Japanese and Taiwanese planes had been shot down. The Chinese absorbed the loss of over seventeen hundred aircraft. The Battle of the Yellow Sea was over.

By noon eastern the battle was finished and the Situation room was a mess. Little sleep, bad food, coffee, and stress left everyone wrung out.

Stallings pulled the senior players to the table for a status poll. "Stansfield can you summarize the far east for us."

The Secretary of Defense looked grey as he read off the casualties. "We lost 109 total air craft at last count. That figure may change based on planes landing out of place, but Kevin and

Grant think its accurate." He listed off the numbers, "thirty nine from Nimitz- four Awacs E-3's, and thirty five attack planes split between the F-35's and the FA-18's. Japan based forces- Forty F-35's along with seven controller planes. The Marines at Smedly lost twelve attack planes, while our Korean units lost another twelve fighters." He let those figures get into people's heads for a second.

"Our allies fared worse: Korea lost one hundred fifty out of two hundred or so. Japan all of their two hundred. The Taiwanese were late and only lost twenty four fighters", Sec Def could not keep the bitterness from his voice.

"We suffered some minor damage to our bases, mostly long range air to ground missiles but none of the airfields are out of commission. We lost no Naval units." The paper dropped from his hand. This was the worst loss in Air Force history in air to air combat. The country was used to seeing individual planes go down, not entire squadrons being wiped out.

And yet this was a victory.

Stallings refocused them. "Our troops fought brilliantly. How many Chinese planes went down?"

"Seventeen hundred, ma'am", Mussman told her.

"Why?" "Why the hell did they do this?"

Paul Marino asked the question on everyone's mind instead of answering the Presidents unanswerable thought. "What purpose did it serve?"

Stallings went around the room. "General Thomas?"

"I don't know, he admitted. This makes no sense by itself. The Chinese have lost three quarters of their offensive strike capability. Of course we have no way to strike them either. At least from our local assets. We could conceivably attack them from Hawaii or even the mainland but why would we want to do that? Punishment?"

"Couldn't we use that carrier, the Nimitz?" Aly Mustafina asked not knowing the capabilities of the forces.

The President shook her head. "Aly the Nimitz has been decimated by losses, we..."

General Graham interrupted. "Madam President, forgive me but you are using that word incorrectly. Decimated literally means "reduce by a tenth"- it's from the Greek." In military terms a combat unit is not considered out of commission until it drops below fifty percent." The Nimitz has lost fifty percent of its strike planes but can still conduct other sustained operations. I realize that decimated has come to mean "wiped out" for the average person but we need to be very precise in talking about our forces now."

"Can we restore the Nimitz to full combat capability, General?" Sharon appreciated being kept on the straight and narrow.

"We can, of course. We have three reserve squadrons so that won't be a problem, but it will take a week or so to get them out there."

"Do it." Admiral?"

She raised her head to check with the CNO. Mooney nodded his head on the vid screen. He and Grant had been popping in and out all morning. Neither had gotten much sleep as the time zones were killing them.

"Will do!" Mooney told the President.

Wellington Thomas and General Graham shared a look. That was just not how Drum would have handled the situation. He would have put off the decision until forced and then he would have ordered without thought for anything else. Stallings was a breath of fresh air.

"Why, Wellington?"

The NSA head lowered his eyes. "I don't know. This has the feel of a false flag or Trojan horse kind of thing. It's not nuclear and they know we won't either." He sounded like he was talking to himself. 'On the surface it looks like just what it was: an operation that got out of control and resulted in a colossal fuck up. They didn't have any anti-ship missiles, they didn't strike US infrastructure. They just took out our strike assets." To what end? Why would we have to strike them? Ma'am, Sharon, I think there is another shoe to drop!"

But no one could come up with what or where.

"People!" What proactive steps can we take? Do we declare war on China?"

That question brought stomachs to feet around the table. Libby told Paul that they might already be in a war whether they wanted to be or not. Marino agreed with a grimace.

The discussion brought a number of action items: The middle east and Indian Ocean carriers would be brought across the Pacific. The San Diego based fleet would leave port as soon as they could be readied. Mooney promised in twenty four hours. The fleet in Hawaii would leave as feasible in the next few hours. The West coast Naval units would concentrate on the Chinese Navy, sitting near Midway. Norfolk? The same. The east coast fleet would be consolidated into a major battle group to provide protection to the major cities, New York, Boston, Philly and DC.

DEFCON 1 was declared and Sharon was going to address the people, Congress and the UN in the next two days.

"Martial law?"

That question brought the most vociferous argument from all sides. A closely run contest that saw Sharon convince the others that the American people would do their jobs as they had always done them.

"Alert EAS and get the reverse 911 system in effect, Paul", she ordered. "We have to let everyone know what is going on." "Check."

"We ought to think Facebook and Twitter. The younger crowd uses social media," he advised. Sharon nodded agreement.

The meeting involved hundreds of items: Where was Fei and the rest of the Military Council? Should they expel the Chinese ambassador? What do they do about the US diplomats in country? What about civilians in the far east? Chinese civilians here? What about reprisals against innocent Chinese Americans?

There were a thousand small things. None of them focused on the Chinese merchants waiting to load US grain.

Tommy was topside while the Ohio exited the basin and went to the middle of the channel that led to the sound and the sea. 0635 and Ohio was leading the procession out of Bangor. The early dawn was cool and a mist hung over the still calm waters. Thoughts and images kept intruding while he tried to lead his line handlers in unhooking the tug from the submarine. The vision of Lynn lying in his arms last night, her head on his chest. The phone call from Noah. *My boy is in danger!* And there was shit all he or his wife could do about it. The boy was south and would have to look after himself. He shook it off. Lynn was going out of her mind but he thought the kid could do it. The look on the CO's face as he told them all about the air battle last night in China was stricken. No it was actually North Korea. Hundreds of planes down. The intel boards from the Radiomen had contained sobering briefs. *Looks like the muppet got some payback!* Muppet being the nickname of the USS Elmo Zumwalt.

The tug pulled off and slid back towards the base as she was required to get Michigan yanked off the wharf and headed for sea.

The rigid hull inflatable boat from the Coast Guard cruised in as the sub picked up speed. Tommy watched the young sailors coil the lines as the kid mounting the fifty cal machine gun on the following boat, swung it back and forth. The Hood Canal Bridge lay three miles ahead as the sub ran up to ten knots. That was much faster than they normally went on this run. And they were early. Kollmansburger and Captain Greene did not believe in waiting, so they shoved off when ready.

Spiegel was perfectly positioned when the white hulled fishing boat roared to life across the channel and started to speed towards the bridge. *"What the fuck?"*
Tommy was not the only one who'd seen the intruder. The lookout was pointing and the Officer of the Deck was shouting along with the Captain from the bridge.

A radio call and the Coast Guard swung into action. The RHIB turned to the threat with a sharp burst of speed. The chatter of the fifty cal was loud as it stitched a line of water spouts towards the oncoming boat and it was frightening.

'All hands, Lay below!" The COB bellowed the order. The twenty men and women scrambled for the amidships hatch. But they did not have enough time.

The fishing boat was ignoring the fire as she kept plugging for the bridge piling.

Tommy looked up in horror to see the figures on the bridge. Wives and girlfriends lining the rails.

The underground wives' intelligence network was second to none in ferreting out when the US Navy was deploying and those faithful family members were up on the bridge.

Bullets walked the bow of the terrorist boat as it neared its goal. Tommy could see the fuel drums stacked up now, ready to take out the bridge and trap the Tridents in port.

Motherfucker!

They were powerless to do anything when the Petty Officer commanding the RHIB made his decision. The roar of the twin outboards went up in volume as the small boat veered to the left. The cross path closing speed was near fifty knots as the boats came together.

Just five hundred yards in front of the Ohio and a thousand from the bridge piling, the Coastie made the ultimate sacrifice. He rammed the fishing boat.

The explosion was bright and deafening.

The sailors involuntarily flinched as the debris rained down. Pieces of the machine gun and the sailor manning it ended up on deck. Tommy would never forget the severed hand bouncing on the deck.

The burning hulks of both ships drifted towards the channel edge as the sub slid past.

The CO was already calling the base to report the attack. It wasn't ten minutes later that a second RHIB came along side. The COB allowed the topside detail to render full honors to the grim faced Coast Guard sailors manning the new inflatable.

Later that morning the Captain addressed the troops before the submarine went deep to complete its transit to the open ocean in relative safety.

"Ladies and gentlemen of the USS Ohio. It appears that we are at war. The events of today are horrifying and fresh in our minds as we go to do our jobs. I know that we witnessed a singular act of bravery today. I expect that every man and woman on this boat will do their utmost to perform our mission as assigned and honor the sacrifice that Petty Officer William Andrews and his crew made for us. Carry On."

Ohio slid silently under the surface and disappeared.

CHAPTER SEVEN

The sound didn't sound like fire crackers at all to Dre. *He knew.* Knew it all too well. Gunfire. Automatic gunfire at that. Once you've heard that sound in combat the rest of your life any gunfire is similarly marked by your ears and balls. It was just the bodies' natural survival instinct.

The gunfire was coming from the docks and it caused Dre to whip his head up from the tire he was helping Manny mount on a rig. The Air Force might be in a war this morning but the three huge ships waiting at the ways meant he had a job to do. Isn't that what the President had told them? "Go to work and do your jobs as Americans and we will get thru this together."

Well, that was what Dre was trying to do.

The Chinese containers ships had pulled in an hour ago. The first one was tied up and had delayed boarding the Coast Guard due to the "incident this morning". Mr. Jenkins had called and told them that the US aid people and the Coast Guard and the State Department boys were trying to corral what was going to happen.

Meanwhile, Dre had rigs to fix.

He and Manny and Tito watched the second big ship dock while the President spoke. The third unit was waiting its turn for the pilots and the line handlers to finish up its sister ships.

"Big puta, eh, hermano?" Tito said.

Dre grunted. From his window looking due west at the docks the giant ships were blocking the view of San Francisco. In truth his view wasn't really of San Francisco. *That's just what he had bragged to Tabatha.* It was towards the Coast Guard Island and the one cutter and five RHIB's docked there. Dre could see the figures of sailors running around the small craft making preps to get them underway. He didn't know what was up their butts. He and the Pacheco brothers went back to tire work when the gunfire sounded out.

Dre could see the cranes positioned inland from the first merchant. The long steel boom was looming over the mid ship's area, waiting to pluck a container from the multitudes of stacks on the ship. The sheer number of the containers was staggering. The Hanjin Leopard held 14,022 containers on board. The units were stacked sixteen high and nine wide at the beam steel cage stations, where the bulk of the cargo would be loaded. The giant ship held twenty-four rows of these 2 TEU containers in the standard rust and blue colors. And she had three more of these stations on board! The forward and aft areas held containers in a piecemeal way to bring the total to the fourteen thousand mark. Various bulk storage areas were located below decks and Andre knew the whole ship was run by a minimal staff of perhaps twenty-five seaman.

Standard operating procedure for an off-load/on-load scenario had the Coast Guard performing the customs and cargo checks in the first hour after docking while the DEA and ICE did the crew sweep and pat down. Once that was accomplished the long shore men took over and the endless round of crane and truck moves began.

The pattern was broken today. The Coast Guard was on board but had not yet emerged. The coverall wearing sea crew was standing at the top of the ship gang way near the forward bulk elevator, when the shots rang out. *Funny the gunfire didn't seem to upset the crew people at all,* Dre wondered.

"What was that?" Manny joined Dre looking at the ship.

"Sounded like shots, Dre muttered. *He did not need anything messing up his rhythm right now…*

A flurry of activity at the gangway could be seen. More crew coverall wearing men appeared at the top and started down the silver aluminum colored ramp. The Oakport employees were just starting to look away when a gun flash appeared and one of the DEA men waiting at the bottom of the ramp went down. More flashes and then all six bodies were crumpled on the docks.

"Oh, shit!"

The sound of gunfire reached the two men as Manny exclaimed in a shocked voice.

Things started happening real fast. Men swarmed out of the ship from every conceivable hatch and hole. Shouts from the longshore gang could be heard as they started to flee.

Flashes from automatic rifles began to wink along the dock. The bright daylight did nothing to dampen the orange flares.

Dre watched in horror as four men began scaling the nearest crane with rifles slung on halyards on their backs.

"Dre, Look!"

Manny pointed to the other ship docked in port, the Tiger. Men began coming out of her holds and hidden crannies as well. The Port officials were not even on this ship, so the troops began running to the wheeled lay down cranes and to the numerous trucks that were lined up waiting to accept loads or drop off. The attackers hauled drivers out by the shirt collars and ruthlessly shot them. One driver out of the twenty-two lined up, managed to pull a gun from his cab somewhere and he at least shot one of the hijackers before losing his life.

Soldiers.

The realization hit Dre as he saw the scene unfold. Two hundred men in matching dark blue coveralls were systematically surrounding the vital areas of the port and executing anyone who stood in their way.

"We got to move!" "Tito, Amir! Everyone! Drop what you doing and get in your cars!" Dre shouted to get the men going. He turned to grab some tools and bags and started throwing the effects into the towing unit.

"Dre, where we gonna go man!" Amir was wide eyed with fear.

The operations building was being breached right now as the eight men gathered at the roll up door to the shop.

"Manny, you with me in the tower. Listen up! There are soldiers or terrorist taking over the port. Won't take them long to make it out here. I'm going to ram the fence along harbor drive with the tower and make a hole. Follow me thru it. You guys head home and watch the news. "I'll call when it's clear to come back." Andre sketched out what he wanted to do.

Tight nods from everyone. What Dre had failed to tell them was that a large group of cars tearing out of a building was liable to attract a lot of attention.

The flash back to Iraq was causing him to sweat profusely. He was a fucking mechanic, not an infantry man. He never was one, even over there when he had to be. But when push came to shove and the Forward Operating Base (FOB) was attacked, he had defended right beside the others. Until the mortar took him out. He fought off the nerves and the memories.

"Ready?"

Manny was behind the wheel and the rest of the men were poised to run for their cars. Dre stood on the runner of the tower rig. Essentially the tow unit was an 18-wheel cab with a small crane and a large tool and storage box on the back. The bright yellow vehicle was not exactly stealthy.

"Go!"

He swung in and shut the door. Manny drove slowly out of the shop and waited while Dre worked the automatic door opener from the passenger seat. Terrorists or not the shop had to be locked up!

The rest of them were in a ragged assembly of beaten up cars and engines roared to life as they went in.

"Go, Manny!"

Pacheco goosed the gas and the truck belched out a puff of diesel smoke. As the truck pulled out and headed briefly west before turning north, Dre had a clear view of the ships, three of them now bumping the piers and disgorging men. A glance to his left as the Port ops building swung into view showed the soldiers breaching the doors and sweeping into the place. Dre knew as sure as shit no one was getting out of there alive. Scattered men, workers and drivers who had been at roadability and the inspection stations away from the main action, were now out and running around the lay down lots. Casualties waiting to happen, Dre figured. He rolled down the window to shout at them as they passed. "East! Head east!"

Manny was working the truck in that direction by shuttling in and out of the stacks of containers in the yard. The best place to punch thru was right where Adeline street became Inner Harbor drive. That was near to the main entrance to the port however.

A glimpse down a long lane of containers revealed the main terminus gates. Groups of soldiers were hauling drivers out and shooting them. This action was causing chaos to the line of trucks waiting to get into the port. Drivers bailed and swung rigs right and left trying to get out of harm's way. Dre saw a last contingent of forty or so men establishing a barricade right in the middle of Adeline. *Was Tabs workin the Brick, this morning? No, she was at his place, thank god.*

He pulled his phone out and simultaneously yelled at Manny Pacheco to head north.

Manny yanked hard on the steering wheel and the big truck protested but got around. Manny watched his rear view and saw their newest employee, Jeremey Collins slow and pull over to take on two struggling drivers. He did not think that was a good idea and that proved to be the case as a team of two light duty trucks filled with armed men crashed his little column. The last two cars, Eddie and Jeremey's both were cut off.

"Fuck!"

Dre spat out the word. Tito, Amir, and Bobby who had Ladarius with him all swerved and managed to stay with the fleeing rig. The procession picked up speed and came north to the commercial end of the port. Several trucking outfits had offices here as well as SSA West, the shipping firm. Most of these offices were surrounded by K rail traffic barriers so Manny could not breach them but he wanted to try to warn the growing crowd of men and women emerging to see what was going on.

"Run!"

He bellowed the word and followed the roadway as it went back east to the right. Dre finally managed to remember what the phone was doing in his hand and he dialed 911. He pointed to a spot for Manny- "There!"

"Hello?"

"911 what is your emergency?" The phone sounded static-y.

"I'm at the port…

"Sir we have a report of a work place shooting already."

"No!" Dre broke in. It ain't a work place shooting! It is soldiers. There are over a thousand that I saw, coming from the ships." He took a long breath.

Shit!

He hadn't been watching and Manny was weaving around and between the stacks of containers and buildings and K rail barriers trying to find a straight shot to the street. And now he'd found his break point. The tow rig shot straight across the parking lot and right into the chain link fence that protected the port from vandals and thieves.

The truck snapped off the pole and the fencing wrapped itself around the front before breaking off, scratching the fuck out of the paint job. The tires sucked the chain link off the hood and the debris shed as the truck bounced onto Harbor drive heading north.

"Sir, did you say from the ships?"

Dre looked at the phone in his hand. "Yes! Heavily armed men, at least a thousand, have taken over the port."

"We have the police responding."

"No ma'am. You send the police in there and they are going to be killed. You need the army!" Stay on inner harbor, it turns into 7th and then bends back around," he said to Manny. The man complied. He turned to see the others following grimly.

Dre couldn't get anywhere with police dispatch and he knew no one in the army so he hung up on the lady. Shit!

7th avenue runs parallel to the BART tracks as they move commuters to and from San Francisco. The giant post office facility that served the east bay went past on the right. "Turn here."

Manny did as the truck and convoy got to Campbell street. The drive to his place was only two minutes from there. Pulling the big truck into the tiny driveway allowed the other three cars to park on the street.

All of them were shaken.

"Did anyone see Jeremey or Eddie?"

A shaken Amir said, "I saw them get shot up." The man sat heavily on the dead grass in front of the house.

Dre's gut seethed. "You guys can go home or come in and watch the TV with me."

Everyone went into the house.

"Tabs!"

His mother was out east visiting the Atlanta relatives. *A thousand of that extra money was gone but that was okay.*

A note on the table put Tabatha at her friend Danisha's place. *That was bad.*

He tried the cell as the men flipped on the TV. The news chopper was hovering over the port showing a long shot. The cell circuits were all busy, dammit! Figures could be seen running and moving all over the port. The news coverage was still calling it an "incident".

Dre looked over his workers and friends he guessed you could call them. Tito and Manny stood near the kitchen doorway. Both short and compact with dark hair. He'd never guess they were thirty eight. Both men looked older. Hard work and the sun had etched lines and kept their dark skin looking like an avocado. That might be unkind.

Amir was the youngest he knew at 22. The thin Pakistani was normally quiet and generally upbeat but now he sat on the couch with a frozen look of fear on his face. Bobby and Ladarious were his newest employees and more different. Robert Tornelda was white and southern while Ladarius Snell was black and from LA. Both were former military mechanics as Dre liked to hire vets.

"You guys can get some to eat if anyone is hungry. I think Tabatha made some stew or something."

The men slowly made their way from the living room couch and chairs to the small kitchen. Dre was handing out bowls and cans of soda while the news crew zoomed in on the soldiers.

"We can see the attackers here setting up a barricade on Adeline street just off the 880. Police have cordoned off the area and are attempting to negotiate with them."

Without warning the picture fuzzed out white and went to static.

"We seem to have lost the chopper feed." The channel three newsman was calm and reassuring. The anchors went into a recap of the shootings as they knew them.

"Flip it to channel seven-ABC," Amir advised.

Dre did so.

The scene on the TV was of a different news camera chopper. The breathless voice yelled as the view swung wildly.

"I'm trying to evade... I have at least one after me..."

Again the flash and the feed cut.

The TV resolved on the shocked faces of the ABC noon news crew.

"We will rerun the last few minutes of Ted Morrison and the Channel seven news chopper footage." The tape cut back to the longer view of the port. The zoom in revealed several trucks being loaded with men and arms. Gantry cranes were swinging the containers down to mate with some trucks that were just pulling out to form up at the exit of the port. Other 2 TEU units were being laid down bare on the concrete pad. Some were even being set up on end.

"You can see here the images from the port. To reiterate, we do not know who these men are but they seem to be coming from inside the containers. We can see at least three to four thousand men all armed, moving with some purpose trying to secure the port." The news and footage had the whole feel of a traffic report.

That changed with the next shot. The three-man team braced the black tube on the hood of a truck cab and one of them sighted down the barrel. The second man unpacked the back end and then tapped the first on his head. The third looked at the sky with his binoculars and then dropped his hand.

A missile leaped from the end of the tube.

The white smoke trail was followed up as the sky bound weapon accelerated up some two thousand feet and a mile off to the east. The police helicopter was hovering just over the 880.

The missile struck with a blinding flash and explosion.

"Oh My God!"

The sound from the news reporter was panicked. A second smoke trial was just visible as the view came back towards the west. The NBC logo on the channel three chopper was just recognizable as the next bird to die as the shoulder fired FN-6 missiles started bringing down anything that could fly.

"I'm trying to evade...I have at least one after me..."

"Mother fucker!"

The men in the living room were shocked. Suddenly the annoying Emergency Advisory System sound came out of the TV. The succinct thirty second report told everyone to return home and shelter in place. Further reports would be issued. Stay tuned.

The men all looked to Andre. "You better get home and see to your families."

Manny and Tito stepped closer. "Our wives and kids are down in Mexico, man," Manny said. "You know, what with Drum and all...". He shrugged but did not have to say any more. Amir, Bobby and Lardi exchanged quick glances. "We got no families here either."

The two other military men looked to Dre. "Boss man, you know what going on here, right?", Lardi said.

Dre did in fact know what was happening. An invasion. Just like when they went into Iraq. Establish a secure operating area and then fan out. Kill anyone that moves. That was pretty simple but it was hard to get his head around the concept. But he was not their boss in this. This was a whole nother level.

"I do but I aint the boss..

"Fuck that! You in charge, Dre. You know what to do. We gotta be ready for when they come!" Bobby Tornado they called him and his voice sounded in the wind. He was scared and charged up and waiting for someone to tell him what to do.

Dre searched the faces watching him. They wanted, no they *needed* him to direct them and to take charge.

Okay.

"Here what we do. You guys swing home quick and grab what weapons you can. Remember ammo! Anyone got a first aid kit? Two hands went up: Manny and Bobby. Bring them. Pack a bag with basics, clothes, food and water. Bring yo medicine!"

"We meet right back here as soon as you can."

The three cars roared off as Dre tried the phone again. Still no luck. All circuits were still busy. He had to find Tabs!

"Focus on unloading the first ship. The reserve ship is four hours behind us. The Leopard had one more part to play in the plan, Bo knew. *They had to get unloaded.*

Zi was down on the docks alternately yelling and pleading with the colonels in charge. Men scampered up and down the gang way without regard to safety. The invasion was more or less on schedule. Two hours ago he had radioed the order to go: 'Zhenge He is at Seirra 2. Sierra 1, Sierra 3, Hotel 1 and Lima 1 proceed with Operation Quinru."

"Colonel Zi, tell them to begin," he told his aide. His plan was working. He had four ships in port under no opposition with one more on the way. Two cruise ships filled with troops were even now landing at the cruise ship terminal at San Francisco pier twenty-seven.

The men had survived the trip over the ocean. Check that- most of them had survived. They did have some casualties. Regrettable but expected given the cramped conditions. The men were isolated three to a container. Another two thousand were permitted to jam into the bulk holds for the trip.

Bo was not sure which one would be worse: Having to share the small 360 square foot containers or sitting in a virtual cell with five hundred other soldiers in one of the bulk holds.

The containers had been outfitted with a vent line and water along with a sewer pipe, but the two week trip had killed nearly four thousand. Most of those in the interior units when the sewer gasses had backed up on the vent pipes. Bo shuddered at the thought of being unable to even open the door to the container to escape the noxious fumes.

He was receiving reports from Elephant and Tiger that they too had some deaths but that it was acceptable. Wei Bo was counting on an initial one hundred fifty thousand man force with reinforcements coming very quickly.

And he was watching the initial wave pour over the port facilities without a problem.

"The trucks are important but the missile system has top priority!" he commented to the messenger. "Tell Colonel Zi that the north end must be kept clear for the surface to air missiles."

He raised the binoculars to his eyes and looked at the cranes dropping the containers end up to his left. *Excellent!*

Giving up precious container space that could have contained troops was a tough exchange but he had to have the protection. His ships could not bring over air craft and he did not have air fields to stage them from, so he devised a two prong attack plan to overcome the problem. General Qi's Air Force in phase one had removed some of the United States' ability to strike back at his invasion force. Nothing in Japan or Korea could be formed up and sent over to attack his troops.

Hawaii and the East coast? They could reach out and bomb the shit out of his forces, but...

He currently had five large merchants landing at Hotel 1 (Hawaii) right now. Any US strike planes would have to be used to attack those invaders. Bo knew that they would kill thousands of his troops but China did not want to take and hold Hawaii. He just wanted to tie up the troops to the island and make them fight in place.

Same with San Diego and Seattle. Sierra 2 (Seattle) and Lima 1 (Long beach) both had more container ships landing today to block the Marines and the US Army's Seventh infantry division respectively.

His reasoning was sound. The United States would have no choice but to use the local forces to repel the invaders. But the US had nothing local to oppose him in San Francisco and Oakland.

Again his main problem was the east coast planes and the US carriers. He *had to establish this missile defense system to mitigate that advantage.*

The large crane strained to lift the container off the stack. The heavy unit went north along the rail tracks as the crane squealed and protested. Reaching the end of the tracks the guide wires reeled in and the closed front end went down to the ground. The container touched down lightly and set up by itself as the lift points were unhooked by the ground staff. The workers climbed up the forty foot steel unit and flipped open the doors. The interior was a canister which held four HQ-9 Fang Dun (defensive shield) missiles. The twenty five foot long two stage rockets were normally carried on a truck transporter but when attached to a generator and controlled by a HT-233 field radar unit the HQ-9 could be devastating. With a 100 mile range and an 80,000 foot ceiling, Bo would not feel safe until the two thousand missiles he'd brought with him were set up. 18-24 hours. He figured he still had sixteen before the US used its air power to wipe him out.

"General, we have a report from Ant force: Alameda island air strip is secured. Proceeding to clear out the rest of the island." The young messenger was pale and gaunt from the trip over. Bo was going to have to feed and water them and let them get some real sleep at some point. But now was not that time.

"Prepare for the landings."

The soldier saluted and returned to his station. Bo went to the other side of the ship. The westward side was bathed in sunlight and it was difficult to focus on the incoming speck that was the Boeing 737-800. The ubiquitous civilian plane was supposed to be flying into Oakland, but things were a little chaotic right now and the local air traffic controllers had lost track. The plane swung out low and slow over the bay and headed for the angled runway. The cracks and weeds didn't bother the pilot at all. In fact, the abandoned runway was in surprisingly good shape. The jet touched down and screeched to a halt at the far end away from the watching General.

Bo had an excellent view of the process. The small trucks of jet fuel he'd brought over were parked at the far end of the island after being driven over on the causeway road. They'd been one of the first things the cranes had unloaded from his ship when it landed. Bo was so prepared that the army had packed a roll up ramp and stuck it in the shipping container. The one hundred fifty troops in the plane had to get off in decent fashion did they not? The luggage holds were stuffed with ruck sacks and ammo cans. The ground crew rushed to get the plane re fueled and off the island. They only had fifteen minutes before the next plane came in. One of the next reports Bo hoped to hear was of the Long Beach team securing Long Beach Airport for the landings there.

The Long Beach theater was the weakest link in his opinion. The force, led by General Zhou Pi was able but had to be spread out. Being asked to secure Los Angeles and then try to pivot and box in the Marines and Navy in San Diego was perhaps too ambitious. Pi had an extra merchant so he had maybe 200,000 men to accomplish his objectives, but Bo was asking much of his men. The suicide ships would be the real key.

"General, we have word from Sierra 2. General Fei's disrupter force was unable to accomplish their mission."

Bo calculated. The force was supposed to isolate the American submarine forces at Bangor. That was bad for his support people. The second surge of ships was due to land in a few days. Each landing spot had a dedicated reserve ship coming right on the heels of the initial wave , but he'd planned on a second landing with five more ships each for Seattle/Tacoma, Long Beach, and Oakland. Hawaii was not getting second wave. The Chinese had run out of men and guns and container ships.

"All forces this is Zhenge He. Accelerate reserve landings at Sierra 1, Sierra 2, Hotel 1 and Lima 1 by one hour."

It would have to do.

"I don't fucking know!"

Rammy could not answer him. Noah was just coming unglued. Too many reports. Too many things that had to be done and now the news indicated that armed men had stormed the cruise terminal at pier 27. The ferry building was closed off. People were panicking and the kid wanted to know about his family.

In a calmer voice she went on. "Noah, I only have the same reports that you do. An unknown force, possibly Chinese, have landed at major ports on the west coast. Oakland, San Francisco, Seattle/Tacoma and Long Beach seem to be effected. Oh and Hawaii," she added.

"But my dad barely survived the thing this morning! Now there are Chinese troops in Tacoma?" "You have to let me tell my mom!"

"Noah, your dad is Navy and has the clearance, your mom…"

"Is the administrative assistant to COMSUBGRU 9." He said it casually and with emphasis on the military slang.

Ms. Pak the NSA's head tech weenie had some soul searching to do. The White House and her bosses at Mclean, Virginia had not been too forth coming about what to do for the last twelve hours. Now they had a report that Zhenge He was accelerating the landings. No check that- a landing.

She was going to make some decisions that were a bit above her paygrade.

"Okay, text her. The cell signals are overloaded. I'm going to use the reverse 911 service to advise people here to leave via the 280 and the peninsula. Can you use that email family gram thing to let your dad know what is going on?"

Noah nodded. He'd explained that submarines had very limited connection to the internet when they were undersea. For obvious reasons. But the Navy had finally figured out that low level messages from home meant something to sailors and allowed a dedicated email server to ride on the standard navy sub broadcast. So subs at sea were getting weather reports, sea borne traffic advisories and notes from home all at the same time. Classified and operational orders still came via the high level radio signals but the low level stuff got copied just the same. Family grams were what the sailors called the messages from home. Rammy marveled at technology.

"My mom is so crappy at texting…" he muttered under his breath tapping keys with his thumbs.

Mom, it's me.

Noah, where are you are U safe?

Fine and here in San Francisco. Don't freak out, but I'm working with the NSA monitoring the Chinese communications for the invasion.

OMG!

Hey, I'm proud of you! U used that right. Is the Admiral with you? The NSA agent has an update for him. The Chinese are going to have another landing very soon. She says it looks like reinforcements. 3-5 hours ETA.

He does not believe you.

Mom!

Convince him she is who she says she is.

The agent says her authentication is whiskey whiskey tango twenty two.

Wait one. OK. He is going to share that with the General at Joint base McChord. Now you get out of there!

I will if you will.

Noah, I have to stay to help the Admiral.

I have to stay too.

The pause was longer this time. *Love U.*

Love U too, mom.

Sleep was the enemy. Sharon was so tired her eyes hurt. The snatched two hours at 1400 hours were not nearly enough. None of them were operating at peak efficiency and they knew it. Especially after the night they'd had with the air battle. The timing of that was now apparent to everyone.

Marino, Graham and Thomas were left as she had ordered everyone else to get four down for sure. Cots littered the White House. It was almost dinner time, five o'clock on the east coast and still eleven am in Hawaii. No it was noon there, they did not go on daylight savings time. She was not sure why that should be something she focused on but she did. Daylight savings time was stupid.

"Madam President we should do this in the morning."

"General, I have to know."

Graham looked at his briefing paper. This was a disaster!

"Ma'am. Approximately three hours ago, forces from the Chinese army landed at four US ports with an invasion sized troop force. The Sand island facility in Oahu, Hawaii along with a ship that crashed into the channel at Iroquois point has Hickam field under Chinese control.

The Long Beach contingent has the port and Long Beach Airport under its control. The Tacoma port along with the Seattle deep water port is in their hands as well as the Sea Tac airport. The port of Oakland as well as an old airstrip at Alameda are in Chinese hands." "A smaller contingent has breached San Francisco via two cruise ships."

The Chairman stopped for a drink of water, his voice hoarse.

"We responded initially with police and swat units but they have some man portable missile units that have knocked down police and news helicopters. We have attempted to gather intel using drones but four have been shot down as well. It will take us some nine hours to retask the satellites from overseas work to the US mainland."

No one was happy about that.

"So we are blind?"

"No, Graham said tiredly. "We have eyewitnesses at all scenes. Hell, we even have one of Wellington's whiz kids right on hand in San Francisco."

"It is going to take us through the night to get a full flight of reconnaissance aircraft up and over the target areas. They do have some anti air capability it seems."

Thomas took over the briefing as Graham seemed to slump from exhaustion.

"Madam President, it now looks like the Chinese intend to occupy the west coast of the United States. The Oakland landings are typical of what is happening. Approximately 150,000 men of the light infantry types are sitting in houses on Alameda Island. We have reports that they brought man portable missiles, guns and small bore artillery with them."

"It seems they have no armor and no air."

Thomas let that drop out by itself for added significance.

Sharon struggled to understand what that meant. "But if he has no air power than we can fly over and bomb them? Right?"

"Yes and no, ma'am." "We can bomb the ports but the main bulk of men are mixed in with the civilian population. Do you really want to bomb Oakland or Long Beach? The civilian deaths would be catastrophic."

Stallings mulled it over. 'What are they doing in there? Why go into the neighborhoods?"

Stedman stirred. "They are living off the land. These guys must be tired from the trip over. They are allowing our people to escape on foot and in passenger cars while they grab the larger trucks and SUV's. My people in the California National Guard think that they are grabbing weapons and ammo as well. "

"The escaping civilians do two things for the Chinese, burden us and get them out of the way of the attackers."

"Recommendations?"

Graham took a deep breath. "We strip the air national guard and the eastern air bases and hit the ports in the morning. It will take us that long to plan and execute the attack anyway. Oh and we have to hit the airports. The Chinese are getting some men in on civilian planes. We have to deny the use of the airfields to them."

"Bomb Long Beach Airport, General?"

The man winced. "We have to. The two F-16's the FAA sent from Travis Air Force base to interdict the flights have both been shot down."

The President shook her head. "What else?"

The head of the NSA had a list of things: Activate the National Guard and civilian reserve components of the Army. Have the FAA shut down the airports in 24 hours. Order martial law in California, Hawaii, Oregon, Washington and Nevada. Maybe Arizona too. Activate the reverse 911 and EAS and get the people out of the way. The major population centers in California, and Seattle at a minimum. Have Congress convene in the morning to declare war."

Her chief of staff who'd been silent until then jumped in. "We have to have a Vice President as well!"

Stallings agreed. She started giving out orders. "General, I want a full briefing at 2:00 am. I want to know where the enemy is and where he is going. I want a full attack plan to close off his re enforcements and destroy his beach head." *That was the right word wasn't it?*

"Paul, you handle Congress. I want a war powers declaration on my desk at 8:00 am. I expect Belkins to be sworn in at 8:02. Check?" "I don't expect any of you to be at the brief. You will all be asleep. That is an order from your Commander in Chief!"

"Able team, move up!"

Sanchez shouted out the order to get her people into place. Orange squad was part of the defensive perimeter surrounding the critical road juncture at the I-405 and the 605. The Marines of Lima company had drawn the duty of supervising the San Diego freeway and the rush of people moving down the coast from LA, specifically Long Beach. This spot would let them continue watching both the freeway and the ultimate prize in the area. Seal Beach Naval Weapons station. The Navy was even now frantically shipping the missiles and bombs held at Seal Beach back down the 405 to the fleet in San Diego. Lima company was the closest US force to the enemy on the mainland. Not that they were doing any fighting. The late afternoon sun had kept the temps at a pleasant 74 degrees and she was happy for that. If it was 90 degrees then these people currently sitting in this parking lot they called a highway would be really unhappy. Not that they were just unhappy. They were fucking scared.

 Check that they would be miserable as well as scared out of their minds. Collins, Armster, Sanchez and Wilkins along with the Major were making sure the company of Marines had the choke point flowing as well as could be expected. The order to evacuate had come down about two hours ago from DC. Lots of people were ready to go but the road system just could not take that volume of people. Even with the 8, 10, 40 and 80 all running both sides of the divider to the east, the traffic jams were horrendous. *But they were moving.* The unending stream was going about 20 miles an hour. Sanchez sincerely hoped the traffic broke open somewhere east of Santa Ana because these folks were going to run out of gas soon otherwise. Some already were.

Orders had come down to make the gas stations fill on an orderly basis. Gas trucks were the only things (besides military and ambulances) getting back into the zone.

The Major had his laptop up and the NCO's and the platoon leaders were grouped around watching TV. Of course it was not TV per se. Drone footage.

The Marines had their AVQ intel drones running over Long Beach.

From a military standpoint the fucking Chinese were kicking ass. They'd managed to land what looked like a hundred thousand man force without a shot fired in defense.

That wasn't strictly true. The Sargent had watched a SWAT barricade be overrun by Chines in coveralls at the Long Beach airport. The light duty truck had a fifty cal machine gun stuck on the bed and the Chinese had simply ran three of them at the cops. The police did pretty well taking out two of the trucks but they were all cut down eventually.

So there was sporadic resistance but for her purposes the invasion was unopposed. The enemy did a good job of consolidating their gains. The enemy troops had taken both sides of the 710 freeway and were ransacking houses in the rough square shape of land between the 710, the 405, the 605 and the ocean.

"Lots of guns in those houses." Collins spoke with authority.

"They going to lose some men and it's going to take a butt ton of time. Plenty of time for us to get the goodies out of NWS Seal." Armster answered with equal knowledge.

Except that felt wrong to Sanchez.

Why?

They did not seem interested in in stopping the Marines and the Navy at Seal beach. Why?

"LT. run that drone back over to the port, she asked her superior. I want to see what they are up to."

Wilkins tapped out his orders to the intel squad running the drone. "They got a unit there already. Delta delta 2, the Lieutenant told her. 'Intel weeines got a lot of spies in the skies up right now. DC got no satellite coverage so the drones are it." He switched the view over.

The port came into view from the seaward side. The huge Hanjin shipping works port was very similar to Oakland with the cranes and the race track configuration.

The Marines watched the massive ships continue with the unloading of the containers. The tipped up missile containers mystified the grunts who had no real knowledge of what the systems would look like. The Chinese could have chosen a dozen places to unload but the middle harbor west basin was central and very close to the 710. There was also abundant fuel at this location, so they didn't have to worry about the numerous trucks that were getting full containers loaded on their racks.

What's in there?, the group wondered.

"Hey, where's the fourth ship?" The question from Collins brought heads back to stop contemplating and look at the screen again. Wilkins tapped furiously.

"They switched it off to the San Diego drone operators to watch." More tapping. "Dammit!" The switch was dropped!"

"Uh oh."

Wilkins immediately got on the radio. "Charlie Oscar, Lima 3/5, request status of number four enemy landing craft. Requesting posit." "Over" Hicks relayed the request over the radio.

Minutes went by as the San Diego Command ran requests up and down the coast to drone operators looking for the ship.

How do you lose a merchant that size? Sanchez wondered.

By the time they found it, it was too late. The huge merchant had off loaded about a third of the containers she'd arrived with. The drone footage showed the vessel back out of port, running flat out about three miles off the coast. The wake the ship left was a white line in the blue water leading to the stern as she steadily came south. The Marines finally caught up with the ship as she passed La Jolla. The bluffs of the exclusive enclave were passing the ship off the port side as she hit 22 knots.

"Holy shit!"

The exclamation from Collins was loud to Sanchez. The Chinese ship was heading south as fast as she could but where was she...

"They are heading for the naval base!" Wilkins surmised it about the same time the radio exploded with chatter.

The Marine hierarchy had obviously figured out that the merchant was a threat and that they needed to take action- but what?

A flight of F-18's from Miramar, scrambled and looped out over the ocean to eliminate the problem.

But the real problem was red tape.

The First Marines relayed the fire request to Hawaii to have Pac Fleet authorize the sinking of a merchant vessel. Precious minutes were lost as the common sense order went from Hawaii to San Diego that the Admiral in charge of the joint bases in the San Diego had full authorization to shot unauthorized forces in the area. No need to bother them.

The F-18's lined up four missiles on the huge superstructure as the Hanjin ship Hippo breasted Point Loma.

The four air to surface missiles struck the ship evenly spaced along the starboard side of the upper container racks.

The bright explosions rolled the ship twenty two degrees to port and hurled crumpled containers high in the air.

But in no way did they sink the ship. The fucking thing was just too big.

The engines made the whole ship shudder as the backing bell slammed the twin screws into reverse. The ship slowed dramatically and turned left into the channel between North island and Point Loma smoke and fire belching. The last of the San Diego submarine squadron fast attack boats was just exiting the port. The Los Angeles class SSN, The Hampton, was pulling away from the pier when the explosions lit up the sky.

The CO of the sub could see the huge ship easing into the channel directly off the Harbor Inn.

Jesus, I've slept in those rooms! Commander Parker thought as he ordered the sub to all stop nose pointing almost due north. The ship and sub were nestled in the upper part of this comma shape that held the key to US Naval forces in this area. North Island was only a few hundred yards from point Loma at this spot. Problem was North Island wasn't really an island. The rest of the bulb of the northern part was connected to the mainland by the strand. The strand being a thin barrier strip of land that connect it to the mainland at Imperial Beach.

"Make tubes two and three ready in all respects.'

Parker still had a hard time comprehending his orders: Shoot the merchant.

This was spearing fish in a barrel.

But he couldn't shoot just yet.

Two destroyers were trying to squeeze by the merchant on the south side near North island before the Chinese ship managed to scuttle.

And that was what Parker feared. If the ship sank where she was there was no way the two carriers and her larger escorts could get by.

They'd be trapped in the inner harbor area.

Warning sirens were blaring from the sub and the merchant and both Burke class destroyers as four ships tried to occupy this small area of naval real estate.

"Get the fuck out of there, so I can blow this guy up!" Parker said over the radio.

The USS Peralta and the USS Finn both stopped shelling the monster and eased out of the way.

"Flood down and equalize tubes."

"Fire two, fire three."

The compressed air made a whoosing sound and a puff of air forced its way up the conning tower trunk and blew back the captains ball cap.

The sub was less than 2,000 yards from the merchant that was by now nearly dead in the water. The MK 48 torpedoes left twin line's in the water as they ran just under the surface for the short run to target.

At 200 hundred yards the two weapons both dove down.

Parker was incorrect when he told the tin can's to move so he could "blow this guy up".

MK 48's do not penetrate the side of a ship. They don't damage the side of a vessel.

The torpedoes skimmed the bottom of the shallow One hundred fifty-foot deep channel. Directly under the merchant both 650 pound high explosive warheads exploded with unbelievable force.

Huge twin gouts of water frothed up on either side of the merchant as the whole ship and the surface of the water seemed to bulge into the sky.

The giant explosion created an enormous void under the twelve-hundred-foot long ship. The middle four-hundred-foot wide section of water underneath the keel ceased to exist.

As the bulge went back to normal the front and back ends of the ship were buoyed up as normal.

But the middle section continued to sag towards the bottom. Ten feet down, twenty feet, then thirty feet and the keel could take no more.

The ship broke in two.

Hippo sank in six minutes taking fifty-five Chinese sailors and army men with her to the bottom. Several containers floated free and scattered around the ship.

The ship had indeed blocked the exit of the port of San Diego for two full US carrier battle groups.

The Marines of orange company turned away from the laptop at the conclusion of action.

None of them watched over the next few minutes as shoulder fired missiles knocked down the ten drones the Marine intel units had watching the enemy.

"Sargent, what does that mean?"

The question from Duarte was quiet and very earnest. The young Marine did not understand what was going on and he asked the person who knew *everything* as far as he was concerned. His Sargent.

Sanchez reeled. She looked out over NWS Seal Beach. Truck after truck was running loads down to 29th street naval base. And Point Loma. And Miramar.

Weapons. That's what they stored at a Naval Weapons Station. Only now none of those missiles or torpedoes or bombs were going to be able to be used. *At least not right away.*

Sanchez firmed up. *Uh uh. Nope. The Chinese Did Not Dictate To United States Marines What Was What In Our Own Country!*

"It means we are at war, Duarte."

The rest of her team looked up at her. The Sargent was laying down the law.

"It means that we have to get our heads on straight and get in the game. You can bet the command staff is preparing a response right now. Until then we follow orders, keep tight and watch each other's backs. Just like always. Affirm?"

"Yes, Sargent!"

Duarte was satisfied. Morrelli Hicks, Olsen and Hill a little less so. The more experienced the Marine the more jaded.

Sanchez turned to stand next to Collins and Armster as Wilkins checked orders from Command. Both the other NCO's were not pleased.

"Wanna know how I know it's bad? Collins asked no one.

"How?"

"They have the Devil Doc's out with us."

Both Sanchez and Armster turned to look at the assigned fleet corpsman with Orange company. Sure enough it was Senior Chief Tanzer. The Navy corpsman was indistinguishable from regular Marines. Tanzer was Fleet and forces qualified. He carried the M-16 just like the rest of them but in addition he had a med bag and two full medical cases. Gunshot wound? Broken leg? The clap? The Doc could handle it all.

"Shit." Now Armster was scared.

Walt Tsuomo was beyond scared. Scared had happened hours ago. Hours that saw him pulling the first bodies out of the water off Sand Island. *How many*? He'd lost count.

The Collen was just pulling in to Waianae harbor from his trip to Kauai. Twenty-six souls aboard seriously overloaded the ship as she plied the rough waters over to the garden isle. Walt would have preferred taking people over to Molokai but that island had no real facilities to house or take care of any kind of the numbers of refugees Walt was sure was going to be moving out of Oahu.

***

The early morning sun had revealed the Chinese taking over Sand island. Poor Sam Chow was one of the first to be killed. Walt had heard it straight from the young port worker he'd fished out of the harbor water. His trip to drop off the morning catch had almost cost him his life. The shooting from the port area was wide spread and seemed to be concentrated on killing as many civilians as possible. Walt could not see much as low on the water as he was but the people running and even swimming out to sea to escape told him all he needed to know about the situation. Swinging the boat back towards Pearl he'd radioed the Coast Guard only to find all hell breaking loose.

A fourth huge merchant had rammed straight onto Honolulu pier without even much slowing down. The fifth Hawaiian Chinese troop ship had blocked the Navy base at the channel choke point off of Iroquois point. The troops aboard her swarmed Hickam field and established control of the air field and the control tower.

Air Force support personnel did fight back. Whole maintenance squadrons and logistics groups dropped tools and picked up whatever guns were available. The battle was in full swing as Walt returned with three badly wounded men from the port. His son Kemo was with him as he tried to make sense of the carnage.

He would never forget the sight of the marine Helicopters topping the Ko'olau mountains in the distance and then use the 63 highway as a sight line to bore in straight at Hickam.

The AH-1 Super Cobra is a four bladed attack craft capable of close in support missions and long distance fire support against almost any type of enemy.

Walt could hear the frantic calls for help over his radio in the clear as the Air Force fought the surprise attack.

The Marines sent fifteen of the attack helicopters in three flights of five to deal with what must have looked like to them a terrorist attack.

The first four helo's, with the senior pilot acting as a spotter, flew low and tight to the Navy/Marine Corps golf course as it bordered the H1 highway. The pilots could see the thousands of Chinese infantry men attempting to take over the buildings on base that housed the planes for the American Air Force.

Several strafing runs from the helo's rallied the US personnel. With the other two groups of Cobra's pounding away at the Chinese, Walt had a brief flare of hope. That died when Walt saw that a swarm of missiles came from every conceivable angle at the US helicopters. He could not count the number of Chinese FN-6s leaping into the air to wreck the Cobra's. Of the twelve helo's actually attacking the Chinese, eleven dropped out of the sky in flaming heaps. The last four attack choppers wisely broke off and headed out to a normal safe distance.

The shoulder fired Chinese weapons had a limited four or five mile effective range. As Walt and Kemo watched while transferring the wounded to the shore, a missile would cook off and head east trying to knock down the orbiting Cobras'. All of them fell back to earth, unfortunately in the crowded housing developments near Aiea. The Marine pilots took video of the situation and similar footage over the port facility. They did manage to fire their longer range Hellfire missiles against the landing ships and do some serious damage. The anti-tank missiles dug deep into the giant ships before exploding, destroying full containers of anti-air missiles. Unfortunately, they had nowhere near the numbers necessary to dampen the attack.

Walt also knew the Navy would be trying to move the fleet out of Pearl and he watched from the safety of the water off White Beach near the harbor entrance, as the first small destroyer risked the trip.

The smaller ship stood no chance against the close distance and the ready enemy. At less than twenty yards, the man portable missile didn't even have to be sighted. The USS Chung Hoon sustained major damage and the loss of most of her bridge crew, including the Captain as enemy teams popped up and launched away with hellish fire. Luckily the Helmsman, Petty Officer Janice Atkins, while badly wounded, managed to steer the damaged ship at a backing bell out of the danger zone and beach her near the weapons loading zone of the west loch.

Walt saw it all and radioed Coast Guard headquarters and then spent some minutes convincing them he was actually trying to help. "Tell, Admiral Nickers he needs to set the Hamilton out near the golf ball and blast the fuck out of them!"

More minutes were lost while the brass at PAC Fleet went thru through their own permutations but eventually they realized the old Navy man was right: Putting the destroyer behind the protective screen of the huge radar platform parked behind Ford Island would allow the USS Paul Hamilton to rake over the container ship and perhaps allow the rest of the smaller fleet units to disembark.

Walt and Kemo left the area as soon as they saw the weirdly shaped destroyer pull away from the pier. He did not know if they could depress the angle on that laser gun down enough to but he knew they could lob rail gun rounds at an incredible fire rate.

The Hamilton and the other Zumwalts in addition to the laser also carried the newest fire support gun in service: the rail gun.

Built to replace the old three and five inch ground support guns that fired shells, the rail guns fired twenty-three pound shaped kinetic loads that looked like tiny space ships. The projectiles could hit speeds of Mach seven and travel over fifty miles. The Navy says the gun could fire up to twelve times a minute. Hamilton fired fourteen shells in 72 seconds almost straight up into the air. The tip over point meant the force for the blasts would be up and down. The effect was devastating. The first hit took off most of the bow section container cage and the windlass for the ships anchors. A steady stream of erupting fireballs walked back aft, killing about a third of the landing crew from the ship. The rest managed to straggle forward to the Hickam field maintenance buildings. The thought being it was better to be in among the American forces where the Navy would not bomb them from above.

Indeed, that seemed to be the Chinese battle plan. They did not have re-enforcements coming in by air here as they apparently did on the mainland. Walt was hearing the Coast Guard and Admiral Nickers staff openly discuss what was going on. They had to. The Chinese were advancing with two hundred thousand plus men right into the heart of Waikiki. Nickers called for the mobilization of anything that could float to take civvies off the beaches and haul them to Kauai.

His first load at Waianae harbor held the most precious cargo, Collen and the kids and the grand kids. The other twelve passengers might not be ohana now but soon would be.

In the midday sun, Walt beheld an eerie sight: The cruise ship Pride of America, carrying at least ten thousand people disgorging them onto Nawilliwillie docks as the small island of Kauai suddenly got bigger.

He spoke with the bar pilot, an old friend.

"Bruddah, the Captain said pull up to the beach and we got da kine out on the tenders." The man told him.

"Dat some akamai jimmy," Walt said, telling his friend he thought the Captain of the cruise ship was smart for getting the people out of the danger zone.

At Three O'clock in the afternoon, the battle lines had been drawn: The Chinese in control of Waikiki, the port, some of downtown and the airport/Hickam area. The Navy, Army and Marines still held Pearl and the rest of the island. No planes were landing more troops but the count seemed to be at least 220,000 enemy armed with FN-6s, some anti air missiles and small arms. The Marines in Kaneohe Bay and the Army in Scofield Barracks would have to unite to try to dislodge the attackers. That was going to require a plan.

Walt prayed Nickers was working on his plan to do just that. He still had another two or three trips to get tourists out of harm's way, maybe more. *Then he would see about the men attacking his home.*

CHAPTER EIGHT

May 19th, 2121 was as busy a day as Washington had seen in many, many, years. The US Congress in a rare joint session had voice voted a declaration of war with the Republic of China, ratified the order of Martial Law as defined by the President, confirmed Senator Belkins as the Vice President and completed a slew of judicial and cabinet appointments. And all of that before nine A.M. It seemed spending bills were up next as the government responded to the crises slowly but with as much force as could be mustered. The spirit of cooperation was a new facet a whole generation of American people had not seen before.

The new Vice President was left in the secured bunker making phone calls to worried world leaders as the news and impact of the Chinese attack spread.

Financial markets were closed today by order of the President and most of the world had followed suit. They would reopen when the world made sense again, Sharon knew.

The rest of the team was in the situation room, or the new oval office as Sharon was coming to think of it. She'd left this room for less than four hours over the last thirty-six.

But she was getting better at the military stuff.

"I want Mooney out of Hawaii and back here ASAP!" Her voice did not rise but she put in it the quiet steel she knew tended to unnerve most people.

"We are trying Madam President," Paul Marino told her, bending down to slip a briefing paper in front of her. "We have to get him to Kaneohe Bay from Pearl harbor and he was loath to leave Grant in the middle without any help."

"He has the entire Navy to look after, not just Grant and Hawaii." She said bluntly.

"General Graham, are you going to do anything with Admiral Nickers forces in Hawaii? she turned to the Chairman.

"No ma'am. I would suggest that the chain of command flow this way: I will retain overall battle management. Grant will be scene commander in the Hawaiian theater of operations. Likewise, General Nethercot in the San Diego/Long Beach theater with General Tedesco in charge of the Seattle theater."

The President had never met Alice Tedesco. The first female line Major General, she would be the first female to lead troops into battle for the United States. General Tedesco was in charge of the US Seventh Infantry Division based at Joint Base Lewis-McCord, in Lewis Washington, just south of Tacoma.

"That leaves San Francisco and Oakland, General, who is in charge there?"

President Stallings was learning a very difficult lesson about her military advisors. Sometimes it was what they *didn't* say that was the most important.

***

Her briefing last night was both frustrating and very scary. The staff and NSA people had mustered everyone they had and tapped some sources to fill in the picture for her.

"Ma'am the Chinese appear to have halted moving inwards from their beach heads at this time." The young looking Army Major was from central casting. Square jaw, high and tight haircut, broad shoulders, he looked every bit the part. Sharon was impressed.

The wall screens lit up the darkened room as video and pictures of the enemy troops filled the screens. The President watched in horror as the roaming gangs of men went thru Long Beach, Waikiki, the Hilltop section of Tacoma and Alameda, California.

"The pattern is the same, the Major went on. "They have secured the beach head and the port areas. Enemy troops have systematically gone into selected inland sections rooting out civilian populations. They are studiously setting up their defensive systems as best they can in each theater. The major brunt of airborne re enforcements are in the Long Beach and Oakland zones. Seattle and Hawaii seemed to be limited to troops on hand."

The President was puzzled about that and had asked why. "The Oakland Army is theorized to be the enemy's asymmetrical maneuver units, so they need to be as large as possible."

That only led to more puzzlement and more questions. The major was thrown out of the briefing room.

"I need someone who speaks civilian!"

Another briefer, this time a seasoned army Master Sargent who served as the White House Communications Senior enlisted advisor was shown in.

The grizzled twenty-seven-year Army vet was from a different central casting office. Coal black skin and two hundred twenty pounds of rock hard muscle jammed into a clean set of digital green cammies, the man greeted his President warily. "Ma'am."

"Master Sargent, what is an asymmetrical maneuver unit?" Sharon asked him.

"Ma'am, that's when the enemy does not use standard tanks and armored personnel carriers to move themselves around." "Ma'am."

"What do they use?"

Master Sargent Luongo grimaced. "Ma'am, they shoot civilians and take their trucks and use those." "Ma'am."

Well that certainly fit what was happening according to the video they were seeing.

"Stop calling me ma'am, Sharon said absently looking at the status sheets.

"Yes, ma'am."

"How many are we looking at, total."

"The enemy? Ma'am," Luongo stalled while some paper got shoved at him. Generals are bad at sliding briefing notes to Master Sergeants, Sharon noted.

A deep breath accompanied the new information from the briefer. "As of one hour ago, intel analysts are saying, over thirty thousand in San Francisco. Oakland has another two hundred twenty-five thousand troops. Hawaii is dealing with that same amount while Long Beach has somewhat less: one hundred ninety thousand. Seattle/Tacoma is right in the middle at an even two hundred thousand."

The Master Sargent looked his President squarely in the eye and said, "Ma'am you should be aware that the enemy is still landing troops at Alameda airfield and Long Beach. Upwards of three thousand men an hour in planes."

The President pinned General Graham with a look. "I thought we had interdicted those flights!"

"They have shot down both sets of new planes we sent out, he lamented. "We did get off some shots but the planes are taking non-standard routes into the areas and then gunning for the fields."

"What can we do about that?"

The question had no good answers. "I think we have to accept that reality until we finalize the air strike we want for tomorrow."

The President took that in. She *hated* that choice but she did not have any alternatives coming in to help her, so she went with it.

"What about civilian casualties?"

That's how you know you've asked the right question, she told herself, *when there is dead silence after you ask.*

"Ma'am, the latest estimate is at least ten thousand and climbing," the Master Sargent said softly.

It's what they didn't say that mattered. She feared that the military would not have even told her the death count unless she'd asked. That angered and frightened her.

***

Once the chain of command was laid out before her Sharon knew they weren't telling her something again. The enemy had been on US soil for nearly twenty-four hours. She had gotten some sleep and so had her team but it seemed they were still a bit in the fog.

"Who is handling Oakland?" She asked again.

Graham cleared his throat. "No one, Madam President. We don't have a command structure or a force in place to oppose the Chinese."

Libby and Paul among all the other staffers watched the President come to grips with that problem.

Sharon knew the issue was a real killer. Enemy troops in danger close to six million civilians and no one to keep them from tearing them up. Bad. Very bad.

"Okay, General, we have to approach this systematically. What is our priority?"

Sharon could see the appreciation in The Chairman's eyes.

"Madam President we have to close off the port and the airport re enforcements first." He stopped while video of the huge China airline 747's landed and grouped at the end of Long Beach airport. Streams of men could be seen pouring down the ramps. "We are seven hours away from a coordinated strike, both the port facilities and the two airfields."

His Air Force Service Chief General Zapata, laid out the coming attack for the room. "Ma'am we have stripped air national guard units from the south and east to base them at Luke,

Hill, Nellis, and Mountain Home air force bases. We have additional units coming in from Elmendorf, Diego Garcia and Guam."

The room was impressed. This was a response on a massive scale. At least six hundred planes would be taking part in the strikes. The sheer complexity of the operation was daunting for Sharon. She let phrases like "aerial refueling options" and "limited munitions options" bounce off her.

"What do the Chinese have to stop us?"

General Zapata frowned. "We have seen no evidence that they have any air units with them, Ma'am." "We will go in with the stealth fighters to hit the radar sites they have setup and then we will take out the missiles. After that we take out the ports with the BUFF's."

Big Ugly Fat Fuckers. B-52's. She did not like that acronym.

"They have managed to shoot down several drones and six of our planes, General. Have we taken into account those abilities?"

General Zapata did not like being second guessed on his battle plan, that was plain from his face. He knew how to conduct an air war, he told her so with arrogance in his voice. That's what they paid him to do after all! Sharon watched it all play out before her.

"Okay, General. Your plan is approved." "Paul, Libby, have the Vice President ready to meet with me on our overseas allies and their plans, check?"

"General Graham, I want a commander of forces for Oakland and San Francisco identified and an army placed at that man-or woman's- call."

The General agreed quickly.

"Kevin?" Admiral Mooney?"

The small Chief of Naval Operations was sitting on the side line chairs after taking a C-17 cargo plane loaded with wounded back from Hawaii.

"I see the Chinese have their Navy and a group of merchants heading east from Midway- I can only assume those are more troops ships. That could be over a million men! What do you intend to do about that?" The Admiral gulped and started planning.

But the President was not thru giving orders. "Stedman, I need to know what the Chinese goal is. Where is that maneuver group going? Who is leading the Chinese troops? How can we counter their moves?" The spy master nodded, getting to work.

"Homeland Security, we have to get the civilians out of harm's way!"

178

"I need options people!"

The fog started to clear a bit.

The normal marine layer of fog burned off quickly in the morning on this hot May day in Oakland. Dre was nervously checking his phone, watching the Chinese through the binoculars, and trying to keep his bladder from exploding.

At noon on the 19th of May, what was left of Oakport Trucking was sitting at what Andre called a forward observation area: The Ask.com building on twelfth and Jefferson in the heart of downtown Oakland. The Ask building was twenty-five floors high and had a commanding view of Lake Merritt, Frank Ogawa Plaza, Alameda Island, the port and the Oakland airport. Dre and the rest of his employees sat on the roof watching the Chinese as they worked to secure their territory.

After a relatively quiet night, the Chinese were again busy sending teams into neighborhoods and shooting anyone who stood in their way. The kill teams started in on the bottoms area at daylight. Manny, Dre and Tito had roused the rest of the men and piled them into cars to escape the fire. Many, many men and women tried to make isolated stands against the Chinese but they could not coordinate against the professional troops and that got them killed. Chaos was evident as people had been fleeing the area for a while but bad traffic had kept many in their homes.

Some had no choice. They had nowhere to go and no means of taking themselves out of the path of the Chinese. Older black, Asian, White and Hispanic residents were killed in the thousands. Alameda was being swept north to south. The chaos was sickening to the watching men. School officials, police and fire men all trying to deal with frantic parents and residents trying to flee on the small bridges. Cell service was spotty at best. Oakland itself was just being cleared around a corridor along the 880/980/580 and 80 highways.

That meant little to Dre as he and his friends were stuck in that corridor. Thousands had been killed and millions were on the move. The highways were clogged with cars filled with refugees. Sirens and emergency vehicles could be seen moving around the city. Dre's cell phone was getting some reverse 911 messages from some place in San Francisco, telling everyone that they needed to get out on the 580 over the Altamont pass and the 280, down the peninsula to the 101 and then east on the smaller 152 or 198 highways. The San Francisco station or people were calling themselves SF 1 and they seemed to have decent on site information from different areas as well as contact with someone in charge as they kept urging people to get out of both Oakland, San Francisco and the rest of California.

And now SF 1 was telling everyone to keep their heads down. Payback was coming.

"What that mean, Dre?", Amir asked looking tired after his tough night trying to puzzle out the strange text from someone in the city.

Keeping his eyes on the port area, watching the men scurry around and the airplanes land regularly, Dre grunted. "It mean the Air Force gonna hit the Chinese."

"What about the port? What about the people in Alameda?" Manny broke in after listening to the two men.

"I don't know man." The words sounded bitter and hollow to Dre. His little unit had done next to nothing, other than make it to this spot. The morning was spent running and dodging the Chinese kill teams as they went house to house. More often than not the houses were empty and the enemy troops just went to the next. Every so often some unfortunate soul would be at home and the gunfire would erupt.

Dre knew the homies on the blocks were killing some of the Chinese but the vast majority were moving on after killing the locals.

It was SF 1 that told them the Chinese were not taking the time to go through the larger office buildings.

That's when Dre directed his friends to the Ask.com building. He felt strange, trusting the text from someone he didn't know but the few authority figures he'd seen: cops and firemen- had no idea what was going on. At least SF1, whoever or whatever that was, knew something. And they were right about the large office buildings. The blue coverall wearing troops just cleared the bottom floors before moving on.

The roar of the missile lagged behind the flash of it lighting off by some two seconds. The huge weapon lifted off from the port area from the upended containers that were scattered around. Missile two, three and then four rocked off in regular intervals some ten seconds apart.

"What are they shooting at?" Tito wondered.

I don't know, Dre thought and he was loath to say it. His employees had agreed to follow him in some kind of patriotic response to the invasion but now they were just spectators.

"My guess would be the Air Force planes", he told Amir, Tito and Manny. Bobby and Ladarius were on the other end of the building watching the east side and the Lake Merritt area.

"I don't hear no planes," Amir complained.

The men on top of the building and all the civilians trapped down in west Oakland watched as more and more missiles lofted into the air. The roar and smoke trails added to the sirens and fires sounding in the downtown area. Fully a hundred surface to air missiles went off in the next two to three minutes.

Dre had an inspiration. He didn't know what was going on, but sharing information seemed to be the only way they were going to defeat the Chinese.

"Amir, man, why don't you respond to that SF 1 text?" Dre told his man. "Tell them the Chinese are firing a barrage of surface to air missiles from the dock area."

"On it." Amir dexterously tapped the message out with the speed of someone born to technology.

"What you think, Dre?" Manny looked for answers as well.

"Maybe they know some about what's going on with our forces. If they do, then at least we warned them."

"Some dude is texting us about the missile launches."

Noah showed his laptop to Rammy as the two sat heavily together in in the break room at the Folsom street building. Papers and the remains of a scrounged early lunch sat on the plastic tables. Vending machine sandwiches and cokes were not the best but the pair was hungry and exhausted.

All morning Ms. Pak and Mr. Spiegel had wrestled with avoiding the roaming gangs of Chinese soldiers, gathering supplies, and moving scared citizens out of their area of the city.

Added to that almost constant contact with DC and trying to figure out where Zhenge He was located, had the two irritable and snappy. The rush back down from the roof had winded them both.

"We were just on the roof, Noah, we saw the launches ourselves!"

"Yeah, but this guy is in Oakland and says there were over a hundred missiles launched. We only saw the ten that went over us."

Rammy silently groaned but grabbed her laptop and inputted the data to DC. She was sure the AWAC's planes knew the Chinese were throwing the kitchen sink at them but better safe than sorry.

"Tell them thanks."

"Sure." Noah tapped out the reply. *"Without giving it away, can you tell us who you are and where you are?"* He added the extra stuff because he was tired of seeing US citizens killed indiscriminately today. He wanted, no *needed* someone to get away from these guys without being killed.

The reply was cryptic. "Well, Jeeves knows where we are and as for who, let's just say some of us wore some green at one point."

The young man puzzled over the text. "Rammy, look at this."

The young woman couldn't figure it out either. "Google, Oakland and Jeeves," she directed.

Noah did so. With typical efficiency Google came up with the answer: "Ask Jeeves was a website search engine in Oakland starting in 1996." It is now Ask.com."

Another search revealed the building.

"So they are some ex-military guys and they are sitting on the Ask building," Rammy mused.

"Tell them to stick it out if they can. We might have some use for them."

Noah typed reluctantly. He did not want to have the Oakport gang killed on account of him.

"They say they will," he reported back.

There didn't seem to be a lull and then the Oakport unit reported more surface to air missiles being launched by the Chinese.

"What the hell is going on?" he asked Rammy.

The NSA agent seemed as confused as he did. She was on her computer monitoring the search parameters they'd set to find the Chinese battle general. DC was very interested in Zhenge He; Noah could gather that by what the higher ups were asking them to do.

He surmised the US Air Force was in the middle of a retaliatory strike but so far it just seemed to be some launches of missiles back at the friendly planes.

"Well?"

The woman looked at her new friend. "Noah, I don't know. We seem to be getting some internet messaging and radio calls to and from Zhenge He. Our top priority is pinpointing this guy's position, not winning the air war. That's the Air Forces job." She was a bit exasperated, Noah could tell.

"But if we don't win the air war, we are going to have a hard time winning the whole war in total, are we not?"

She had no good answer to that question, so she just kept trying figure out where the man known as Zhenge He was located.

That very man was at that moment sitting at a kitchen table at a small apartment complex in Alameda, California.

The Point Alameda apartment complex sat at Central avenue and Ballena road on the north end of the island. The four story apartment buildings, six of them in a rectangular configuration with a courtyard, looked like any one of a million complexes in the US. Lap siding, aluminum windows, sliding glass patio doors, beige carpet and basic kitchens- the units still went for large dollars in the crazy real estate market that was the bay area. The small pool and club house were busy as the command staff took their ease.

General Bo watched his men swim in the pool and barbeque in the provided pits. Muted gunfire could be heard from the south end of the island and every so often a cluster of anti-air missiles would cook off from the containers to head east, south or north.

The strangest air battle ever fought was coming to a head. And Bo knew they were winning. He knew it because it had taken the Americans until noon to attack him. Knew it because the US was not ready for the kind of air war he was proposing.

Any aircraft that flew was hostile and therefore a threat. Shoot it down.

That sounded like a deceptively simple thing when he'd planned it way back in the Peoples Hall six months ago for the ruling council. Simple but radical. Lin Wei Bo had no air cover for his forces.

So he was reliant on the fact that he did have missiles. Lots of them. His radar operators were scattered around the docks and the port buildings and he had them turning the radars on and off. The HT-233 radar could frequency shift and it could shift modes quickly. What made the total anti air system so robust were a few key factors: The missile itself had a heat seeking mode and a terminal radar for added redundancy. That coupled with a huge range and search limit of sixty nautical miles and eighty-thousand-foot height meant that the missile could be fired and forgotten.

That fact was going to save his men's lives. The search radar only had to get the missile in the neighborhood and it would do the rest. Another life-saving factor was the sheer number of the radar sites he had operating. He had redundancy and he had some surprises for the Americans built in as to where he'd positioned his men. One of very first containers off the Hanjin Tiger was the lead air search radar. Two back up trucks with men and a generator had gotten onto the highway system before anyone had suspected a thing. Now he had a radar site sitting on Mount Hamilton, the highest peak in this area providing a hundred nautical mile look around the area. The US planes would be vulnerable.

The B-52's provided the best example. The ancient flying bomber was still an immensely destructive platform. A three plane cell could deliver over one hundred fifty- dumb bombs. They had as recently as 2016 in Iraq against the forces of ISIS.

While the B-52 H could deliver a massive payload, the planes themselves were very, very vulnerable. America's air force was built to fight a conventional static war. Simply put the plan was always, send in the stealth planes (F-117's F-22's) and have them knock out the missile radars and missile sites. Then send in the strike craft to mop up. The whole crowd was protected and directed as they said. Protected by the fighters against enemy air and directed against the targets by the AWACs boys. The whole gang was refueled by the aerial tankers and you have the classic air strike package as seen in Baghdad, Tripoli, and any number of hotspots around the world.

Only this time, the Chinese were not playing fair. Bo had limited the strike air craft and the radars were spoofing the HAARM weapons (High Altitude Anti Radar Missiles). He figured the US could muster about three hundred strike craft from the various Air National Guard units and active Air Force squadrons around the eastern mainland. Those planes were to be used to hit his Oakland troops. Similar numbers were going to try their luck against Seattle Tacoma and Long Beach as well. Hawaii was a special case. The numbers were way down as the US only had the current Navy carrier planes and the Marines for the Chinese to worry about. Maybe fifty total craft. True they could get to his forces very fast but Bo did not concern himself with those. It was the mainland strikes he was really worried about. And the B-52's were going to lead those strikes. If the sixty-five-year-old planes could survive against a brand new missile.

The reports had been coming in for an hour now. Both from spies he had out observing the US bases in the east and his own radar data. He was again not playing fair with that information. The Chinese were not getting a huge influx of coded radio messages that screamed to the Americans: "Here is my headquarters, please come and bomb it!"

Instead he was getting text messages and cell phone calls.

The steak came off the grill medium rare at the apartment grills and he tucked in with a will. *Never pass up a chance to eat sleep or piss, you never know when you are going to get another one.* Words for a soldier to live by

Another salvo of missiles went off headed for the south. About three hundred fifty missiles expended now. Seventeen hundred to go. Bo suspected things were going to start blowing up near him soon. And he wasn't wrong. He also suspected the US was in for some nasty surprises. And he wasn't wrong about that either.

"Something you want to tell me General?" The question came out more sharply than she maybe intended.

Major General Zapata at least had the decency to look guilty. "Ma'am the Chinese have managed to shoot down the strike element coming in from Diego Garcia." As soon as he said it the man knew he'd made a mistake. Sharon could see that by the way the man almost physically backtracked.

"Sorry ma'am, Zapata said holding up both hands. "The nine B-52's from our base in Diego Garcia that were coming to hit the port of Oakland have been shot down."

"How did they manage that, General?" The President put every bit of winter ice into her voice.

"The anti-air system they have is a new generation surface to air missile. It has some capabilities we did not anticipate."

The room was silent. Every set of eyes was on the two people at the table. The situation room had gotten stale. Lack of sleep and the stress made most of them look like zombies. Dark circles and grey pallor was the order of the day. The President and her General were no different. All the zombies in the room knew the seriousness of what they were discussing.

"Summarize our losses."

The Chief of the Air Force hesitated and then firmed up. "We have sustained a total of sixty-two planes shot down in all three theaters. Hawaii has not yet been attacked. Admiral Nickers is reluctant to bomb Waikiki, so we have had no losses there and have regrouped to try a different tactic."

"And what damage have we inflicted on the enemy, so far, Sir." Again the hushed silence that told Sharon she'd come to a critical question.

"None so far, Ma'am. We have managed to launch some missiles around and at Oakland but the effects have been negligible."

The president sat back in her chair. This was bad, she thought. You did not have to be a military genius to know that someone had screwed up this attack. She stared right at General Zapata. "What is our next move General? We have to stop those flights into the enemy airfields. We must prevent the port facilities from allowing more cruise ships to dock…"

"Madam President, I am aware of that. We should not give up on this plan." "We have another two hundred strike craft ready to form up and hit the enemy as he lies…"

"Thank you General, that will be all." The soft command stopped the man in his speech and stunned him.

Sharon turned to General Graham. "Mr. Chairman, pull the planes back to our bases. We need a new direction. I would recommend consulting with Admiral Nickers to get what he is thinking. Our goal remains to destroy the docks and airfields the Chinese are using against us."

A subdued Kevin Mooney led General Zapata out of the situation room. Sharon hadn't fired him, just made it clear she would no longer listen to his recommendations or approve any of his battle plans anymore.

Stedman Graham returned to the table after passing out orders to his staff. He exchanged a look with the President. "Yes, ma'am. The definition of insanity: trying the same thing over and over expecting different results."

The woman nodded to her military chief.

Graham paused a moment and addressed the whole room. "We are at a difficult moment. We've been attacked by an intelligent, determined foe. Fei and the Chinese are not interested in set piece battles or any exercise in strategic thinking. He wants to kill Americans and drive them out of California, so they can take it. Same with Washington state and Oregon I'd guess. We've responded with predictability and a lack of imagination in regards to the real situation as it sits on the ground." 'That has to stop."

The staff people, Paul Marino, Libby Kaufman and the rest all roused a little at the words. "We have been too timid and too confined in our thinking." "Madam President it is time for the truth."

Sharon nodded her go ahead, and Graham continued with a will. "We are going to have to order Grant Nickers to destroy Waikiki and all of Honolulu if he has to, in order to defeat the Chinese in Hawaii."

Sharon absorbed that last statement. Try as she could to work around it she knew the man was right. She agreed with the Chairman and the man went further. Turning to his subordinate, the Chairman of the Joints Chiefs said, "Kevin, I need options in order to close down the docks on the mainland. Up to and including a nuclear option."

Horror shown in the eyes of everyone on the room. Graham was resolute. "We have to think about it. I'm not saying that should be our first option but it is one of them. The President needs to have ways we haven't explored brought to her for brainstorming. We have to get the Navy unstuck from San Diego and Hawaii in order to get them in the game." He watched his colleagues from hooded eyes.

All eyes turned to the diminutive CNO.

The Chief of Naval Operations leaned down on the table and spoke equally bluntly. "I am going to kill a lot of civilians with these plans, ma'am."

The President bowed her head. "What did you have in mind, Kevin?"

***

Well, at least they'd killed someone, that was the good part. Dre and the Oakport trucking company employees were shivering their asses off at Miller/Knox Regional Shoreline park in Point Richmond. The last two days had been the most frustrating he'd ever been a part of. The "kick ass" response from the Air Force was anything but kick ass. Three small explosions were all they'd seen from the Ask building. Dre could see the radar stations the missiles had managed to blow up. Mangled wrecks and the crews all dead. But the enemy planes had not stopped coming in to Alameda. And the big surface to air missiles had stopped firing as well. The Chinese had only launched five hundred or so. Even SF 1 was pissed. Manny and Tito and the rest of them had discussed it and texted SF 1 to ask what the hell was going on but the station had no idea either. "Await further instructions."

What the fuck was that supposed to mean? The six of them had dropped off the Ask rooftop and headed for the north. There was a noticeable lessening of people out on the streets, that was evident to Dre, right away. The evening of the 19th was quiet. The weather held as beautiful and the Chinese remained confined to the highway corridors and the Alameda stronghold. The big planes kept coming in and every so often a flash could be seen as a drone or stray F-15 tried its luck at knocking them down and got blown up in the process.

What little national news the group had heard was pretty rudimentary: China in control of the cities/docks and airports in Seattle, Long Beach, and Oakland. Hawaii looked to be pretty fucked up. The cable TV at the house they'd broken into off of Shattuck in Berkeley was working and the news was on a loop. The men scavenged a small meal and managed to take showers and get some sleep.

Try as he might, Dre still had not gotten in touch with Tabatha. Cell was working okay but he just couldn't get her to answer. Tabatha's message board filled up quickly. Disappeared. That was what he thought. He had talked briefly to his mom. Safe in Atlanta, thank god!

Tito and Manny and the rest stayed up until full dark to talk over their situation.

'Got to keep track of what they doin for the Army, right Dre?"

Amir had it correct.

"Yeah. We watch and report. When someone makes a stand, we get our shots in then, cool?"

The next morning was shattered by the sound of gunfire and explosions.

The house where they'd holed up backed in to Shattuck and was actually on Walnut Street. The tree lined back yard blocked his view so Dre went out to the fence and hopped it. His friends followed right after.

Creeping down an alley/walkway he edged out to Shattuck proper. Sticking his head out Dre looked up and down Shattuck avenue in Berkeley. He could barely believe what he was seeing.

The wide Avenue ran north and south through the Peoples Republic of Berkeley as they liked to say. Up to his right half a block away was the junction of Shattuck place, Vine and Shattuck. The huge Safeway fronted the road there and that's where the National Guard thought it would be a good idea to attack the Chinese.

For their part the enemy had set up a small barricade at the natural choke point with four or five trucks parked across the road and about twenty men standing behind piles of crap. The troopers had thrown anything they could into the cover formation: shopping carts, branches, trash cans, concrete blocks, whatever. Dre and his friends had had no idea the barricade was even there when they pulling in to the Walnut street house last night.

The California National Guard thought they had the advantage when they spotted the Chinese. The platoon sized group had three Humvees and an armored personnel carrier. As they made the turn from Shattuck place they'd spotted the barricades and deployed some infantry. Maybe ten guys humping it next to the Safeway store. Small arms fire to start with as both sides probed to see how serious the resolve was to fight.

The Chinese set the bar pretty high when they rocked off a HJ-8 anti-tank missile. The armored personnel carrier went up like a candle and brought Oakport trucking to the party.

Dre looked to his left and saw that the explosion had brought others as well.

Two blocks south at Virginia was the University apartment complex. The enemy was using that as a staging base/rest area as another hundred or so troops poured out, scrambling for parked trucks and vehicles lining the street.

Dre had a moment to gawp as the blue coverall wearing soldiers reminded him of office workers running after the work bell sounded.

'Fuck!"

Manny had it right and Dre's awareness snapped into place.

"Manny, Tito, Amir across to the Cheese Board," he said pointing to the store area. It was located behind the Chinese positions. "Watch me. When we get into position, open up with everything. Got it?"

Tight nods from the men and he dropped his arm.

The three men sprinted to the indicated spot. Dre took Lardi and Bobby Tornado up the other side of the street. Right to the porch of Chez Panisse, Alice Walters fabulous restaurant. Dre hadn't had the pleasure.

A bare second for everyone to get weapons up and ready when Dre shouted "Now!"

The six cut loose with assorted 9mm and .357 magnums.

The Chinese didn't even know there was anyone in their rear until most of them were dead. Another two minutes of concentrated fire from both sides killed the last of the Chinese.

Dre stepped out cautiously. The National Guard seemed to be rethinking its attack plan. The remaining twenty-five or so men and women hauled around the surviving Humvee and the troopers retreated right back up Shattuck place. They left sixteen dead. And one slightly wounded, dazed soldier.

Shit!

Dre glanced back. The University apartment regiment of the enemy did not seem to be in a big hurry to charge at the small group of men for some reason.

Dre took advantage. "Amir, go with Manny. Get the car and the truck and meet us over there," he pointed to the food store. Tito, take Bobby and get our stuff from the house. Lardi and I will help the grunt and we meet in the Safeway parking lot in one minute. Right? Anyone late gets left!"

His men scattered.

Ladarius crept across the intersection, past the bodies of the Chinese soldiers. A low moan escaped one of them and the man from LA put one in his ear. Dre nodded tightly. Sucked, but it had to be done.

The US soldier was face down wriggling away. The body was not trailing blood so Dre figured he was just shocked by the blast. In the confusion he never saw where the private was located in the fight.

The two men reached the figure and gently lay hands on him to turn him over and…

A woman.

The young white female stared up at the two black men looking down on her.

Dre worked his mouth to say something comforting.

"What!?!"

The woman yelled looking confused.

Dre knew she was deafened by the blast of the missile. He'd seen it before. So had Ladarius.

The smaller, thinner mechanic put a hand down and helped haul the woman to her feet.

The vest, helmet, tactical pack and gun all together weighed just a few pounds less than she did.

When did the California National Guard start taking children?

The thought struck Dre quickly and he just as quickly realized he was wrong. The woman was small and skinny but not a child. Twenty-five, or six somewhere in there, Dre thought as he pantomimed 'Are you hurt anywhere".

The woman, who was a Sargent named Miller, according to her name tag yelled, "NO! I'M JUST DEAF FROM THE BLAST!"

Lardi and Dre both grinned showing white teeth. The roar of the tower rig diesel engine came to them as the bright yellow truck hooked the left onto Vine from Walnut and then the right into the Safeway lot from Shattuck. Dre and Lardi assisted Miller over to the truck. The old Toyota of Amir's screeched into the lot with Bobby riding shot gun yelling, "Hurry- Hurry!"

Lardi got Miller into the back seat of the rig, while Dre went to his accustomed passenger seat in the tower rig with Manny driving. Amir waited until Ladarius was safely in the back of the Camry until he pealed out and smoked away from the ambush.

His unit was blooded.

The first time they'd taken lives and it worked out okay. At least none of his people had gotten hurt and they'd accomplished what they wanted to do. He turned to look at Miller and the woman was slumped on the bench seat head back and a slight grimace on her face. He let her rest.

"We got to get away from these Chinese and get some direction from some who knows what is what."

Manny agreed but there did not seem to be a good answer to either problem. Every time they worked to get near a highway the concentration of Chinese troops seemed to be bigger. Manny kept working back streets north and west until he found himself in a relative area of calm near Point Richmond. The vast majority of Marin county seemed to have figured out that the 80 was a bad way to escape the bay area. The back-up of cars was just now thinning out. The northern people had stayed on the 101 north until getting over to Redwood Valley. The 20, a nice two lane road, suddenly became a life line as the fleeing hoards cut across the state to Williams and then went north on the five or hooked back up to the 80 to go further east near Blue Canyon. Dre heard from SF 1 that 80 was controlled by the police and the army and had been turned both directions to east bound traffic. Reno was a parking lot as the authorities were putting refugee cars on the Rosewood Lakes Golf Course, according to SF1. Evacuation flights were running people out to Denver and Chicago as fast as the planes could pull in and out. Portland and Eugene were taking in their share of refugees but an evacuation was underway there as well. The 8, 10, 15, 40 and 70 were all jammed taking the millions fleeing from Southern California.

The Shoreline park area was deserted as the bedraggled crew stopped at ten am to assess.

Dre was texting SF 1 for the third time that morning. The San Francisco people now wanted to know where he was and where the ambush was staged.

He sent the details. Miller broke away from the back seat of the rig and joined him.

"Hey."

"Sargent, how you feeling?"

Denise Miller smiled wanly. "Not too bad. Headache and some ringing on my ears still."

"Stay out the bright light," Dre advised. The fog was burning off quickly and it would soon be bright sun.

Miller nodded and held up a pair of tactical wrap around eye protection. The iridescent yellow shades looked bug like and cool.

Dre nodded. "Iraq?"

"Yeah. You?"

"Mechanic in 16. Stationed at FOB Greenway."

Miller looked at him with respect. "That was the thick of it."

Dre just nodded. "Where were you at?"

Miller looked away. "FOB Granite for a time. Then not."

That statement told Andre a whole lot. Just the way she said it. Not that Forward Operating Base Granite was more or less dangerous than where he was stationed. Just- she'd obviously had some problems in Iraq.

And Dre could just guess what kind of problems those were.

Harassment. Assault. Maybe even rape.

Shit. Dre knew it was hard for a black man in the army. A woman? Harder still. And yet here she was. Still serving. Still doing her part.

"What were your orders?"

Miller snickered. "We were just supposed to help secure the 80 corridor so the East bay could escape. The Chinese sent groups to probe our positions all night last night." "They did not seem to care where we were as long as we helped the civvies get out."

"Why in the fuck you attack them?"

"Not me! My stupid Lieutenant. The dickhead wants to get some revenge and he orders us to reconnoiter the Shattuck off ramp. We just kept on the road until we ran into the Chin."

"And they left you."

Miller shrugged. "Yeah. Probably thought I was dead."

A grunt from Dre.

"Anyway, thanks."

Dre grinned at her. The girl was tough. "You from around here?"

Antioch was the response. The eastern suburb was generally poor and white. "What you want us to do? We could hot wire a car for you. The Richmond San Rafael is still open, you take that across and hook up with the Guard in Marin."

"Who are you texting?" she asked instead of answering.

Dre explained about SF 1 and how they seemed to be someone or something in charge. "They sayin' to stand by- they got some for us to do."

Miller got an interested look on her face. "I believe I could hang out with you fellows for a while."

Even Bobby Tornado laughed at the Trading Places line.

That found the now seven of them at Miller shoreline park shivering in the early morning darkness of the 21st. The fog had rolled back in and was thick. The moon was also down so the blackness was almost total. SF 1 had said to be here and they would be contacted. The city people didn't say the who or the how, Dre noted. Or the what.

Typical government situation. Kept in the dark and fed bullshit.

'What's that?"

Lardi pointed out to the beach area. A floating bag could be seen moving towards them about twenty yards in the distance. The bag should not have been moving like that, Dre knew.

A figure rose from the depths like the Creature from the Black Lagoon.

Well, in reality it was the Navy Seal from the San Francisco Bay, but the scare effect was the same. The gun in the man's hands was stubby and all business and it was pointed right at the group.

The crouched figure moved towards them with practiced movements. After a brief moment the gun was lowered and the night revealed the man.

"Well, you did spot the bag and you are in the right place at the right time, so I can work with you." The voice was rough and not even winded.

"Did you just swim the whole bay?" Amir was awestruck at the proceedings.

Instead of answering the man turned to Dre and said, "detail someone to help with the bag. There are two actually. I need to see the transportation options and a clear space for my check in."

How the man determined that Dre was the leader of this small unit, he never figured out.

A motion to Bobby and Lardi and the two men went to the water edge to retrieve the surprisingly heavy bags.

The Seal moved off a few feet and spoke into a small wrapped box he pulled from a water proof liner in his suit. None of the group over heard the conversation.

"What the hell you got in here?" Lardi asked as they hoisted the trailing bag up on the little picnic table they were using as a staging area. Again the information did not flow from the large man as he went to the water's edge and drove in a stake that the group had not noticed before.

"What is that? Some we need to know about?" Dre asked on his return.

The Seal looked him up and down. 'Just securing my Swimmer Delivery Vehicle." He turned to Amir, "No I did not swim this whole distance. We have an underwater sled we use to get in from the ocean."

The man took twenty-five minutes to strip out of his wetsuit and into the various items the bags had produced.

The amount of gear was incredible. From a Kevlar vest and helmet, to night vision goggles, along with tactical shooter knee pads and combat boots, the man was hung over with equipment. Dre noted the man was large and very fit as he wriggled and dressed.

"What do we call you?" Dre asked as he finished up.

"Senior Chief, Joseph Smith."

Dre made introductions for his team. Nods from everyone involved.

"What's next?"

"Transport."

The seven men and one woman took up the bags and their own gear and went to the two cars parked on the deserted road.

The sight of the bright yellow tow truck put a frown on Smiths face.

"Its big, it has a winch and a crane, which we have used once before to clear the roads, it uses diesel that is available, whereas gas is not." And it can hold a hell of a lot of stuff." Dre listed off the benefits of the tow rig.

"Yeah. Dig up some mud and cover the paint job."

The seven made short work of it. "We are going to need another car or truck at some point, Smith noted to Dre.

"What is the op?" Miller asked the Seal.

Smith looked over his new teammates. "We have to mark some targets for some ordinance coming in."

"That sounds dangerous," Miller told the man.

"I don't know if you are keeping track here or not but we are getting our butts whipped, Smith said quietly. The National Guardswoman had no good response to that.

"The Chinese have been really smart with the incoming planes. The commercial jets have come in at all altitudes. The latest seem to be hugging the sea deck. It makes for long difficult flights but they don't care. The planes down south actually over flew Mexico for the last few hours. We had a bunch of Navy planes out to sea looking for them when the flights appeared from the east and the south. Not good." Smith paused a second. "Our pilots have been reluctant to launch on Boeing jets squawking IFF codes from United Airline flights."

Amir had to be told that IFF was Identification Friend or Foe. "The military uses that to let them know it's a friendly aircraft or not." Dre told him.

Smith nodded. "The conventional attack we sent a couple days ago did not go so well."

The Oakport trucking employees knew the truth of that.

'So we have a back-up plan but it involves some new toys." Smith motioned to the boxes in his duty bags currently stored in the truck cargo boxes.

"Here's the deal, a lot of the targets are fixed. The runways at Alameda and the Oakland airport for example. We have to knock those out. The dock and port facilities are known and not going anywhere as well." The Senior Chief eyed his helpers to see if they were following. "But the problem is the anti-air stuff the Chinese brought in. Those containers have to be lased."

Dre, Miller, Lardi and Bobby all knew what that meant. The Pacheco brothers and Amir had to be told. "He means that someone, namely us, has to go down there and put a laser marker on those missile containers." Dre told the other three.

Smith nodded emphatically. "You guys are familiar with the port area and the layout around here. You know where the missiles are." "And not just that but the radars and concentrations of enemy troops."

That took a moment to penetrate for Dre. "That's going to be tough." They aint stayin in one apartment complex more than a few hours."

Smith swore. "We got to get to high ground and observe. We have at least a day for the bubble heads to get into position. More like two. In that time, we can mark where we think the enemy will be and what we want to hit."

Smith made it sound easy but Dre knew that was deceptive. This was going to be dangerous.

CHAPTER NINE

The days were beginning to blur for Lynn Spiegel. She seemed to be constantly at the base helping Kollmansburger deal with the attack. Bremerton was separated by the sound from the Chinese at Tacoma and Seattle. General Tedesco had resorted to using cars and boats and going around the sound to get to the base. Or the Admiral had gone to her on occasion. Joint base Lewis-McCord was in Lewis, south of Tacoma by a few miles, and the two had to consult. So far the Chinese seemed to be content to stay near the Tacoma dome and the downtown Seattle area while the Navy, Army and National Guard tried to evacuate everyone and gear up for the coming battle. Helicopters were being routinely shot down and the radio communications were spotty after the towers had been felled by the Chinese.

Yesterday's visit to McCord marked the first time the Admirals convoy had been fired upon. Lynn was with him in the car and the shots scared her to death. Not as much as her brief texts with Noah had scared her though. It seemed to her the Spiegel family was at personal war with the Chinese.

Noah was in San Francisco dodging gangs of Chinese troops while Tommy was speeding back to this side of the Pacific Ocean to help stem the tide of the Chinese advance. And now she was under fire. *Fucking great.*

The real problem for Alice Tedesco and Brent Kollmansburger was that the 7th Infantry division, the main weapon they had to fight back with, *existed only on paper.* Someone in their infinite wisdom had decided that the 7th ID would have a command brigade, which Major General Tedesco proudly led, and they would have "associate units".

The idea being that the deep water ports of Seattle Tacoma and the alignment of Sea Tac airport made the place ideal to mate up troops and equipment for that long, slow developing foreign war. Bad part, Lynn knew, was that it was badly undermanned for an actual invasion of the United States. The "associate units" were not actually stationed along with their commander officer.

Tedesco could field a few Stryker brigades and an artillery unit but she did not have the twenty thousand troops ready to be supported by air cover and armor that she should have.

198

Instead she had the Oregon and Washington National Guard units that could be spared, some thrown together admin units from all over the region and some adhoc civilian teams from the huge numbers of retirees located in the area.

You went to war with the army you have. Fucking Rumsfeld. Lynn knew the saying but it bit pretty hard right now. Especially when her husband and her son were part of that army.

The whole situation meant the staff and COMSUBGRU 9 were trying to consult with the General to come up with a comprehensive plan to deal with the Chinese.

And they had to contribute to what Lynn and the Admiral both figured would be the biggest Naval battle since WWII.

The Chinese had two hundred thousand men, give or take, dug in to the downtown Seattle and Tacoma areas. They were killing some civilians as was the case in the other theaters of operations. Kollmansburger had managed to get all of his subs out to sea, despite the terrorists and the chaos.

Now Mooney was calling on him to use those subs to fight back.

Lynn sat in the Admirals office and listened while the staff went over plans.

She was horrified. And more horrified still to know that her husband would be on one end of the missile barrage being planned and her son on the receiving end.

"Can't be helped Lynn. The NSA says they are taking steps to protect SF 1, but the CNO wants us to shut down the port and the avenues where the re-enforcements are coming in." "That means we have to hit them and it has to be coordinated." The Admiral was not unsympathetic she thought. He was just caught between what she knew he needed to do and what the consequences of those actions was going to be.

'CNO says we have to get the subs to their launch points in 29 hours."

"It's a mess but we have to move them quickly."

She typed up the movement orders and handed them off to the ops staff. They would actually plot the courses and speeds and deconflict the movements so that no US forces would fire on the subs as they approached the US mainland.

"What the hell is the old man thinking!"

Commander Greene complained to no one and everyone in control. The USS Ohio was coming out of the stovepipe after copying the broadcast and housekeeping evolutions.

A submarine had to check in for radio traffic every few hours to ensure it had current orders. The messages were in three different categories: "eyes only", "Operational" and "Routine". The first level was instructions to the CO's right from the command authority itself. The op stuff was just that: movement orders, help troubleshooting equipment and ocean assignment areas. The routine things were weather advisories and family grams. Even at a time of war the subs were getting traffic.

The housekeeping functions were the drudgery of submarining. The air had to be replaced every so often. Subs used compressed air to roll valves and operate some controls, so the air banks got used up. The compressors took a suction on the normal, breathable air to compress it down, from the various compartments on the ship. So eventually the ship started to take a vacuum when they were not pumping air back in. So they had to snorkel or ventilate. Which meant using the huge diesel generator as a pump to swap out the air in the ship. Problem was the diesel was very noisy. Ventilating meant just sticking the giant vent mast up and opening up the valve. Like a straw, the air could rush in to the vacuum of the ship. That allowed for a natural swapping of the air. It just took time. So the swap out was noisy and fast, or slow and quiet.

Same with making water or pumping out sanitary tanks or shooting trash. 160 men and women living underneath the ocean generated a lot of shit and a lot of trash. Both had to be gotten rid of. And darn it people actually liked to shower. So water had to be made. And grey water pumped. Most subs grouped these housekeeping evolutions to ensure they took care of them and to ensure any noise they put out would be minimized.

Ohio was good at the game. Her crew was trained in being quiet and the equipment they had was second to none as far as not putting noise in the water. The sub took a turn monitoring itself every six hours to ensure it was not radiating sound that could allow itself to be detected.

Sound in the water equals death for a submarine at war.

As she dove deep and cleared the stovepipe, Ohio noted no other contacts in the area. She'd gotten a sniff of Michigan one day ago, but no other submerged contacts could be found. Stennis and her surface escorts were still in the area but south of them. The last three days had been horrifying to everyone. Chinese invading, airplanes being shot down, civilian deaths. And they could do nothing but wait. But that looked like it was coming to an end.

Greene read over the orders again. "Move to So Cal Op area "William". Establish contact with "Lima 3/5" at 0230 local 21 May to obtain target designations. Use best judgment to determine ordinance and configuration for Tomahawks. Objective: destroy middle harbor dock facilities Port of Long Beach. Destroy Long Beach Airport runways, taxi ways, op tower and facilities. Destroy designated port area and surrounding targets as set by Lima 3/5. COMSUBGRU 9 for the CNO."

Wow. The XO and Weps both read over his shoulder. "Thank god," the Weps mumbled under his breath. "What", Commander Greene asked.

"We aren't hitting SF or Oakland. Senior Chief Spiegel's kid is right in the middle of this thing."

"I bet Michigan has Oakland port and the airfield there", the XO told them.

"Yep." The CO agreed but had to focus on his job. "Nav!" "Get us to William." "COB, XO, let's go over the battle stations watch bill. We have to hit these guys as hard as we can."

'Duarte, you stay right here. Shoot anyone coming up that gangway who isn't one of us," Sanchez told her youngest Marine. Duarte nodded tightly. The Marine unslung his M16 and placed a load of grenades for the 203 launcher near him in case he had to use it. An extra can of ammo came out of the pack Wilkins was humping and he set it near the grunt. "Stay alert." We got about half an hour before the fun starts."

"Ohh rah!" came soft and low. Duarte was already stacking some sandbags that had been keeping signs from blowing over in the wind onto the chairs scattered around the deck. Lieutenant Koster helped him get a more fortified position at the top of the civilian gangway to the USS Iowa.

The huge battle ship was now a museum and moored on the San Pedro side of the West basin in Long Beach. The giant ship was deserted and more importantly, her central mast and bridge stood two hundred fifty feet above the water line. Lima 3/5 was going to use that bridge as command central to attack the Chinese.

Wilkins and Koster led Sanchez up the after gangway and past the enormous sixteen inch turrets. Connie had a moment of whimsy. She'd love to see those guns turned on the Chinese air battery stations right now. Just the concussive shock of the guns firing would be enough to knock the Chinese out- let alone the two thousand pound shells.

Well, she would just have to settle for the Tomahawks.

Lima Company had picked up Lieutenant Koster as the expert in the TOMCOMM system and had spent the last 24 hours wriggling their way to the port and the surrounding areas from their duty spot near Seal Beach. Armster, Collins and the rest of her kids had the hard part: They were scattered out all around the port ready to lase targets. Sixteen two man teams had gone dark and behind the lines and Sanchez was sweating it. She knew Hill and Morrelli and the others could hack it but that didn't mean she would not worry. That was her job after all.

The bridge door itself was locked and Wilkins duct taped off the glass in the port view window to allow Koster the muffling he needed. The M16 rifle but made short work of the glass and Sanchez wormed her way in and undogged the door.

The harbor spread out before them on the south and east sides. West was the ocean and north was endless homes for the millions who called LA home. People like her abuela. The veteran Marine did not want to think about her grandmother right now. She had had no word. Not on any of them. Her family was tough but they were right in the path of the Chinese. She hoped they got out.

'Christ how many planes do you think have landed?" Koster was focusing the binoculars on Long Beach airport in the distance. The lights of the landing planes could be seen popping on a few seconds before landing. The planes were approaching from all angles. Scuttle butt said that Mexico had thrown in with the Chinese. She didn't know about that, so she did not respond to rumors. The planes landing in front of her? That she knew about. That she was here to do something about.

"Too many," Wilkins replied to the question.

Sanchez and Koster busied themselves setting up the TOMCOMM unit and the laptop. No fewer than nine intel drones were up in the air supporting her team. It was 0205 local. They had twenty-five minutes until the sub contacted them. None of them knew what the Chinese ESM or Electronic Surveillance Measures, were like. The intel weenies had told them it was unlikely the Chinese could triangulate on their signal but Sanchez did not want to bet her life on that thin assurance.

"This is going to happen quickly, Koster told them. Ohio will have itself at battle stations with the missiles spun up. The hard target birds might be last off the sub, so we have priority. I assume the CO will want to mix in some hard targets with the hand controlled shots." The Marine lieutenant spoke with grudging admiration for the bubble heads.

"We have to establish the laser connections first," Sanchez reminded him.

"Easy, Sargent. You are on the laptop because you are the best we have at that. The sub will launch and you assign the targets from the laser locks. Just move down the list." Wilkins coached his top enlisted person like a champ. Sanchez snickered. *Shave tail Lieutenant trying to work me!*

"Affirm!"

There was nothing much to do for a period. The three of them tried to spot the missile canisters from the battleship bridge. They could see five clusters they thought might fit the bill scattered around the laydown pads at the port terminal. Wilkins marked each of them carefully. If they had no lasers and extra missiles he wanted to try to get those. Especially if none of his people had already marked them. They also looked for five scant minutes to ascertain where the Chinese were keeping their troops.

"What's that?" Koster asked pointing.

Almost due north of their position was a cluster of apartment buildings. At least fourteen groups of three story white roofed buildings were laid out in a square with a building on each side. The units were a half block long so perhaps ten apartments were on each floor. That made it thirty units per building per cluster.

Wilkins tapped on his command pad to call up the map of this area. "Rancho San Pedro housing project," he informed the other two.

Connie did some quick math. "Four per room. 6,700 or so in there."

Wilkins marked it. "That's worth three cluster bombs."

0230 came on all too quickly.

"Ready, Sanchez?" Wilkins asked. A tight nod from his Sargent answered the man. Koster worked the TOMCOMM.

"Lima 3/5, this is Sierra, authenticate 2356. I say again, Lima 3/5 this is Sierra, authenticate 2356."

Koster was on it. "Sierra, this is Lima 3/5 roger. Counter 3210. Lima 3/5, counter 3210."

A lag time that was in realty maybe ten seconds that felt like hours to the three marines and then: 'Roger Lima 3/5. Sierra is ready. At your discretion."

"Sierra, Lima 3/5 requests sixteen, I say again sixteen TOMCOMM units and then all hard targets. Final launch will be TOMCOMM up to the max level."

Sanchez was vigorously nodding her head. She fucking concurred with that! Let the sub launch a quick group of sixteen for her and her troops to control and then rain down the destruction on the airfield and the porta as the hard targets. That would allow her marines time scamper to new targets or bug out in the confusion. She would then put the remaining missiles in a racetrack orbit and pick and choose where she went with the rest- based on whatever happened.

"Lima, be advised, Sierra concurs. Hard target numbers look like thirty-six units. Sierra will launch forty."

Wilkins and Koster consulted. Max level of missiles for this op was seventy-five. That left nineteen secondary TOMCOMM missiles given that The Ohio was going to use forty and their initial flight of sixteen birds. That was if her people were ready out there.

"Roger that Sierra. Lima requests a group of three MK 2 variants in the last launch."

"Affirm Lima, Good hunting!" Sierra out."

Sanchez didn't have to wait long. She had no idea where the sub was located but in three minutes the TOMCOMM unit fed the laptop data and suddenly the tactical map showed fifteen laser markers being picked up by the incoming missiles. All she had to do was to assign the targets to the birds as they came on. Just highlight and designate, highlight and designate. The last bird went into a racetrack orbit. It was much easier than typing in the raw GPS numbers, which she could do, but that would suck!

Why only fifteen?

She could not worry about that, guessing one had had a mechanical failure. The streaks of the missiles were becoming visible. The sound was low but starting to get loud. A glance at the tac map showed the anti air sites as scattered around the port but relatively close. One was on the Harbor Park Golf Course which was up the 110 freeway due east of them. She pointed. "There first!"

The missile rocked in at a low altitude. Sanchez did not know it but Hill had the laser right on the side of the upright canister. The radar and generator were very close so she didn't even have to split the difference.

The explosion was very distant and small for Sanchez. For Hill it was ear splitting and crazy. "Move," she told Hicks. The pair had one more target they wanted to get.

To Sanchez it seemed that points of light started blooming all over the skyline. Fifteen different explosions hit around the port.

Wilkins and Koster were scanning the local area. "Uh oh!"

Sanchez risked a look around at the words. Ants were coming out of the Rancho San Pedro buildings. That wasn't going to be good. The port was not very bright but some lights did pop on. Crews were running around and trucks cranked up engines.

That was lost in the back ground as the first hard target missiles hit the port.

Sanchez had been in some missile attacks before so she knew what was coming but the power of the Tomahawks still jolted her. Directly across the main channel from them lay a cluster of ten cranes. The missile impacted on the concrete directly behind the giant steel machines. The fireball lit up the whole battle ship. The wrecked metal looked vaguely like art after the smoke cleared.

Bet Duarte is scared shitless! Sanchez thought. The kid had not said anything on the radio as the bombs went off though. A point for him.

She stopped counting as the next flight of missiles were up in the air talking to her laptop thru the TOMCOMM. She read off configurations to find her cluster bombs. Seven new laser targets had been picked out by the Lima Marines and she assigned birds to each one as they came onto her screen. The rest got put into the race track formation above the port. She returned to her three special missiles and targeted them in from Wilkins coordinates at the San Pedro complex.

At the last second she grabbed her radio and told Duarte, "head down, incoming!"

The cluster bombs were not the big high explosive weapons the cranes had been destroyed with. The individual bomblets were not much bigger than tennis balls. Still the effect when the three missiles lined up and started popping off bomblets was chilling. The carnage was even worse.

Koster strangled out a "that got them", comment but Sanchez was not listening. Two more laser markers had been detected by the missiles. She detailed the birds. Lima 3/5 was still working hard tonight.

Over the next thirty minutes she got four more laser targets and got satisfactory explosions from each of them. Wilkins was scanning the area again. They were down to the last two missiles.

"Oh, shit Sargent! Right there! Put them on the 110!" Wilkins pointed and shouted.

Sanchez could see why he was upset. In the thirty minutes since the destruction of the Long Beach airport, three planes had attempted to land. All three had blown up. She surmised that the airport was out of business. So had the Chinese pilots.

Now the incoming plane was trying a new tactic. The 110 freeway was cleared of traffic for a short stretch. The commercial liner was trying to land on the road.

Sanchez tapped furiously. Wilkins ground out the coordinates. The birds dropped out of the race track to glide smoothly over the freeway. The sudden nose dive into the ground could be seen by the three watchers.

The back blast from the bombs hit the 737 and the thin aluminum frame could not take the debris being thrown up. The plane dug in and exploded in a huge fireball.

A moment of silence as the three Marines looked at each other.

"Let's move!" Sanchez got them going. *Don't give them time to dwell on the fact that we just killed a lot of people.*

Packing up seemed to take no time and then they were humping down the ladders to the gangway.

"Duarte, it's us. You good to go?" she called, not wanting to get shot.

"Affirm Sargent!"

"Good work Marine."

The group paused a second to look out over the rail at San Pedro.

"Why didn't they launch any missiles or counter attacks?" Koster wondered.

"What did they do, Duarte? Sanchez asked the young marine.

"Not much Sargent. When the missiles hit they all just jumped in the cars and trucks they have and took off," Duarte pointed to the side streets that seemed to have a lot of brake lights on them to Sanchez' eyes. Especially in a city that was supposed to be evacuated.

Wilkins listened. "There's no shooting."

He was right. Occasionally from where they could see, a FN-6 went off and a drone died but for the most part the city was quiet. Small fires were in evidence but nothing huge.

Koster frowned. "It was like they were expecting the attack and they just moved to secondary locations."

"Sir, we have to rendezvous with our men and women." Sanchez reminded Wilkins.

The short trip to the Wachon Basin harbor marina was uneventful. Well not uneventful but not critical.

The four Marines watched a plane try to land on the water while they moved. The wing tip clipped a wave and the plane cartwheeled violently into the water. They could not see any survivors. The Sargent did some math with Wilkins for his after action report: four planes an hour, fifteen hour trip from China to the west coast. Sixty planes on the way to the US. Two hundred fifty men per plane. Fifteen thousand men were potentially going to die because of this.

Wilkins paled a little. He did not want those men getting onto American soil but neither did he want them dying because of something he'd done. Sanchez made him feel a little better. Or a little worse. "Look there," she gestured off to the left.

A block away a small crew of Chinese soldiers ignored them and kept on with what they were about. Setting fire to the empty row of homes that bordered the marina.

'Yeah, fuck them," Wilkins said bitterly. The Chinese roared off in trucks to start more fires and the Marines could not afford to get into a fight right now.

The rest of the company straggled in two by two. Collins and Armster leading the way. Hill and her wingman, Hicks briefed Sanchez on the op. "Piece of fuckin cake," she said in her squeaky voice.

Yeah, not so much. Armster reported that two of his people- Thompkins and Gonzales were killed. "Caught in the blast near the canisters," he told Wilkins. "The airport is out of action, though."

Sanchez supposed that was all that mattered. Her Marines had taken some scrapes but no major injuries. The thirty- eight Marines of Lima company plus Lieutenant Koster boarded three stolen boats for the trip down to Pendleton. Sanchez knew they'd be coming back this way again very soon. The trip down south was sobering watching the growing flames. The night sky was clear and very dark. The light sources from the city were knocked out in a lot of places. Duarte sat next to Sanchez in the boat. The kid looked tired but exhilarated that they'd pulled off the mission. Everyone talked in low voices about the mission and the mood was generally upbeat. Sanchez felt that too, but she knew more. She knew the real dying was coming.

"Madam President."

Stedman Graham, sat heavily at the table. The east wing dining hall was starting to look like a goodwill kitchen. Bedraggled staffers and soldiers coming thru at all hours grabbing coffee and a sandwich or whatever and then right back to work. Sharon was glad but the pace was killing her people. *Thank God, Coleman was back!*

The Chairman of the Joint Chiefs started spooning eggs and a few strips of bacon onto his plate. Strong black coffee was placed in front of him as he started eating methodically. A soldier never forgets how to eat: Quickly and with purpose. Sharon smiled inwardly while Paul Marino, Libby and Vice President Belkins watched in horror.

After the chow was demolished, Graham leaned back and frowned. "Sorry. Just finished with a conference with Kevin."

'Well?"

Graham paused. "It looks like it was a success. Both Alameda and Long Beach are out of commission. Drones say the Chinese have not successfully landed a plane in the last three hours. He went on to tell them of the attempted water landings in So Cal and the possible ramifications.

Libby gasped. "The same with Oakland?"

"Yes, ma'am," Graham told her. It's good news for us. We managed to park maintenance vehicles on the other airports in the area and to sabotage the runways in different ways before we evacuated the critical personnel." He paused. "It looks like the Southern California army is topped at about 280,000. We undoubtedly killed some last night but how many is still a subject for debate. The Northern Army is the most formidable. Three hundred maybe three hundred ten thousand is the best estimate."

The table absorbed that news.

"Is there any good news?" Sharon asked. She had to address the people tonight and she wanted to get them working on something.

Graham nodded. "Yes, it looks like the evacuation is working. It's taken four days but it seems the people coming out of LA and Oakland are down to a trickle. Anyone still in those cities are liable to remain in there. Same with Seattle and Honolulu."

"Any idea how many people are trapped? General", Paul asked softly. Graham hesitated.

It's what they didn't tell you. Sharon thought.

"We estimate about a million still in the LA basin. Two hundred thousand maybe more in the east bay, with a similar number on the peninsula for the Bay area. Seattle and Honolulu are a little harder to gage. Five hundred thousand in the northwest corner and fifty thousand on the island. The tourists are out but now its residents that are trapped..." "And the next attacks aren't going to get any easier."

The President braced for what she knew was coming. Graham had told her it was going to be bad. "We have to force them out of the downtown areas. Especially in Honolulu and Seattle. We hit them with the Navy very soon."

"And what is that going to do to those people left in Honolulu?" Marino added.

Graham had no answer to that. At least none he was willing to voice aloud.

"Madam President you cannot allow this!" Paul was adamant with Libby backing him up.

Sharon rose and started pacing the historic room. This was what it meant to be the President. Life or death.

"Paul we have no choice! We have to do this! We can't have the Chinese tying up the Hawaiian fleet or the Marines at Kaneohe Bay." We have to be able to send them to the mainland to help with the battles here."

The man was not pleased. "What about Fort Hood? Fort Stewart?"

Vice President Belkins cleared his throat with a little smile on his face. "Madam President If you will allow me?" Belkins had been on the phone with the NATO allies and other leaders. He knew the whole global picture.

"Paul, we have consulted with our NATO friends and we do perceive a true threat from Mexico. Hollings warned of a China Mexico overture before he went sick. The basic deal is the Mexican government gets Texas and Arizona back in exchange for throwing open the borders and letting her people steam north."

Marino was confused. "But they haven't."

"No not yet. But that means we have to keep the Fifty thousand soldiers in the First Army Group West right where they are." Otherwise, 'we'd get carved up like a turkey, piece by piece," Belkins noted. "As for Ft Stewart, the Third Mech is not going anywhere for about one month."

He reviewed the Cooper River Bridge problem again for everyone.

"Paul, we do have some aces up our sleeves but we have to let General Graham play out his strategy. It's not pretty but I think it gives us the best chance at victory," the President told him and the rest.

Graham preened under the praise. "Madam President we have some steps we have to take: Seattle and Honolulu are the next after the sub bombardment. Then we have the actual land battles. But before then we are going to get a little help from our friends."

Again, Belkins smiled.

'England, Germany, France and Australia are going to hit China for us."

The people in the room shuddered at that statement. This was truly a world war now.

"Stedman, our main problem is still that army in Oakland. Zhenge He is in charge of that group. I need, America needs- to know where that army is going and what its goals are!" And we have to get our opposition force going!"

"President Stallings our best bet on that is still the Fourth ID from Ft Carson, Colorado. General Lemonge will be mobile tomorrow at the latest. He has his full division plus all support personnel. We have been able to augment his forces with national guard troops from Colorado and Utah. They are going straight over on the 80." "We expect the army group to pick up adhoc units along the way plus others." He said the last with special emphasis. The President knew but kept her mouth shut. This was tricky.

"As for the Chinese goals. We just don't know. The tomahawk attack seems to have destroyed the enemies anti air capability. We intend to test that out over the next three days. However, we are dangerously low on strike aircraft. The losses in the Yellow sea and our first attack have put us at critical levels. I've spoken to The National Guard and Air Force reserve units. Unauthorized attacks on Chinese forces are not helping the situation. "The... Graham searched for the right word, "loss... of General Zapata has opened a leadership vacuum in the Air Force. They aren't coordinating their forces with the rest like I want." "Those single plane attacks are just getting shot down."

Sharon motioned him to silence. That was a discussion she wanted to have on another day. Not now not in front of every one.

"How much intel are we getting, Stedman?" she steered the conversation back onto safe ground.

The General shrugged. "Thomas' asset in the San Francisco office is providing a lot actually. They have pinpointed Zhenge He in Oakland. Near the Port. We sent in some of Seal Team Six to assist. One has made contact with a resistance group in Oakland, while the rest of them have proceeded with Operation Safeguard as we discussed ma'am."

He ignored the questioning looks from everyone who'd heard that. The President was the only one who needed to know that.

"Part of what they are safeguarding are the NSA assets General Thomas is so fond of."

One of those assets awoke that same morning very stiff and sore and very hungry. Noah Spiegel had had enough of war and destruction. Sleeping in the office where he and Rammy were trying to help lock down where Zhenge He was located was starting to get old. Catching a whiff of his own odor he thought, *when was my last shower? Tuesday? What was today Friday the 2ndth? No Saturday the 23rd.* Six days. He was going to have to get to the bathroom and take a bird bath.

The Seals had started taking baths last night. Shifts of three had gone in and used buckets and made a huge mess. Socks and underwear and body liner shirts were hanging all over the stalls. The special operations soldiers did things in groups of three.

Assholes, was the young man's position on Seal Team Six.

At least the members who'd found him and Ms. Pak two nights ago were assholes. When the guy burst in the door Noah did not know what was bigger, the dude or his gun. Both looked to be huge to his eyes.

"You Whiskey Whiskey Tango Twenty two?"

Rammy could have been knocked over with a feather.

The next guy thru the door took in the two sets of Asian features staring back and him and the man grimaced. 'Figures" came out low but audibly for the two civilians. The white Anglo Saxon soldier apparently was not of a high opinion of the eastern persuasion of his assignment workmates.

The boy had had some dealings with racism but the casualness of the remark incensed him.

"Yeah, fuck head! The white guys who were with us all chickened out so fuck you- we are all you have!"

Rammy gawped at Noah and moved to hold him back. In no way could the kid possibly take on the soldier. "I'm whiskey. What are we doing here?" The Seals ignored the outburst from the kid like they would have if an ant had thrown a hissy fit. Inconsequential.

The nine-man seal team moved in to the office building on Folsom and started using it for a base. They all made contact with another teammate in the east bay who was with the Oakport group and with the USS Michigan for the bombing. Noah was eternally grateful it wasn't his dads sub doing the dirty work. His latest family gram to Ohio had some oblique mentions. He was sure his mom was the one who typed up the orders to bomb San Francisco. Funny. The bombing that night did indeed take out the Alameda airstrip along with the Oakland International airport and the port facilities. The east bay team was insistent about knowing where Zhenge He was located. Noah and Rammy tried as hard as they could but they could not triangulate to more than "near the port".

'We have to have any information you can get with regards to intentions and goals," the man Smith asked them from across the bay. The east bay people were still dealing with the laser targeting from last night. The Oakport men told them it was "not fun." Noah could believe that.

The pair had no way of dealing with the elite military unit. To them the Seals were just hard eyed killers. Unfortunately for the world it was a time for hard eyed killers. Over the next hours the men would ghost out of the building in three man hit squads. They returned in few hours and another group would go out. Gunfire would sound out from around the city but the pair could never correlate it the US servicemen.

What they didn't know was the Seals operational routine was set from long ago. The men operated in three man three shift teams. One set out on the firing line while one was in high spotting nests, both finding targets and reporting any enemy closing in on home base. The third set was sleeping or washing or mending the inevitable small hurts they would take.

Noah glared as he slipped on the wet tiles as the man opposite him in the bathroom poured a bucket over his head. His muscled torso sported a huge bruise on the ribs, and his thigh had a gash that was hastily sewn up. The young man tried not to stare.

"Kevlar vests spread out the force of the bullet- but it still hurts like hell."

Jesus! This guy got shot.

The boy said nothing however as he used a bucket to wash himself. The two dressed and went into the server farm office to find Rammy head down over the latest printouts.

"Good, you're here. Lieutenant, Noah, look at this." She let the men read the papers.

Noah got thru it first. "That is the countermove from the bombing. We have to get this to DC."

The Lieutenant concurred. '24 hours to commence Operation Magic Tapestry," he read. "what is that?"

"It's obviously the next goal of the Chinese," she said.

"But what is the goal, I mean?'

The two batted the idea back and forth while Noah sat at his little desk. He was remembering something Kimmy from back home was teaching him last winter. *In between kissing sessions*, he blushed remembering. Something about a story from China called the Magic Tapestry.

He tapped on his computer and called up Google. All those crazy games/scenarios where aliens attacked California were coming up roses as the search engine was still online. He read thru the results and tried to call up a website. He found out that the Chinese culture site was not as robust a website as Google. 'Shit!"

"What?" Rammy looked over.

"I remember something, a story a…friend, once told me about a Chinese legend called the Magic Tapestry. Supposed to be an ancient story with a moral about today." He covered up the "girlfriend" remark that almost slipped out. Rammy smiled at him. She knew. "Most of these websites are down", Noah went on, showing her the sites he'd try to use to find the actual story.

"I'll mention it to DC. They can do the legwork, too."

"Do the names of operations have special meanings?" She asked the Seal.

The Lieutenant shrugged. "Sometimes." "Let us know when you have some actionable intelligence." "Meanwhile keep looking for the Chinese bastard for Smith. He's got the bullet for him."

The civilians gulped and watched the man leave.

"Stop glaring at those guys!"

Noah grunted. "Just type up the shit for DC. I know that message has something to do with Zhenge He and where the Chinese are headed. Meantime I think we can try to work up something to make the Chinese talk more and get Zhenge He to show his head."

The two got back to work. More gunfire sounded from outside. Muffled. Sometime soon the Chinese were going to wonder what was going on in these buildings. Then things would get hairy.

Walt stood on the bridge of the Colleen and cried. *My beautiful home.*

The Collene was off of Waikiki about a thousand yards on a breezy afternoon of the 24th of May. The crystal blue waters and bright skies mocked the black smoke issuing from the pink building. The Royal Hawaiian was burning from the shelling the Navy was putting on the tourist area. The destroyer Hamilton was outside about five miles off shore. Her rail gun rounds made a ripping sound as they tore through the atmosphere and into the hotels lining Kalakaua avenue. Another ship could be seen ready to join up on the Hamilton. The USS Preble DDG 88 was fresh off of blasting the merchant blocking the entrance to Pearl Harbor to smithereens. Walt had heard and even felt the explosion from his position. The black smoke was still rising over the hulk burning at the waterline. It took a lot of ordinance to move 200,000 tons out of the way. Luckily the Preble had MK 36 torpedoes and contact depth charges she set next to the hull. Setting off five oil drums of high explosives with a torpedo was as much fun as the Preble CO could have asked for.

Bombing civilians was not so much fun.

The two ships systematically pounded the square between Kapahulu-near the Zoo, and Ala Moana. The shore to the ala wai canal set the other boundaries. There were Chinese troops in the area. Walt could see them moving. He could also see some kama aina in the danger zone.

His conversation with Admiral Nickers earlier was brief and sobering.

"Walt, I need you and some of your friends to be ready to move wounded back to Pearl."

He'd agreed but so far only one guy had managed to stagger into the surf and reach his boat. Kemo hauled the man in like he was a marlin.

Bodies could be seen floating nearby. Some in board shorts and some in blue coveralls. Walt ignored the second and checked the first. At least ten other small craft were ferrying wounded out of the area. The shells took on a different sound as the angle and range adjusted and the mall at Ala Moana took five direct hits. The Marines and the Navy had drones in the air, directing fire for the destroyers. The Chinese responded by launching missiles whenever they could get a good lock on the aircraft. The Marines and the Navy planes were staying out of the fight so far.

Kemo had the wounded man wrapped up in some beach towels. His wounds didn't look so bad but Walt feared internal injuries. He heeled the boat out of the zone and started west for the base. The Coast Guard boat followed him in and gave him the once over. His asian features were a cause for suspicion.

Eh brah! You look at every face around here for Chinese or Japanese looks you gone be finding dem all day!

Sliding past the smoking merchant was scary for the local man. The channel looked open to his eyes but he didn't have any of the sonar data. The inner harbor was a buzz of activity. The transfer to the aid station on the USS Arizona Visitor center and the Bowfin pier. The real triage was being setup and conducted by the Army in the Aloha stadium parking lot. Fatigue wearing

215

men carried the towel wearing patient on a stretcher up the pier. Walt never learned his name. Thank god the rest of his family was safe.

"Look, dad." Kemo pointed back towards the main base piers.

The Vinson was getting underway.

The Nimitz class carrier was huge and grand and vulnerable. Three other destroyers were serving as escorts while the ship ran the blockage. The John Paul Jones and the John McCain joined the USS Chafee with the two John's out front. Bracketing the carrier as she built up speed for a run past the enemy.

The three ships tried to get up to fifteen knots but the tight space and the short run inhibited that. The Mc Cain went thru first. The carrier was right on her heels as the giant ship came abreast of the wrecked Hanjin ship.

The first HJ-8 anti tank missile came from the west side. Somewhere on the plains of Ewa Beach the missile streaked in towards the vessel. The carrier was at full battle stations with all guns manned and all systems ready. That included the phalanx system. The R2D2 looking white tin can gun system was mounted on the starboard forward sponson. The radar had less than half a second to detect, lock on and fire. Since the Phalanx was a CWIS system, that task was within its operating parameters. CWIS stands for Close in Weapons System and it means close in. R2 made a "whirr....BBBRRRRTTTTTT" sound. Thousands of slugs of depleted uranium spat out in the line of travel. The missile exploded less than a thousand yards away from the ship.

Most of the expended rounds fell onto the deserted grounds of the West Loch Weapons Compound. Most of them. Some tore up two houses on Hanaloa Street near the golf course. Two civilians died in one of the houses.

The destroyers sprang into action. Helicopters risked it and rose off the decks of the destroyers. Fifty caliber machine guns opened on imaginary targets on the line of travel for the missile trail.

That action caused some ruckus. More missiles, both the FN-6 anti air and the anti tank variety came at the carrier and the helo's from Ewa and the Sand Island directions. The first destroyer was past the choke point now and she turned east to better target the Sand Island side of the missile barrage. The CWIS on both sides of the carrier cranked out rounds and three more missiles were shot down. The helo's returned fire down the lines of travel to target the Chinese missile teams. Explosions could be seen Ewa side and at the port area. The off shore destroyers got in on the action dropping shells and rail gun rounds on both sides of the channel to inhibit any more fire.

The carrier cranked on the speed as she hit the wreck of the merchant and an ominous scraping sound could be heard by her sailors, but she never slowed. The green entrance buoy bobbed up and down at the wake made by the giant ship. A last desperate missile did sneak past the carrier defenses to impact on the after end of the ship. The damage was spectacular looking as a hole was blown open on the upper stern hull plating below the flight deck. However, the deck was not warped and the effected spaces were not critical.

Chaffee followed the carrier out of port and the Pearl Harbor fleet was finally out in the open ocean ready to roam to do some damage to the enemy.

The radio crackled with an in the clear update from the coast guard. "Pac Fleet has announced that the blockage in San Diego has been cleared away and the Reagan and Bush Battle groups have left San Diego in good order."

Walt knew that Admiral Nickers was announcing that to boost morale among the people of Hawaii. Oahu still had the same problem: a dug in enemy in the downtown and residential districts around the urban core. He feared the house to house fighting that he knew was coming.

My old department head better have a good plan for that, he thought. He and Kemo returned to fishing wounded out of the water.

CHAPTER TEN

Amir didn't look so good.

Dre sat by the man at the small fire. "Hey."

"Dre."

The two men ate coldish soup straight from the cans. The spoons were none to clean but that was okay as neither were the men. The night of the 26th of May was cool and overcast after some high clouds but bright sun during the day. It was still dry though. They were three days into Operation Magic Tapestry and it was telling.

Amir had a scruff of beard on his face but that wasn't it. It was the eyes. Amir's eyes had the tight, haunted cast of a man who had seen too much.

Dre watched his employee (*no, friend!*) shovel food into his mouth because his body demanded it. He was sure Amir's soup tasted like his did. Ashes.

"I was two weeks in country in the desert in 16." Dre's voice was low and he was speaking to the fire. The small flames were for psychological comfort not real warmth. Amir let him speak. "One day a woman wearing the hijab approached the gate to the FOB." A spoon full of soup went in.

"The guards- they order her to stop in Arabic. She don't tho. Just kept on comin."

Amir was watching him now. "Two three more steps and the one grunt walks out to get her to stop, thinkin she don understand." I was fixin the duty vehicle, watchin."

"I swear she looked right at me, her eyes so bright, so beautiful. Brown as can be."

Dre's voice was hypnotic. "I could *see* her smile even tho I couldn't, ya know?"

"She blew up the suicide vest just to take out the one American guard."

Amir stopped looking at Dre and concentrated on the fire.

"Why?"

Amir's question was so simple and so hard. *Why?* "Why war? Why do people treat each other so bad?" I don't know man. I just know we did no wrong. It was them that did it." Dre spoke with authority to let his friend know it was okay.

"You reach the point where you can't. You can't." "You walk on- okay? No shame- no blame."

He let Amir make his own decision. They all had to make that call.

The little resistance group had lost one person earlier today. Guy just sat down on the ground and started rocking back and forth. Smith, Miller and Dre had all tried to move him but it was no good. Dude was catatonic. Dre could barely remember his name. Hansen? Hansel? No- Hopkins. That was it.

***

Hopkins had joined them at the start three mornings ago.

Smith had them lasing targets during the tomahawk attack and that was bad enough. Then early that same morning he started them hunting. The seven-man unit picked up an eighth and then a ninth and tenth person very quickly. White guys. Hopkins was a construction guy, about thirty-five just trying to defend his home. Smith took Miller and the three new comers in two cars on the east side of the 880 and Dre led his men in their two mud covered cars and followed.

A series of looping, running attacks as they ran down south on San Leandro Boulevard hitting the over and underpasses on the access roads that led back to the highway and the Chinese troops massing there. Smith had them a couple blocks off the highway, running parallel. They took to driving up, spotting the Chinese as they controlled the access point to the Nimitz freeway, and cracking off a couple of shots. The two groups would alternate who went first and who hopped over to the next spot.

It went pretty well. The Chinese would respond or not depending on how well they were prepared.

Dre took the time to watch and observe what was happening, between the Davis Street Bart station parking lot and the highway. The Chinese had occupied the groups of homes on either side of Davis. The typical suburban housing development was perfect for commuters: all roads dumped onto Davis which in turn connected to the freeway. This group of Chinese troops

219

had survived the attack last night in good order and were ready for the next phase. Whatever that was.

When his men came to the intersection, the Chinese barricade was thrown up down near Thrasher park. Amir pointed it out and told them he'd skateboarded there as a kid.

The men sighted carefully from the cover provided by the Bart track pillars. Six or seven shots rang out and at least two men were killed that they could see. They roared off before the Chinese could react.

It was Marina Square where everything went to shit. The area around the Marina Boulevard entrance to the 880 was suburban industrial and commercial. Loads of Auto dealers and a little strip mall meant fewer homes. That also meant the Chinese were more ready.

The Chinese were down there picking out some of the newer model trucks for their use. And they had some American volunteers to help them. They watched six men tie a cop to the roof of a Ford F-150.

Smith watched through his scope and let Dre take a look. "Sumbitch!" *So that's where all the cops and firemen and ambulance crews have gotten to.*

The Seal shrugged. "Saw ISUL do the same thing at Mosul." "Keeps us from running a predator drone over the top and blasting their column as they move." Bet they have some news people as well. Let's confirm this."

Amir lost it with the little girl. The thin eleven or twelve-year old was tied to the rear trunk portion with wire from a spool. The blood was showing red on her arms. The more the kid struggled the more she bled. The Oakport employees watched as she went completely berserk in the hands of the Chinese. The wailing and crying cut the air at the 238 juncture with the 880 and could be heard plainly. The city being unnaturally quiet. The men were watching from the top of the Century 16 Bayfair movie theater. The natural rise in the land let them see the mile or two down to the junction clearly. Her struggles weakened as she lost blood. Soon enough she was passed out on the trunk.

"Aint we going to do nothing?" Amir had asked, anguished at the sight. Smith said nothing shaking his head. Dre took Amir off to the side.

"Can't do none for her today." We got to report that they getting ready to move. Then we got to track them. Report it all back to SF 1."

That did not set with the young man. It didn't set with a lot of the unit. But Dre knew Smith was right. The ten of them could not fight the entire Chinese invasion force.

Hours later the men were perched on the top of the Crockett Hills regional park area near the huge Phillips oil refinery at Rodeo, California. The refinery was right next to the 80 highway and the storage tanks were huge and white in the bright sun. Tito and Bobby were independently counting trucks and trailers as they slowly rolled past the watchers.

"Just get an average of four or five individual one minute counts and then we multiply, Smith told the two men.

The bald hill tops were deserted and Dre was worried the Chinese could spot them up here.

"They won't slow just to get us unless we start to fire at them. Amir and Lardi were all for that, but the rest were content to let Smith take the lead.

After conferring with SF1, the unit was directed to observe the 80 and where Operation Magic Tapestry was taking the Chinese.

Some worming their way thru the city led them to the Richmond San Rafel bridge to see about a thousand men on each end setting up positions. A quick check with the San Francisco people told them that the Chinese were detaching about twenty thousand of the contingent in San Francisco and were hustling to the Golden Gate and the other side of the Richmond bridge.

Dre and his friends watched as the huge snake of cars started out to the 80 and then saw them go south on the 880 to hook up with the 580. The text from SF1 wanted them back up north to see if the Carquinez and the Benicia bridges were in Chinese hands.

They were.

Smith put them on the hill top by the refinery to get some hard numbers on the troops.

The line of big rig trucks stretched far back as they could see. Survivors and emergency people were tied to the cars here just like the 580.

The column of trucks stretched back all the way to Berkeley. The men could see soldiers and some missiles but mostly the line of vehicles had big rigs and containers. *What was in those?* Dre wondered.

The best guess was about 6,000 vehicles in total. Smith scowled and texted SF 1.

"We have to figure out where the rest of them are."

Bobby looked back over his shoulder. "That aint all of them?"

Miller took that question. "Mr. Tornado, you have to do some math. If the Chinese have three hundred thousand men in Oakland how many are they going to leave behind to protect their rear?"

Bobby looked at Dre who shrugged. "Fifty, sixty thousand, I'd guess," his southern drawl coming out when he was tired like now.

"That's a pretty good number I think. So say they have three hundred thousand and they leave fifty. That's two hundred fifty that gotta move. How many cars is that?"

Dre said, "I'd guess four men per car."

Miller nodded. "That means sixty-two thousand five hundred."

Lardi whistled while Bobby figured in his head. "So that's what they been doing? Collecting cars."

Smith agreed saying, "yeah, and gas and guns and ammo and food."

"So where the rest of those cars?"

Smith did not answer Dre's question, instead he asked, "how are we going to get to that side of the river." He pointed back at the water.

"Bay," Miller told him, letting him know he was looking at the bay not a river. "I know how we get across, I'm from Antioch. We take the Rio Vista bridge."

***

The unit texted in the data to SF 1 and then took the 4 over to the Rio Vista bridge a long ways to the east of where they were. By the time they worked their way back north and west on the 12 where it joined back in to the Eighty at Fairfield it was late. Full dark was at eight at night this late in spring. They did not spy the Chinese column moving on the road. After searching they found them in Cordelia Junction.

"What the fuck are they doing?"

Dre had no idea. The trucks were mostly parked right along the highway. The troops were decamped out of their vehicles and ransacking the small subdivision north of the highway. Most of the trucks were parked but a steady stream of big rigs were peeling off and heading up Green valley road.

Another hour of working their way around found what the Americans were looking for. A California Department of Transportation depot yard. A depot yard where the highway folks had their dumps trucks and their graders and other equipment. All of it stored and lined up ready for work that would not be coming anytime soon.

The yard had one other important thing: Gas pumps.

The CDOT people could of course fill up those dump trucks with diesel without draining local filling stations. And since those local stations were empty, the tanks here were the only fuel around. The Chinese were gassing up trucks and filling drums as the trucks came up.

Smith grimaced. "Smart." "This fucker is smart," he said meaning the Chinese commander.

They set the ambush as carefully as they could. "Move!" Every minute is more trucks filled." Smith drove them. Hopkins and the other guys worked down to the edge of the yard fence. The Chinese had guards but it was late and they were tired. As soon as the SUV carrying the guards went back to the light and the gas pumps, Smith took careful aim. His first shot sparked the pavement but did nothing. The second got the enemy moving and pierced a truck tank.

The fuel leaked as the rest of them opened up- shooting at the Chinese guards.

The last shot from the Seal sparked again but this time the effect was devastating.

The "whump" of the fumes igniting was barely audible. The light and the heat was intense when the explosion hit them.

What got Hopkins was the local on the hood of the truck. He was burned alive and he screamed the entire time. Two other trucks waiting to get filled were caught in the fire and their hostages added to the carnage and the screaming. That and the smell of burned human.

The pumps themselves were now on fire and the fuel lines added to the blaze.

"Time to leave."

Smith and Dre got everyone back to the rendezvous point without much trouble.

Except that Hopkins was not functioning. The group left him some food and a blanket and drove off.

Two more nights of ambushing the Chinese as they continued to drive east on 80. Smith figured it out early and it was not rocket science as Dre quickly found out.

"They stoppin at government fuel depots," he told Manny and Tito that first night. "We just got to figure where and beat them to it."

The second evening found them leapfrogging forward from a spot Smith figured from his tactical map. The city yard at Davis went up at three in the afternoon. The blaze throwing black smoke into the air. A complete victory for the beleaguered resistance unit. The talk among them that night was that they'd slowed down the Chinese by a couple days.

But the enemy learned as they did. When the Chinese started out the next morning after scrounging around, they sent a convoy of fifty or so vehicles ahead to secure the Sacramento city vehicle depot at Raley boulevard and I-80.

The advance guard met three things: A barricade across the highway, a full regiment of California National Guard and a very pissed off Smith.

The Seal kept arguing with the Guard commander. "Major, you can't win this battle. Blow the fuel and help us harass them!"

But the man would not listen and the Battle of the Raley Boulevard off ramp was a disaster.

The two hundred figures across the barricades looked like the peasants in Les Mis to Miller. She said as much to Dre who just looked at her. He wasn't a big Victor Hugo fan.

The Chinese just popped off five or six missiles and blew up the barricades with the men and women behind them. The Major died right along with the rest.

Dre and his crew picked up the few survivors and raced the enveloping Chinese trucks and SUV's up Raley to see who could get to the pumps first. The Americans won but just by a few minutes. The Chinese decided to not waste missiles at the dull tower rig parked at the end of the parking lot. Fifty or so men dismounted their vehicles and advanced in good order to occupy the facility.

Dre with Tito, Manny, Bobby and Lardi, backing him up, opened up from their not so hidden spot behind some bright orange dump trucks. The ping of return rounds off the sides of the trucks and the pavement scared the piss out of them. The men had some regular rifles now they'd picked up from various encounters and they put a concentrated fire back at the enemy. Dre watched at least five bodies fall from the fire and the Chinese tried to close the hundred yards in the open.

But Smith was moving on them and they had not seen the man.

That was a mistake because the special ops sailor with Amir and Miller backing him up started a controlled walk from the right side of the lot. Sighting and squeezing the trigger he kept putting men down. The steady "pap, pap", "Pap, pap," sound of his gun was punctuated by the screams of the enemy.

For about five seconds the wolf ran among the sheep with impunity. Smith took full advantage. Pap, Pap. Pap, pap. Pap, pap. More shots and screams.

The shock wore off and troops on both sides reacted. Miller and Amir added to the fusillade while Bobby, Lardi and Dre's bunch methodically worked at the guns.

The Chinese broke under the onslaught.

The remaining thirty guys or so ran back to their trucks and moved back up the road towards their main body.

Smith handed Amir a hand gun. "Put down the wounded." He walked away.

***

That was what had Amir so spooked that evening. He'd never killed up close before. Now he had technically committed a war crime. Not that anyone was going to prosecute him on that. But up close killing had affected the young man and had him rocking in the night.

"You do what you gotta, Amir", Dre told him finishing his soup before going to find Smith and Miller. The Pacheco brothers were seeing to the new men in the band.

The two real soldiers in the group were going over the contents of the bags they'd found in the SUV the Chinese had left behind when Dre joined them.

"Food, ammo, this looks like a looted first aid kit," Miller said laying out the items.

The cell phone was in Chinese and none of them could read it.

"Forward the numbers and texts to SF1." "See if they can make sense of anything," Smith directed.

"I think they are going to be here two or three days. We got to round up the resistance people and start being an effective force." The Senior Chief laid out his case to Dre to solicit his help. Smith was the killer but Dre was a leader among the rank and file of those he had to work with. Even the professional soldier, Miller, would look to Dre for leadership on occasion. As things sat, Smith wanted to get Dre onboard with his plan.

"Yeah. That sounds good." You still lookin for that Zhenge He dude?" Dre asked.

Smith nodded. His body language told Dre and the National Guardswoman the luck he was having.

Well somebody better do some different cause we aint doin so well, Dre thought to himself.

***

"We are quite well positioned, Colonel." Bo told his aide. Zi nodded and went outside.

The two men were less than ten miles from Dre and Smith, sitting nice and cozy in the looted house off of Norwood avenue. Glenwood Meadows was a lovely subdivision in Sacramento. Tree lined streets, tidy single family homes. It looked like middle America.

To the Chinese General it looked like paradise and everything he hated about the US. The homes were decadently huge to his eyes. The fact that these people had left and there were still many cars scattered around showed the unimaginable wealth the Americans possessed. The back yard pools were just confirmation.

It rankled Bo that the US system was better at providing the creature comforts of life for its citizens and not the Communist one. All Communism had ever done for China was to provide a handle for the elite to keep the peasants down.

He was here to change all that.

The man was very pleased with the invasion as it stood right this second. He was receiving reports from Sierra 1 and 2 that they were on schedule as well. His troops here were actually ahead of schedule and still in good order.

Not that everything was perfect. The San Diego Naval base was open again as was Pearl Harbor. The Americans had cutoff the half of his contingent down south, and forced a way thru the strand. The thin barrier was no match for the Corps of Engineers and the two battle groups had left this morning. Bo was aware of just how much fire power the US Navy was capable of throwing at his re enforcements. His initial goal was ten of the ships reaching the Oakland port, but he would take five or even two. The Hawaii action was never meant as more than a diversion and it was still working. The carrier Vinson was at a point to threaten the convoy of ships steaming in the northern Pacific. He was unsure whether the US Commander would risk his lone carrier or wait until the full four battle groups were merged into a super element.

Bo had prepared for this eventuality but that did not mean he preferred it.

The reports continued to be ferried to him at the strange house. The convoy was one of the fingers he had working its way east. Magic Tapestry was still in effect. To that end he had to get his goodies to Sun Valley just like the story said. Only then would the manufactured reality of the tapestry come true.

An aide handed him a phone. Bo read the text with a nod. The Southern California groups were proceeding up the 99 and the five to the east leading byways. Another week and he felt they would be at the meeting spot. If.

If things went to plan. So far the US did not seem capable of mounting a sustained engagement with his forces. With their air power and armor neutralized, the National Guard units had been easy victims.

Not so much with the Marines at Sierra 1. Bo had great respect for the American elite fighting units but he knew they were badly outnumbered. Just as he knew the Sierra 2 units were a paper tiger at this point. But he knew the US would get its shit together as they liked to say.

He still had some surprises ready for when they did.

"Send out the teams into the neighborhoods. Food gas and whatever guns and ammo they can get in three hours. A four-hour sleep shift and then we move up a few blocks. We will repeat this until the trucks are gassed and reserves are up to level. It does us no good to arrive and not have the fuel." Bo told his aides this as they hovered around the man. Zi was outside now supervising the pillaging. Some of their hostages were dead and needed to be replaced. Luckily there seemed to be an endless supply of the frightened civilians just waiting around.

The one troubling thought came in to his mind: *where was Fei and the rest of the ruling council?*

The three-member panel had been very difficult to get ahold of lately. Bo was speaking to Fei just before they left Oakland when the call was interrupted by an attack. Fei and his friends were supposed to be in Shanghai arranging for the phase three ships to be loaded with the ten million workers it would be necessary to have to grow enough food for the transplanted people.

Instead they were in Beijing under bombardment by the Europeans. Bo had paid little attention to the rest of the world since landing. He was unaware that the Uighurs that he'd spent so much time pacifying, had carved out the west for themselves. The Russians and the South Koreans had also annexed provinces near the border regions as the carcass of China began to stink. He could just guess what the Tibetans were doing right now.

No matter. None of that was his concern. As long as he had the time he could finish off the American military and then sue for peace. That might prove tricky but the person who had the land had control. He firmly believed that.

"Paul, how do you think I look?" The President asked her Chief of Staff.

Marino looked his boss over with a critical eye. "Power suit, power hair, power jewelry." "Fantastic," was the pronouncement. This session before the press needed to go well. Ostensibly the President was there to talk about the war but in reality she was there to reassure the American people and the world that the US leadership was in control of the situation. And they did have some good news to pass out. And a plea.

The briefing room at the White house was down to a select few cameras and reporters. Most of the Washington press corps was preoccupied with trying to get an embed within the war theaters. The local crews had gone dark and that boded ominous. Sharon knew that would be a question: What were they doing to ensure the safety of the press in the battle zones?

She started with a brief statement at the lectern. "Ladies and gentlemen, we do have some good news: Our assessment of the recent European strike on the Chinese mainland has been upgraded. The major military and infrastructure targets in the Beijing corridor have been rated as eliminated. We continue to position our forces in the US mainland to bring the invading troops to battle. As you know, the inner downtown areas of Honolulu and Seattle was well as Long Beach and Oakland have been severely damaged."

She took a sip of water. "The movement of civilians out of the affected areas along the coast has continued even to today. We estimate that thirty million people have been moved out of California alone. Resettlement of these families has been set with our survivor program. People as far away as Maine have taken in a refugee family."

Sharon caught a glimpse of Paul wincing over the refugee word. They'd debated how to say that: Refugee, survivor, displaced person. All of them had been suggested and they'd went with refugee. Paul hated the word and had argued vigorously against it. She had made the decision. Calling them displaced people did not lesson the problem, it just made people feel better.

"We are making progress in our overall battle plan. General Graham will brief you on specific aspects that we can release right after my briefing. *This is the part I have to hit hard.*

"My fellow Americans. We are in the midst of a great struggle. An enemy has ruthlessly attacked us and against all bonds of decency has tried to drive us from our homes. This will not stand!" I, my entire government, and the US military are striving to bring this war to a swift and successful conclusion. I need, and the nation needs men to help in this effort. If you have prior military service or want to be involved in the fight, the rally point is Salt Lake City. Our forces under General Lemonge are heading into the Northern California zone with the intent of meeting the enemy head on. Your country is counting on you."

Sharon pinned a glare at the camera. *That's for you wanna be assholes!*

She had hashed out the need for more troops with General Graham two days earlier. The Fourth Infantry division could field about thirty thousand men. With the Colorado National Guard and Utah's contribution, Lemonge had about fifty thousand as an effective fighting force. As it stood he would be outnumbered five to one.

'We can't win that kind of a battle unless we can control the skies and we have the heavy mechanized units in place." Graham had told her. "Without that we need more men."

One solution was obvious and the General told her what they wanted to do on that score. "But we need more than that," he concluded after their discussion.

Sharon shrugged. "My whole life, I've been told that the United States is gun crazy. That we have scores of guys running around in the woods, training for this very occasion! Where are they?"

Graham stared right at her. "The militia people have not come down from Michigan or Idaho." "We have reports they are holed up in their own homes protecting themselves only."

The President shook her head.

Now back in the briefing room, Sharon called upon any loyal and available men and women to come to the aid of their country.

The reporters in the room dutifully wrote things down and would broadcast the message but they seemed to be in a state of shock. The country desperately need a victory right now to bring up morale and energy for the coming battles.

Leaving the stage after taking some questions, Sharon felt like the briefing had gone well. She moved back into the oval office for an update from the Chief of Naval Operations. Kevin Mooney waited for the President outside her office. His normally open and honest face had a grey cast and dark circle sunder his eyes. Coordinating the movements of eleven carrier battle groups and over thirty-five submarines in two huge elements for the attack was taking its toll on him. Many sleepless nights were spent trying to figure out where the Chinese would mass together long enough to take their shot.

"Kevin what do you have for me?" Sharon led the man into the oval office. The Resolute desk was once again the place where she sat. President Drum had the desk removed to storage when he'd taken office. He did not want to sit behind the same desk as Obama. Sharon had had it returned the hour after she was sworn in.

Admiral Mooney went at ease at her question from his ridged stance in front of the President. "Ma'am, we are moving the Norfolk groups into the gulf now. I have the Army and Air Force liaison officers being air lifted onto the carriers now. They will coordinate with Lemonge and his staff to direct air cover and fire. Admiral Kollmansburger and General Tedesco are gathering Oregon and Washington National Guard units with civilians for an attack on the remnants of the Seattle/Tacoma Chinese troops. The rest of the Chinese are heading down the 84 and the five south. Admiral Nickers is concentrating on Hawaii. The Marines are moving out from Kaneohe right now. We expect them to link up with the 25th at Schofield barracks soon. Maybe as early as tomorrow. Then it's a slow slog out to the Honolulu area to root out the Chinese. We expect it to be house to house." He paused to make sure the Commander in Chief knew what that meant. Sharon did. Vicious fighting for every home and block from Aiea to Waialae. Both of them expected the islands forces to overcome the invaders but it would cost dearly in terms of lives and destruction.

When Sharon nodded for him to go on, Mooney laid out a chart of the mid Pacific area. "This is the sat picture of the Chinese Navy and the merchants they are guarding. Here are our forces." He pointed to two separate blobs.

"Are they ready?"

"We have to start the radio and ESM signals part tonight. We are ready."

The President nodded. She was ordering four ships to their deaths. The ships and all the men and women in them. *It had to be done.*

General Graham burst into the office. "Madam President! I know where the Chinese are going!"

Tommy Spiegel was in Control when the orders came in from Radio. *I know Lynn typed these up.* The darkened room was quiet as a grave at periscope depth awaiting instructions. The Ohio had run back to the mid Pacific to help shadow the Chinese, but none of them was sure what part they would play. The tactical Tridents did not usually play attack submarine in the normal scenarios. Not that they couldn't. It's just that their purpose was for something else. This patch of the ocean was getting crowded.

A glance at the tactical display showed what the CO *thought* was the relative positions of the Chinese submarines. The Sonar girls had a track on at least five Chinese Shang class SSN's so those tracks were solid but there were several displayed that were several hours old at best. The newest boat being produced out of the Chinese military industrial complex, the Shang was on par with older Los Angeles class units. As such they were quiet but not ULTRA quiet. The main problem was that the Chinese had a butt ton of those boats! Intel put the count at thirty-five. The subs were set out in a standard ring pattern, or so they thought. The five the Ohio had pretty well locked down were the units out front. The next level of tracks was further west and more spread out. The last ring of what they thought was going on matched the intel sat picture they had: a noisy group of surface targets surrounded by a protective layer of subs encircling them. That was a formation the US subs were used to seeing and used to dealing with. Most of them could individually wriggle their way into the flock of sheep, but they hadn't practiced wolf pack submarining since World War II. Some coordination would be needed.

Two days ago the Ohio had "conferenced" with two other US subs. Captain Greene had ordered underwater comms with the USS Jimmy Carter and the USS Bremerton. The unlikely trio were all in the same stove pipe to conduct housekeeping and copy traffic. The sketchy and lengthy underwater comm units were a terrible way to talk to each other but they had no other option. None of them wanted to risk surfacing and exposing themselves, so the funky underwater hydrophones were used.

The gist was pretty simple: Bremerton was to head back south and west and corral the eight other Hawaii based boats to stay down in that sector: Carter was going to lead the front on attack area as she was the best and most capable at battle group operations. Ohio would find the San Diego subs and lead them more to the north axis to prevent any of the enemy from escaping that way. Once the subs were taken care of, they would see about the surface targets. The last bit of talk among the captains was the orders from Washington and what they would contain. All three men felt that the higher ups would give them broad powers to freelance during the naval battle. It was what they did after all. The agreement was that the orders from DC would override any plans they had made but in the absence of real tasking from PACFleet or the CNO, their ideas would be the best option.

Spiegel sat in the dive chair watching the bubble. The trim of a submarine is called the bubble and it has to do with how the boat sits in the water. Since the sub grossed 18,000 tons, a lot of people assumed the thing just sank straight down. But! The submarine is a big steel pipe, and its hollow, plus it has many voids and tanks. All of those factors make the sub buoyant. So much so the boat has to take on water to make it submerge. Part of the daily chore for the diving officer is to calculate what the trim of the ship is. Hydro dynamically the ship wants to be at a slight up angle and neutrally buoyant at around one hundred and fifty feet down. Once there the ship can use its engine and planes to make itself glide thru the water efficiently and more important, quietly at whatever depth it wants.

Several factors affect the trim of the ship: speed, how much water is in which tank, where that water is forward versus aft, even the temperature and salinity of the water affects the buoyancy. So cold, salty, water is more dense and therefore more buoyant. Spiegel's job was to bring on or take off water, move it around and order the fairwater planes and stern planes to whatever angle he needed to get to the desired depth. The fairwater planes were analogous to wings on an airplane. Some subs have them on the bow and some have them on the conning tower. If they are on the coning tower they are called fairwater planes. If they are on the bow, then obviously they are called bow planes. His job was very simple and very complex: reach and maintain ordered depth by any combination of planes, ships angle, or speed. It is entirely possible for the speed of the ship to mask being heavy or light. So the faster you go the heavier you can be and still stay at the same depth. The problem comes when you slow down: you sink. Same for when the ocean has a thermocline or a change in temperature, and suddenly a "hole" opens in the ocean. Tommy had seen it many times: the sub is tooling along and then out of nowhere starts to sink out. Pumping water off as fast as possible usually arrests that problem, but it is noisy to run pumps. The best diving officers watched the bathymetry and anticipated when the current and the temperature was going to change and took actions to head off the depth excursion. But the job was even more complex than that. The Diving officer supervises two watch standers: the helm and the planes men. Both of those sailors sat on the dive station and worked the control yokes to make the sub change course and speed and depth. Tommy directly supervised those two but he also had to contend with a Chief of the Watch who worked the ballast control panel to move the water he needed. In addition to a million other things the COW performed, he also interfaced with the auxiliary man of the watch who physically operated the pumps and the valves that they need to move water and air and electrical systems.

All of it added to the team necessary to make a submarine function. The aux of the watch could mess you up. The Dive could be unaware of something, the Chief of the Watch not paying attention, the helm lacking in her attentiveness. The sailors of USS Ohio were very good at their jobs right now because they had been practicing for this for the last forty years.

What separates the US Navy from all other navies of the world is the operational tempo. The US practices for war. Every day. The daily watch routine for the sub was nothing but the normal now that they were in a shooting war. The watch bill was little shorter in that Tommy had to come off to launch missiles but now that that was done, here he was standing his normal watch. Same practices: quiet professionalism and high standards. Everyone on board had seen the stakes first hand. Screw up now and you could die. The Captain had ordered some machinery shut down to ensure extra quietness. Along with some small accommodations such as toilet seats being removed on the heads and stall doors removed, the sub was running as it normally did.

The control room was unusually quiet. The new orders were anticipated but the uncertainty was causing the crew angst. Tommy watched and waited as the COB came up to relieve him.

"I got it." The Master Chief added the last part to the more formal litany of the watch change. Spiegel grunted.

"We're still in the same box: watch the 180 course, the cross current doesn't flow right and she wants to sink out. I got a good one third trim less than twenty minutes ago after we came down from periscope depth." "CO and XO are holed up in his stateroom." Tommy hinted with this last part that he wanted the COB to bust in and find out what was going on.

The Master Chef grinned at his friend. "You'll find out right along with the rest of us."

Tommy hauled out of the chair. "I stand relieved"

Other watch standers were being relieved as well. It was 0525 on 28 May. The sun would be up in about twenty-five minutes. Spiegel was not tired or hungry. He'd gotten some sleep on his off watch period and since the ship wasn't doing drills or cleaning or paperwork, Tommy had some time to kill. He'd eaten six hours ago and he wasn't thrilled with breakfasts onboard since the real milk had run out two days ago. He hated UHT milk!

He wondered over to the nav chart the quartermaster had setup in the after corner. The electronic display was large enough that the light had to be covered by a screen to shield it. Tommy looked.

The whole northern Pacific was on the screen. The great spread of ocean between the US west Coast and the far east with the Hawaiian Islands as a series of diagonal dots running southeast to northwest was in view. The Quartermaster had the ships position as a green dot located a thousand miles due west of Portland, Oregon. At this far view the other tracks were right on top of own ship but the targets were dimmed out. The Quartermaster, a First class Petty Officer named Robert E. Lee, had the major ocean currents called up on the display.

The Pacific had two major currents that everyone worried about: The Alaskan Gyre and the Pacific Gyre. Very simply- a gyre is a current that makes a circle. The Gulf of Alaska had one that ran counter clockwise while the much larger Pacific gyre ran clockwise around the whole northern half of the ocean. The Kuroshio current runs north along the eastern seaboard of Asia. It bends east way up by Japan and becomes the North Pacific Current as it heads straight for North American. The ocean river current crosses thousands of miles of water before bending southward as it hits the coast and becomes the California current. Southward to the equator, near Baja California, the California current bends back east as it crosses back over the entire ocean to feed the Kuroshio at its start.

The CO and XO came into control and they joined Tommy at the Nav chart. The men nodded to one another and the Senior Chief made room and started to leave.

"You can stay Senior," the Captain told him. I'd like to know your thoughts on garbage."

Garbage? What the… oh.

The XO grinned at him. "The CNO has a plan for the Chinese. I think the details are from Nickers but it looks very good!"

Tommy bent down to look at a huge swath of ocean near them. It was labeled: Pacific Garbage Patch.

"That's going to suck, sir!" Tommy told him.

"That your professional opinion, is it?"

The OOD and the Weps now joined the men. News always traveled quickly on a sub. New orders were a reason to be woken up.

The CO spoke up. "COB can you get a relief and join us?"

The off going OOD was qualified as a dive and she decided to stay in control and listen to the bull session. The other six watch standers seemed to find reasons to remain in the area while listening. This was important!

Once the Chief of the Boat was packed around the chart the CO spoke. "CNO and PACFLEET have ordered us to do basically what I discussed forty-eight hours ago with the Carter and The Bremerfish." "We are to head to this point and rendezvous with a wolfpack of San Diego subs. Looks like Scranton, Hampton, San Honolulu, Pasadena and Alexandria."

The Co listed them off with a look at the XO. Everyone around the plot grinned. The XO was stationed on the USS San Francisco along with Captain Kevin Mooney when the sub had smashed into an uncharted sea mount. *That must have been hairy,* Tommy thought. The Navy decided to chop off the front end of the decommissioning USS Honolulu and weld it to the San Francisco, which gave them the nickname of San Honolulu. The XO always said Mooney had gotten them thru the worst of the situation with a calm determined attitude. *That's why he made an excellent CNO.*

"Our group is to establish a picket line, here," the CO continued and drew a slash north of the Current area and well north of where they were currently located. "We have to drive the Chinese surface navy and the merchants south into the patch."

The Pacific garbage patch. The gyre made for some weird conditions in the ocean waters. One of them is a swirling closed off zone in the ocean well south of them where any plastic or garbage that floated in the ocean, naturally collected. Tons and tons of the discarded bits of man waste littered the ocean waters. Merchant ships and the Navy tended to stay out of the gunk because it played hell with intake systems. Since most modern naval engines (even nuclear) tended to be seawater cooled, any plastic garbage bag clogging up the valve that took in the sea water, was not very helpful. The Navy had retrofitted some puffer systems onto the hull valves that allowed them to blow the debris off. Trouble was they tended to work only sporadically. Surface ships suffered more than subs because the debris littered the surface more than the depths but some trash was down there as well.

The other untried issue with the garbage was the effect it had on sonar.

The way sound propagates thru water is effected by temperature and salinity and surface noise, but the garbage acted as a sound absorber and added to the ambient noise. Tommy and the Ohio had played around in the patch before but it was dicey. The Sonar supervisor had joined them in the control room to add his expertise on what they wanted to do.

"We have to drag the Chinese first ring boats with us when we run south to make contact with the San Dog boats, sir. How are we going to do that?" The Sonar sup sorted out the main problem.

"Well…." The CO told the others his plan.

Shit! That could get a person killed, Tommy marveled.

CHAPTER ELEVEN

The smoke and ashes were thick, obscuring vision and making breathing difficult. The Marines of Lima company were set on the right side of the Santa Ana River as it passed under the 5 freeway. The 22 highway joined in just south of them and the Outlets at Orange were further to their right as the company tried to sort out the mess.

Oh my god early the V-22's had dropped the leading elements of the first Marine in the Anaheim Angles parking lots to begin the operation against the Chinese. Nerthercot was putting them all in. Every man, woman and child was armed and loaded onto the choppers and trucks as the sweep had to begin now.

The Chinese were burning LA and trying to kill everyone they could. Sanchez and the Orange Squad were assigned to be right in the middle as the strategy was simple: The 55 was the north south boundary from Costa Mesa to Yorba Linda. The Marines lined up units along that line and told them to keep going north and east until they were dead or they hit Santa Monica.

They did have help. Civilians had been coming out of the woodworks for the last two days. Gang Bangers, Some cops and fire men (those not killed) a few National Guard troops, really anyone who could fire a gun was taken. They needed people.

Sanchez and her group with Wilkins had at least thirty auxiliary troops under their direction. She hated using them as shock troops but it was house to house and vicious fighting.

The Chinese had a few missiles, both anti air and anti-tank with them, as well as grenades. They had numbers but no air cover and no heavy weapons.

The Marines at least had mortars and some tanks. And they were making good use of them. The first hours of the battles had been unit sized. The Chinese tried to setup tank killing traps but the Marines had seen through that. Any barricades were shelled with mortars. The tanks kept moving and firing.

The Chinese could not stand up to that and had broken apart quickly. The only response from them was to move into the neighborhoods and the houses. That forced the American forces to walk block after block in Santa Ana. Eastside, Wilshire Square, Madison Park, Bristol Warner, South Coast, every neighborhood had to be cleared. The civilians provided a bit of intel about where the Chinese were located as they entered. Wilkins ordered the Aux teams to form on the entrance to the subdivisions. The Marines with a few of the more "battle hardened" civilians would walk through coaxing shots from the Chinese. Any random shots brought swift retaliation from the Marines. Especially stubborn spots were taken care of by the tanks or by shelling the house with a few artillery shots.

Block after block was liberated.

The Santa Ana river was dry with a thin stream running in it that provided no real obstacle as the smoke from the fires obscured everything.

Sanchez ordered Duarte to take a group of civvies and head over to the mall area.

"Run thru the mall quickly. If you run into any size force report that ASAP and we will call in a fire mission."

"Affirm Sargent!"

The young man took up his gear and called for the volunteers in an authoritative voice. Even Hill was impressed.

Orange squad Marines were taking a short break to re supply and rest up. The past seven hours had been hard fighting and the body could only take so much. Even the Chinese were tired. Sanchez could tell. They seemed to be abandoning positions quicker as the Marines marched on.

Wilkins came up to his top Sargent to confer.

"The Major is worried." "He thinks the enemy will try to ditch those coveralls and try to blend in."

Taking a swig of water, Sanchez contemplated the problem. *Suicides?*
"As we get the new civilian volunteers, we should vet them," she suggested.

"How?"

The Lieutenant had a point.

It was Morrelli who spotted the first one about twenty minutes later. The young man was dirty, pale and obviously Asian. He looked thin and exhausted. *Of course they all did, all of the civilians trapped here.* Sanchez thought when the PFC pointed out the man. He stood a few feet apart from the other volunteers. Swaying just a bit in ill-fitting jeans, he looked around furtively.

Wilkins, Sanchez, Hicks and Olsen moved to surround the man.

The enemy soldier noted the movements and brought a hand gun out from his waist area. "Gun!"

The man got off one shot before he was killed. Fortunately, no one else was hurt.

"It looked like he was wearing the same kind of jeans my mom wears", Morrelli noted as they examined the body.

And he was. The body was dirty and very thin. He had a cell phone, the gun and a fanny pack of explosives which would not have detonated even if he would have been able to trigger the device.

Wilkins called in the Major who swung by a scant few minutes after they radioed in the call to be wary of infiltrators. The two officers conferred and Sanchez told them she felt like the troops they were facing were a rear guard action. Just there to tie them down, not really win a battle.

"Why?" They must have a hundred thousand men. They still outnumber us", the Major noted.

Sanchez thought hard. "The Chinese are spread too thin, Sir. If they concentrate, they know we would be able to hit them with an air strike or even tanks or artillery. If they stay spread out they can cause maximum damage and keep us in this theater."

The Major furrowed his brow. Wilkins nodded to her assessment. They placed a call to Nerthercot. *Be advised the possibility exists that the troops here are a holding action for prosecuting another target.*

The shit problem with that was Command concurred with their assessment. They *knew* that was the case.

But that did not help the 3/5 Marines nor the rest of the First MEF. They still had tanks on the ground and choppers in the air and troops running through houses. And what's worse they had Marines dying.

Sanchez unit did not go unscathed. Washington died late the night of the 28th. His civ group had come upon an apartment block of dense units across from Disney that housed some Chinese troops. The parking lot fronted S Walnut street and the Hermosa Village apartments were four streets in towards the west. PFC Washington was acting as a squad leader for a group of Latino and black gang bangers. The young men were outfitted with Tec-9's and some other submachine guns so they were heavily armed. The Chinese had responded with the HJ-8 missile when confronted.

The gang dudes panicked and Washington tried to organize them to provide suppressing fire as they retreated down CLL Del Mar towards the south. He took several rounds in the back and died almost immediately. The last two men from the twelve newbies who'd gone in, came back and reported the engagement. Wilkins ordered in an artillery strike that took out the six block square. Sanchez insisted on recovering Washington's body. *No Marine left behind!*

That seemed to be the way of this battle. The day of the 29th saw the Marines moving steadily west and north bunching up the Chinese. The enemy kept trying to isolate out pockets of American troops and crush them with superior numbers but the Marines were too smart for that. Mosul, Fallujah, Somalia, you name any other hot spot and the Marines had been there and had practiced house to house fighting. They knew the drill. Any time they needed something they called in a predator drone or an artillery strike.

The tanks the Marines used, the M1 Abrams, was the finest tank on the battle field today. It was vulnerable to the man portable missile the Chinese were using, but the command for the Marines was making each tank count. The armored behemoths were scattered all along the front, not concentrating them and tempting the Chinese.

But the Marines and the civilians were winning the battle. Slowly, the Chinese fell back and regrouped. They got hit again, killing more and causing more destruction to LA but they fell back again. The Marines were down about five thousand dead with another twenty-five hundred wounded. That was seriously wounded. Anyone who could lift a gun was kept on the front lines.

The civvies took the brunt of the casualties. At least thirty thousand dead in the brutal fighting. The Marines were taking a steady stream of wounded back to Pendleton for treatment. The hospitals in San Diego and southern LA were being pressed into service to treat the wounded.

The number of dead for the Chinese was harder for Sanchez and Wilkins to estimate. Forty thousand? Fifty? They had only captured a few dozen soldiers. Most of those believed they would be immediately killed. The battle shock was very evident as they were grouped in the Disney parking lot for holding. The Marines guarding the prisoners were constantly keeping the civilians from killing the unarmed Chinese. Such was war.

Olsen died late on the night of the 29th near midnight. Hicks followed on the 30th. Sanchez was getting numb to her people going down. They were doing the job but it was killing them. A few hours after Hicks went down, Sanchez mustered her squad. Hill, Morrelli, Duarte, Tacks, Harper, Gonzales, Roberts-Morris, Brown, Boyer, Glamm, Weitlisbach, and Manor were all resting where they dropped. Water, MRE's and ammo were all being fed to her troops. She barely knew the names of the civilians who were sitting right with them. Briles? Was that the ladies name? The thin African American woman was crazier than Hill, but not as tough. Still, she and Parker and that other guy had survived and gotten good at this type of war.

This was the most brutal Darwin winnowing ever created. If you could not learn the lessons of this, you died. By definition, anyone who was still alive at this point was a battle hardened mother fucker. Sanchez made sure the civvies got food and water. Not too many shaking hands she noted, good.

Wilkins appeared thru the smoke and confusion of the rally point to find his people. The Major was right on his heels. Sanchez was very impressed with the Lieutenant as the shit kept flying. Wilkins kept her in the loop, took her advice, interfaced with command and let her, Collins and Armster do most of the yelling and ordering. That seemed to be a good working relationship for her.

The other two top Sargents joined her as the Major and Wilkins drew up and faced the enlisted.

"We got orders." Wilkins put it out bluntly. The Major was just there to assign transport.

"Unass to Anaheim Stadium", he barked. "We got the V-22's ready. You Marines have more fighting to do. Real fighting, not this mop up shit!" "Pick out as many civilians as you think can hack it and take them with you."

Oh oh.

Quinru California

"General Graham it's been three days!"

The President was getting impatient. Graham had told her the destination of the Chinese but she had yet to see the solution.

The timing on this has to be right, Stedman Graham kept telling her. He was scared, Stallings could see that. It took her several hours to see the problems the first time Graham had gone thru it with her.

***

"The Magic Tapestry story is an old Chinese fable," he'd told her three days earlier in the Oval Office. Kevin Mooney looked up from his preparations for the naval engagement to listen.

"The NSA agents in San Francisco have tapped into the fact that they are calling the invasion "Magic Tapestry." "We think that it has significance to the story and to the operation."

The President gestured for him to go on.

"SF1 thinks and we concur that the Chinese rally point will be Sun Valley in Nevada. We think that because in the story a young peasant woman weaves a magical tapestry. The Magic Tapestry or Carpet as it came to be called, could alter reality. When the woman needed a cow for milk, she wove it and the cow appeared. She made the tapestry give her a husband and a house as well."

Sharon listened intently without interrupting.

"As word of this miraculous Tapestry carpet spread, the authorities wanted to take it from her. So she built a well-fortified, well provisioned beautiful city called, Hangzhou, for the good people to live in. The City was near a beautiful lake and had access to many weapons to defend itself with. She was saved and the people were saved all living in the Magic Tapestry." "The fable says that Hangzhou was located in "Sun Valley".

Sharon pursed her lips. "And you think that the story Sun Valley corresponds to our Sun Valley?"

"I do, Ma'am and here is why," Graham spread out a large map of the Western states: Washington, Oregon, California with Nevada and some of Idaho thrown in. "Our satellites show the movement in its beginning stages for the three theaters: Tacoma/Seattle, Oakland/San Fran and Long Beach/LA."

"Zhenge He has split his forces into multiple movement groups." He paused to see if she was keeping up with the military jargon. Graham came down a notch, "The Chinese battle leader is moving his forces in smaller groups to negate our air power and our missiles. See here a column is moving along the Eighty, and the five eighty, but also on these smaller east west highways: The Fifty, Eighty-Eight, Four and the One-Twenty as far south as Yosemite are routes we think they are going to take." The LA group is moving up the Five but only to access the One Seventy Eight, One Ninety, and One Ninety Eight. All of those routes will eventually hit the Three Ninety-Five." That's the same thing the northern group is doing."

Graham looked at the President expectantly. Mooney coughed, telling him he need to explain it. "Ma'am the three ninety-five is the only north south highway on the east side of the Sierra. It ends at Sun Valley."

That she could understand.

"So they can't go further east on those routes and they already have LA so they won't go south." She summed it up.

Graham nodded. "The other prize is not just Sun Valley. They know an army is marching for them, and what's the one advantage we have?"

"Armor," Mooney answered for the President.

Graham vigorously head bobbed yes. "The Navy boy is right, Ma'am. We have tanks and artillery and they don't. They could not bring those heavy, bulky weapons with them on the ships." "But they could capture some."

Sharon stared in horror. "What?" *God Damn it! It's what they didn't tell you!*

"The SF 1 agents raised the possibility that the Chinese are driving for the Sierra Army Depot," The General took a deep breath and launched into the explanation. "The Depot is a store house for tanks and artillery pieces. Thousands of them. Tens of thousands." "They are stored in a preserved state ready for use." He went on to relate the numerous trucks, water purification rigs, and power generators stored at the facility. "It is where we keep all the things we would need for a war on someone else's soil," he said finally.

All three were repulsed by the thought of the Chinese with half a million men mated up with US equipment. That force could overrun the entire US!

"We think the container and truck rigs in the columns have parts, tools and ammo for the tanks. They would need a solid month with the gear before the items are usable but once they are there…"

The General did not go on.

***

"Why can't we Nuc it," The President said with finality after yelling at The Chairman of the Joint Chiefs about his delay in coming up with a solution.

"Madam President, using nuclear weapons on our own soil to destroy our own equipment, killing some of our own people…"

"To deny the enemy the use of the weapons, right General?"

She was faced with a very difficult decision. Paul and Libby had turned up enough examples that told a scorched earth policy could actually work. Still, to be the person who ordered the bombing of a US state? Was it any different than the Navy's bombardment of Honolulu? They were talking degree here. Not to mention the fact that a group of National Guard troops from California was on scene and guarding the facility, just like they were supposed to do.

"That will be our last resort, ladies and gentlemen", she announced after hours of debate. If we can't stop them at Sun Valley, we go with Option B."

Sharon hated herself right then. *Option B was a dry clinical way to describe something so heinous.*

"General Graham it is time to put everything we have on the ground in Nevada."

"The planes will be rolling in the next few hours, Ma'am."

"Admiral Mooney, tell me you have the Navy ready to deny the Chinese the next wave of troops?"

"Yes, ma'am I do."

The city was quiet. The 1st of June was typically dry and moderate in San Francisco. The sudden exit of two thirds of the Chinese troops meant that the number of people left in the city was quite small. Maybe nine thousand Chinese troops, another five or six thousand homeless and abandoned city dwellers. Two NSA agents, well really one NSA agent, a very young half agent and six Navy Seals completed the roster for the forty-nine square miles of some of the most expensive real estate around.

Not so expensive any more, Noah thought. The view from on top of the building was excellent in the mid-morning light. Rammy was down texting the resistance groups the rally points and the battle plan. They'd never found where Zhenge He was explicitly, but they figured out where he was moving towards and that was good enough. The Magic Tapestry story was out and the President believed them, so that was all that mattered to him.

Not all that mattered.

He'd been able to text his mom in Silverdale a few days ago. She was okay as the Subase was on the other side of the peninsula from the Chinese. She was busy with the Admiral and the General coordinating the Seattle resistance army and their movements within the President's battle plan.

He knew it was coming down to the serious "take a stand" kind of times. If the Chinese ever got to the Sierra Army Depot, the war was lost. General Tedesco and the Admiral were rallying the Oregon National Guard troops and the Washington state contingent along with whatever units of volunteers could be spared from the house to house fighting to follow the Chinese down the Eighty-Four towards Herlong, California. That was the name of the fly speck town where the Army Depot was located. Noah knew as sure as anything his mom would be right with the command contingent. She would not take no for an answer he'd be willing to bet.

Kind of like dad and me.

His dad. Ohio had gone silent, so he hadn't gotten any more replies to his family grams. He knew from the NSA chatter that the Navy had a huge battle upcoming. It did not take a genius to know that every ship and sub available would be used in the fight.

Like what he was doing right now.

The binoculars the Seal lead had given him were gyro stabilized and very good. He was glassing the surrounding buildings for movement inside that marked the Chinese snipers.

The enemy had figured out where they were down to a few blocks. The Seals had continued to conduct raids even as the bulk of the troops left the city. The primary mission was a bust, in that they hadn't gotten the enemy leader, but they had completed a secondary task: The Golden Gate Bridge was mined with explosives…

If everything went to shit, the Chinese would not be using San Francisco bay as a docking port.

But someone had to be alive in order to trigger the charges. To that end the two computer wieners were taking turns acting as spotters. They would mark where the enemy was and relay that info to the Spec ops guys. Now the seals were just hunting people until their ammo ran out. And they still had boxes of bullets as far as Noah could tell. He was up to bat.

The game had become deadly as three Seals had been killed. Two were dead on the park grounds but the third man had died in the office right on the floor. There was nothing any of them could do, as the man was too badly injured to save. The amount of blood had been shocking to the young man.

The past two weeks had seen the boy grow up. Noah did not doubt he was then oldest seventeen-year old in the world right now.

A sudden flash winked at his eye. Way north. Someone was on the top of Nob hill looking around. Not one of theirs. He texted the info to the Seal, Mathers. The "K" response was what they were using as code. Yesterday it was an emoji. Just a small security thing the military guys had worked out with Rammy. That way they knew the person sending or receiving the text was a good guy.

That was smart.

More movement directly below him drew his attention. Two more Seals going out.

They'd broken pattern today, shifting from night time ops to day light. The two-man team was going out to relieve the other two.

The men wore rags and were pushing shopping carts. Noah thought that was way smart too. Even in the craziness of the invasion, the homeless dudes still prowled the streets with carts loaded with huge black plastic bags tied on. Even the Chinese eventually stopped killing them. Too much trouble. They weren't a threat and they couldn't go anywhere, they just *were*. The Seals took advantage.

The men disappeared down the street. Noah could not see anything else.

A gun shot echoed from the north.

Scratch one Chinese watcher.

He glassed the whole area to see if any troops were going to respond to the killing. Sometimes they did and sometimes they didn't. The US troops were good at this cat and mouse game. They seemed to love to trap the trappers and the Chinese were learning. Noah watched the Americans use one man as bait days ago and then catch twenty or so Chinese as they surrounded the man. It took seconds for the other Seals to kill the Chinese.

But the odds caught up to them eventually. The two guys in Golden Gate Park, and the other one now dead. Only eight of them left against thousands. The odds didn't seem so good. He texted the all clear signal.

Rammy came onto the roof. Noah thought she was looking to get out of the office area. The smell and the closeness was stultifying and he looked forward to being on the roof.

She squatted next to him with her back to the low wall that ran around the building top.

"Hey."

"Hey," she responded.

"Any news?"

"Yeah, some of it good. The Oakport guys managed to stall out the group heading up Eighty."

Noah grunted. He tended to think of the Oakport resistance group as "theirs" because they were the first people who'd contacted them and they had lasted the longest and done the best against the Chinese. Internally he grudged that it might be because they had the other Seal with them but he was being unkind towards the Seals.

"They hit them hard last night and managed to block the highway right near the California Nevada line."

"Awesome!"

Rammy smiled at the enthusiasm. "Yeah, thought you'd like that. The Oakport guys are now calling themselves the Antioch Army."

"Huh. Why that", the man asked.

"I guess one of the people they picked up was a National Guardswoman from Antioch California and she recruited from the survivors around there when they needed them." "She told me they have a hundred plus guys right now and are picking up more all the time."

The ramifications of that hit home for Noah.

"How are all those new guys going to talk to one another?'"

"That's what I'm doing up here. DC wants us to come up with a text code for them, kind of like what we are doing with the Seals."

"Let's go!"

He texted the two-man Seal team that he had to run on orders. The sad faced emoji came back quickly with a "K". Yeah, everyone had to adjust.

Fucking batteries. World War Three was being run on a huge box of looted Costco batteries. That and some quick use cell phone chargers.

Dre dug in and grabbed four new ones and loaded the charger. He connected up his cell and then slumped against the tower truck seat exhausted, while his phone grabbed a few more operating hours.

He looked out on the airport grounds in amazement. *Yeah, this shit right here is huge!*

The Reno airport was the location for all the activity but the golf course was the crazy part. The lakes course was not only where the bulk of the fleeing bay area Californian's had left their cars, but also where school busses were parked. And A/C transit busses, along with flatbeds and what seemed to be thousands of other vehicles all jammed anywhere they could go. No one was going to play on this course for a very long time.

He'd spent the better part of the morning arguing with Smith and Miller and acting like some kind of officer. They were wrangling with a bunch of things before the real Army and Marines came in to the area. Word was the Jarheads flew in today and the Fourth ID was rolling up I-80 right now. SF 1 was getting together a text code so everyone could reasonably talk to everyone else.

Dre marveled at the logistics that were happening right now all around him. The Army had sent a contingent of technicians to secure the Cal ISO electrical grid operating station in Bakersfield, so the electrical grid between northern and southern California could operate in some fashion. That meant spotty electrical power as individual substations were knocked out by the Chinese but there was electricity and even some running water around the state. A food tent was setup and someone was cooking stew while showers and some basic medicines were available for the Oakport people and their Antioch friends. Reno itself was reasonably intact as the bulk of the Chinese troops were south on 395 or West and North waiting to connect up for the attack.

That this was going to be the battle front was a foregone conclusion at this point. Smith was running most of this until some dudes named Lemonge and Nethercot got here. Dre was fine with that.

He looked around to see Manny and Tito teaching some of Miller's Antioch boys how to hot wire busses. There were probably three hundred resistance fighters in this vicinity and the roads in held one or two cars it seemed at all times carrying more Americans into the fight.

But Dre knew the best was due in in about two hours. That's why they needed to hotwire busses.

Amir came up and reported that they had fifty vehicles capable of carrying about a thousand men ready to go.

"That's nice man but we need ten times that number." Dre hated to burst the young man's bubble, but it was the truth. Ten times might not be enough.

Lardi swept by and told him that all of the Antioch people were fed and had gotten guns and ammo. The man was still down about the loss of Bobby Tornado two days ago.

Buried in the avalanche that blocked the highway by the Truckee River, Bobby was gone before any of them could react.

Lardi had taken it hard. Dre talked to his friend and said some consoling words but the thing that got Ladarius moving again was this: "Take it out on the people who are responsible. Take it out on the Chinese!"
Dre hated using revenge as a motivator but sometimes that was all that kept a man moving.

His phone was fully charged and in his pocket when Miller came by the truck.

"Put this on." She handed him a blue armband handkerchief, just like she was wearing.

250

"When you hear the call for "Officers meetings" that means you," she told him.

Dre just looked at her. Miller and Smith had been having the same conversations with SF 1. Their little resistance units were going to get melded into the regular army very soon. Looked like DC wanted to get some of the leaders of the resistance groups involved in the meetings to pass out the information they need to let the troops have.

He put the hand on his right arm and told her they only had about fifty busses ready.

"It will have to do. Detail Manny, Tito and the rest of your boys. They want the first four busses for the Officers to go up with Lemonge and the others to scout out the ground, she told him smiling.

Dre nodded. Yeah he could do that. "Gon be a big battle and a tough one."

The woman looked at him. "To the death Dre. DC already said we can't allow them to pass to the depot."

He knew the truth of that. The fuckin Chinese with tanks and artillery? No thanks.

"Be ready in an hour," Miller advised him and went on handing out arm bands.

Dre went to find what was left of Oakport Trucking. He wondered if he would ever work at the port again. He knew it was destroyed right now, but assuming the US won this little fight he was sure they would need to get supplies into the area to rebuild. That meant ships and that meant work for Oakport. Hell, just maybe Tabatha was still alive. If he was going to daydream, he should do it all the way.

Dre went to tell his people what they had to do and to be ready.

The time passed quickly and then he was on a bus with Manny driving and some fifteen men and women riding while they drove east on the eighty freeway.

Miller and Smith were on the bus with him while Lardi, and Tito and Amir drove the other three rigs. The small procession went swiftly for the thirty or so miles they needed to go.

The area was deserted. Even the huge Tesla giga factory was evacuated.

The Fallon Wildlife refuge area sat hard on the freeway some thirty miles east of Reno.

As the busses pulled onto the hard packed sand and alkali flats, vehicles could be seen rolling up the highway towards them. Huge American flags were stuck out the windows as markers of the occupants. Even though the armored personnel carriers and flatbed trucks were obviously part of the US Army.

"That's the lead elements of the Fourth Infantry division," Smith told them standing at the doorway. He checked his phone.

"SF 1 says Lemonge is in one of the first personnel carriers,"

The first three vehicles pulled up next to the busses alongside the highway and they disgorged US troops in full battle gear. Several officers joined the twenty or so grunts on the ground. The seven Officers, all Colonels or above went right to the bus carrying Dre, Smith and Miller.

Dre was impressed with Major General Brad Lemonge. Tall, trim and very fit looking his salt and pepper hair gave him a slight grandfatherly air. Olive green digital cammies with the two gold stars on the collar marked him as the Man. The high shine boots and holstered 9MM gave off a more deadly vibe.

"You the Oakland people?" The man asked in a deep voice as he entered.

Smith took charge as the two sides eyed each other. Some of the Colonels on Lemonge's staff did not look too happy to be dealing with "locals". The Navy Seal set them straight. "Treadwell and his group were AT the port when the Chinese hit, so they've been in this fight the longest. And they survived and hit the enemy, hard, so you gentlemen should show some respect."

The staff looked at Manny and Dre a bit differently. Most noted the blue arm bands for both of them.

Lemonge was talking quietly with Miller and Smith.

"Should be any time. Whitworth and his division from Kansas are behind us a day. The Marines are due in first," the General told them.

A honk from Lardi's bus made heads look around. The men outside were pointing up in the air.

The assembled group made their way off the bus and out onto the flats a little way. The sound was just becoming audible. The steady chump of the huge twin rotor Osprey's as they came into view. At least twenty of the huge transports flying low in the air from the south.

The Marines were coming to town.

Nethercot had taken a chance and pulled himself and a regiment out of LA to come to grips with the real enemy. A second flight of the hybrid plane/chopper could be seen now behind the first.

The lead Ospreys on the scene were slowing and changing rotor configuration to land vertically. The dust rising as the five lined up perpendicular to the run of the highway and touched down softly a few hundred yards from the waiting people and busses.

The Marines dismounted in an impressive fashion. Again in full battle gear and a few surprises came with them: some motorized artillery pieces. Nothing huge, but 55 millimeter shells could ruin anyone's day.

The V-22's held twenty Marines and most of their gear so the extraction took a few minutes. General Nethercot was on the first bird down, so he marched up the distance like Caesar crossing the Rubicon. He was followed by a platoon of tough looking sons of bitches.

"General Nethercot, welcome to Fallon," Lemonge told him shaking hands.

The two men didn't know each other so a small ceremony was held. Technically as a three star, Nethercot would be in charge of the battle. But he only had about five thousand men and women with him. Lemonge was bolstered by the majority of the Colorado National Guard and the Wyoming contingent as well, so he had about thirty-five thousand men under his flag. Both of those Colonels were with his staff officers trying meld them into a unified whole. The Utah Guard was with the Kansas based "Big Red One" First Division as well as the Kansas and more Midwest guard units. They would be bringing another thirty to forty thousand men to the battle in addition to some heavy artillery and tanks. The transporters were laborious and slow but they dared not leave them behind.

The augmented divisions were badly needed.

Dre found himself standing next to a female Marine Sargent while Lemonge and Nethercot exchanged pleasantries with each other's staffs. Smith and Miller were mixing in shaking hands and taking.

"Who's the swabbie?" The female Sargent asked with a bit of 'tude in her voice.

"That Smith. He a Seal Team Six dude." Dre told her.

"Huh. How you meet him?" she asked surprised.

Dre found himself telling her the story of Smith rising out of San Francisco bay and then the rest of it.

Connie Sanchez was impressed. "Sounds like you guys have seen some shit."

"Yeah. What about you guys? How is LA?"

The Sargent told her about the missile attack and the fighting so far. "LA was burning but it looked like we were going to be able to root most of the Chinese out of there."

The Oakland man was impressed right back. Lasing targets was not his idea of fun.

"What are we waiting on? I got fifty busses ready to shuttle people to Reno." Complaining was a time honored tradition in military service and Dre was doing his share.

"My Lieutenant," she nodded over to the group of officers, "Wilkins by name, says we are waiting on the showoffs to arrive."

"The showoff's?"

But she wouldn't say any more. The last of the Marines landed. The twenty Osprey's immediately went back to the Forward Operating Base at Edwards where the rest of the Marines were waiting on transport. They had as many round trips as the busses

They only had to wait another fifteen minutes more for the showoffs to arrive. A hand pointed to the East and up. Heads followed the hand.

Planes were visible.

Big planes. Lots of them started appearing as little dots and then grew rapidly. Dre could see these were the big four engine jobs. The transport types.

The C-17 Globe master is a big ass plane. Four jet engines, a distinctive "T" shaped back end and a flat wide fuselage, meant the two-hundred-million-dollar craft could hold and haul a lot of shit. Or lots of shits. The first plane lined up on the Fallon salt flat and swooped in to an altitude of 5,000 feet. Three lanes were being established as the next sixty planes lined up. Not all of them were the Globe masters. Dre could see the C-130 prop jobs mixed in. The smaller, older transports were led by a gaudily painted blue one.

"Is that fucking Fat Albert?" Dre asked Sanchez, his voice taking on a wondering note.

The Marines Sargent grinned right back. "Yeah. The scuttlebutt at Edwards said the Seal instructors and staff people requested that plane."

Amir, Manny and Tito joined Dre by the busses to watch the largest parachute drop in the history of the world.

The United States Airborne corps had arrived.

Strings of men leapt out the lowered aft cargo doors and pulled up on static lines, chutes billowing. The wind wasn't bad and there was no enemy fire, so as a combat drop this one was a piece of cake.

The roar of engines sounded louder and louder as more and more men hit the ground. The 82nd and 101st both brought division plus sized contingents. One of the first men on the ground was Lieutenant General Ashleigh Whitworth. The Three star soon found his way with his staff to the confab point where Lemonge and Nethercot awaited.

"That's a lot of brass sittin at one spot", Dre noted to Sanchez. He took out his phone and snapped a few quick pictures of the landings and the Generals. Even he knew the immensity of the historic moment this was.

"Shit, look at that, Dre!" Amir pointed.

A much louder engine was on the scene.

A C-5 galaxy transport came in as slow and low as she dared. The back door was open and fucking building dropped out the back end.

That's what Amir was pointing at, but it wasn't a building. It was a tank. Dre whistled and nudged the Sargent. "I didn't think they dropped those bad boys from planes."

Sanchez shook her head. "We don't." "Duarte, look at that!' she called to one of her young Marines. "That is an A1 Abrams main battle tank being air dropped into a combat zone against all regulations. The rule book says we fly them in and land them, right?"

"This must be some kind of shooting war, Sargent."

Lots of overloaded things and planes running around in the sky today. Dre knew there was only supposed to be 125 dudes on a C-17 static line but it looked like they'd packed in 150 or so. And every one of those men and women had packs with them. Guns and ammo and food. Other shit was coming in as well. A few Humvee's, more tanks. More special forces as the Delta Force made a showy low altitude opening right over the Generals. Dre hoped they would take Smith off his hands. That guy scared him a little.

More murmuring from the crowd as a new group of air craft approached. Same haze grey fuselage's but the tail sections had a large red maple leaf on the upright.

The Royal Canadian paratroopers were joining the fray. Five thousand of his majesty's finest joined the soon to be Seventy-five thousand strong US airborne force. Tito asked Dre if he thought there were any parachutes left in the military. The man did not think so. It looked like they took every swinging dick and hairy vagina that could jump out of a plane a moved them to the desert.

He did some quick math. A few Marines, some Canadians, a division of US Infantry- no two divisions. The airborne portion. It looked like one hundred thousand. Maybe up to one twenty-five with the civilians they were getting. They would still be outnumbered three to one, Dre figured.

That was going to be bad.

"Let's start moving them!" Smith, Miller and Sanchez moved out from the staff meeting and started yelling. Damn, that Sanchez could holla!

Men, women and equipment started the long trek to Reno. Manny was driving the bus with the Oakport people and the Marine squad they'd been talking to. The Lieutenant-Wilkins was his name, talked to Sanchez and she asked Dre if he wanted to hook his people up with them.

"The general consensus is that the civilians are going to be folded into the army units at a squad level. If you want to bring in three or four fire teams we can make you a 3/5 Officer," Sanchez told him.

Dre hesitated.

"Better with us than being a grunt in the Army", Sanchez teased.

Amir and Manny said yes so he decided to go with the jarheads. Wilkins came over and sat by him and the two men talked over Dre and his people. What they'd experienced, what they were capable of, that sort of thing. Wilkins went back impressed, Dre knew. He also knew that they only had two or three days to get things ready for the Chinese.

The enemy was coming, and everyone knew that. This time they had to be ready for them.

CHAPTER TWELVE

"Form up at the end of the street and sweep straight down it", the Private First class instructed the civilians. "If you contact the enemy, sing out and we will concentrate fire. Everyone needs to be aware of friendly forces, Affirm?"

"Ya, Bruddah we da kine."

The trade winds were up in the islands making puffy white clouds scoot across the blue sky. Walt and the half of Waianae that decided to stay and fight were standing on the Eva Beach side of the plains, near the highway. Kemo was standing next to him as the two men readied to sweep Kapolei to round up any Chinese and help concentrate the invaders down near the downtown corridor and Waikiki.

The 2nd of June saw the most intense fighting to date in the Hawaiian theater. The Chinese were dug into their positions and ready for the Marines to boil out of Kaneohe Bay and roll their tanks down the Pali highway to cut them off. The intel and satellite feeds showed Admiral Nickers what the Chinese had planned: teams of anti-tank missile trucks were hidden on each side of the highway in enveloping fields of fire. As soon as the Marines came down the roads the missiles would arc out and touch someone. In the bad way.

Nickers was too smart for that. The Marines at KBay did indeed boil out of their barracks and their base. But at the Kamehameha highway they turned right instead of left.

The Admiral pulled an end around, literally. The Marines went up the east side of the island to the north shore and down the famed pipeline beach side. At the old school fishing harbor of Haleiwa, the Marines bent left with the road to head inland.

Up and south they travelled along the pineapple fields past the Dole plantation the column of trucks, tanks and Bradley's started to collect a motley group of camp followers. The Kama Aina were out to fight. The people from Wahiawa, Nanakuli, Kailua, Pearl City had come to defend their homes. The assembled horde stopped at Wheeler Army Air field to pick up its leaders and get basic strategy.

Admiral Nickers joined General Zelazny of the 25th infantry division based at Schofield Barracks.

The two men were in agreement on the strategy part: March to the enemy, close, and kill him.

It was that basic.

Clearing out Mililani as they started down the H2, was the only training they got. Very few Chinese had managed to penetrate to this part of the island, so the small suburb was a good test case for the tactics they would use.

"Stay at the top of the street until you get the word to go in. When, WHEN the word is given, knuckleheads, you will enter the houses and clear each and every room. Empty houses are marked with a "X" on the front side." The Major from the 25th was a huge scary looking black man. No one wanted to test his bad side so the locals followed orders. Walt and Kemo had hooked over the top of the Waianae mountains and on Trimble road right to Schofield's back gate. That five or six thousand people were with them ready to fight was all the ID they needed.

Now they were starting in earnest with Kapolei and Ewa Beach. Walt knew there were enemy soldiers in these houses. He'd seen them from his boat days ago. He had to assume they would still be here. Creeping down Kapolei parkway Walt kept his head on a swivel. Two clusters of homes were on each side of the roadway here. Varona Villages on the right and the larger Ewa villages on the left. The right side was not his responsibility. The Ewa side was however.

At least the Colonel in charge had listened to the locals. Walt and five hundred or so men, a mix of Army, Marine and civilians were on the Parkway while another thousand were further north creeping across the open fields to the north to get to the 12th hole.

The Ewa Beach community had golf courses just like all of Hawaii. Walt and a few of the others had suggested that the trees bordering the fairways and providing a screen for the houses would also make a good screen for the advancing Americans.

The Colonel liked that thought.

At a signal from several Non coms, Walt's group ran across the road and over the scrub land to the manicured green of the fairway. They stopped in the trees about fifty yards from the fronts of the tidy homes on Puhiko street. Kemo was wheezing right next to him as they waited for the final signal to attack. Fishing is not particularly a cardio workout.

The bullhorn rang out in the midmorning calm. Several men screamed out their fear as they ran to the scattered cars that were still in the area.

Amazingly to Walt they'd maintained the spread as they ran and he just took the house in front of him with at least ten other men and his son. External sounds seemed to be damped but he did hear some firing but not anything to be scared of.

The guy in front, reached the door and kicked at it. The door rocked but did not open. Another man grabbed the knob and turned and the door swung open easily. Both Civilians grinned at the absurdity and then everyone was rushing thru the door. *Thank God it was empty because we could have all been killed with a single bullet,* Walt thought.

The search took moments and the house was declared empty. The "X" went on the front and the men stepped to the street to see others coming out of their own target houses. Several houses north of them a crack of gunfire sounded out. Several rounds and then screams lit up the day. A huge volume of return fire sounded for fifteen seconds or so.

"God damn it, stop firing!" The voice of a hardened Army Sargent growled out in the distance. Kemo and Walt joined the general crowd watching the hotspot. A fire team of four soldiers went through the door again. This time they did it by the book: covering corners and each other. Two shots came in rapid sequence. The all clear rang out a minute later.

The Colonel had the men go into the house to see what the cost was: Eight civilians and one soldiers killed by three Chinese troops. Two of the Chinese were killed by the concentrated external fire. The last two shots had put down the last wounded Chinese trooper.

His boy was white and gulping to keep down the small breakfast they'd managed to eat while Walt and Kemo looked at the dead. *He has to see this. See what happens if we don't do it by the book.*

Again, Darwin weeded out the ones who would not learn the lessons of war.

The enemy response was varied. Sometimes the Chinese waited until they got into the houses to fire. Sometimes they started in as they ran towards the doors. In Pearl City several groups were banded together and behind barricades. This was more Marine and Amy fighting stuff as Walt and his friends just provided a flank guard position.

"Just shoot anyone who comes down that street who isn't one of us", the Marine told him. Seemed simple enough. The fighting at the barricade raged for a hot thirty minutes. The Chinese seemed to want the Americans to bring the tank out to take a few shots at them. As soon as the armor made an appearance, the HJ-8 missile made its. The tank did manage to get some hits in and kill most of the thirty or so men at the reinforced position before it died. The last Chinese troops were killed by a grenade thrown in close.

"We can't trade a tank for a position, we only have sixty-two of them now, Colonel Jennings said.

What they did have were mortars and some artillery.

The next heavy spot was easier as they learned how to crack the trap the Chinese were setting.

The tank setup two miles away out of sight of the Chinese. Raising the massive barrel, the crew loaded a phosphorous round. The thump of the gun going off pounded on Walt's chest.

The white hot round exploded and threw bits of burning metal all over the scene.

The screams and the smell and the carnage did make Kemo vomit this time. But they did learn to use some standoff weapons on the Chinese to preserve lives.

The human tide flowed over the outer suburbs of Honolulu.

The boy killed his first man hours later at Pearl City High school. The massive housing development was a planned community and the school was built right at the top of the cluster of fifteen hundred homes.

The Chinese had obviously planned this area to be a kill zone. Several fortified positions were setup and the enemy troop concentration was in the two to three thousand range.

Nickers and Zelazny let the Colonels figure this nut out.

Problem was there was no easy answer. The first wave of attacks lost five tanks and over three hundred soldiers of the 25th division. They managed to push half way into the streets, but kept running into mobile shuttles of Chinese troops as they supported one element or another against the American thrusts.

The civilian teams were backing up the troops as the fighting raged in the late afternoon light. Walt, Kemo and his group were backed up against some stacked cars occasionally winging shots into the house where a group of Chinese had taken refuge.

"Keep them occupied." Walt directed. He went in search of an artillery team.

He found the gun emplacement on the grounds of Manana Elementary school. A few minutes with the crew and the maps gave them the target.

The five round cluster pattern impacted the wood framed house with thunder and splinters, killing the Chinese.

"That's a better way!" The Lieutenant Colonel running the gun battery told Walt. 'Trap them or get them stationary and then we hit them!"

Walt agreed and that became the pattern: fire until they ran for cover or were pinned down and then a text to the gun batteries with the target. Twenty-five houses went up over the next hour as more and more Chinese were caught in the self-made tombs.

Quite suddenly, the Chinese broke out of back end of the complex and made a run for the highway. The thing that killed them was the thing that made Oahu hell for everyone: traffic.

Komo Mai drive was not built to take several hundred cars all trying to exit the subdivision at the same time. A well timed shell hit one of the lead element cars as it tried to enter the Queen Liliuokalani highway which slowed or stopped all the rest of the transports.

The guns now walked shells back along the line of vehicles as fast as the crews could reload.

The rout was on as enemy troops bailed out of the flaming traps.

Fleeing Chinese soldiers were shot in the back as they tried to wade Waimalu stream. Pearl Country club golf course became a killing field as the seven hundred survivors desperately ran to the next concentration of Chinese positions at Aiea Heights. The Americans upped their fire rate. Fewer than fifty of the enemy made the safety of the houses.

Walt and Kemo were back in Pearl City sweeping thru the subdivision house by house to find and eliminate any stragglers. The High school grounds were quiet as the light faded and the twenty or so civilians with the man and son went through the buildings.

It was just an ordinary classroom. Walt pointed to Kemo that the door was slightly opened and put a finger to his lips. The young man nodded and gripped his 9mm tighter.

Walt went through the door first. Turning right he swept the side of the classroom. Kemo went left and Walt heard two shots.

When he looked he saw a young Chinese soldier slumping down behind some desks. Kemo was facing the man and holding the gun out as it smoked just a little.

The look of surprise on his face was heart breaking for Walt.

He quickly searched his son to make sure the enemy shot had missed. It had.

"I shot more out of reflex than anger, dad." Kemo admitted in a small voice.

"I know."

"He looks so young. Not much older than me."

Walt looked at the Chinese soldier. Scruff of beard on his face. Thin and pale in his blue coverall which was clean except for the blood.

"What was he doing here, Kemo?" Walt asked.

"Huh? I dunno."

"You have to understand, he chose to come here. He chose to invade us. He has been killing and living in these houses for a couple weeks now, eh?"

Kemo nodded.

"He had a choice. We did not cause the problems in China. Mother Nature and their leaders did that. But he was here trying to kill us and we are going to do everything possible to prevent them from killing any more of us, so don't hesitate. Shoot first and question later, ya?"

The young man seemed to accept that. *Tough thing to kill someone,* Walt thought as they continued their sweep. They'd both seen a lot of death so far and Walt was scared it was going to get worse before it got better.

The stench was terrible and the chaos worse. General Fei tried to deal with it as reasonably as possible. He put on the mask and ignored the bodies.

Shanghai was virtually destroyed. The ruling council had left Beijing days ago after the allied bombing attack. The air battle had been a stalemate, but that didn't mean much. Qi's forces had managed to shoot down sixty or so planes but the rest of the four hundred plane raid from the European forces wreaked havoc on an already chaotic city. Many cultural centers and government offices were targeted and destroyed. The Generals didn't care one way or another, but the Imperial City was destroyed. *Old China is dead anyway,* Fei thought as he watched the thousand-year old structure burn.

The Peoples Hall didn't fare any better. Several direct hits with five-hundred pound bombs had caved in the roof, killing thousands.

The ruling council made their way out of the doomed northern areas and went south for the meet up with the ships taking the third wave over to America. New China it was going to be called.

Fei stood at the Baoshan base officer's facility and watched the shuttle of people and materials going onto the ships in the distance. The planes hadn't yet gotten to the southern areas. Maybe they never would.

Fei was much more concerned with Lin Wei Bo. The General had not contacted the ruling council in over three days. Reports were still coming in so he knew that the plan was proceeding but there were problems. The forces Wei had left behind were encountering civilian reprisal attacks. Bo had planned for this Fei knew, but the crazy Americans were killing a lot of his men in all theaters. Seattle, LA, and Hawaii were all locked in vicious house to house fighting. If those three areas were vicious, Oakland was off the charts. The level of ferocity of the American response had shocked Bo and Fei both. The two architects of the plan felt that the US civilian population was too soft to mount a serious defense of their homes. Too much television and easy living had made them ripe for the plucking. They were mistaken in that assumption.

The civilians and the government both had responded in ways Bo had no concept that they were capable of. Bombing the Honolulu downtown area? Wantonly destroying houses to kill Chinese troops? Kill squads in San Francisco? The reports from his agents in Bo's forces were highly disturbing. And now he hadn't heard from Bo himself in days.

Fei knew that the initial attack had gone very well as the Americans had wasted too much time responding. But now it seemed that the harassing counter attacks were slowing the march of Bo's forces towards the American arms depot that was so vital to the success of the mission.

To top that all off, he knew the Navy was headed for a giant battle in the next days that would go a long way to determining the amount of re-enforcements Bo was going to receive. The Navy assured him they had a plan to defeat the US ships and submarines. No modern Navy could withstand the amount of missiles the PLAN wanted to throw at them. The carriers would be destroyed! And with that the last power projection the US possessed would be gone. They didn't have to have the docks to land the three quarters of a million troops on the container ships. Any beach would do along the coast.

Long into the night Fei stood and watched the bustle around him. He was due to board the ship in five days. He had to kill Qi and Yuan before that point but he had plenty of time. Zi was going to take care of Bo, that had already been arranged.

Another two weeks should see him in New China and the head of his own empire.

"Madam President, its time."

"Thank you, Paul."

Sharon Stallings rose from her desk and went to the Situation room with Paul Marino. The now familiar cast of characters was already in attendance. Stedman Graham was conferring with Kevin Mooney. Wellington Thomas sat at the table texting SF 1- she could see the exchange on the vid screen above his shoulder. Libby was in the corner briefing the Vice President. It seemed that every conceivable staff member was in here.

They know the future of our country could ride on this battle.

She sat in the middle of the table to provide herself a good look at the tac screens as they held the satellite images and the radar overlays from the various units monitoring the naval battle. Graham and Mooney broke off talking and Kevin came to stand in front of the President.

"Ma'am we think the initial salvo's will commence within a few minutes to perhaps an hour." The CNO was under enormous pressure. Men and women were going to die today. A lot of them, even if it went perfectly.

"What are we looking at Admiral," she invited the man to talk.

"Madam President the area you see before you, is about six hundred miles due west of Portland, Oregon. The box outline is approximately two hundred nautical miles on a side. That is roughly four thousand two hundred square miles of ocean." He paused to see if she was following.

She was.

"The red triangles are the Chinese surface Navy ships. You can see the designations from their destroyers to the lone aircraft carrier the PLAN possess, right here," Mooney used the laser pointer on a triangle surrounded by escorts. That was standard naval doctrine for most battle groups. The Chinese were no different. "The white squares are the twenty-five merchants ships we think hold the second wave of troops headed for America." The ships formed a double line and were spaced out over a fairly large area. The carrier was actually in the middle of those ships while the escorts circled the whole formation.

"The yellow circles are the Chinese submarines." Mooney swung the display out wider to show the rings of subs and their locations. Now things got confusing for the President.

'Go through this again for me please, admiral."

Mooney nodded. "Ma'am, as we have talked about, we ordered the Ohio south to rendezvous with the San Diego based units. Their job was to get the advanced ring of Chinese attack subs to follow." "Captain Greene did that in a truly spectacular fashion by shooting a torpedo at them and running."

Graham snickered at the puckered assholes that must have caused both sides. *That was one way to accomplish his mission.*

Mooney continued. "Ohio did rendezvous with the other submarines and they managed to sink two of the Chinese before the enemy ran back to the formation." "Greene and the rest then took up their assigned positions." He again shifted the display to give the President the overall look at the forces arrayed.

"So we currently have this for a tactical picture: Ohio and the other tactical Tridents: Michigan, Florida and Georgia along with the Hampton are north of the formations and hiding in the Kuiosho current thermal layers." He pointed out five orange circles arranged in a picket line east to west.

"The Chinese subs are here with regards to their surface forces." Again he pointed out the three layers of subs that was doctrine. Three units in front with a further ten riding west of them and more in a semi-circle with another seven back around the carrier and the merchants.

"I thought they had more subs Admiral."

"They do Ma'am. Our Tac system picture will blank out any tracks older than twelve hours. We think they have another fifteen units encircling the flotilla." Mooney highlighted the side list headed: Unaccounted for Chinese subs.

"Where are our surface units and the rest of our subs?" She wanted to get to the other symbols she could see.

The subs you can see in two groups besides the Ohio group. The Los Angeles groups: Bremerton, Lajolla, Chicago, and the other fifteen are west of the Chinese and are the back stop in case anyone cuts and runs." "The other group is here: More circles appeared south of the enemy. "The Carter, Seawolf, Connecticut and the six Virginia class units are located in the garbage path hiding among the trash." Nine wolves ready to feast on the sheep.

The President knew that was something they'd never tried before. The Admiral was taking a risk. Well. They all were. She'd approved the plan after all.

"Our surface groups are here," he tapped the pointed on the large number of green triangles that represented the huge contingent of US ships.

Everyone in the room swelled with pride at the thought of four huge aircraft carriers along with full escorts heading into battle.

But that wasn't all. More symbols marking US ships were right next to the carriers. USS America, Wasp, Kersarge, and Boxer were designated.

Mooney was ready for the missiles.

The two forces were about one hundred nautical miles apart which was the limit for the newest Chinese anti-ship missiles. The game would be played out long distance and danger close by the two forces.

The Battle of the Garbage Patch was about to get underway.

"Missile launch detected, Admiral!"

"Mark time: 1204 Eastern standard time, 3rd June 2021." History was about to be made.

Mooney sat with the President and murmured in her ear as the reports came in. He wanted her aware of what was going on.

Out in the Pacific Ocean the choppy seas and winds were causing problems for the surface boys. The Chinese missile cruisers were ready to launch but the waves kept rocking the boats, literally. They wanted to launch before the American carriers could get their planes in the air. The Chinese carrier Zhou only had limited VTOL aircraft and the anti-ship missile load out far and away dwarfed the anti-air missile numbers. Overwhelm the carriers from far away when they only had the normal five or six screening aircraft in the skies like they did now, not the eighty odd plane flights they were capable of unleashing. The plan was sound. Two hundred fifty missiles in the space of twelve minutes.

No carrier could withstand that, no matter the destroyers or cruisers the Americans possessed. The missiles boasted a look down targeting system, which meant that the internal radar would turn on and match targets with the inputted data in case the target ships maneuvered mid-course. It would only be a fifteen-minute flight if the weather would cooperate.

A slacking of the wind hit just after nine local and the order was given. "Launch with radar data!"

The arcing trails from twenty ship launches stood white and was quickly lost in the wind. The missiles rocketed up to begin the dance.

"Madam President the Chinese have launched their missiles as we expected. We are executing Plan Z." Mooney was shaking slightly in his seat next to the President.

The order had come down: Execute!

Four Nimitz class carriers rode very close to the huge Helicopter carriers in the seas. This was strictly against policy and common sense. A one hundred thousand ton vessel next to a forty-five thousand ton vessel was a nightmare for ships control parties. Especially in the rough waters of the Pacific.

But Mooney's plan was to invite the missile attack. He had to give them the target: The carriers. But he also had to spoof the missiles when they went to internal radar.

The Nimitz carriers, Reagan, Bush, Vinson and Stennis all heeled under a hard right rudder and reversed course. They sped directly away from the group at flank speed.

The four helo carriers of the America and Wasp classes, were as large as the Chinese carrier Zhou, itself. They marched merrily on the same course and speed as before.

Of course they held minimal crews and maximum readiness factors. No troops or ordinance was on board. Except for CWIS and self-defense measures. Extra anti-missile placements had been seated on deck.

Mooney didn't think they could survive, but every sailor aboard had volunteered to be there. It brought a tear to his eye to think of their sacrifice.

Stallings gripped his arm hard as they waited.

Seven minutes for the Nimitz class ships to escape. They managed to put significant miles between themselves and the Wasp in that time. Flank speed for a carrier is very fast

"Radar aspect change on the missiles!" "Ten, Admiral!" Only ten." The tech could not keep the excitement from his voice.

Mooney leaned in and said, "That means the Chinese missiles are using their internal radar to find the targets. Since ten of them have changed aspect that means they are locked onto the Nimitz fleet not the decoys."

Sharon understood that. "Two hundred forty bombs headed for those brave men and women." She looked at the reverse situation the decoys found themselves in.

Mooney bowed his head. 'Yes ma'am." "But the escorts for the carriers should be able to handle the incoming ten."

That was the important thing.

Things started happening real fast. Missiles tipped over midflight and began a final dive to target, wherever that happened to be.

Weapons systems went on auto and anti-missile missiles came off decks to hit incoming threats. Escorts put themselves in harm's way to protect what had to be protected.

Flashes lit the sky and dropped towards the deck.

The Kersarge was hit first. The warhead screamed over and impacted the forward area blowing a huge hole in the bow deck. That was followed in rapid succession by three more strikes. The ship was a flaming wreck as more hits came onto the other ships.

Mooney watched the data feed almost wincing as every hit came in. A whoop from a tech as the last missile targeting the carriers was destroyed with a single hit, but the joy was lost on the Admiral. USS America got eleven of the incoming missiles but was still blown out of the water. Boxer and Wasp followed shortly. Twelve hundred sailors lost their lives.

'Get the planes in the air!" "Signal the subs."

The battle now took on another phase.
 Ohio and the picket line was ready to go. The distance was at the extreme end of the range for their torpedo's but they didn't expect to sink anything. They had to get the surface ships moving. Of course they had to do that without getting killed in the process.

"Fire tubes two and three!" Greene kept the order quiet. He had Tommy and the rest of the ship at battle stations after working their way into the thermal layer at two hundred feet. Since sound propagated differently at the warm/cold layer boundary, Green felt they could count on at least a little confusion as to what was happening. Maybe.

The other four subs launched two torpedoes apiece right after his and the ocean exploded with noise.

"Contact bearing 235! He's pinging active sir!"

"Match generated bearings, range and shoot, tube one!"

US policy called for a quick reaction tube to be ready at all times and they practiced this almost every day. Tommy tapped buttons on his console furiously as the data became available in sonar.

The range was a relatively close ten thousand yards and the contact was almost dead abeam of them.

"Ready!"

"Fire tube one!"

The whoose of air made ears stuff all over the ship. Forty-two seconds. The book said less than a minute so they were good.

"One away!" Tommy called. The Weps took over.

"Wire connection is good," Lieutenant Archibald said. "Run to enable five thousand yards, tube one is normal."

"Weps make tube one ready, reload with one Mk 48 ADCAP." "Dive make your depth 90 feet, Helm, left five degrees rudder, set course 180." The Captain spat out the orders.

Heads snapped up. *What?*

"Do it, god damn it!"

The CO *never* cursed at them. He was the boss so…

The orders came back smartly and the USS Ohio turned right towards the Chinese submarine and rose to an absurdly shallow and difficult depth to keep.

The COB was standing dive and was struggling to keep the ship from broaching in the rough seas. The surface suction the wave action produced kept wanting to suck up the ship and expose it the air.

Bad things happened to submarines who broached.

"Sierra 12, the Chinese sub has changed course to North!" "He's deep!"

The sonar report brought a smile to the CO's lips. "Wep's, enable the weapon now, cut the wire after."

The Weapons Officer acknowledged the order and breathed easier. *That was some ballsy shit!*

Tommy finished enabling the internal active sonar on the torpedo to start actively pinging for the Chinese sub, now, not in another three thousand yards when the sub would be too close to do anything with. *The CO knew the Chinese sub would not go into the garbage patch and would come north and go deep. Son of a bitch!*

The Ohio was hiding in the surface noise and the unexpected change of direction while the Chinese did what they always did and it was going to cost them.

"Unit is active!"

"Unit has acquired!"

"Final homing!"

The sonar reports came fast and furiously.

The explosion could be heard throughout the ship and it brought shudders to the whole crew.

"Dive make your depth two hundred feet, maintain course south. Sonar update the CO's display! I want to know where those surface ships are!" 'Radio launch a comms buoy! Up load relative data!"

"Madam President we have some updates," Mooney read from the piece of paper. "The carriers are turned back around and have launched the strike package. The initial sub attack has moved the surface ships and merchants into the garbage patch as we'd hoped. "We think an initial loss of six Chinese subs. We have better track on the remaining units as well.

Sharon looked at the display. Even she could tell the Chinese were disorganized. The surface ships had shifted south where they wanted them. And more importantly: The subs had not moved enough!

Mooney and Graham watched while she absorbed that part.

"Yes, ma'am. The surface ships are between the Chinese subs and ours. Their subs can't shoot at us!"

The Chinese commander of the flotilla was very angry. "Move my submarine screen further south!" Order the helo's into the air and start active sonar from the surface ships!"

"Where are those airplanes?"

He was about to fucking find out where the US Navy's F-35's and F-18's were located.

And he was about to find out where the destroyers were located as well and what they could do to his ships. The US ships drove themselves in closer and made the Chinese screening ships react. The whole Chinese group came fully into the garbage patch.

The Angels flight planes from USS Ronald Reagan began their attack runs at less than twenty nautical miles. At that distance the radar returns for the weapons were enormous.

The missile blast came at a low altitude and scared every Chinese sailor aboard and the huge explosion rocked the Zhou. The carrier completed launching her planes but the thirty or so she managed to get into the air were just going to be fodder. They had no air controller like the US versions and they had no real combat experience. Another three incoming US missiles were knocked down by the ships defensive systems. That was the good news. The bad was the next eight US Harpoons zooming in to try their luck. Three of the huge missiles impacted the hull and flight deck and blew the interior of the carrier into a burning twisted wreck. The huge ship fell off the fleet pace of fifteen knots and she started settling low in the water. There didn't seem to be many survivors when she sank.

More missiles started impacting the rest of the Chinese surface fleet. The F-18's could only carry two anti-ship missiles on the wing hard points. But they still had two anti-air missiles and guns. Once the last of the missiles were launched at the Chinese birds, the planes took actual strafing runs on the merchants.

The Stennis group and the Vinson coordinated to take on the lead five cruisers. The Reagan's planes targeted the carrier and then the other escorts as they could find targets. Bush's jets went for the annoying J- 24 planes from the carrier. This time they had the advantage.

And payback was a stone bitch.

The Chinese planes started dying right away as they tried to interdict the US fleet. The look first-shoot first capability of the twelve F-35's came into play and paid huge dividends. The initial barrage killed ten. The second pass caught eight. By the time the next flight of Super Hornets entered the fray the Chinese were trying to close for suicide runs.

The Navy pilots tried not to let them, but some still got through.

Meanwhile, the Chinese escort ships were taking missile hits. Flares and chaff and radical maneuvers only had so much effect at the close ranges the Americans were getting for their shots. Six and then eight and then fourteen vessels were flaming hulks or dead in the water from the planes.

Mooney sighed and reported the progress to the President. "We aren't out of this yet!" he called to keep the enthusiasm down. They'd lost the Florida to a torpedo and the Cowpens to a kamikaze attack but overall things were going well. If you forgot about the four large capital ship's they'd already sacrificed.

"Order the subs to press our advantage and tell the destroyers to close and fire," he ordered the aide.

The Zumwalt and two of her sister ships, the Monsoor and the Johnson closed the gap between the US ships and the Chinese. The garbage was bad in this area and the Lyndon Johnson was overheating their primary Main Seawater Cooling pump. The CO ordered the puffer system to max capacity to blow the shit out of the strainers and he hoped that would be enough. The man never told anyone the problem other than his crew and he never slowed or considered slowing. *They had to be in this fight!*

The remaining Chinese escorts had abandoned the merchants and the dead carrier and other vessels. Of the fifty-eight fighting ships in the enemy fleet, only twenty remained undamaged. The four large cruisers and sixteen destroyers and frigates tried to form up and respond to the Americans.

The newest US destroyers came at them with a closing speed of nearly fifty knots. The wave chop was such that the gun solutions were being thrown off, but the tin cans didn't care.

The dull whoosh of the rail gun firings kept pace from all three ships as they launched the kinetic energy rounds. The launch of Tomahawks and Harpoon anti-ship missiles were causing streaks of smoke to flare up at regular intervals.

The Chinese came back with five-inch gun rounds of their own. A large scale naval battle between surface combatants has not happened since world War II. Airborne missiles and torpedoes are much more effective at sinking surface ships than guns or lasers.

The confusing tactical picture for the Chinese got even worse as the American destroyers closed and started firing. The amount of noise in the water: engines, screws, waves, active sonar and bits of garbage all contributed to fire control screens looking crazy with tracks and blips of noise all over the place.

Zigging to throw off the rail gun "dumb" shots, the Chinese tried to answer with more of their own shells. The huge gouts of water looked impressive but only succeeded in killing fish. The real problem for the Chinese was the air and surface threat was the most immediate and the most visible, and they were reacting to that threat. The silent service was about to make itself known.

"Helm, All stop. Rig ship for Ultra quiet."

The CO of the Jimmy Carter was taking a huge risk.

The Seawolf class sub was doing what it always did. Penetrating the escort screen to get close to the enemy and destroy them.

The huge sub was shallow as the US sub fleet recognized its advantages were multiplied by the ambient noise up at the surface.

Three Chinese destroyers were less than five thousand yards abeam of them and heading right over the top of the sub. The CO knew if he could hang here and let them zoof over the top, there was no way they could detect the firing once the sub was in the surface ship baffles.

The baffle is the sonar "dead zone" astern of a ship because own ships engines make enough noise to mask anything competing to be heard by the ships sonar.

And now that the Carter was Ultra quiet, she had shut off as much machinery as she dared to make herself a virtual hole in the ocean.

Of course if any crew member did something stupid like slam a hatch or drop a wrench on the deck, that sound would be transmitted right into the water and would be picked up by the Chinese ships. Or worse: the dipping sonar that the Chinese helicopters were deploying in a desperate attempt to locate the US subs. The fact that several US helo's were also in the area only added to the confusion.

"Make all tubes ready in all respects."

The Carter flooded down and equalized her tubes. All eight of the tubes held MK 48 torpedo's. The flooding down was the noisiest thing they would be doing. Until the REALLY noisy thing, the actual firing of the weapons.

The intent was to give the three destroyers a two shot spread each and keep two weapons for quick reaction in case a Chinese sub took exception to them blowing up their countrymen.

Course plans don't always work out.

The sound of the destroyers passing overhead and off a scant six hundred yards sent shivers up every back.

Twenty-seven agonizing minutes after the CO's initial call the Carter had drifted her way to firing position.

"Match final bearings and shoot!"

"Fire, tubes one, three, five, two, four and six."

"All units away, all units enabled!" "No!"

The Weps strangled out the last. "Unit in tube five has shut down!"

"Post launch tube five."

The litany was quick with the tension very high in control. The crew only had six minutes to wait for their weapons to finish the run to target. The enemy ships were very close.

"Torpedo in the water!"

Orders flew from the CO.

"Helm all ahead flank, cavitate!" Dive make your depth six hundred feet!" "Weps cut the wires." "Sonar where is that incoming unit?"

Men and women scrambled to obey orders or give status reports as required.

"Active unit bears 165, range four thousand yards."

That was close. Where had that shot come from? With the sub at a dead stop for the firing position, the vulnerability of the Carter was huge. The speed of the ship built very slowly as she cavitated her screw, which meant to thrash the water into a million noisy bubbles but in this case the sound didn't matter because the torpedo coming at them overrode the machinery noise problem.

An agonizing minute when there was no sound except for the "bleep, bleep, bleep of the active homing threat detector unit in control. The sub scrambled to build up speed to get out of harm's way but it wasn't working.

"Sonar!" "Range and Bearing?" the CO called over the open mic system to the most important position feeding him information.

"Unit bears 170, range three thousand." "Conn, Sonar, incoming weapon is classified a MK 32!"

"Son of a bitch!"

The swearing from the CO scared the shit out of the control room personnel. They all knew a MK 32 was an air dropped US torpedo from a helicopter. It was friendly fire incident.

The sub desperately tried everything it could to lose the US made weapon.

"Launch countermeasures!"

The hollow thud of the six inch launcher going off could be heard throughout the ship as the deck vibrated. The countermeasures put acoustic noise makers in the water, hoping to spoof the homing of the internal sonar as it searched for them.

The MK 32 is a fire and forget weapon. It has a set pattern and a slew of internal guidelines to follow. If it detects a target in front of it, the torpedo will lock on and destroy that target. Even if it's a friendly unit. Even through countermeasures.

"MK 32 is active, final pinging!"

"Dammit. Dive standby for emergency blow!"

In a last ditch effort, the Captain had the ship ready to pump thousands of pounds of compressed air into the ballast tanks to force out the water and propel the sub to the surface. The thought being the sudden shift upward of the target would fool the incoming fish.

"Chief of the Watch Emergency surface the ship!"

The sailor flipped the switches and the huge rush of air made every ear plug. The sub rose the final two hundred feet to the surface in seconds, with the surface alarm klaxon wailing.

The sub was on the surface when the torpedo exploded beneath them.

The hammer blow warped the hull plating and caused two huge cracks in the people tank almost six feet long each. The explosion also caused the main engine shaft to be knocked out of alignment by a bare half inch.

That was enough as the reactor shut down and the shaft locked and stopped turning.

Emergency lighting came on as the power in the sub flickered and died.

The nightmare continued as the reports of flooding came into control. No power, no engine and water coming in. This was as bad as it gets.

"XO, take a party aft, open the aft escape hatch and abandon ship. COB take the mid ships hatch. Weps- forward. Everyone abandon ship!"

The seldom practiced event was a cluster fuck in the dark and confusion of the chaos below decks.

Of the Carter's, 145 person crew, only eighty managed to get to the deck. The sea was swamping the rapidly sinking sub as water poured into her lower holds and compartments.

The fires and explosions from the Chinese ships could be seen in the distance as the torpedo spread Carter had directed at the enemy hit home.

Now sailors from both navies were going into the waters of the Pacific.

USS Jimmy Carter slid beneath the waves and sunk to be crushed in the abyss of the Pacific twenty-two minutes after being struck. Less than thirty of her crew were recovered. The Weps was the only officer.

The Chinese merchant ships panicked at the ferocity of the American attack. About half tried to swing back west towards home but all they did was run right into the Hawaii and Guam based contingent of US subs waiting for them.

Bremerton, Lajolla, Chicago, Topeka, Cheyenne, Oklahoma City, Columbia, Tucson, all aligned themselves as the targets came on running at high speed. Since they had no defensive measures the outcome was easy to determine.

Five of the giant ships broke apart as the subs fired multiple torpedoes at them. More than one CO watched in horror thru the periscope as the containers slipped off and sank as the ships went beneath the waves. The Commanding Officers had been briefed on what the containers actually held. They knew thousands, hell- tens of thousands, of men were dying out there. But then again so were thousands of Americans on land right now.

A flight of F-35's struck the seven fleeing Hanjin ships. The missiles impacting the waterline area of the ships causing more than one to capsize. Two more subs got a merchant apiece as the US victory was almost complete. Captain Kosinski on Bremerton got the last of the westward merchants with the final free weapons he had available. The subs had to keep two shots in reserve for the last fifteen Chinese attack subs lurking to their north.

The second group of the running merchant ships tried to close with the last remaining Chinese cruiser and three destroyers. The muddle was packed very tightly as they attempted to put on speed to get out of the area.

The Zumwalt and her friends concentrated on the warships as they fled. The destroyer only carried eight anti-ship missiles and she was perilously close to being out of ammo. But she managed to hit two more ships and leave those targets dead in the water. The Johnson got another and the Monsoor took out the last two while sustaining some serious damage herself.

The carrier planes took the final blows on the Chinese. Flights from the Stennis and the Reagan re armed and dropped anti-ship missiles on the merchants. The last explosions left the ocean filled with flaming wreckage and bodies. Some Chinese helo's fled the scene to God knows where. They didn't have enough gas to get to land and the last three tried to attack the US fleet to devastating consequences. The attack runs lasted all of three minutes before the stout ZF-12's were knocked from the skies. The major battle was over.

Admiral Mooney quickly scanned the paper his aide handed him. *Thank God!*

"Madam President, the battle of the Garbage Patch is over. We have some mop up work with what we estimate are twelve remaining Chinese submarines, but we think that the rest of the resupply ships and subs are destroyed, as well as a majority of the Chinese Navy." His quiet voice was hard to hear in the crowded room.

"Thank you Admiral. I want everyone to know that the Navy has won a critical victory today. Without their sacrifices the enemy may have been able to land more troops on our soil and prolong this war. Well done!" Sharon embraced the small man warmly. Scattered clapping and cheers broke out around the room. General Graham had a huge smile on his face as he hugged Paul Marino and then Libby.

Sharon kept receiving congratulations from everyone like she had fought in the battle. She knew she had not but yet she felt as if she had. She felt every loss: The four Wasp class helo carriers. Jimmy Carter, Florida, Cowpens, the USS Momsen and maybe even the Monsoor. Other ships were damaged. The Vinson herself had a huge hole in her. They'd lost a few more planes and helo's today. Men and women had died out their today because she had ordered them to war. She had allowed the command structure to develop the best plan they could and then they had executed the orders. That was all anyone could ask of her. That was all she could ask of the people under her. And this time it had worked out.

But the government had another huge battle to get on with. And one that would be even more costly in terms of lives and would seal the fate of both countries.

CHAPTER THIRTEEN

'The code for the next six hours is the third ingredient in the Big Mac jingle," Noah informed Rammy.

He was reading from a list of small code phrases and words they'd used over the last four days to ensure that the people following their texts could ensure it had come from them.

Their group text numbers were becoming huge as more and more people pinged them back. The first twenty-four hours had been assessing the "Americanness" of those strange numbers. The two used various tricks to assure themselves they were dealing with US forces. Or at least someone who knew hell of a lot about American culture.

The tests were simple, sometimes childish things: "What's a Pirates favorite letter? "Aaarrr"

"Complete this phrase: "Home, Home on the range…" If the respondent didn't come back with, "Where the deer and the antelope play" within a few seconds, the number was blocked.

They even had to pull the Seals away from killing duties to help. In the end they had good codes, good intel and orders to help coordinate the land battle and had finally managed to convince DC to shut down 'Google" as a website. Even the map function was aiding the Chinese. They couldn't have them googling the answer to "What number is associated with Ketchup?" (Heinz 57). The manageable group text was to eighteen hundred or so cell phones which they were pretty certain belonged to Americans.

"Lettuce it is", Rammy told him. She looked back at Noah. *I hope I look better than that,* she thought.

It was past midnight on the 7th, no 8th of June now. The city was very quiet tonight- Seal asshole number one came into the office with a new scalp wound. The team only had four members left alive. The rest were all injured to some degree or another. Both of the civilians knew that without the Seals they would have long since been dead but that didn't mean they had to like the way the special ops sailors treated them. The Seals thought of the civilians as stupid cattle as far as Rammy was concerned. They'd said as much to them. It made for some awkward exchanges as the Seals would fight off a Chinese push to kill them and then berate the pair for some offense. The Lieutenant had bad news and worse news: "The Chinese got the last drone drop of ammo and food. Won't matter though. The Chin are massing to do a sweep. Maybe start in the morning

The pair of them hadn't left the office in days. Make shift meals, make shift showers and make shift sleeping was all they were getting. People needed to know what was going on and they were serving as the vital link between the knots of information and the players involved. She had even directly texted the President of the United States. Generals? They were on a first name basis now.

"I think tomorrow", Rammy texted to Oakport trucking. "We have good intel on where the Chinese are and they seemed to be heading right for you guys. Everyone needs to be lettuce," she typed incongruously. Noah chuckled softly.

Lettuce indeed.

He hoped his mom was okay. Funny he felt that she was in more danger right now than himself or his father. A brief message from the Admiral thru his mom had said he and the Ohio had come thru the Garbage Patch battle okay. The Tridents and the fleet were massing for a new mission, but they first needed to know what was happening back on American soil. Admiral Mooney had him using a back door family gram and text chain to communicate with Ohio and Admiral Kollmansburger.

Why in the hell had mom chosen to accompany the Admiral and General Tedesco as they went after the Seattle based Chinese as they came south?

But the young man knew why she had done it. Just as he knew why his dad was at sea right now and he was stuck in San Francisco. Someone had to!

"Where are the Oakport people?" Rammy asked.

"They are on the top of Adams peak, or actually the bluffs leading up to the peak." Noah looked at the map the desk held.

Quinru California

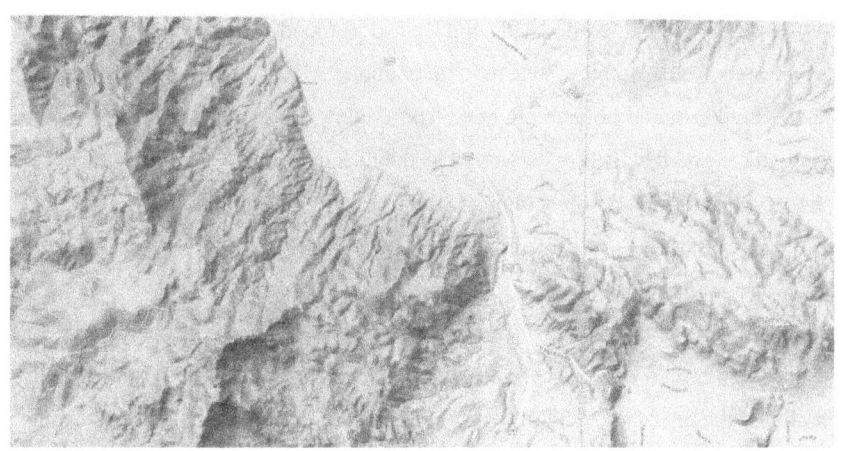

Reno and the California/Nevada border area along I-80 and 395 was shown in detail.

Sun Valley was north of the city itself as the 80 and the 395 made a tee through the Biggest Little City on earth. The area around the 395 was flat and fertile as the road followed a natural valley as it bent north and west like a lazy "7" some five-mile north of the target city. The valley itself was only ten or so miles wide and was surrounded on both sides by two large peaks: Adams and State Line. Both of those mountains funneled rain water and snow melt down to a small creek that fed Pyramid Lake to the east. The small town of Doyle was at the top of the twenty-mile long valley and that little town served as the turning point to the Sierra depot facility proper. The mountains surrounding the valley had no more snow clinging to the tops near the bluffs and the folded ravines that dominated the landscape. The bottom land was green to dry brush, this late towards summer.

Oakport and the civilians had been shuttling Marines and Army units the last three days as the Chinese had been forced by the Dre and Smith's landslide to swing south of the highway. The enemy paralleled the big roadway until the frontage road they were on coupled back into the 395 highway near Washoe City. But they were delayed by at least four days. And the grouping of the Chinese forces turned out to be a cluster fuck according to Andre. The whole mess of them, nearly five hundred thousand men and vehicles had spent three days lounging by a lake south of them. From what Dre reported to Noah and Rammy anyway.

Now, Dre and his five hundred civilians were attached to a Marine regiment and they were manning the bluffs near Adams Peak, some sixty miles away from the Chinese.

Noah knew the Generals, Nethercot, Lemonge and Whitworth, had very *carefully* picked their ground. They'd had to. The two agents in San Francisco had listened in while the Generals and the National Command Authority had debated about where to meet the Chinese.

This battle was going to determine most things in the war. If the Chinese succeeded in getting close to the Army depot, the DC people might have no option but to use a small nuc to avoid the enemy from getting the stores of materiel at the facility.

But the use of that weapon on American soil by an American President might cause the people to rethink who they wanted to be the President. The Chairman of the Joint Chief's had also argued that he felt the Chinese leader would not be so stupid as to bring his whole army to the depot. He would leave them blocking the entrances and let a smaller group of technicians bring the weapons up to working conditions. After the nuc went off he reasoned that it would leave a zone of inhabitability where no one could get close to the Chinese. Left alone, they would kill every American on the west coast and dig in for the long inevitable charge of the rest of the US armored divisions from back east and the south.

And who knew how that was likely to turn out?

Certainly not Rammy or Noah. Better to win right here in Sun Valley. This was the spot where the Chinese had to funnel and attack the Americans, not the other way around.

"I hope those guys stay safe in this battle," Rammy noted the look of concern on Noah's face.

The young man shrugged. 'Everyone is going to be in danger. The Chinese are getting ready to come after us here, you know."

"I want you to cut out. One of us should survive this. You need to get back to your mom and dad."

Noah was silent a minute. "No." "Not without you."

The woman smiled, grateful for the support. "I guess we are going down with the ship.'

He winced at the metaphor.

"Tell everyone in the next text that the weather for the next two days is going to be optimal. And don't forget the lettuce."

The woman started thumb typing.

"Sir, the report ends with "Don't forget the lettuce." The messenger dropped the cell phone on the seat of the H2 hummer Bo was using as an office/bedroom/tank buster.

"The Americans are just using the code words again, Su, that is all."

Bo slumped in the seat. He was *so* tired. So were his men. The past two weeks had been a night mare of furtive cat naps and hit and run attacks. His plan had succeeded. To an extent. He had gotten almost four hundred eighty thousand troops landed in the US and to this area. Four hundred with him and the other eighty thousand massing near Susanville. *They were so close!* They had weapons and transportation to achieve the objective. They had anti air missiles in what he hoped were enough numbers to blunt the American advantage. His men had enough anti-tank weapons to negate that piece. He had numerical superiority in the local area and with the actual technician force coming down from Seattle.

He knew it still might not be enough.

The Americans had surprised him with the landslide and the air drop. His southern California forces were setting up their air defense missile systems when the Screaming Eagles had landed. He figured the timing was a coincidence, but it galled him. The first operational radar they'd manage to erect and get operational near Washoe city showed the Osprey's and the Globe masters flying serenely away from the area while they could do nothing about it.

His men had taken only eighteen hours to setup the initial HJ-8 quad launchers in the shipping containers during the initial invasion. But they'd been relatively fresh then.

Now it took them three days to get the mobile launchers up the small mountain track and connected to the portable generators and radar units. Sixty launchers were spread around the lake near Washoe City ready for the battle. The other twenty were in the western edge of the battle filed with his Seattle based troops. The small town of Susanville was at the exit of 395 as it disgorged into the valley where Honey lake sat next to Herlong and the Sierra Army depot.

Three critical days where the US had managed to beat him to the spot. The enemy had figured out his objective and had brought a considerable force structure to ground. Bo and Zi had put heads together and figured one hundred thousand, based on the radar returns of the transport planes.

Three days of screaming and yelling and dodging calls from Shanghai had left Bo exhausted. He'd been avoiding the calls from Fei because they were a distraction. Simply speaking about what he was doing took away the focus he needed to make the plan a reality. He knew the ruling council was getting anxious. The chaos engulfing China had reached a crescendo and the defeat of the Naval re enforcements was a huge set back but...

Bo knew that the chances of the Chinese Navy defeating its US counterpart were not very good. He'd always considered the re supply by that flotilla to be a low probability. He also considered the order of battle with the US fleet and the overall military in the United States.

He estimated the US was running out of torpedoes and planes and missiles.

The sums went thru his head: 1400 operational US or carrier based strike planes. 5,230 cruise missiles of all varieties on or near US soil or carried by ships, planes and subs. 730

torpedoes carried on the US subs, helo's, and ships. How much of that was left? *That was the critical question.*

The next batch of merchants should be massing off of Shanghai even now, ready to break for the US coast. Not in a convoy, no. A jailbreak of zig zagging ships. Of the sixty older, smaller vessels ready for the transit, his plan called for half of them to be sunk. But if thirty ships landed along the US western states, and he could get the Army depot's riches, he would be ready when the American armored divisions made the trek from Texas and Georgia to confront him. He was betting the US reserve of torpedoes was not large enough to sink all of them. He was betting the US didn't have enough anti-ship missiles left to sink them. Short of a suicide attack, there was no way the Americans could get them all. Some of them would get thru and bring needed men and material to the area.

By then he hoped to have the first crops harvested for the people, while sheltering the New China populace in the remnants of the American cities.

So he was not talking to Fei. Nor was he telling his men of the naval defeat. They didn't need that distraction from him. They had to concentrate on the task at hand. Fighting their way up the 395.

He moved off the seat and out to drink some water and sit at the camp table setup by his aides. Maps of the local area were spread around. He could guess that the US commanders were doing exactly the same thing right now: trying to guess how the battle would progress.

Speed and timing, the whole thing came down to those two factors, he thought for the millionth time.

"Su, get ready to start the orders for the deployment," he called to the messenger loitering nearby. 'Where is Zi?"

"He is personally passing on the rotation schedule for the radar units, Comrade General."

No doubt he was. That was the most critical part of the timing. They only had eight stations, no-nine, with the one north west of them. They couldn't be on at the same time for the duration of the battle. Just like the air raids at the docks, Bo was certain the enemy would strike at the radar units as they operated. It was too tempting a target for the HARM weapons for them not to. High altitude, Anti-Radar Missile; he was sure the US had plenty of those.

A last look at the map and the man started giving out the assignments. More and more messengers arrived to begin texting out the Chinese movements.

General Graham, Wellington Thomas, Paul, Libby and Admiral Mooney all had a working lunch with the President on Monday, the 10th of June, 2022. The executive dining room was set for just this kind of occasion: an evolving US government response to a lengthy situation or crises. In this case the impending battle with the Chinese.

Two days ago, the table was almost the scene of Armageddon.

***

The Russians had tried to steal the Ukraine while the attention of the world was focused on the far east.

Not content with taking huge chunks of territory along their former border with China, Putin had tried to sneak two divisions into the rest of the Ukraine from his salient that the former Soviet state had squeezed out in 2014.

The US had scrambled to arrange its response while the major players got some lunch and dinner. They finally called Putin and Sharon let him have it.

"Mr. President, I am ready to end the world right now!" She put every ounce of her frustration, worry and rage at the Chinese and the Russians into that almost gleeful yell.

"Madam President, what are you taking about and why are you screaming at me?"

"Fuck you, asshole!" "You have one hour to move those tanks back from the Donetsk area or I will Nuc Moscow."

Putin chuckled. "Madam President, you are in no position to dictate to me where we grab territory, not while the Chinese are at your throats."

"You know Vlad, you are right. I don't have the time or patience to negotiate with you. I just have time to end the world." Sharon looked up to get a signal from the Air Force liaison.

"That interruption you are getting Mr. President, is a call from Colonel Gagonov, the Moscow Air Defense Chief. You should take that." She put her hand over the phone and breathed deeply. Everyone in the room was silent and pale. They'd agreed to this but it was very dangerous.

A few silent minuets went by. Putin came back on the line furious. "You crazy bitch, you blew up my dacha!?!"

"Yes I did. And I am crazy. Ready to start the nuclear war? Because I am." Thomas felt that switching to calm at this point would help confuse the dictator and Sharon maintained calm even though she wanted to continue screaming and yelling. *It felt so good!*

Putin spluttered and threatened, while stalling. He wasn't sure if it was a bluff.

"Vlad, I just signed an order changing US currency over to military scrip. Do you know what that means?" The negative response got a smile from her that the man couldn't see. "This is my area of expertise, see. As Treasury Secretary, I know how the globally connected economy works. The US dollar is the world reserve currency. Every bank in Russia has a substantial amount of money in good old US greenbacks in their vaults. Well, not really in physical form, it is just electronic sums now. Point is, anyone who has the majority of their wealth tied up in US denominated assets is now going to have to come to the US government to get that money exchanged." Sharon waited while that sank in for Putin.

"Yeah, all that money you have in Switzerland? It's in US dollars. Poor Vlad. I'm sure someone told you that the strong US dollar was a great investment and that cash was king, but twenty billion? That's too much liquidity."
A deep breath got this next line out.

"I think we have just enough bombs to take out both China and Russia at the same time, but you and I will both be gone, so who cares if a few stray cities in Siberia escape instant death?"

Putin was stunned. This was not the response his advisors had told him the weak Americans were capable of.

"You got forty- nine minutes left to move those tanks or face the death of us all."
Sharon broke the connection.

She kept her head in her hands mostly while the next minutes played out. Libby was gently rubbing her back which she appreciated.

"They're moving east!"

The aide announced it in a clear loud voice, short of the deadline.

"Wellington, stay on him. Tell him, I haven't yet decided when to implement the scrip order." The President told the head of the NSA while everyone else celebrated.

***

"Madam President, SF 1 is reporting that Zhenge He is making major calls and texts from the area south of Reno." Both Thomas and Graham were looking at the reports and eating soup. The Chairman gave the assessment. "That probably means tonight or tomorrow."

That wasn't a surprise to any of them.

Sharon grimaced. "What's the code word for tomorrow?"

"The first one is: The Founding Father with the most musical ability," Graham glanced at the text.

"Hamilton," Paul Marino supplied while everyone else furrowed brows.

"Oh yeah, good Paul," The President smiled at him.

"General, are we ready?"

Stedman Graham nodded while sitting at the dining room table. "We are madam President. General Whitworth is in position with the airborne forces and some civilians and Guard unit's, in the northern part of the killbox ready for the Chinese troops. He hasn't had much time to prepare so that is going to be tough fighting. "Lemonge and Nethercot are going to be on either peak, while General Atkinson with the Big Red One and the Kansas people are deployed east to keep the Chinese from swinging around the trap in that direction."

The President could see the plan laid out on the maps the military provided. She thought the little red and blue dashed lines that indicated positions should have had more resemblance to the actual people who would be manning those lines.

"What about the Air Force?" Sharon asked without looking for the liaison.

"Ma'am everything we have combat ready will fly," the aide told her. "And I do mean everything."

Sharon wanted to ask what he meant by that but she decided to keep silent. No need in bringing up the fact that they could only field about two hundred strike fighters. They had other attack planes but they would not do well in the missile environment the Chinese had already shown they could muster during an attack. If they couldn't knock out those launchers, the numerical superiority of the Chinese would overwhelm the US troops.

"Admiral?"

A glance at Mooney and the trim Admiral nodded his head. "Our ships and subs are in position, but without lased targets, it's going to be inaccurate fire. We have some TOMCOMM capability but it is limited to what Nethercot could bring with him."

A scowl marked the President's face. *It's what they didn't tell you.*

"Stedman, tell me the rest."

The Chairman of the Joints Chiefs took a dollar from Wellington Thomas. He'd won the bet on whether the woman would want to know the bad side of things as well. *Sucker bet, Thomas hasn't dealt with her like I have these last weeks. She wants to know*, Graham thought.

"Madam President, we have several problematic areas for this battle. One is Susanville." A sip of coffee helped. "General Tedesco and Admiral Kollmansburger have been trailing the Chinese on the way south and they had to swing around to get into position in front. The Joint base McChord forces are being tasked with protecting the front gate to the Sierra Depot. "The lead elements of the command structure are there but not the rest of the troops."

"Not much of a General without someone to boss around," Paul said in a voice that should have been quieter.

"Alice Tedesco is the toughest fighter this side of Audie Murphy, son," the man shot back. "She will do what she needs to because she has to."

Sharon nodded to that.

"Two, we are running out of ammo or we didn't have that much to begin with, Stedman reminded her. "Our plan is to run the Chinese into a kill box, here," he indicated the valley that followed the 395 highway on the way to Sierra. "Don't make it much of a box if we can't stop the Chinese here because we don't have shots for the few tanks we have." The southern drawl came out when the man was stressed.

That was bad, the President could feel that coming off in waves from her General.

"And three, we only have a limited number of artillery pieces and those are deployed on the heights. I think we are going to be limited to three or four big barrages." Silence greeted that.

Graham drilled on. "Once that is over it is going to come down to hand to hand fighting."

Too many if's in this battle, Sharon thought. *If we can take out those launchers, we will have air superiority and the other strike planes can come into play. If we can stop the advance with the tanks and shells. If we can get to the field with enough troops. If...*

She took a deep breath. "That's fine, General, I understand." She stood and everyone stood with her. 'We are at a critical junction in our history and in our fight. I know that every American will do his or her duty to the utmost of their capabilities. We can ask no more."

She paused. "I will have a speech ready for tonight for the troops and the American people, check?" When there were no questions she said "Thank you." She left to go find Coleman. She needed to be close to someone right now.

The morning sun was just giving way to the first clouds of the day around 12:30 pm island time. Walt and Kemo paused in the dorm room at the University of Hawaii, Manoa campus to linger before going back out. The men had had two down days away from combat. Nickers and Zelazny wanted whatever remained of their fighting forces to be in top shape for this push.

The last days were a blur of killing and fighting for everyone. The Chinese had been pushed back to the area near Diamond Head. The ancient crater held the last thirty thousand or so Chinese troops out of two hundred fifty thousand or so to start with. Well over half a million enemy troops, natives, tourists and US military members laid dead on their ruined home isle.

The bitter fighting came down to this: Did the last twenty thousand US civilians and military people have anything left? Did the Chinese?

Downtown was a waste land. Waikiki was as well. Thousands of homes were burned or destroyed outright.

Nickers had ordered the rotating down time while continuing to press the Chinese. *They couldn't have any more missiles, right?* Walt figured it wouldn't matter how many they had left because the last US tank and helo had been shot down or blown up three days ago.

After a lukewarm shower, small meal and a solid night's sleep, Walt had gone over to the command tent to see if anyone had any news on the rest of the world.

Zelazny and Nickers were head down over a map trying to coordinate something. A brief nod and smile from his old shipmate, the Admiral, was all the acknowledgement Walt got. He didn't mind that, the man had things to do. A pale, shaken Army Second Lieutenant was on the radio talking or texting to someone in San Francisco, as far as Walt could see.

"Eh, Brah, Howzit with the rest of da kine?"

A mirthless laugh escaped the man. "You mean with the rest of the war and not the forgotten island where we are?"

Walt laid a hand on the man's arm gently. "Dey tryin dey best, brah."

The man nodded ashamed he'd spoken so bitterly. "We've been nothing but a holding action here." Seattle/Tacoma, Long Beach/LA/San Diego, and Oakland/San Francisco are all fighting back. Civilian resistance groups are rising to fight for their homes." "Cities are pretty tore up and there have been a couple million killed." The Lieutenant hauled in a breath and went on, steadier. "Been a big naval battle out near the coast of Portland a few days ago. Big US victory and we still lost ten ships and twenty planes." But, they did sink most of the Chinese fleet and prevent some more troops from landing is what I'm told."

"That's great!" Walt told the man. 'We gon' get some help here now?"

"Maybe. Gonna be a big land battle tomorrow or the next day in California or Nevada. The government needs everything for another mission or two." The bitterness crept back in. The brass is trying to get a destroyer or two to be detailed to help us." A jerk of his chin over his shoulder told Walt what the Admiral and General were trying to do on the radio. Well, Nickers was a four-star Admiral in charge of the Western US forces, he should be able to get something for Hawaii. *If they had anything to give him.*

Admiral Nickers approached Walt. "Master Chief, how are you holding up?"

"Fine, sir. Le'ahi is gon be tough nut to crack."

Nickers smiled at Walt's use of the Hawaiian name for Diamond Head crater. 'We just need to keep them attached to the crater for another couple of days. DC has promised us help."

Tsuomo was grateful for that. He didn't want to have to charge up the top of those slopes to force the Chinese from the tops. *Kamehameha may have done it but I aint no king!*

He bid good bye to the Admiral and went back to find Kemo. The pair were due to relieve some others on the Kalanianaole highway tonight. Walt snickered as he remembered some of his white friends' attempts at pronouncing the name of the highway. "Unpronounceable Hawaiian word that begins with a K" was his favorite. He whistled on the way. He had a duty to do.

CHAPTER FOURTEEN

"Senior, can't sleep?" The CO asked Tommy as he wandered into control.

'Thought I'd give the COB a head call if he needs it", Speigal told Greene.

Members of Ohio's crew were all exhausted and keyed up and had taken to roaming the ship at all hours. The COB shook his head. "The Chop was just in and took care of me." The Chop being what they called the Supply Officer on board.

Speigal grunted. "Any idea how this is going to go, Captain?"

Greene grunted back, "We are going to have to wing it, Senior. We have no hard intel and no hard orders, other than "be at spot Delta at 0600 local on 10 June at launch depth ready for anything."

Tommy winced. Since the Navy and Army secured intel links had gone down they were getting as many orders from the text/family gram line as the regular broadcast. At least he knew the person on the other end of those texts.

The Captain looked at his Fire Control Team leader. "Senior do you know who the most musical founding father is?"

Tommy grinned in what felt like the first time in forever. "Alexander Hamilton, sir. We took Noah to see the play when they came to Seattle last year."

Greene nodded. "That was our assessment as well," he pointed at himself and the XO.

"Well, the Nav says we will be at Delta in a few hours, well ahead of the launch deadline, you better get some sleep." The CO was being proactive in assuring his crew got some shuteye so they would be at their best tomorrow.

"Conn, Radio, receiving eyes only flash traffic." The announcement jarred everyone in control. *A message for only the CO's eyes was a big deal, Tommy knew.* No way he could leave control until the CO had doled out whatever he would of the new news.

The aluminum clipboard had a cover that flipped up to conceal the message. Tommy noted the Seal of the ship on the cover as the CO signed and took the board.

He read the message with a frown and a then a smile.

Now Tommy was intrigued.

"Tommy, hand me the 1MC", Captain Greene asked him. Speigal grabbed the mic and pulled the cord over to the Captain's chair. All eyes were on the man.

"Men and women of the USS Ohio. I have message from the President of the United States," he said in loud, clear voice. The ships speaker boxes were piping the words all over the huge submarine. Even to the crew trying to sleep.

"My fellow Americans. Our nation stands tonight at the crossroads of history. Based on consultations with the Joint Chiefs and our intelligence services, we believe a large land battle will take place near Reno, Nevada between our forces and the invaders from China. I will be completely honest with you, in that despite our recent victory in the Pacific Ocean over the Chinese naval forces, our troops will be badly outnumbered and the outcome of the battle is very uncertain."

"I call upon every American to do his or her utmost to aid in our efforts, even if that aid is simply prayers. To our men and women waiting tonight on the edge of battle, I ask the most of all: The full measure of your devotion."

"The heroes of America's past are calling upon you now just as I do. There exists a direct line that runs from the frozen soldiers at Valley Forge to the defenders at Gettysburg. From the doughboys at the Somme, to the Screaming Eagles at Bastogne. From the men at Inchon and Chosen, to the grunts sweating at Khe Sanh, or the deserts of Iraq, that line points directly at you. This is a time that demands heroes."

I tell you now that no quarter will be given and none will be asked for. This fight is for the right of the United States to exist, not for high ideals or to prevent aggression. Not an inch of territory will be surrendered without blood being spilled. I ask of you what Roman mothers told their sons before going off to fight in their wars: Come back with your shield, or on it." "The fate of our nation hangs in the balance of your actions and I am proud to be your leader.

"May God bless us in our terrifying labors and grant us victory."

Greene paused a moment to let everyone wrap his or her heads around the President's words. He spoke solemnly into the mic. "We have a part to play in the coming battle. You have performed brilliantly over these past weeks and I know we will do our best to help the ground forces defeat the enemy. Stay focused and be ready. That is all." He handed the mic back to

Tommy to be hung up in the overhead clip. Speigal did so with silence. *Where was Lynn? Where was Noah? What were they doing?*

Lynn Speigal was at that moment digging a hole in the ground. The dark was full on around them but someone in the team had setup some portable lights and they were digging fire positions into the northern side of Honey lake. The semi dry lakebed was crusted over in the early summer heat but the ground gave way to mud a few feet down. The shovel made a "splurge" sound but she kept at it. They needed the holes.

The last ten days had been a crazy nightmare thrill ride that made her shudder when she thought of them.

Admiral Kollmansburger had been dead set against her accompanying his staff as they joined with General Tedesco as they battled the Chinese in Tacoma and down the highways first towards California and then the final turn East to Herlong. Lynn just ignored him and became one of his runners, ferrying messages to various commanders in the units accompanying the mobile rolling retreat. She'd seen more than one ambush as the Washington National Guard and the Oregon folks came together to defend their territories.

But the Chinese were relentless as they came on.

And now they were here at Sierra. A destination her son had figured out as a matter of fact. Funny, she was talking to him more by text that they had before the war. She laughed under her breath to think about that and then continued digging.

Ten other men and women were out prepping positions on Honey Lake this evening. Tedesco and K14 had been here for twenty-four hours, but the vast bulk of their forces were still on the move.

The artillery pieces and the few tanks they possessed were still on the Modoc line rail trail moving into position above the lake.

General Tedesco knew her business. The area around the army depot was dominated by the lake and the "Angels ridge". The Chinese on the march down had chosen to cut away from the 5 at Red Bluff and take the 36 over to Susanville. The General had broken off at Redding, north of the Chinese and swung the US troops around Lassen Peak on US 44. The narrow winding road joined back to the 395 north of the depot at a fly speck town called Brockman. The

Army had picked up an entire contingent of Hells Angels at Brockman. Thirty-five burly bikers with beards and guns and tattoos. Lynn thought anyone ever looked better in her life. They came from all over. Karlo and Thermo. Viewland and The Crossing. Small towns dotting the California Nevada line. Like the bikers, they just joined up in whatever vehicle they could run with. She didn't even know if they had weapons and ammo.

They must have because they were all sitting on the Angels Ridge right now waiting for the enemy and the rest of Tedesco's forces. The 395 highway bends around Honey lake as it passes near Sierra. The most direct route becomes Wendel road. That road follows the foothills and the lake and then dumps into the front door to the depot right at the Amadee Army airfield. But to get to the depot the Chinese were going to have to pass under the "angels ridge." The formation looked from the air like a person under a blanket trying to do a snow angel. A large central spine ran perpendicular to Wendel road with two flanking ridges standing out like arms.

The high ground provided the best clear view of the entire valley, especially the view back west towards Susanville. Tedesco had ordered the artillery up the Modoc Line trail to get to the ridge and establish the best field of fire they were going to get.

And to facilitate that fire, Lynn was digging holes on the lake where more men and women would try to stop the advance of the numerically superior Chinese. She dug deeper. *If it was Noah in the hole' I'd want it deep.*

Twenty minutes later the Colonel in charge of the Lake forces called them off. Lynn and her crew moved back by truck to the Depot, as men and women moved to occupy the fire positions. The Admiral was at the airfield in the command tent losing his mind.

"Do not leave this tent without my direct permission," he thundered.

Lynn said nothing.

Kollmansburger backed down. "Text SF1. Find out what's happening, if they have any orders from the President."

Lynn knew the President's speech had affected the man. *Not an inch of territory surrendered without blood being spilled.*

"Noah, K14 would like to know if there are any orders from DC? Oh, and Hamilton."

"Mom, I recognize your number and the code doesn't start until 0600 local." "DC says to expect the attack in the morning, with the bulk moving at first light. We are trying to coordinate support here so I am busy."

"You are okay, right?"

"Fine mom. Love you, gotta go. Stay safe!"

Noah Speigal was anything but safe. He looked up from his phone at his mother's text as the Seal died in the office. Rammy had brought the severely wounded man down from the roof top an hour ago. He'd bled out since they could do virtually nothing for sucking chest wounds...

The blood, gun oil and unwashed body smell all converged to make him gag.

Three left, he thought. *Maybe.*

Rammy Pak turned from the body to Noah with tears in her eyes. It was just past midnight in San Francisco. "We're not going to make it, are we?" Her voice cut through the young man.

He debated what to say and then went with the truth. "No, probably not. Best we can do is to keep texting out until they storm the place."

The woman nodded and bowed her head. She moved next to Noah. "I don't want to be alone right now."

Noah held her for a moment and then the two made their way back to the mats they'd been sleeping on the last few days. An hour of closeness was all they would get. The war would come calling after that.

General Graham took the paper straight from the printer. The tech eyed the Chairman as he read the report. "Okay, Lieutenant, I'll take this to her." The young woman squeaked out her thanks.

The Situation Room was again the place where Sharon had chosen to ride out the battle. It offered her the most in the way of up to date information but little in the way of psychological comfort. *This place needs some plants. Just something living to offset the gravity of what always happens in here,* she thought.

Her head came up as Graham approached. "The final tally is 541 planes total. Only 221 strike craft, Madam President."

That wasn't going to be enough, she knew.

Graham continued, "We did not get any planes off from the Indian Ocean Carriers. They had to back track to cover the raid on Putin's dacha, so those eighty are out."

"It had to be done, General. It's not your fault."

"Ma'am, we still have some tricks up our sleeves. We are at a disadvantage but we can still emerge victorious."

Sharon didn't know if he was trying to convince her or himself. A tech appeared next to them. "Madam President, General, the carriers are turning into the wind."

Just past three am. In DC and on the three Norfolk based carriers: Roosevelt, Truman and Eisenhower, which were now in the Gulf of Mexico, people were being awoken for their respective tasks. Pilots and support crews to launch the sorties, DC staffers to deal with the fallout one way or another.

The Stennis and the other three carriers in the Pacific were also ready to start operations. Their crews were luckier, they had less travel time so they got to sleep in an extra hour. Sharon didn't envy them the sleep. It was hard to come by for her. She figured the actual participants in the battles would be having a difficult time sleeping.

But she would be wrong about that. Andre Treadwell was sleeping like a baby. In that he was crying every hour and waking up. But he was getting some sleep. Exhaustion or "other" factors were preventing some of the Oakport people and the Marines of the 3/5 from getting some much needed shuteye.

When Dre woke he could see the "other" factors lying in twos on the mountain around him. *When it's your last night on earth its strange who you hook up with.* He rose slowly and silently as to not disturb anyone. He stepped over Amir with his arms wrapped around that Marine, Hill, he thought her name was. Tiny girl. Both looked to be smiling. Manny and Tito were off somewhere in this mess, he didn't know where right off the top of his head. Lardi too. A moment of sadness hit as he realized the rest of his friends were gone. Killed by the Chinese.

A figure was just visible on the bluff face, outlined in the dark sitting on some rocks. He went over. Sanchez.

"Mind some company?"

She shifted over so he could hook a hip on the boulder but said nothing. The two sat in companionable silence. Then pair had been working shoulder to shoulder since the Marines had landed in northern California. Dre marveled at her energy and sheer competence while they wrestled the troops and material into position. He had briefly considered asking her to sleep with him last night but he was just too tired. It wasn't loyalty to Tabatha, he realized. He was aware of the fragility of human life and the need to hold back the darkness as much as the next guy but he was so dog tired from hauling shit up this mountain he couldn't have gotten it up for Beyonce.

The combined civilian and Marine forces were situated on the top of some rocks near the summit of Adams Peak on the California side of the border. The troopers had dubbed these rocks "The Citadel" because of their commanding position along the 395 highway. The knob bulged out at the crux of the "7" shape the road took as it continued its merry way to Herlong and the Sierra Army depot.

Nethercot had setup his command tents in these rocks and trees and kept Sanchez and Orange Squad close due to her knowledge and possession of the TOMMCOM units. The bulk of his twenty-thousand man force was dug in along the ridges and gullies, protecting their artillery pieces. Guns that the men and women had broken their backs on hauling up hiking trails over the last three days. The boxes of shells were stacked neatly next to the guns as they had to be close when the barrages started. No resupply possible since Sierra didn't carry that much ammo for the howitzers. They had plenty of bullets though, which was cold comfort for Dre.

Still he would rather be here than with the three thousand man blocking force along the 395/70 junction about five miles to the south. Nethercot was afraid that the Chinese could flank them around the little town of Chilcoot-Vinson. If they managed to work past the blockers the enemy could come at them from the west after going thru the trees and up the actual slopes of Adams peak. That whole deal had a "Custer's last stand" feel to Dre. Not that the President's speech had given them any leeway. *Not an inch of territory surrendered without blood being spilled.* Dre had turned green at that part last night.

"You scared," Sanchez asked softly.

"Yep."

She snorted and he could tell she was smiling. "How come you didn't ask me to hook up last night?" Again her voice was soft.

 Instead of answering, Dre asked back, "How come you didn't ask me?"

"Too tired, she said. I might have managed it if Denzel was here, but sex before a battle just keys me up too much."

It was Dre's turn to smile. "That's God's little joke on the universe: sex for women is a charge up. Sex for men is a drain."

Dre knew all about the exchange of Chi between men and women it seemed to her. *He is a good man.*

The warm moonless night was almost over. Both Dre and Sanchez watched Miller and Duarte part with a kiss after waking up below them about thirty yards.

Miller and that boy? Dre thought the young man from Oklahoma was cool and all, but he thought Miller might have been with Smith. *Huh.*

"I got some word from the advanced scouts. Can't seem to get ahold of SF1. Chinese have been up since midnight assembling down south. Looks like a couple hours before they get here." Sanchez gave the report without much inflection or emotion.

"We should get them up now. Give everyone a chance to eat and then shit right before it starts," she told Dre.

"Yep," he replied.

She slid off the boulder and offered him a hand. Dre grunted as he stood. "Hey. If we live, would you like to get a cup of coffee?"

"I'd like that a lot."

Man and woman made their way to the tents to get Wilkins and Collins and Armster. Although they were already up and alerted the same as Sanchez. In ones and twos, the command structure made its way to the largest tent on the mountain.

The Army tent smelled of canvas and unwashed bodies. Portable desks and chairs were setup along with a larger table. A large scale map was taking up the bulk of the surface area. The ubiquitous lines and shapes representing the Chinese and US positions were scrawled over the map. The glow of computer screens and a few battery powered electric lamps gave a greenish tinge to everything.

Nethercot and his staff, four big bodied Colonels largest among them, were arrayed along one side of the table. The other side held the officers and blue armband wearing civilians that would direct this fight. Dre and Sanchez stood to one side while the General gave his orders.

"We have drones in the air and the scouts all agree that the Chinese are mobilizing. The distance to Lake Washoe is thirty-seven miles, so the lead elements will arrive at 0730 or so." The General paused while his XO confirmed Sanchez plan to feed and relieve the line troops.

Nethercot took up again. "The big question in this is air support. If we can't stop them, or we can't get them clumped together for our air to ground strike packages to be effective, then it's going to be bad. That is assuming of course we can get some planes to survive the Chinese missile barrage that is likely to come…" The man trailed off.

Too many unknowns, thought Dre. Sanchez had a similar look on her face.

"What about the TOMCOMM, General?" Lieutenant Wilkins asked into the silence.

The Marine grimaced. "LINK 11 is down. We have lost contact with SF 1 so we can talk DC but not the ships and subs that are supposed to be out there." "I'm literally phoning up Lemonge and General Tedesco and Whitworth." As soon as I get comms with the firing platforms I will move on the missiles."

A grumbling came with that. In order to make effective use of the missiles they had to be able to coordinate with the platforms firing the birds and the units that needed the help. That was going to be difficult with the battlefield spread out like it was.

"Listen up people!" "I will deal with the communication problem. I will get you targets, but you have to be ready to direct the missiles as they come."

The General paused and looked at his aide. "Colonel Timms?"

The large man stood even straighter. "Sir, ladies and gentlemen, we have placed the markers as indicated on your maps."

Dre pulled his out of his jacket pocket. The 395 and the valley were shown with range markers set out at distances put in as dots. The markers were the key points where the artillery pieces and the tanks all had sighted in for the coming battle. The markers were little mile posts every one could use to detail fire missions for the guns as the Chinese came on. The hope was they Marines could use the markers as points for the missiles. If. *If they could contact the fleet and let them know when to fire,* Dre thought. He glanced at Sanchez. She was the one with the most experience with the new unit and the technology. The Oakport team had lased targets for Smith but Sanchez had actually controlled the missiles inflight. That made her valuable. Wilkins and Sanchez got some extra love from Colonel Timms and the General.

The General finished up and concluded with this thought. "You all heard the President last night. Our orders are clear. Trust the man or woman next to you and kill the enemy. Good luck."

The troopers left the tents. Dawn was a hint coming from the east.

CHAPTER FIFTEEN

Lin Wei Bo was already exhausted. He'd only slept a few hours and the call to start the mobilization was at midnight- nearly six hours ago. The day was dawning bright and cloudless. The 10th of June was normally warm in this area he knew. The tops of the Sierra still had snow but this part had been bone dry for a month. *That's why the depot was put out here,* he thought. Dry and cold made for better storage for the tanks.

His Humvee was a looted civilian version of the military vehicle and was very big and it sucked gas. Fuel that was in short supply. But they had enough gas for this last part he knew. Colonel Zi was in the back seat next to him as the driver slowly crawled along the 395 shoulder. His car rode about one fourth of the way back in the column. The Chinese were worried about mines and traps on the highways. The forces coming up from southern California and the troops from Seattle had all been subject to the same hit and run attacks as his troops, so they crawled along until Bo gave the word to accelerate.

The two messengers in the last row seats were juggling multiple sat phones, cell phones and radio handsets. Bo knew he couldn't get a perfect formation deployment but it was critical to get it as close as possible. He wanted to hit the Americans at four sites as near to simultaneous as he could get.

But that was tricky with this many cars and trucks. Over twenty thousand vehicles were jammed onto four lanes of the 395 highway moving north at twenty miles an hour. The first five thousand or so would sprint ahead at Bo's signal to try to drive straight to Doyle along the normal route to the Depot. The next three quarters of Bo's massed forces would hit a point and peel off in two directions: one group towards the north east and State line peak to try to swing around the US troops dug into the area west of Pyramid lake and the second would attack due east towards the Adams peak area. The fourth group was the Susanville forces from Seattle and they would drive directly for Sierra and its stores of tanks and artillery.

But they were vulnerable now, Bo knew. Crawling along the highway the mass of trucks and cars would be a tempting target for any American attack plane. *But we are ready for that!*

"Order the radars to operational mode. Track the incoming US planes. Be ready to launch missiles." Bo gave the order to Zi who relayed it to the messengers. The young officers were honored to be riding with the General into battle.

"Commence Operation Magic Tapestry," Bo told his aide.

Zi practically shouted the order to the Officer on the phone. Bo could just make out the tail end of the first group start to accelerate away from the rest of the cars which maintained their speed for now. The Chines passed a sign that read "Sierra Safari Zoo." *Who would put a zoo put in the middle of nowhere?* He thought was broken by a gigantic sonic boom.

The air was dry and clear from Dre's point of view. The sun would be in their eyes for a bit while it rose but that should only last thirty minutes or so. They had a great view and could see the Chinese trucks barreling up the road below them. *The group ahead is going faster. Good strategy, get them through the kill box quickly he thought.* The cars were approaching forty miles an hour it appeared to Dre.

"Can we hit them if they are going that fast?" He asked Sanchez with concern.

"No we cannot. We have to get them stopped."

At that second a huge boom reverberated over the valley.

"What the fuck?"

"I guess DC has called everyone out to play," Sanchez looked at her phone. "That plane is one of ours!"

The two searched the skies for the noisemaker but they could only catch glimpses. Another loud double boom indicated the plane cracking the sound barrier. Wilkins wriggled over to their position.

He grinned at Sanchez and Dre. "Aurora!"

President Stallings and General Graham did have all their toys out. The Aurora was America's newest secret plane. The black, sleek machine used experimental technology to achieve some nearly impossible speeds. Mach six was the rumored top end. Dre could believe that. The plane swept along the valley right over the Chinese at a thousand feet. So fast it was blur. The distinctive thrum of its pulse detonation engine and the donuts on a rope contrail were the only markers of its passage. Two missiles streaked skyward from far to the south towards the blended wing plane.

The radios near Sanchez blared with the pilot's voice: "Darkstar is gone!"

The plane took it vertical and poured on the liquid methane fuel. The anti-air missiles were no match. At ninety thousand feet the plane leveled off and watched the pursuing missiles falter and drop away.

The Marines and civilians had thought that the plane was through but not so…

Again the plane rocketed down towards the Chinese, pulling fantastic gees as it cracked the sound barrier and windows from Doyle to Susanville to Reno.

"Holy shit!" Dre was impressed.

Sanchez was not that thrilled. "Yeah it sounded great, but he only got two missiles fired at him. I was hoping the Chinese would be less disciplined and cook off twenty or so at the ghost."

That was not to be. Aurora went back to Area 51 and the mothballs.

"Jesus that looks like the 15 on the way to Vegas on a Friday evening!" Dre pointed at the 395.

Despite the interruption, the Chinese were hauling up the highway at dangerous speeds- as fast as they could go as tightly packed as the cars running from LA to Sin City ready for a weekend of gambling. Sanchez had done that run a few times. *Eighty miles an hour and three lanes packed from Barstow to the strip.*

Off to their right an artillery gun went off. The boom sounding soft after the Aurora. The shell impacted the line of cars about fifty or so from the front. A large truck was hit dead on and it shredded and came apart under the 88mm explosive. Several cars and trucks rammed into the destroyed vehicle adding to the carnage. Bodies could be seen flinging away from the wreck. Dre and Sanchez watched as the Chinese dealt with the situation by driving around the smoking truck. The bubble of slow cars parted and flowed around either side, churning up dust as they went off road. Sanchez grunted as more shells went off. The next group of five impacted the road in front of the enemy.

The Chinese remained disciplined as they drove around the potholes and craters and kept going north. The lead cars were nearly even with Dre's position on the mountain. The Chinese seemed to have other places to go as they went past. The air was rent by a shell launched from Lemonge's forces on Stateline Peak. The Army artillery units from Colorado had a better angle than the Marines as they were perpendicular to the highway and could line up better than Nethercot's people. Again the explosions from the guns took out cars and trucks filled with

Chinese troops. More bubbles of slow movement built and rippled through the lines of trucks. Sanchez did some quick math in her head. "We can only take out about a tenth of them with the guns," she told Dre. The Sargent relayed her thinking over to Wilkins who ran it up the chain. *They had to have those cars stopped and clustered so they could take out more!* The guns fell silent.

0712 and things looked bad. The flash and smoke of the liftoff of twenty huge anti air missiles from the far southern edge of Dre's vision added to his bad feeling.

"The Chinese are attacking our planes but I can't see any of them!" Dre raged at Sanchez.

"Watch the south! The plan should be to take out the radar's directing the missiles. Once those are gone they are in a world of hurt!"

Dre raised his glasses as Amir came up to their position to scan as well. The young man was dirty and even scrawnier than when the war started. Dre felt a flash of guilt. Two quick explosions lit the Lake Washoe area in sympathy to his guilt.

"Those are the anti radar HARM missiles!" Sanchez shouted. A ragged cheer went up. The Marines and civilians watched the Chines column continue to move despite more shelling and the missiles from the south being shot off at regular intervals. Long distance air warfare was hard to follow from the ground. Wilkins came back from a briefing at the command tent.

"The General says the Chinese are knocking the hell out of our planes again," he said sadly. "We may not get the air support."

Both Sanchez, Dre and the other leaders noted the despair in the body language of the Lieutenant. She took the man aside and spoke quietly to him. They were less than fifteen minutes into the battle, there was still time. "We need those Tomahawks, she told the Officer. "Recommend calling Sierra one-that sub- just like last time," Sanchez said trying to steady the man.

Wilkins shook his head. "The LINK is down. Nethercot has been trying to have DC coordinate but it is too much with the air battle going on. He'd getting overwhelmed."

"Then go get his phone, and tell him you are going to direct the missiles for him!" Go through Timms! That is why we had the briefing this morning!" It was as close to yelling as she ever got with her boss.

More and more contrails and dull roars could be heard from the south as what looked like the last of those missiles went off after the unseen US planes. Three more explosions rocked the area.

"How many of those Radar sites do the Chinese have? Dre asked Sanchez while watching the stream of cars.

The Sargent shrugged. "Intel says ten or so." "What have we destroyed? Five? Six?" She asked the man. Dre had no good answer. He began to feel helpless. He saw Manny Pacheco rush by heading for the command tent. Manny and Tito were coordinating a group of troops whose job it was to respond of they felt the southern flank down at the 395/70 Chilcoot-Vinson junction was threatened. Dre raised his binoculars to look. A group of cars and trucks were indeed pulling off the 395 ready to attack the nexus point. Manny grabbed other Marines and the two brothers rushed off to get their people ready to go into action. Dre watched them go with pride and fear.

He glanced at his watch. 0734 and the day was barely started and it could not get any worse for the Americans. Distant flashes could be seen on the horizon as more American planes were shot down. *This sucks.*

This is intolerable! Bo fumed waiting for his messenger to give the status report for the Susanville forces. His initial strike team of four thousand trucks and eighty thousand men were past the bend in the 395 and hurtling towards the little town of Doyle. His drones had told them the US was dug in with a tank force enfiladed by the highway. The timing was critical for his attack. The Susanville forces *had* to be down the highway and ready to attack from that direction while his other teams made their attacks on the high ground.

"Sir, Colonel Chu from Tiger force reports they are past the blockade and moving towards the objective."

Finally. He let none of that show on his face however. Zi was getting antsy next to him.

"General, the last reports have us down to 27 Fang Dun missiles."

"How many targets are we tracking and how many sites do we have left?"

"Forty-one American planes and we are down to two radar sites, comrade." Zi was flushed.
now.

My god we might pull this off! "Very well." "Have them launch the last of the missiles. If any planes leak through we can use the shoulder fired units to take care of them".

Bo's Humvee was around the left bend in the road and approached a small farm railhead on Constantine road as it joined to the larger highway. The owners of the spot had long since departed the area, but Bo was soon out of the SUV and directing the split for his men. Groups of trucks turned right or left since Bo was almost on a line between the Adams Peak citadel rocks and the highest point of Stateline peak. Lemonge had his Fourth ID forces with their National Guard attached units spread along a line between two natural springs about two thirds of the way up the mountain: Bootlegger Spring to the south and Willow Spring to the north. Homestead Ranch road ran along the bottom of the mountain and Bo wanted his troops to run out along that road before turning up the hill to take out the American guns.

In the same way his forces on the opposite peak were to do a similar run along the rail spur siding road that ran parallel to the 395 on the Adams peak side. His Chilcoot-Vinson attack force was just an ace in the hole against an American surprise or if they proved to be very tenacious. Ten precious minutes went by while the plan unfolded perfectly. Scores of trucks packed with Chinese troopers who grinned madly and waved in their coveralls while they passed the General on their way to their respective sides. Lin Wei Bo watched the last of his anti-air missiles blast off from the south and the Susanville reserve bunch.

0744. Almost ready, Bo thought. *I need twenty more minutes for the troops to get into position and then we shall see how well the Americans can fight!*

"Goddamn it! Radio, Conn! I have Nethercot's personal cell number! You patch that thru to Control, right fucking now!"

Captain Greene was furious. Ninety-one minutes USS Ohio had been at battle stations, at launch depth waiting for an order. DC didn't have the information needed to tell them where or how to launch. The normal attack link was down. That spy group in San Francisco was gone apparently, so he tried the only thing he knew: reach out and touch someone. The phone in his hand started ringing.

"Hello."

Green gripped the phone tightly in his hand. "Who the fuck is this!"

"This is Lieutenant Wilkins, of the 3/5 Marines, I need to speak to the CO of the USS Ohio."

Greene closed his eyes in thanks. "Speaking son. Ohio is standing by for fire orders."

"Thank god. Uhh... sir. I'm going to have you talk to my Sargent. She has the TOMCOMM unit and laptop." Wilkins handed the cell phone to Sanchez.

"Lima 3/5 ready for Op control, Sierra 1. Request flights of sixteen every five mikes until exhausted starting time now!"

"Roger, Lima 3/5", Greene said into the mic. He turned his head to the station off of the raised Control platform and asked Senior Chief Speigal, "Got all that Senior?"

Speigal raised his head and reported "Fire Control ready, Lima 3/5 will have full op control. Four flights plus an orphan of eleven, sir."

Greene nodded to his man and told the Marine waiting that she had four full flights of sixteen heading her way with an additional flight of eleven.

Twenty minutes between first bird and last he thought. Only eighteen minutes of flight time. God I hope they are ready, Greene thought to himself as his ship made ready to fire. Ohio would be out of the game once these missiles were gone. She had zero weapons left afterwards.

Wilkins and Sanchez exchanged glances. *Crap, these birds are on the way!* Sanchez realized.

"Dre! I need that list of GPS positions versus the marker numbers the Colonel laid out for the artillery!" She pleaded with her new friend. Dre hustled back to the command tent to get her the information.

"Lieutenant, I need you to interface with Lemonge and Nethercot. He has to coordinate an artillery barrage to keep the Chinese busy while the birds are incoming."

The Officer nodded his head and followed Dre to the large tent to talk to the brass.

"Hill! Sanchez scanned the rocks and ridge line to find the diminutive Marine. The skinny girl materialized with Duarte, and some of those people with Dre: Amir and Miller. She took in all four. "Your team are my coordination with the Doyle and Susanville people. Call Whitworth and that General Tedesco, ask them where they want the missiles." Before her forces could scatter she stopped them. "I need to know the GPS position or the artillery marker number when you ask them."

The combined, Marine, National Guard, and civilian fire team scurried off to get her what she needed.

Sargent Connie Sanchez raised her glasses and watched the snake of Chinese cars move out and split up. *In another thirty minutes it won't matter. They will be attacking us and not able to be grouped up anymore.*

General Bo scanned the American positions above him on Adams Peak. The dust from his cars and trucks was bad but he could see the guns protected by hastily dug berms. Another ten minutes and he would signal the att....

A droning sound reached his ears above the sound of truck engines. A dot approached the line of cars both still on the 395 and on the spur line. Bo raised his binoculars. Three planes low and slow were coming straight in.

My god the American timing is incredible! Air to ground attack planes were lining up to attack his forces when they were at their most vulnerable. The vehicles in a full and complete line ready to slow down to dismount their vehicles and start the attacks. *How did they coordinate that?*

"Colonel Zi! Notify the force commanders, American air planes coming in. Have them stop and deploy the short range missiles."

The large aide to Bo immediately started dictating orders to the phone and radio messengers.

The planes were close enough to be identified now. The distinctive twin tail configuration of the A-10 warthog materialized out of the haze. The US Air Force had managed to get a few attack planes thru the Chinese anti-air missile envelope and arrive on the battlefield.

The A-10 warthogs in the air were museum pieces, Bo knew. *The US deactivated them nine years ago,* he remembered. They must have worked overtime to get them ready for the war. He also remembered what the planes were famous for: The road to Basra.

***

During the Gulf war in 1991, Iraqi forces fled Kuwait when it became apparent that the war was lost. The Iraq Army grabbed whatever loot they could get their hands on and threw it in whatever car they could hotwire and the whole group tried to flee the country on a single road to Basra, Iraq.

The A-10's caught up with them and the pilots lined up on the road and strafed the whole column. 2,000 cars, tanks, and armored personnel carriers were destroyed on the Highway of Death in mere minutes. And the A-10 was the main attack plane.

The Warthog was slow and old but she was incredibly tough and heavily decked out with weapons. The main one being a chin mounted 30 mm chain gun. The twin barrel gun could spit out armor piercing rounds at a high volume. Thousands were killed and the cars turned into twisted wrecks by the fire during the Basra raid. Bo knew The Iraqi's had stood no chance because the US controlled the skies and the A-10's operated with impunity.

***

But the Americans don't control the skies today, do they?

Both Zi and Bo watched in fascination as the US planes formed up on the 395 and started a run. The "brrrrruuuup" sound of the gun was delayed in covering the ten or so miles distance to them as they stood at the small farm house. What wasn't delayed were the effects.

The large rounds punched thru the cars and trucks like a hot knife through butter. Several cars exploded and bodies were hurled into the air. Surrounding trucks and cars pulled out of the road and tried to evade. Some even had success. The planes managed one short twenty second pass each and then pulled off to begin to sweep around for another.

As they did, streaks of white smoke reached up from the ground towards the planes. The FN-6 type man portable missiles could only could range out about five miles at the most. But the Chinese had twenty of them in the air for the three US attack planes.

Three quick explosions knocked the planes out of the air. The warthogs are armored but they cannot fly with the rear mounted engines blown off.

Bo heard more explosions and gun sounds from the north and he swung the binoculars around to watch two more three plane elements of Warthogs attack his Doyle and Susanville groups.

The same pattern held out as the planes succeeded in getting in an initial pass but then were quickly knocked out by the more advanced missile systems of the Chinese.

"Are we tracking more of the US planes?" he asked Zi. The Colonel consulted with the staff members. Meanwhile Bo urged his forces to complete their split and form up to charge the Americans on their mountain strongholds. He had to have those guns and army groups defeated before they could sack the Depot at their leisure.

Zi started to return with his plane count when a ripping sound split the air. Fifty guns on each mountain, both Adams and Stateline opened up with a coordinated artillery barrage.

His little knot of cars and trucks was targeted and Bo found himself hurled to the ground by the concussive force of the blasts.

Dre watched the explosions run down the line of Chinese cars. *Artillery shells are a sure way to break up the orderly formations of the Chinese*, he observed. The group across the valley that was threatening the Stateline peak forces of General Lemonge, was especially hard hit. A huge clump of fifty or so cars were right near a marker point and the guns racked them over with devastating effects. Dre figured hundreds died in the first bursts.

Missiles crossed the sky as the small dots that were the A-10's got clobbered.
He felt sorry for the pilots. No parachutes came out at all, as the fly boys and girls tried to crash the planes into the enemy. Ballsy.

The few tanks the US had managed to transport to the battle filed now got off a barrage as the artillery re ranged and shot again. Dre didn't know how many rounds the US had but he knew it wasn't many. A third round of shots all rang out and the Chinese finally figured out that the cars were the targets and they abandoned them en mass.

But it wasn't quite the cluster fuck it appeared. The Chinese unassed their vehicles intact and with all of their weapons.

The troops started to form up along parallel lines with the roads and began a slow advance up the mountains.

Booms and the staccato sound of gunfire sounded throughout the valley as all of the smaller groups were coming into contact.

Sanchez crawled next to Dre with the TOMMCOM laptop and the two of them were surrounded by Wilkins, Collins, Armster. Duarte, Hill, Miller and Amir also crouched next to the two on the rocks near the top of the ridge they occupied.

"You got those GPS coordinates?"

"Yes, Sargent", Duarte shouted.

Everyone instinctively ducked as the sound of a large explosion reached them. A huge plane had just crashed against the base of Stateline Peak.

Everyone strained to see through the smoke.

"What the fuck?" Armster asked into the noise.

Another four engine plane was running directly up the valley following first I-80 and then the 395.

An AC -130 gunship.

Armster and Collins whooped as the killing machine managed to open up for thirty full seconds against the Chinese threatening the 4th ID and national Guard units of General Lemonge.

The AC Cobra gunship is an older weapon system that was first used in Vietnam. The troops there called it "Puff the Magic Dragon". The plane sported a waist mounted 30 mm gatlin gun in its cargo area. The gun 'puffed" out thousands of rounds per second.

And puff it did. Its twin was already down but again the words of the President rang in every head: *Not an inch of territory surrendered without blood being spilled.*

Ignoring the certain death of the missiles coming at it, the 130 completed its run up the valley. The gun ran out of ammo right before the three missiles took out the plane in mid air. But not before it did an incredible amount of damage to the Chinese. At least two hundred cars and trucks were flat out destroyed. Tens of thousands of soldiers were sent scrambling for the safety of ditches along the base road, Homestead ranch. Sanchez could see the carnage and had a flare of hope. Between the A-10's and the AC 130's the Chinese had received a serious blow. Thousands had been killed in just a few passes by the planes. *That's what we needed!*

The other battle fields were receiving visits from the Air Force. The service had pulled out every plane it could muster and since the long range Chinese missiles had destroyed the combined carrier based planes and whatever modern strike aircraft, the dregs had been sent to do whatever they could.

A lull hit the fields as the last of the gunships went down over the Angels ridge forces. The fiery wreck could be seen sending a huge column of smoke into the clear air.

Dre emerged near Sanchez from the cluster of people scurrying back and forth on the mountain. He had the page with the GPS coordinates on it.

Sanchez was setting up the laptop on a flat rock near the edge of the steep slope that led down to the enemy.

"Duarte, you and Miller take the markers in front of us. Armster, find Collins and coordinate where General Tedesco wants the ordinance up near the Angels ridge place." Sanchez paused to connect up the TOMMCOM to the laptop. "Hill, you and Amir take the Stateline peak area." She looked around. "I need someone to work the Doyle area."

Wilkins came to stand in front of her. "Sargent I will work that part." "We need to know time on target?"

Sanchez worked the keys furiously. The birds were in the air and on the way, she knew. A quick check of the time let her know she only had a few minutes. 0804. *That late?*

Dre watched the laptop display establish interfaces with the incoming missiles. Fifteen status lines were filling up the screen. *Must have lost one,* he thought.

"Okay, I'm ready to start assigning birds. Who has a cluster and a marker?"

Sanchez looked up from the laptop. Faces stared at her. "Anytime people!"

Bo came struggling to full consciousness from the fog. His ears rang and his shoulder hurt from the impact on the ground. But he was alive and most of his staff was as well.

"Status!" his voice cracked and strangled out as he attempted to gather info on what was happening to his attack.

Zi materialized like a magicians trick next to him. "Sir, the Americans have inflicted damage across our battle groups. The Susanville group is within range of the guns mounted on Angels Ridge. They are only a few miles from the Depot airfield." His report was breathless. ZI appeared unhurt by the artillery blast to Bo's eyes.

"Colonel Zhou reports he is near to making contact with the tanks and Army soldiers in place near Doyle at the head of the valley. Colonel Li is bogged down on Homestead ranch road. He reports many casualties." Zi wound down.

Bo grimaced. The enemy had struck a blow but his men had been too passive.

"I can see our troops here have started up the slope towards Adams peak. Order a general push among all groups. Troops are to dismount vehicles wherever they are and move to engage the enemy. Start the charge with a barrage of RPG's and destroy the US tanks with the HJ-8. That has priority, Zi!"

The staff around Bo picked up phones and started texting and calling the team leads in the clear. At 0805 a huge cluster of enemy calls went out.

***

Noah drank from the canteen trying to wash out the blood from his mouth. He'd bitten his tongue and it hurt like a bitch, plus he hated the copper taste and smell that dominated his senses.

The gun was very warm in his hands. He was down to three clips left. A quick glance a Rammy and the two sprinted for the edge of the roof top. Reaching the low wall the pair popped up and leaned over the protective railing. The light machine gun was from one of the dead Seals and it still could be fired by an untrained person. The group of Chinese soldiers trying to break in the door way were killed in seconds as the two fired into the soldiers.

The killing didn't bother the man any more. That was the third try the enemy had made on the front door.

He and Rammy ducked back to the middle of the building, near the air conditioner unit. They been playing ping pong all night up here. The three remaining seals had divided themselves up. One was barricaded near the front door. The last two were at the loading dock. The plan was to put Rammy and Noah on the roof to bounce to whichever side the attack came from and provide support.

The plan had worked very well. Much better than Noah would have guessed. *I thought we would be dead by 0200. It's seven fifteen and we are still alive. I wonder why?*
He didn't say anything to Rammy however. The two were saving their breath and their ammo.

The fog was burning off and it made for weird reverbs and sound dampening in the city. The Chinese had been making a coordinated effort to kill them for hours now but they were also under attack from other places in the city.

The sounds of battle echoed and rang out near the office building. Noah didn't know how many Chinese were in the city but he knew the forces had been seriously depleted. The majority were stationed near the two bridges and that's where the main gunfire sounds could be heard. In the local area maybe a thousand were trying like hell to kill them.

The phone jingled near them. In coming text.

"I hate that sound," Rammy Pak said dully, picking up the phone. "Back door," she said reading the text.

Noah figured the Chinese had wanted to arrange the two attacks simultaneously, but they couldn't pull it off. *Sucks for them.*

"Let's go." He told her and they scuttled to the western side roof wall to observe how the Chinese soldiers were attempting this one.

Pretty straight forward, he saw. Ram the dock door with a truck and charge in like hell. About fifty men stood back waiting for the truck to find out the problem.

What Noah could see from the roof was something the Chinese could not: The street level and the door level were not the same. From where the enemy observed the place, it looked like a straight shot to a door on the same level as the ground.

That was not so. The short dock area was sunken and sloped right at the street juncture. The loading dock door was raised about four feet, to allow easier truck access by forklift.

Too late for the Chinese. The truck hurtled down the street and cranked into the dock zone as fast as the driver could reasonably go. The crash was at twenty-five miles an hour and killed the driver. The ten men in the back were hurled onto the street over the cab and none of them got up. The Seals and the two on the roof didn't even bother to shot them. They concentrated on the frontal follow up charge by the remaining forty or so men. A few RPG and missile rounds did impact the building door and walls, causing enormous damage, but the fire from above and inside soon enveloped all the enemy. Only a few soldiers were left struggling to crawl away on the street.

Noah ducked back down when he heard the sound of a car turn near the cross street. *Jesus! How many times are they going to do this?*

He risked a glance at the incoming car. The Oakland Raider twin flags flew from the side windows of the gold Lexus SC 430. The Silver and Black come representing.

A large black man got out of the car and methodically started shooting the Chinese as they lay or crawled. A white man with a pony tail soon joined him.

Noah was dumb struck.

"Hey!" Rammy yelled next to him.

Both men looked up.

"Hey, we are here!"

"You okay?" The black man shouted and then looked around at the bodies. "You guys been giving them hell, but we are here to help!"

The pair slumped back down. *Maybe they would live.*

Ten minutes was all it took for the army of the peninsula to rescue the NSA outpost.

The three seriously wounded Seals and the two civilians met with Kerry Woolridge, a Fremont cop and National Guardsman and Oakland raiders fan.

"We heard the President and finally figured that we had to try. Started up the 101 last night and made it this far," Kerry said.

"We have a group heading for the Golden gate bridge, since it looks like our men met with some Oakland folks coming across the bay bridge earlier today," the white guy, Rich Hopper told them.

"We are going to take a minute," the Seal Lieutenant told the civilians.

The men laughed. "You guys rest up. We got this!"

And the battle for San Francisco was over for them.

Noah and Rammy hurried down to the office to see what could be salvaged. Power was still on and the office was cluttered and full of dead friends but the basic computers still worked.

The young man sat at his desk and tapped the screen. His Zhenge He search program was up and merrily collecting its data.

Rammy went to her office to report their survival to DC. At least some good had come of their mission.

"Hey! Hey. Hey! Look at this!" Noah's voice rose with excitement.

The woman went out to see.

The screen held a cluster of messages from their target. Zhenge He was transmitting! Not only was he transmitting, it was in the clear and there were a lot of them.

"We got to get back on the air and tell our people," Noah said excitedly. He grabbed a phone from the desk.

***

"Its assigned!" Sanchez shouted as the loud explosions started. As she tapped the laptop, the next missile in line came active to get its coordinates.

"Anti-personnel variant! I need one for a cluster of troops!" The Sargent looked at Dre and the rest for a line on the next target. Collins gave her one near the spring at Stateline peak. *Those people at Pyramid lake must be getting clobbered,* the thought struck fear in her. Collins gave her the marker number from the sheet and the GPS equivalents came from Dre. Collins radioed Lemonge's staff and told them "Heads Down!"

The tomahawk missile dropped form the race track it had been flying to home in on the new spot. Two hundred feet from the ground it leveled off and flew a slow path parallel to the frontage road. Starting right at the marker and continuing for a few seconds smaller explosions came of the body as bomblets dropped off the missile.

The small "bangs" caused the mass of Chinese soldiers to look up for a second.

Not that the second mattered. A strip two hundred yards wide and five hundred yards long became a killing field. The sub munitions exploded ripping thru the men. Five hundred men ceased to be.

But Sanchez was on to the next target. She was on flight two with another inbound already and a third launching. The Ohio was doing its part. Sometime ago, she only was vaguely aware of it, the American forces had begun their second artillery barrage. A larger more concentrated barrage of the artillery and tanks rounds they had remaining. Every one of them had to count. Wilkins reported the Chinese massing and coming up the hills for them. *Not good!*

The top of the slope where they were provided a nice view but also a nice target. The RPG and anti-tank missiles made a wreck of the rocks as the Chinese decided they hadn't been playing offense enough during this battle.

The explosions ripped thru the area hurling dirt, trees and rocks into the air along with people.

Sanchez couldn't be bothered with the carnage. Knots of fire teams from the Marines and others began firing back as the two side closed together.

"I need three bird's danger close!" Dre told her. Pointing out the spots and the coordinates.

None of that registered for the woman. Point and assign, click and assign. It didn't matter what happened after that.

The three missiles came down nearly on top of the citadel. The slope below them was obscured by the fire and smoke as the high explosives shook the ground.

The carnage was unbelievable as the smoke cleared. Hundreds of bodies were in view. And some of them American.

"How can they do that?" Bo was dumbfounded. He slumped against the farm house wall as the after effects of the missile blasts became clear. *How many of my men are dead? Eighty? One hundred thousand? My god its only 0845!*

Lin Wei Bo ordered his men to regroup and make a maximum push to close with the US forces. He knew they stood no chance against the missiles without some kind of armored protection. And since that armor was waiting for them at the Army Depot, they had no choice.

More tomahawks could be heard at the distant battlefields as the Americans had to divide up their weapons. Bo shuddered to think what the missiles were costing him in terms of men.

He watched his remaining men, now about forty thousand in the group in front of him, start to climb again up the steep slopes.

"Zi! Order the Chilcoot-Vinson force to break thru and approach those rocks from the west." Bo had planned the smaller force as a last resort and now he'd been pushed into it. More coded cell calls and radio phone messages went out.

"Here they come again!" The voice was tinged with fear and Sanchez had no idea whose it was. Dre was crouched down next to her reading numbers while she willed her fingers to type them in correctly. They were on flight four and she didn't lack for targets. Collins, Armster, Hill, and Dre all demanded she drop missiles where they wanted them.

"They need help at Angles ridge!"

"Stateline Peak has three large concentrations!"

"Sargent!"

Sanchez blocked them out and concentrated. Missiles began dropping out of the sky as the US guns opened up with what she thought was going to be their final barrage. The boom and thud was punctuated with the Chinese response of the numerous rocket propelled grenade and anti-tank missile noise makers that they possessed.

Dre looked up as Sanchez got the final flight number four birds assigned and was thunder struck. Explosions, fire, smoke and debris were hurled into the air all around him. He could see the effect on the adjacent mountain as those forces clashed. The distant sounds from Doyle indicated those people were having a bad time as well. The Susanville folks were as busy as he was, according to the Marine Lieutenant who was shouting into his phone.

His phone vibrated in his hand and he glanced at it. The screen read "SF1"

Holy shit!

"Hello!"

"Dre! Can you hear me?" The young voice was barely audible over the din.

"Hey! You're alive?" Dre asked the boy.

"No time, Dre. We found Zhenge He, that guy you were looking for?" The statement came out in a rush as Dre paused to think about it.

Zhenge He was the Chinese leader for this battle. He knew that. Smith was lookin to kill that dude! But where was Smith? Where was the target, this Zhenge He dude?

"Where is he, man?" Dre asked excitedly.

"He's making a bunch of calls from a tower near a cluster of houses on a road named Constantina. Its right off the 395," Noah paused to take a huge breath. "I, we...think he might be right below your position if you guys are where we think..."

Dre jerked his head up and could see the cluster of buildings below and to his left. The Chinese troops could be seen milling about the area. There were only about a hundred but there seemed to be a large concentration of larger SUV's and Hummers. *That could be him! Where's Smith?'*

"Got it! Thanks dude!" he hung up.

"Sanchez!" he screamed at her not to target the last few missiles.

Connie looked up as Dre yelled her name. She was down to the last flight, four missiles left. She needed to make them count.

Dre came up to her breathing hard, looking around. "Where's Miller and that boy, Duarte?"

Sanchez searched the small knob of the hill. She spied the pair taking swigs off a canteen. Her throat suddenly dry in sympathy. Her hand thrust out pointing.

Dre followed the arm and yelled. "Miller!"

The National Guard woman and the young Marine rushed up to Dre and Sanchez. Both were filthy and had suffered some cuts from flying debris.

Dre spelled out the conversation with SF 1. He looked at Sanchez for confirmation, but he ordered them. "I need you to find Smith. Tell that motherfucker he is up. Kill that fuckin Chinese dude, and end this thing!"

Miller nodded soberly. "I think I know where he is, but Dre why don't we just drop some bombs on that guy?"

Dre and Sanchez exchanged looks. *Yeah we could target that farmhouse with the four remaining bombs and kill the guy... but.*

But Sanchez knew the Chinese were close to pressing thru. Pressing thru in a few spots. Susanville and Chilcoot-Vinson being the two most pressing. She had fire missions for those last missiles. Important fire missions. Did she dare make this call?

CHAPTER SIXTEEN

I hate that clock, Paul Marino thought for the millionth time. Once again he was in the Situation Room while the fate of the nation hung in the balance. *Is it possible to be this tired for this long?* He looked at Libby. She had the grey cast to her skin from extreme exhaustion like many in the room. *When this is over, I'm going to ask her to marry me and we are going to move to San Diego and never be inside again,* he vowed to himself. There was that little problem of would she accept. He smiled to himself. She would.

Paul looked around the room. Noon Eastern time. General Graham and Admiral Mooney were collecting reports from the battle field and were trying to make sense of them for the President. Marino now knew what the real meaning of "Fog of War". Graham approached Stallings.

"Ma'am we are holding on but barely. The Chinese have penetrated to near the Army airbase at the Depot itself. General Tedesco has mobilized her forces to roll off the mountain at Angels Ridge and come down on the Chinese but that is desperation. Whitworth and the airborne troops are dug in at Doyle. Most of their tanks have been destroyed but they are holding their own." He read from the paper. "The Stateline Peak force has stopped the Chinese and will be able to hold them from rolling around by Pyramid lake. The Adams Peak Marines are in a tough spot. They may have to move off their positions to attack as well." He paused. *She wants to know it all,* He thought. "The small force at Chilcoot is vulnerable. That may be our weak spot.

President Stallings frowned. "Isn't there anything we can give them, General? More missiles? Don't we have any more planes?"

The Chairman of the Joint Chiefs shrugged. "Not for this attack. We have to keep some planes in reserve for the case where they manage to obtain some armor at Sierra."

Mooney looked sick. He'd pulled the Pacific carriers off this part for the next phase of the operation. *Those eighty planes would be vital right now,* he thought. Coulda, woulda, shoulda. The carriers were vital to what had to happen next, he knew. *But would there be a next phase if they lost this battle?* His stomach churned.

There was some good news. SF1 was back on the air. And it seemed that the people had taken back San Francisco. Reports from Oakland and LA indicated that groups of civilians were fighting back very successfully. Teachers, Firefighters and truckers all ganging together to fight for their homes. Seattle was a dead zone as no good intel was coming from there. And Hawaii? Mooney knew Hawaii was a sheer battle of attrition. He had a report that the Chinese were grouped on the top of Diamond head resisting waves of attacks. He detached a part of phase two to help with his home island. But the cost?

It was horrific. Mooney knew the Chinese were not concerned with their own losses but he was about American lives. Millions were dead. Major west coast cities were ruined. The US was being threatened by other nations- even despite the slap down of Russia.

They had to win this battle.

Graham had no eyes for his compatriot. He concentrated on the President. "Madam President, the battle is in the hands of the Privets right now. General's will have nothing to do with it."

Well the General was only half right. A couple of Privates were involved, but the real decision came down to a Sargent and a Lieutenant, along with a civilian.

"Fuck it. It's that squid's job to kill the guy. We need to drop these last four birds where they will do the most good." Sanchez made the pronouncement and brooked no back talk.

Once the pecking order was established, people moved. Duarte and Miller went off to track down Smith. He was somewhere on the mountain they knew. Hill, Amir and the others went back to marking targets.

Wilkins approached her. "Sargent, the General says they are massing near the air field. She needs two anti-personnel types up there ASAP." He gave her the marker coordinates and she sent the packages on the way. Two left.

Dre scanned the mountain down south. He had a bad feeling. That little road juncture was starting to look like Little Big Horn. *Manny and Tito were down there!*

His stomach flipped over.

"Sanchez! Connie, please! Send the last two down to the south," he pointed out where.

The Marine typed in the codes and numbers and assigned the birds. She slowly closed the laptop. Nothing more to do than wait for the charge.

Lynn Spiegal watched the Chinese troops from the sandbag position bunker near the main gate to the airfield. Kollmansburger was next to her. *He was mad, but fuck him. She had as much right to be here as he did. Maybe more!*

The work she had done the night before had almost kill her! The hills and the dug in fire pits had helped to funnel the Chinese into a huge grouping. Right at the front door to the airfield. Right where she was at.

The enemy was bunched and walking at a steady pace towards them. Rifles and small arms fire predominated. It seemed they had run out of the RPG and the anti-tank rounds. That was nice because the Americans were out of tanks and artillery shells, Lynn knew.

At least Noah is safe. And Tommy.

The five thousand man (and woman) force was grimly dug in waiting for the range to shorten down a bit.

She peaked over the top. Two streaks caught her eye. She watched two missiles make an almost left hand turn over the depot to line up on the airfield road.

The smaller puffs as the sub munitions came off, baffled her.

But not Kollmansburger.

He grinned at her, "Way to go Tommy!" he yelled as the explosions started. Ten seconds of intense noise and smoke obscured the enemy.

Lynn strained to see. *What had Tommy had to do with that?*

The scene was beautiful and awful.

Thousands of Chinese soldiers were shredded on the grounds. Blood stark and red against the alkali flats of the lake and the roadside.

The survivors in the back of the Chinese formation were stunned by the sudden loss of their comrades. Another ten thousand men waited and watched from the rear about a mile back from the base.

But the McChord killers, the Ivy division of the 7th infantry were not waiting.

Led by a small woman with flame red hair and sporting pearl handled 45's, the twenty thousand of them ran off the mountain straight for the Chinese.

The shock of the Tomahawk attack and the suicidal charge of the wild men unnerved the Chinese.

They broke.

The group in front turned and tried to go back the way they came. They ran head long into the reserves milling about.

As the lead elements of the Seventh crossed Wendel road, they poured gunfire on the enemy.

Unable to maintain discipline, the Chinese surged back south across the lake to get away from the maniacs coming at them.

And ran head long into the bikers and civilians from the local area waiting in the holes.

The trap was complete as the two forces pinched the Chinese together.

Kollmansburger did not miss his opportunity.

"Let's go!"

He charged out of the bunker towards the Chinese brandishing his M-16.

Lynn was shocked.

The others in the area did not need encouraging. They charged the foreigners with little regard for their own safety.

Shots rang out as the Americans pressed the Chinese on three sides.

The dwindling group of Chinese did not attempt to surrender. Nor did the Americans give any notion to accepting that convention. Thousands died on the sands of Honey lake.

This was payback as the Chinese dropped arms and ran straight back towards Susanville. The Seventh and anyone who had a gun in hot pursuit the whole way.

The twin explosions stunned everyone on the small triangle of land between the dry riverbed, the rail spur and the 70. Chilcoot-Vinson was a small farming community when the rains cooperated.

The small US blocking force was straddled along the 70 between two hills that forced the Chinese into a natural choke point. The three thousand or so US troops were bolstered by a full contingent of Navy Seals as the Coronado based instructor group had chosen this assignment when Nethercot asked for volunteers. Manny could see the Chinese recover from the missile attack in pretty decent order. There looked to be ten million of them. He was dug in deep above the road side about thirty yards or so. Tito was in the next position over and below.

There wasn't going to be any subterfuge here, just men walking into bullets.

Manny was ready to shot those bullets.

"Ready hermano pequeno?"

His much larger younger brother laughed.

The enemy came within range and the US force opened up. Dug in and sighted in for the area, the first volley wilted the Chinese. Men writhed on the ground screaming as blood and bowels poured forth.

The return fire was punctuated by the few RPG's and hand grenades the invaders had left. Men slumped as shots found bodies.

The Chinese found whatever cover was available and tried to mass for a charge. The only hope for them was to get as close as they could as quickly as they could to the Americans.

A sudden rush of soldiers came at Manny. Hundreds of men shoved thru the road gap and started climbing directly at him.

Cold rage washed thru him. Manny took sight and shot.

Sight and shoot.

He was not seeing faces, just chests and stomachs as his rounds hit home.

Sight and shoot.

A quick reload as he became aware of screaming around him. He was unconsciously matching the Seal instructors as they lined up shots.

Cold rage. Screaming.

Men were hurling their voices at the Chinese the same as their bullets on both hill sides. More shots rained down on the enemy. Several positions below him were overrun as Manny continued to fight.

His gun was scalding hot but he was pure ice as he swung the rifle back and forth squeezing off rounds.

The last of the Chinese reserves- about a thousand men- tried to break thru the road as the human wave continued to wash up the hill sides. The wave skimming over with blood.

Manny did not see Tito go down. He was too busy fighting off the three men who had managed to reach his hole. He shot the first and swung the rifle like a club catching the second man on the side of his head, caving it in. Blood and brains dotted the butt of the gun. The piercing pain in his side lanced thru him as the third attacker shot him.

Manny couldn't scream as his lungs were filling with blood. He did manage to get the gun up and squeeze off his last two shots, killing the Chinese youth right in front of him.

Manny Pacheco of Oakland California via Veracruz Mexico lay on his back watching the blue sky of Reno Nevada fade from sight.

General Bo turned to gawp at Zi. The ferocity of the Americans had stunned him. His reports from Susanville, Doyle and the Chilcoot forces all confirmed the Americans dying at their posts. Willing to sacrifice themselves in order to take out his men. *If you want to see how hard a man can fight, back him into a corner...*

No more than eight or nine hundred men from the ten thousand man force at the little road junction had managed to get to the west side of Adams peak. That was far too few to do any real damage, he realized.

"I have never seen this level of fighting my friend," Bo confided to Zi. These devils have to be on drugs of some kind. Americans are too soft for this level of commitment."

Zi said nothing. The battle was quickly becoming untenable. The last person left alive on this ground might well be Chinese but he would be alone, Zi knew.

The battle line right in front of them wavered as the US Marines made their last desperate charge off the hill towards his comrades.

Propelled by superior height and zeal, the Marines were yelling and literally growling as they hurled themselves at the Chinese. Savage hand to hand fighting was breaking out all along the rail line that the Americans had driven them back towards.

Bo was fearful of being overrun when he ordered his staff back into their hummers to order a reconsolidation of the remaining troops.

He might be able to fight his way back to Oakland or LA and try to commander some ships to take him some place…

Bo paused on the way into the SUV. He needed one last look at the battle field to rally his troops…

He heard the shot clearly.

The round punched thru his heart almost dead center of his chest. He slumped to the ground and Zi was at his side, clutching him, the pain flared as the world tilted. Lin Wei Bo's last thought was 'How did that happen…?"

Twenty minutes earlier Smith worked the bolt action to load the chamber on the fifty caliber sniper rifle. Duarte and Miller lay on either side of him taking the occasional shot at the Chinese soldiers who dared interfere with his mission.

Twenty minutes ago, Smith had gotten another bite at the apple. Miller had found him and told him where Zhenge He was located.

He stopped killing the individual Chinese troopers who were foolish enough to come his way and went to cutting off the head of the snake.

The three-person fire team worked their way off the Citadel slopes and down towards the cluster of buildings that SF 1 indicated held Zhenge He. Enemy fire was spotty as the rest of the Marines were rushing down at the line of Chinese men. Smith wanted to take advantage of the chaos.

At a thousand yards a small clump of rocks made the only high ground position Smith was going to get. He set up the rifle on its tripod carefully.

A good bit of glass work with the scope identified the man. A bit older. Trim. Non descript uniform. But…clean and tailored. And the target was clean and tailored.

The large Colonel next to the man was surely subservient to him. Several other soldiers came periodically and gave him reports or took orders from him. Zheng He.

Smith sighted carefully. Miller made the wind call and Duarte worked the range finder with ease.

Several clicks on his sight as the Seal worked to control his breathing. *This is my job*…

3, 2,.. 1.

The shot echoed out on the hillside.

"Got him", Smith said with satisfaction, as Bo crumpled to the ground, blood spraying. *Dead center of the chest.*

For good measure he shot the large colonel as he clutched Zhenge He. *That was a good bit of shooting.*

"Miller, text Dre. Tell him to tell Nethercot the Chinese are going to take off their uniforms soon. We should kill any naked people we see."

Dre was next to Sanchez who was in turn next to Hill. Amir was on the tiny woman's other side. Wilkins was next to his old employee. More Marines and civilians made up the skirmish line as they advanced down the mountain. His phone buzzed but he needed to ignore it right now.

Right now was killing time. Dre had watched as the Chinese had their way on the Oakland docks all those weeks ago.

Those guys were not soldiers. Those guys were truckers and longshoremen. *Those guys were my employees and my friends,* he thought about Jeremy and Eddie. About Hopkins and Bobby. All gone now, killed by the Chinese.

The Chinese who were lined up toe to toe with them now, all subterfuge gone. Dre worked his gun and fired as fast as he could. The concentrated fire was having its effect on the enemy. Men whirled and dropped when shots hit them.

Dre paid no attention to that. He had things on his mind. Friends old and new, gone. Tabatha maybe dead. He hadn't seen or heard of her in some time. His mom. His gun heated up.

Sanchez was directing fire more than shooting herself. Sergeants yelled, they did not pop off rounds.

"Dre, move that weapon off full auto and put in three round bursts Marine!"

"Hill, four 203 rounds, right 35 yards- Time now!"

"Amir! Shoot that motherfucker!"

She risked a glance at her phone when it buzzed. A text from Nethercot. "Press hard"

"Harder Marines!"

The line upped the fire rate as the Chinese seemed to waiver. Both Sanchez and Dre watched some kind of information work its way through the Chinese lines. Men hesitated down there. They looked at each other. *What?*

"Push harder Marines!"

Sanchez backed up her words by moving off the rock formation and starting down the hill. She brought the rifle up to shoulder level and pumped out some grenade rounds to mark her thunderous passage along the trail.

Dre had no choice but to follow her as she mowed down the enemy. Hill, Duarte and the others all came along as the whole of the 3/5 and the civilians crashed down upon the Chinese. Miller and Smith appeared next to their lines and joined the fun.

The blue coveralls held for a few minutes but that was all.

First in ones and twos the men threw down their weapons and moved off the battle line, then in dozens and then hundreds.

They were sadly mistaken if they thought the Americans were going to show them some mercy.

Dre was soon sick of shooting men in the back but he kept at it.

Hours later the Marines met with the forces of the big red One at basically the east side of the 395 highway. The Chinese had succeeded in getting the US troops to take them prisoner when they took off their coveralls. About five thousand men were huddled, naked on the highway with their hands tied behind their backs. The blue coveralls made fine ties.

Five thousand out of one hundred eighty thousand? Dre was sickened.

The combined military watched a group of civilian cars move up the 395. A new group of volunteers coming from Denver and points east to help them battle the Chinese.

"We don't really need the help," Sanchez complained.

"Speak for yourself", Dre told her.

Nethercot and Lemonge were talking and directing the newcomers to take care of the prisoners while they moved to relieve the airborne forces at Doyle.

Dre and Sanchez walked with their friends up the 395. They had a nice ten mile walk.

Amir broke the bad news about Manny and Tito to Dre. He'd been near the Command tent when the results of the Chilcoot battle were detailed. Almost all of the defenders were dead. *Manny and Tito!*

Some Marines were still searching for the final remnant of the Chinese who'd broken thru.

"Funny, they never showed up in our rear," Dre said. "Hey, anyone seen Lardi?" Dre was looking around like he'd lost a sock in the dryer.

Sanchez eyed him as he said it. The man was pissed about his friends. She didn't have the heart to tell him that Lardi had died on the mountain. *Let him find out a little later, when he can handle it,* she reasoned.

The Marine forces were re organizing by unit level and more and more of their friends came in. Hill, Morrelli, and others all arriving to tell tales of the battle.

Miller, Smith and Duarte related their mission to take out Zhenge He.

That's what they found out about, Dre realized. Their CO was dead and that was it for them. Their lines broke after that.

When they finally got there near evening, the Doyle airborne tanks and troops did not need to be rescued but it still felt nice to be able to shoot some more Chinese in the backs as they had them pinned against the tank fronts.

Another six thousand prisoners joined the mass near the south end of the valley.

The Generals all met with Whitworth and they congratulated themselves on the victory. Soon the force needed to move on. Dre and the gang walked onto the sands of Honey lake. These people did not need any rescuing either it seemed to the man. The buzzards and the smell were overpowering as some men worked to separate enemy from friend among the piles of bodies. A mass grave for one, an honored burial for the other. The Susanville Chinese troops were trying to negotiate a surrender. They still had ten thousand men arranged on the road west of them and Dre figured that would be sticky.

He quickly scanned the area as Whitworth, Lemonge and Nethercot joined the other two, Tedesco and that Admiral. Dre estimated the US troops at about forty thousand. *Holy shit!* Only five thousand of his combined Marines and civilian friends had walked off that mountain. The Airborne troops had fared better as did the Kansas unit but still, Eighty or ninety thousand American men and women had died out there today.

The Chinese? He didn't much care but, it looked like four hundred thousand casualties. There would not be many wounded on either side as medical care was almost nonexistent. They just didn't have the men to spare. Every corpsman was out there with a gun.

Dre spared a glance at his watch. Five thirty in the evening. They still had a few hours of daylight. Still time to bury the dead. *Half a million men and women gone in eight hours?* Flesh and bone against missiles and high explosives just did not make for a fair fight.
Dre paused to take a swig of water. He didn't think he could eat anything. He was exhausted. *Where in the fuck is my towing rig?* He'd left it somewhere but couldn't remember.

He went to find Sanchez and Amir.

General Tedesco and some Admiral named Kollmansburner, or some such were holding a confab with the three other Generals. They were talking to DC. Dre couldn't work up much interest. He sat on the hard ground of the lake and some tears were leaking from his eyes. Sanchez held him.

"Generals, Admiral and all the troops in the sound of my voice", the Presidents voice came over the phone setup and the speakers they had rigged on the sands. Troops surged forward to hear clearly. "Your nation owes you a debt of gratitude that can never be repaid. The hallowed ground of Sun Valley, Honey lake, and the Peaks will join the pantheon of American victory. She paused.

"You roared like lions out there so that this nation will continue to be a beacon of light for the world. You have my thanks and the thanks of a grateful nation. God bless you and God bless the United States of America."

Sanchez kept holding him.

The twelfth of June 2022 was a nice day in Shanghai China. The early morning sun was bright and the winds had blown off most of the smoke so the place looked normal. At least as normal as it could look these days.

The port area was the busiest part of the city. With so many deaths and the lack of food anyone working or moving around was a sight to see. But the soldiers and the people moving onto the ships took no notice of their surroundings.

General Fei also took no real notice from the bridge of the huge merchant ship. The city was in ruins but that did not affect him. His calls yesterday to Bo and Zi were useless. That made no difference to him. He was undocking this ship today and sailing for someplace. Maybe one of the islands in the south china sea. He had plenty of gold and diamonds with him. He'd killed those two idiots, Qi and Yuan last night. They seemed to delight in telling him about the defeat of their forces on the mainland, so the gunshots to the face locked in the slightly surprised expression for eternity on both.

Indeed, the last group of fighters they had left was the stragglers on Hawaii. There did not seem to be any way to stop other countries from carving them up like a prize goose. Even Vietnam had taken a large chunk off the border.

Fei did not care. He was getting out. He'd removed his uniform last night. Today, this morning, he was a private citizen of a failed state. A very rich private citizen. Switzerland or perhaps France would grant him asylum. The rest of them could go suck it.

The submarine was hovering at launch depth, and since USS West Virginia was an older Trident II submarine, that was difficult with her older noisier, hov pumps. She had the latest mods to her fire control and weapons systems though and she had the special mods that Senior Chief Speigal had helped install before they'd fled the home base at Bangor.

And she had one more special item loaded. Well many special items in reality.

"Conn, Weapons, Nav, ship is at 1SQ," Captain Borges relayed over the open mic.

The diving officer had preceded that report by the CO by telling him that the Dive was at 1SQ. SQ being submarine quarters. Since every ship or weapons platform had its own language no one could expect the submarine force to use the surface Navy's lingo, could they?

What would happen to military discipline if everyone just went around saying: "I'm ready to kill. Are you?"

Borges had that stray thought as he waited for the weapons at 1SQ call.

Five minutes later the giant nuclear missile carrying submarine was at battle stations with missiles fully spun up and ready to launch.

Tubes 6 thru 20 were ready to be hurled into the sky, Borges had an authentic launch message from the National Command Authority and he was in the window.

The target area had been deconflicted and the valid combination to the launch key safe had been transmitted to the sub.

DC is serious about this, Borges thought again. The broadcast had contained valid launch messages for six other Trident II submarines. Only Nebraska was being held in reserve.

Tennessee, Wyoming, Pennsylvania, Maine and Rhode Island were spinning up just as he was, if he could read the messages right. And the US Navy payed him a lot of money to read those messages correctly. Louisiana got the unlucky break of being the "spare part boat". She would spin up her missiles and wait for any mechanical failures to take out other subs missiles. If any misfires happened, then she got to play. If not… no joy.

But did he feel joy? A nuclear missile is an awesome responsibility. Borges knew lobbing a nuclear weapon around never happened with impunity. He thought the Russians would have something to say about this. But he also knew the Russians had no leg to stand on.

"Captain, Ship is at 1SQ, window is open, request permission to fire." The muffled voice of the Weapons Officer came over the speaker unit.

Borges rose and inserted his key into the Captains Indicator Panel. A hard turn to the right, set the fifteen missiles to red status on the board.

"COB, Sonar, Torpedo room, this is the Captain. I'm about to give permission to fire. I don't know if there are any Chinese subs out here tracking us but I want to be ready for that. At the first hint of an incoming torpedo I will return fire and continue launching, affirm?"

Sailors swallowed hard in control. The Captain had basically announced that in the event an enemy sub tried to take them out, the ship would work to launch all of her missiles rather than try to save itself.

The Captain got three acknowledgements of his wishes and he pushed the button for number six missile. "Prepare six."

The litany started: "Denote six, prepare twenty."

The tube hatch cycled open on the superstructure unseen under the waves.

"Six ready."

A discrete signal ignited a small rocket motor stored on the side of the missile tube. This motor did not launch the missile. Instead it ignited and flashed a small store of pure water underneath the missile into steam. That steam ported thru a huge pipe directly under the missile and started pushing the 130,000 pound weapon out of the tube. The missile broke easily thru its protective cover since the space between the missile and the side of the tube was measured in millimeters. The rush of steam continued as the force of the energy shoved the weapon out of the tube and through the water.

"Six away. Denote twenty, prepare seven."

The litany started for the next units. Meanwhile the first missile was one second out of the boat and braking the surface of the water. Enough energy had been unleashed to throw the missile ninety feet in the air. At the first downward moment of inertia, another discreet signal ignited the internal first stage rocket motor.

The unit roared off on its voyage.

The hatch cycled shut and the next unit was at the ready.

Fifteen missiles were hurtling skyward in mere minutes. As the last hatch cycled shut, and no return fire was noted, the CO started to breathe again. And then to worry more. *He'd actually launched his weapons!*

"Conn, sonar, we are hearing launch transients from a great distance, at least eighty nautical miles. Could be the Rhode Island, sir."

"Very well, sonar. Dive lets go deep, Nav we need to complete our launch clearance maneuver and then we will surface and make contact with DC."

He left the worst part out. *If anyone was left alive in DC, after all this is over.*

***

Marino screamed into the phone, "I keep telling you it is just like Georgia!" "Just wait another twenty minutes and you will see!"

Several members of the Presidents staff were on phones talking to various governments around the world. Early warning networks were going crazy, even though the President had forewarned some administrations.

Paul happened to know the Russian Ambassador to the US pretty well. He reached out and contacted him as the operations were starting. The Russian was livid. Paul kept repeating: "This is just like Georgia!"

***

Out in the upper part of the atmosphere, the "bus" reached its destination. The bus was what the military called the platform that the warheads from a Trident SLBM were hung on. A Trident II is a MIRV, or multiple independent Reentry Vehicle, weapon. The bus tipped over to point its cargo at the ground.

The warheads are not guided or powered in any way on a nuclear missile. The whole thing relies on gravity, trajectories, inertia and math.

The arc of travel reached a critical altitude, attitude, speed and spot, and the warhead detached from the bus. The platform continued dropping the "kids" off at points along its line of travel over the country of China.

Gravity took over as the warhead dropped like a stone. A heavy, heavy stone.

Streaks of lights were beginning to appear in the sky over Shanghai. The glowing tip of the warhead as it reached terminal velocity, plummeting to the earth.

The first impact was to the dock area at Diatzhou island.

The warhead hit the huge merchant ship with stunning velocity and an enormous explosion.

No nuclear mushroom cloud bloomed over the blast, however.

It wasn't a nuclear warhead, that the US had launched.

The West "By God" Virginia, and the other SSBN's had been outfitted prior to deployment by Senior Chief Speigal's team with a new type of weapon. A kinetic energy weapon, attached to the regular submarine launched ballistic missile.

The warhead was basically a huge lawn dart. Heavy, and rugged, the thing was made of depleted uranium and other exotic metals.

And the great thing about it? If you drop a heavy object from a great height, the boom, is really really, big!

The other nice thing? The Trident II can carry a lot of the warheads in any one missile. Plus, lots of missiles.

The problem? As Borges knew, and Paul Marino was explaining, the launch of the missiles initially looked like a full scale nuclear attack. Stallings and her people had very carefully called the Russians and told them the plan, right before they started launching.

After all, the Russians were the first nation to use conventional warheads on a nuclear capable missile when they invaded the former Soviet state of Georgia in 2008. Several ICBM's were launched in support of their operations carrying normal explosives. Putin and his people had no leg to stand on in the moral outrage department. Once the reality that no radiation or fallout was spreading the world shrugged its collective shoulders. China deserved the attack after all.

Phase two of the plan to counter attack the Chinese involved reaching out long range and killing the country's ability to ship out its weapons of war and the infrastructure that supported it.

The seven Tridents all launched fifteen missiles each which carried multiple kenetic warheads.

Soon hundreds of streaks of light were appearing over Shanghai, Beijing and other military facilities.

Baoshan was completely destroyed as was a large merchant ship carrying Fei and his party as it waited for the tide to allow it to undock and escape.

Several US surface ships and other submarines all launched Tomahawks and even some strike sorties to smash the Chinese military, or what was left of it. The Pacific Carriers were even now recovering their aircraft.

***

The two destroyers were back in home port waters. The Choon and the Hamilton, slowed to bare steerage way, and raised deck guns to a high angle of elevation. The breezy puffy clouds were cotton balls in the sky. Hawaii lazy under the wind and sun it was famous for.

The first round rocked the rim of the Diamond Head crater. The arc of the shells went over the top and impacted the interior and totally destroyed the visitors center. The Chinese inside were stunned and demoralized. Only thirty thousand had made it into the crater a week ago. Now less than ten thousand remained. The rest either starved, succumbed to wounds or had thrown themselves off the rim to escape the coming retribution.

The shots kept pounding the area for thirty minutes or so. The drone feeding the ship targeting data was remorseless.

Unable to escape, or mount a response, the Chinese decided to charge. The back side of the crater near the tunnel offered the best vantage to escape the shelling.

Walt and Kemo were stationed at the farmer's market just across Diamond head road from the enemy. Eight or nine thousand kama aina were manning points on this side waiting out the invaders.

The charge was dispirited and pointless and doomed to failure.

But there were a concentrated bunch of men all shooting at one side. The initial salvo killed hundreds of the islanders as they started returning small arms fire.

Walt sighted, shot and screamed for Kemo to get down.

The filthy human wave breasted Diamond head road as the Americans got organized.

A withering volley seemed to erase the first part of the Chinese lines.

The screaming soldiers had no other option as they hurled themselves forward.

Walt was only too happy to shoot them.

He swung left and right squeezing off rounds as more and more men converged where he was crouching, next to a cart selling tee shirts.

Kemo rounded to his left as the man in front of him went down. He caught a glimpse of more enemy soldiers as he brought the gun up to shoulder level. The trigger was stiff as he shot, and from the corner of his eye he saw his dad stagger.

Walt took the bullet right through his calf and it caused him to lurch. That lurch saved his life as several rounds impacted the cart behind him.

Kemo moved in front like a wall to cover his pops.

Screaming, cursing and firing the young man savagely beat a Chinese youth who strayed too near.

More and more men kept pouring into the confined area and the scene was chaos for an intense few minutes.

Shots continued to ring out as individual men were killed, but suddenly the kama aina were standing and the Chinese were down.

Almost all of them dead or dying in the parking lot. A few remaining stood shell shocked, not offering any resistance.

Kemo rushed to his dad and grabbed a tee shirt from the rack. Wrapping the wound as Walt's leg gushed out blood. Kemo was barely aware he was crying.

The Kaneohe based Marines had a basic first aid station setup on the kalanianaole highway a mile or so to the north.

Men rushed Walt to the station, with Kemo grimly hanging on to the make shift tourniquet.

Admiral Nickers found his old shipmate at the tent for the wounded, hours later.

"It's over Walt, we won!" he told the barely conscious man.

And it was over.

EPILOG

The USS Ohio docked at Bangor Subase with little fanfare. No civilians were allowed down to the wharf on the 4th of July. Well, no one but admin assistants to the Group Admiral.

Lynn hugged Tommy and would not let go.

Hours later after all the bullshit involved with their arrival was taken care of, the couple had a moment to catch up at home. Lynn told him her story with stark words and no superlatives while they ate dinner on the couch. Tommy nodded along but he had already had a vivid account from Admiral Kollmansburger. K14, the Rock of the Sierra they were calling him.

"That guy is crazy", Lynn said when Tommy remarked how insane everything was after she finished her story.

That guy is crazy? What about you? He wisely shut up. She had cooked this meal after all. And it looked like they were together again, so…

"Have you talked to Noah?" he asked instead.

"Almost every day," Lynn told him. "He and Rammy are down in San Diego. Some people they met or helped in the war or something, are starting a truck repair business down there." "I guess one of the truck guys is sweet on some Marine or something. You'll have to ask him." Lynn shook her head.

"Gay?"

"No, you pig! She is a female Marine Sargent."

"Oh. Okay." Tommy shrugged. The Marine part was way worse than the gay part as far as he was concerned.

'Are we concerned about Noah and Rammy?" he asked getting serious.

Lynn thought for a long time. "Yes. No. Maybe." Look- it is a difficult situation. The boy...no man! is bright and mature and has just been thru the worst experience imaginable. Someone once told me we were going to have to trust him." She used Tommy's own words against him.

Tommy agreed. *If you come through that kind of hell, killing people and all, you get to decide your own life.* He didn't think anyone would be so mindful of his age. What he was really worried about was the shape of his eyes. Both him and Rammy.

Several ugly instances of hate crimes had been perpetrated on Chinese born Americans and US citizens during the war. All because rednecks hated. *Well, that was above his paygrade. The President was going to have to figure that out.*

He wrapped an arm around Lynn and snapped on the TV.

The Generals were leading the parade down the National Mall.

Tedesco, Lemonge, Whitworth, and Nethercot all walked proudly along, ahead of a motely group of soldiers and others, waving and smiling. The government decide that the interservice nature of the battle and the throwing together of civilian and military called for an untraditional parade. They let the participants march along as they pleased.

Marines walked with Army people. Civilians with Air Force and Navy. Anyone. The camera showed a young woman in a Marine uniform. Her name patch said Hill. Tommy thought her gun was bigger than she was. She walked next to a California National Guardswoman and another Marine- a young white guy, next to them was a civilian, an Indian looking guy. All of them waving and smiling for the crowd. *Takes all kinds.*

Kollmansburger should be there, he thought. Then he decided that maybe the Admiral just wanted to sit on his couch for a bit.

The setting sun was warm and the calm of the ocean helped his mind. Andre Treadwell sat on the cooling sand and tried to make sense of things. He'd never found Tabatha. One month after the war had ended, and he was sure she was dead. Just another nameless casualty of the conflict. He thought about things he'd lost: Tabatha, his mother (staying in Atlanta), his father (disappeared) Eddie, and his employees and friends. Tito and Manny. His business. Gone. Lost.

The breeze shifted and he glanced at Sanchez. He couldn't think of her as anything but Sanchez. "Connie" didn't seem to fit. In all the loss, he'd gained her.

And that was a considerable gain.

He'd even made some new friends. That kid Noah was sharp as a tack and Rammy had helped him get started on his new repair shop, down here.

He had already begun thinking of them as "my old war buddies".

Funny. That's how he planned to introduce them to his kids. Whenever he could talk the Sargent into it, that was.

"Madam President this is better suited in the Situation Room," Paul told her.

She *hated* that room.

Going down there last week to wrestle the Chinese reserve currency dollars from the Swiss was very painful for her. But they had to have that money. The US was confiscating Chinese reserve US dollars from all over the world. *Where ever we can get them*, Sharon thought at the time. They were also confiscating Chines property and cancelling debts owed the Chinese people and government. *Its going to be a long time before anyone can ask us about that part*, she thought.

Paul was bringing up more painful issues with the folder he was holding. The Governor of California wanted to sue China. California had three major cities to resurrect after all. That was just one plate spinning: The rebuilding of the military, the restoring of the economy and the restoration of civil rights. She was grappling with huge problems and trying to plan a wedding, so Paul had better not test her!

Coleman had finally popped the question.

Indeed, it seemed that weddings were happening all over. Libby and Paul? She knew it was a consequence of the war, but that was one of the better ones.

"Paul, I will call Governor Newsom as soon as I can." She was silent a moment. She thought about her activities the last month or so: giving out medals, then taking money from private Chinese citizens. Giving speeches lauding the bravery of people and then coming up with rules for dealing with Chinese nationals suspected of being agents.

Sharon Stallings was determined to try to set an even keel on these things. The United States was beacon of freedom but it needed to be vigilant against those who would do her harm. They needed a strong military and a free and open press. *We try to be open and honest in our relationships with other countries and then we spy on them*, she thought.

"We are such a study in contrast, Paul," she said.

"What do you mean Madam President?"

"I mean that we have so much and give so much, and then take so much. We squabble all the time and then we help each other. We can't get anyone to agree on anything and then we all come together to defeat the Chinese." She sounded confused.

Paul thought a moment and just said, "That's who we are. Separate states, united. Different people, together." Competing ideas, debated." "That is the fabric of the United States, he told her sagely. "That is what our enemies don't understand about us." "We can yell at our neighbor for his dog barking and then rush to aid him in his time of need." He looked at President. "We have a unique outlook and responsibility as a people. All we really need is someone to point out the things we already know."

Sharon smiled. "Let's get back at it."

The End.

www.ingramcontent.com/pod-product-compliance
Lightning Source LLC
Chambersburg PA
CBHW062015170626
46813CB00001B/177